CW00821038

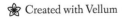 Created with Vellum

BLACKBIRD BROKEN

KERI ARTHUR

With thanks to:

The Lulus
Indigo Chick Designs
Hot Tree Editing
Debbie from DP+
Robyn E.
The lovely ladies from Central Vic Writers
Jake from J Caleb Designs for the amazing cover

CHAPTER ONE

H ell's Gill looked like any other slot canyon. Situated in the northwest sector of the Yorkshire Dales and sharing a border with the Lake District National Park, it was a narrow five-hundred-meter-long slash in the ground, created over the centuries by the clear, cold waters that still ran at its base. Although not particularly deep, it had become a favorite haunt of cavers and scramblers alike, all of whom had no idea that this was one of the most dangerous places on earth.

Hell's Gill wasn't *just* a slot canyon.

It happened to host the main entrance into Darkside—a reflection of our world that existed on a different plane.

It was also the home of demons, dark elves, and who knew what other nasties.

Though no one these days remembered how, multiple gateways had formed between our plane and theirs. Most of these were considered minor and, until recently, the only demons that came through with any sort of regularity were juveniles seeking to hone their hunting skills. Every gateway was both magically warded and regularly checked, and the witch council in the nearest town was generally responsible for dealing with any incursion.

The magic protecting the main gateway had never fractured. Not since Uhtric Aquitaine—the last Witch King to hold the great sword of power—had closed it after the last major incursion hundreds of years ago, anyway.

Unfortunately, all that was about to change. Three hours ago, Mo—who I called my grandmother even though she was centuries older than that—and I had flown over to King's Island, where Uhtric's sword had for centuries been encased in stone, and discovered it gone.

A new king had claimed it.

One we believed was already in league with Darkside.

I peered over the edge of the old stone bridge that spanned the Gill. A pool of dark water lay directly below but narrowed into another gorge several meters further on. Vegetation spilled over the edges of the canyon, hiding much of the sides and the water-smoothed cutaways deeper down. Though I couldn't see the main gate—aside from the fact it was night, it was basically under the bridge and deep within a cavernous cutaway—I could feel the pulse of protective power that emanated from it. It spoke of fierce storms and deep earth, of cindering heat and the violence of the sea—Uhtric's magic, still in place, still protecting us.

But for how long?

I looked up and studied the gently rolling hills of the surrounding area. There was no indication the night held any life, let alone any danger, but that didn't mean something wasn't out there. Darkside's inhabitants were very good at concealment.

I gripped my two daggers in my claws, then fluttered down to the main section of the bridge and shifted back to human form. The De Montfort line of witches were not only healers able to both give *and* take life, we were also the only line capable of taking a secondary form—that of a blackbird. Mo had once said this was part of the reason it had become our duty to guard the king's sword—few ever suspected or even looked for watchers in the sky. Which, given many demons were winged, really didn't make much sense, especially when—as birds—we had no real capacity to fight.

Another blackbird soared up from the darkness of the Gill and swung toward me, her dark brown feathers shimmering in the moonlight as the shifting magic crawled over her. Mo landed lightly beside me in human form and shook off the beads of moisture dotting her bright orange coat.

I leaned back to avoid getting smacked in the face by her long plait of gray hair and then said, "Any indication our new king brought the sword here to test it?"

"No, and that's worrying." She wrinkled her nose. "I'd have thought it would be the first thing he'd do."

"Unless he's well aware *we'd* be thinking that and has reacted accordingly."

As if in response to that statement, something stirred out in the deeper darkness of the night. I scanned the immediate area again. The gently rolling hills remained empty, but I couldn't escape the growing certainty that something was out there—that someone was watching.

"Possibly. The bastard's been one step ahead of us from the get-go." Mo strode over to the edge of the bridge. Though her right leg was still in a protective boot after she'd fractured it in a fall down the stairs, it really wasn't hampering her movements in any way these days. "I'm thinking we need to place a wall across the gateway's entrance."

I frowned. "How will that help? He has the damn

sword—he can simply blast both your wall *and* the gateway open."

"Not if I build it strong enough. Not without some effort on his part, anyway."

"Hate to say this, but he hasn't exactly had too much trouble unpicking your magic up until this point."

"That, my dear Gwen, is because no one fully understood what we were dealing with—"

"A murderous, bloodthirsty would-be king intent on destroying his rivals, the monarchy, and anyone else who stands in his way, you mean?"

I kept my voice deliberately light, but heartache nevertheless slipped through me. Two of the people he'd destroyed were my cousins, and both had suffered utterly brutal deaths.

"Yes." Just for an instant, something shone in Mo's blue eyes. Something that spoke of heartache and great sadness.

It was a stark reminder that she'd lost far more than me —not just over the last few weeks, but also during the long centuries of her life. She'd buried children, grandchildren, great-grandchildren, and who knew how many others, all because none of them had inherited the so-called god gene that extended her life. In all likelihood, she'd bury both my brother, Max, and me just as she'd buried our parents. Unless, of course, her genes suddenly kicked in and extended our lifespans—and given I hadn't even inherited the De Montfort ability to heal, that was looking ever more unlikely.

"However," she continued softly, "now that we *do* know, we can react accordingly."

"So, what are we going to do?"

She cast a smile over her shoulder, her eyes shining with power. I'd always known she was capable of far more magic than her De Montfort heritage should have allowed, but it wasn't until a few days ago that I discovered why. Mo was a mage, and one of only three still alive. Mages differed from witches in that not only did they have a mega-long lifespan, but they were capable of performing a vast range of spells and had the capacity to harness the power of the earth and the skies. Four other witch houses—there were seven in all— were capable of harnessing an element, be it earth, air, or darkness and light, but the dilution of bloodlines over the centuries now meant there were varying degrees of control. The Aquitaine line of kings could technically manipulate fire, but their main skill set was the ability to syphon energy from all elements—though it was only via the king's sword that it became a usable weapon against Darkside.

"I'll create the wall; you deal with any demons or dark elves that might approach before I'm finished. It should be quite simple, really."

I couldn't help a wry smile. "Yeah, because everything up until now has been absolutely simple."

"Well, the law of averages does say we have to strike it lucky sooner or later. Ready?"

No. I took a deep breath and then nodded.

"Then let's get back down there."

I frowned. "There's not a lot of room for fighting at the base of the Gill. Wouldn't it be better if I remained up here —at least I've got more chance of spotting an approach—"

"Except if they send another warrior demon. You won't spot them until they're almost on you."

"True, but how likely is—" I cut the sentence off. In truth, getting hit by one of the red-winged bastards was far more likely than being attacked by either foot soldiers or dark elves, as they could get here far faster than the other two. "I'll follow you down."

5

She shifted shape and disappeared into the Gill's darkness once again. I studied the surrounding area one more time, then flew down after her.

Despite the fact that the last few days had been mild by English standards, it was still winter, and the water at the base of the Gill was not only running high, but also damnably cold. It meant the few perching options that existed in summer were currently underwater, leaving me with little choice but to get wet feet. I strapped on my daggers, then waded to the opposite side of the canyon. From there, I could see both upstream and down, while keeping an eye on what Mo was doing. I could also see past her to the far end of the cutaway, where the gateway was situated. I might not be able to actually see *it*, but I'd feel any disruption to its protective magic and see the shift of shadows if something or someone attacked from that area. When it came to Mo's safety, I wasn't about to take a chance. She, my brother, and my cousin Ada were all the family I had left now.

I tugged off my backpack and hooked it over an outcrop of rock. It held a random selection of potions and charms, most of which wouldn't do a whole lot against demons. But it also had a first aid kit, and I had a bad feeling we were going to need it.

Mo's magic stirred, and the night thrummed with the force of it. If there were indeed demons or even dark elves out there in the shadows beyond the Gill, they'd feel its rise.

And they *would* react.

I flexed my fingers and tried to remain calm. Positioned as we were under the bridge, we were at least protected from a sky assault. To get at us, they'd have to come in from either side and, even then, the canyon's narrow confines prevented any sort of swamping maneuver.

Of course, dark elves didn't need to swamp. They could just unleash their magic. And while some weird twist of genetics had made me immune to magic—this despite the fact shape-shifting was a form of it—Mo wasn't. Hitting her while she was engaged in raising the wall could have deadly consequences.

A chill raced across my skin, and I hoped like hell it was born of fear rather than intuition.

Mo's wall continued to rise out of the wet stone, an invisible but powerful force that gradually crept upward. Though she'd trained me to see and understand both the construction and purpose of spells, I couldn't read this. It was something I'd never seen before; something that came from the elemental portion of her mage powers, rather than magical.

From the depths of the canyon to my left came a whisper of noise. It was nothing more than a splash of water and, had it been day, I might have put it down to fish jumping. But it was night, and the feeling we were no longer alone continued to grow. I gripped the hilts of the daggers, ready to draw them, my gaze searching the shadows, looking for the threat that was still too far away to pin down.

I took a deep breath and released it slowly. It didn't do a whole lot to ease the gathering tension, but then, it rarely did.

I glanced back at Mo. Her shimmering wall was almost at the halfway point. But sweat now trickled down the side of her face, and her cheeks were starting to gain that gaunt look that said she was pushing her limits.

Another splash, this time accompanied by a soft scraping sound. Someone—or something—had slipped and hit the edge of a rock.

I drew Vita and Nex. White lightning crawled down

the sides of both daggers, a clear indication that what approached was demonic in nature.

My grip tightened, and from deep within the hilt of each dagger came an answering pulse of power. The two blades—whose names literally meant life and death—were ready for action. De Montforts these days might be little more than healers and potion makers, but we'd once been warriors who could both give and take life; daggers such as these had been the means through which the deadly side of that power had been channeled. I'd once thought it inaccessible to me for anything more than a brief defense, but when I'd destroyed the red demon that had been carrying the Darkside witchling aloft, I'd forged a deep connection with both blades.

It was a connection that came at a cost, of course, but then, all truly powerful magic did.

Another scrape. Tension wound through me as the lightning pulsing down Nex's sides strengthened. She was eager to taste the blood of those who approached ...

I took another of those useless deep breaths and glanced across the Gill. Mo's wall had gained another few centimeters. I doubted she'd finish the thing before our attackers got here.

Another sound bit through the night—not the scrape of claws against stone this time, but rather the throaty roar of a vehicle approaching at speed. It was some distance away, but I couldn't help wondering if it was our rogue heir. Perhaps he'd sent his new allies here to secure the area before his arrival. It'd make as much sense as anything else that had happened recently.

The light pulsing down Nex's side increased frequency. The demons were getting closer, even though I still had no sense of them.

I risked another glance at Mo. Her wall was higher, but sweat now darkened her silver hair, and her breath was a harsh rattle that sang across the night. If not for the roar of that engine, it would have alerted the demons to our presence.

Though there was every chance they already knew, especially given the stealthy manner in which they were approaching.

Part of me wished they'd just attack and get it over with. I *hated* waiting.

The ever-growing closeness of that engine drowned out all other sounds, leaving me with only the energy pulse in Nex's steel as an indicator of the demons' growing closeness. I flexed my fingers on her hilt, more to allow the cool air to caress my palm than to ease the tension.

Mo's magic reached toward a peak. She was close, so close, to finishing.

Maybe lady luck was on our side tonight. Maybe we could fly out of here before the demons arrived—

The roar of the engine faded as the car moved further away, and silence crept back. Silence, and anticipation.

They knew we were here.

I flexed my fingers again, trying to remain calm. While I couldn't see them, I could now feel them. *Smell* them. Their ashy, acidic scent flooded the air, and they were no longer making any effort to conceal their presence. And there were at least a dozen of them approaching.

Fuck.

I pushed away from the wall and walked into the center of the canyon. Defensively it wasn't a smart move, but I needed those demons to concentrate on me rather than Mo. No matter what else happened, I had to give her time to

KERI ARTHUR

finish her wall. The fate of life on earth might well depend upon it.

White lightning flicked from the sharp points of both daggers now, sizzling lightly as it hit the water. Steam rose, curling around my legs, a gentle fog that in no way hid my form. I waited, my heart pounding so fiercely it felt like it was about to tear out of my chest. They were close now. So damn close.

Then the darkness shifted and a scaly brown shadow launched at me. I held my ground, waiting, as it arrowed through the air, reaching for me with brutally sharp claws. At the last possible moment, I dropped low, raised Nex, and sliced the bastard open from neck to genitals. As the black rain of his blood and guts fell all around me and his body flopped lifelessly into the water behind, I pushed upright and waited for the next attack. It was tempting, so very tempting, to unleash the combined power of the daggers and cinder the whole unseen lot of them, but I'd only just recovered from the effort of killing the red bastard, and I had no idea what sort of toll unleashing the daggers so soon after that would have on me. Better to wait and only use it as a last means of survival.

There was no immediate response from the narrow darkness of the slot ahead. No sound to indicate they were still on the move. Either they were waiting to see what *my* next move was or they were deciding whether it was feasible to sneak up on me from the other side of the bridge.

I shifted stance so that I was slightly side-on and able to see both ahead and behind.

Mo, I noted, was almost finished. A few more minutes was all she needed ...

With a roar that echoed across the night, the demons attacked. Not just one or two, but at least a dozen of them.

They rushed from both sides of the canyon, their claws and yellowed tusks glinting in the fractured, eager light being emitted by both daggers. I swore and attacked, twisting and slashing, cutting fingers and arms and legs. Sliced faces and chests, dodging and weaving as best I could in the slippery confines of the beck. And still they came at me, a never-ending flow of stinking, bleeding scaly flesh.

Three more dropped over the edge of the bridge and arrowed toward Mo. I screamed a denial and clashed the blades together to form a cross. Power surged—one that spoke of storms, not magic, and a force that came from deep within rather than the sky—and then twin bolts of lightning shot from the ends of both blades. They peeled away the night as they arced across the canyon, cindering the three demons in an instant.

Something hit my back, a weight that bit and tore even as it drove me into the water. I screamed again and slashed back with Vita; felt a moment of resistance and then the spurt of liquid across my neck. The weight fell away, but others leapt closer, eager to take its position. I swore and whipped the lightning around the canyon, cindering every one of the bastards. As their ash fell around me, I sucked in a deep breath and thrust fully upright again.

Another scrape of sound ... I spun around, daggers at the ready. Saw a shadow, then the gleam of a blade, and flicked the lightning toward it. Then awareness surged. I swore and recalled the bolts.

This was no demon or dark elf.

It was my goddamn brother.

CHAPTER TWO

I sucked in a breath to steady my nerves and then said, "What the fuck are you doing here?"

"What the fuck do you think I'm doing? I'm certainly not here to enjoy the damn scenery." His expression was a mix of annoyance and concern. "How badly are you hurt?"

"Lots of bites and cuts, but I'll survive." I shoved the daggers back into their sheaths. "How the hell did you know we were here?"

"How the hell do you think I knew? I met the Blackbird at what remains of our bookstore." He paused. "How did *that* happen?"

"Long story short, we were attacked by a Darkside-raised witchling with the ability to raze buildings. And Luc couldn't have known where we were, because the last time he saw us we were flying toward King's Island."

"Why were you flying there?"

"Because we feared the maniac who's been killing off heirs might have gone up there to draw the sword."

"And had he?"

"Yeah."

"Well, fuck." Max swept a hand through his short dark hair. Unlike me, he was full De Montfort in looks. The males of our line all had black skin and hair, while females tended to be brown, but both genders had blue irises ringed by gold. Sadly, I'd been born with Mom's Okoro coloring—though not her gifts—and had white skin, pale blonde hair, and black eyes. Strangers rarely ever guessed that Max and I were twins.

"To put it mildly, yes," I said. "Hence our frantic flight up here and the wall Mo's raising."

His gaze narrowed thoughtfully. "One that almost appears to be a mix of personal and elemental magic."

"It is, and that will hopefully mean it'll take the bastard with the sword longer to break through it. And you didn't answer the question."

He raised an eyebrow, though amusement lurked in his eyes. "What question?"

"How could Luc have told you where we were when he didn't know?"

He gave me the look. The one that suggested I was being an idiot.

"Put together a missing sword and the fact you two weren't home, and it's not hard to come up with the correct answer as to where you'd gone. He's not dumb, Gwen, even if he *is* an annoying prick." He glared at me for a second, and then added, "Why am I getting the third degree? If you don't want my help, just say so. More than happy to fly back to the evening's entertainment. He's keeping a nice bottle of champers on ice for us."

I raised my hands. "Okay, okay, sorry. It's just been a stressful few days."

Which technically wasn't true, as I'd actually been unconscious for the last three days; it was hard to be stressed when you were oblivious to everything that was happening around you.

"Yeah, well," he growled, "there's no need to take it out on me."

I was tempted to bite right back, but resisted. Anger wouldn't get me anywhere; it certainly wouldn't get me answers. I'd learned *that* a long time ago. I trusted my brother—I really *did*—but we now believed someone within our small circle was passing information on to Darkside, and Max *had* to be a suspect. Maybe Darkside had infiltrated his circle of friends, or maybe one of his lovers was being paid to gather information. It certainly *wouldn't* be the first time they'd tried that tactic. They'd hired Tristan Chen—who'd been my first boyfriend, and someone I'd remained close to even after we'd broken up—to get information not only from me, but also from the sister of at least one heir. Of course, Tris was now dead, killed by a single shot to the head when his usefulness had ended. I didn't want the same thing happening to my brother, however peripherally or unknowingly involved he was in this mess.

"This man you have waiting for you ... are you sure he's okay?"

He gave me another of those looks. "I always use condoms, Gwen."

"That's not what I meant."

He rolled his eyes. "He's not another Tris, if that's what you're saying."

"How can you be sure?"

"Because I am." He glanced across the Gill. It was only then I realized Mo had finished spelling and now walked toward us. "Where the hell did you learn to create something like that, Mo? It's not a De Montfort skill."

"Healing isn't the only thing I can do, my boy, and if

you stayed home longer than it takes to grab clean clothes, you might be aware of that." Though her tone was tart, it was softened by the smile tugging at her lips. "Better yet, you might even be able to help your sister fight a demon or two."

His grin flashed, though that spark of annoyance gleamed once more in his eyes. "Gwen was doing perfectly fine by herself."

"Gwen's barely out of her deathbed."

She stepped off the rock and splashed toward us. Her wall shone behind her, a haze of magic so complex and powerful it momentarily left me speechless. A couple of minor threads of magic remained tangled around her fingers, but they had a very different intent to the wall.

When she was close enough, she cast them toward Max. Oddly enough, he didn't seem to notice.

I resisted the temptation to follow their progress, not wanting to draw his attention to them, and kept my gaze on Mo. Her cheeks were sunken and her skin an odd gray color; she really did look like death warmed up. And though I knew she'd recover quickly enough, it nevertheless sent a chill through me. I didn't want to lose her and, for the first time in a long time, I realized that was a definite possibility. She might have a god gene, but that didn't make her immortal.

"Hey," Max retorted. "You and Gwen were the ones who told me to keep my head down and lie low. Don't pile shit on me for obeying."

"I wasn't talking about recent events," Mo said, "but now is neither the time nor the place to be arguing—"

"On that, at least, we agree." He waved a hand toward her wall. "Will that be enough to protect the gateway from the sword?"

"For a while, yes."

"Against all comers, no matter how powerful?"

"Your tone suggests you believe otherwise," I said.

"Oh, for fucks' sake Gwen, what's that supposed to mean?" He motioned at the bodies surrounding us. "You think I'd choose them over my own damn family?"

I wanted to believe he wouldn't. I really did. But he *had* been in contact with Tris, and Tris had been up to his ears involved in this whole thing.

Before I could actually say anything, Mo said, "Gwen, some of those wounds are already starting to fester, but I haven't the strength to heal them right now—is there any holy water in your backpack?"

"Yeah." I waded across and pulled out several bottles. "Max, can you treat the wounds on my back?"

He splashed over and plucked one of the bottles from my grip. His fingers briefly brushed mine, and just for an instant something felt off-kilter. Out of place. But before I could pin down the sensation, he pulled back and motioned with one finger for me to turn around. I hesitated and then obeyed. He poured the water over several wounds, and I gritted my teeth against a scream. Holy water on demon-caused cuts and bites reacted in much the same manner as acid did on skin, although—unlike acid—holy water at least only burned the badness away. I sucked in several breaths then repeated the process on the wounds on my stomach and thighs; thankfully, none of them looked particularly deep. After several very painful minutes, the holy water's effect eased. I wiped the wounds dry with a clean cloth and then applied Mo's sealing concoction. The thick green goop hardened within seconds, forming a waterproof seal that would allow the wound to heal from the inside out while protecting it from infection.

Max applied it to the wounds on my back, then grabbed the pack from the rock and swung it over his shoulder. "You'll tear open the bite wound if you wear it."

"Fine, but I need my phone."

He handed both it and the charger to me, then glanced at Mo. "Do you want me to call Kiri? Sunrise is hours away, and these bodies are going to stain the water downstream pretty badly in the meantime. At the very least, she can filter the demon bits and blood from the water."

Kiri Okoro wasn't a relative of ours, but she'd attended the Okoro Academy at the same time as Max and now worked with him at the Department of Weather Guidance. Her skill set was the control of running water, which was extremely handy when it came to flood situations.

"If she's close, that would be good," Mo said. "The last thing we need is the environmental bods coming down on us for fouling the waters and killing the fish further downstream."

The environmental bods would actually have a hard time pinning these deaths on us, given neither elemental nor personal magic had been involved, but I guess it was better not to take any chances.

"I'll ring her now," Max said. "You heading home?"

Mo shook her head. "I need to rest, and if Gwen flies too far with those wounds, it'll just hasten the spread of any remaining infection. We'll head over to Kirby Stephen and stay there for the night. You want me to book you a room?"

"No." He hesitated. "I only flew back to England to attend Gareth's and Henry's funerals tomorrow."

Mo frowned. "I'm not sure that's wise, Max."

"Why? If the sword's been claimed, there's no longer any point in hiding."

"Unless the heir wants to ensure there's nobody else to contest his claim."

Max snorted. "And how would he do that? He drew the damn sword out of the stone—the throne is his. Besides, he can just smite any challenger with the sword's power."

"That depends on whether he can access it without first being crowned. There's some conjecture that he can't."

His brows furrowed. "Says who? Nothing I've ever read mentions that."

"There's a lot of things they don't mention in history books, my boy, in part because many were written by scholars *after* the event."

He rolled his eyes. "I went to the Okoro Academy, remember? They've one of the finest history archives in the country. Nothing I ever read there said anything about the crown being necessary to access the sword's power."

"And yet Darkside has been searching for the crown," I said, "and in fact stole the fake one kept in the Tower of London."

"That wasn't fake—it's the crown Layton wore when he married Elizabeth."

Layton Aquitaine had been the very last Witch King. Not only had his marriage to Elizabeth of York combined human and witch royalty and signaled the end of true witch rule in England, it had also handed his descendants a means of curtailing any magical attacks on human monarchs—one that was still in force today.

Whether it would protect them from a mad Witch King and the sword of power was a question no one could currently answer.

"True," Mo said, "but said theory also suggests that the coronation needs to be with Uhtric's crown, not Layton's."

"Why on earth would that even matter? The crown's just a symbol—"

"In theory, yes. In reality?" She shrugged.

He raised an eyebrow, skepticism evident. "I take it these theories are yours?"

"Mine and a number of others. And you'd better pray that we're right, otherwise this country is in deep trouble. Are you sure you don't want us to book you a room tonight?"

He shook his head. "Given your advice *not* to attend the funeral, I might as well head back and enjoy the evening's entertainment. Will you be home tomorrow?"

She nodded. "We've a builder coming at eleven for a quote on repairs."

He grunted. "Then I'll meet you there and pick through the ruins. I might as well see what survived and what didn't."

Mo nodded and looked at me. "Meet you at Kirby Stephen—probably The Green Lodge if they've rooms available."

As she shifted shape and flew out of the Gill, I unstrapped my daggers and lashed them together. Their blades were silver, which meant they were immune to the shifting magic that took care of everything else. "Be careful, Max. Not only might there still be demons in the area, but there's every chance the heir will come here to test the sword."

He snorted. "If he had any brains, he wouldn't. He'd wait until all the fuss died down."

"He might not be that cunning." Which was unlikely. Everything so far suggested we were dealing with someone who meticulously planned each and every move. He wouldn't have kept ahead of us otherwise, even with inside help.

"It doesn't take cunning to understand rushing into anything is never a good idea." He shrugged and pulled out his phone. "I'll make the call to Kiri now. You'd better head out, otherwise Mo will be back here telling us both off."

I half smiled. "Enjoy the champers and your man."

"Oh, I intend to. I'll see you tomorrow."

I altered shape, grabbed my knives in my claws, and flew out of the Gill. I didn't go far, though, landing in the long grass a short distance from the bridge to wait for Max. He appeared a few minutes later, his dark plumage merging with the night, making him harder to see. I followed at a safe distance, keeping close to the ground so there'd be less chance of him spotting me if he happened to glance over his wing.

Thankfully, he didn't. Once he'd reached the road, he resumed human form, made a phone call, and then climbed into his racy red Jag. Relief stirred through me. Part of me—a tiny, very distrusting part—had feared he'd be driving a silver Volkswagen Golf rather than his own car. Tris's control—who he'd met in Ordsell and who no doubt had ordered him killed not long afterward—had been driving a Golf. I'd tried to follow him the night he and Tris had met, but a blackbird's wings were no match for a car driven at speed. I'd given the number plate to Luc but, as yet, we hadn't discovered the registered owner.

I watched Max leave, then flew on to Kirby Stephen. As tempting as it was to follow Max to his destination, I couldn't ignore the growing ache from my wounds. Shifting from one shape to another didn't magically heal them, and whatever wounds I gained in one form, I had in the other. I guess it was just lucky the demons hadn't done any major damage to my arms. Walking to Kirby Stephen would not have been fun.

Although I could have asked Max to drive me—his reaction would have been interesting. Aside from the fact he was fastidious when it came to his car and certainly wouldn't have wanted blood on the seats, he'd left the area pretty damn quickly ... which was only sensible, I guess. Hell, I'd have done the same thing given the threat of more demons or the possible arrival of a mad heir. It seemed that the tiny niggles of distrust wouldn't entirely go away, even though as yet there'd been no concrete, legitimate reason for it.

It took me a little bit of time to find The Green Lodge, as Kirby Stephen was bigger than I'd expected. The Lodge was a two-story stone-built building with a slate tile roof and a lovely old thatched veranda covering the main door. Warm light shone from at least half the windows, but there was only one room that had a window open and the curtains pulled aside. I swooped in and shifted shape, landing lightly in a half crouch between the two single beds. For several minutes, I didn't move. In truth, I *couldn't* move. All those cuts and bites that hadn't seemed so major were suddenly making their presence felt, and nearly every part of my body goddamn *hurt*. I needed painkillers, but they were sitting in the first aid kit in my backpack, and Max now had that.

The sound of running water told me Mo was in the shower, but she must have filled the kettle before she went in, because it boiled and then clicked off. I forced myself upright and, with a soft groan of pain, hobbled over to make myself a cup of tea. A hot cuppa always made things seem just that little bit better.

Mo came out of the shower ten minutes later, a white

towel wrapped around her body. Though her face remained gaunt, there was at least some color back in her cheeks. "So, what did your brother do when we left him?"

A smile twitched my lips. "How did you know I was going to keep an eye on him?"

"Because it was the sensible thing to do, and you're an eminently sensible girl." She waved a hand, amusement creasing the corners of her bright eyes. "That would, of course, be my genes coming out in you."

I laughed softly, then winced as the slight movement sent pain slithering across my back. Mo immediately frowned. "Just how bad is that bite?"

"I don't know. I can't exactly see it." And didn't really want to, if I was at all honest.

She tsked. "Go have a shower. You stink worse than Hades, and I can't fix anything with demon crap all over you."

"You need to rest before—"

"I'll be fine, darling girl. Besides, with Darkside's spotlight on us, the last thing we need right now is you getting sick."

I snorted softly. "It's not like they've any reason to come after me now that the sword has been claimed."

"I wouldn't be so sure of that."

I raised an eyebrow. "Meaning what?"

She waved a hand. "Later. Go shower. The air in the room is becoming unbreathable."

I'd learned long ago straight answers and Mo weren't often companions, but I nevertheless shook my head in frustration. "You are so annoying sometimes."

"Only sometimes?" She tsked again. "I'll have to pick up my game. Go."

I gulped down the remains of my tea and hobbled—

wincing all the way—into the bathroom. After plugging my phone into the charger, I flicked on the shower and grabbed a fresh bar of soap. It was lavender scented, which would go some way to erasing the demons' stink from my skin. Nothing would ever erase it from my clothes—they'd have to be burned when I got home—but I could at least wash the worst of the blood and muck off them.

Mo was on her phone when I finally came out of the bathroom, but waved me toward the bed. I lay on my stomach and closed my eyes, only half listening to the conversation. From the bits I could hear, she was talking to Barney—who was not only her current lover, but also the head of Ainslyn's witch council. He didn't sound happy.

"We've a meeting with the builders at eleven," Mo was saying. "But we can be at your place by one, if that's okay."

Though I couldn't hear exactly what he said, it sounded tetchy.

"I know, and I'm sorry, but building a secondary line of defense across the main gate has drained me. I can barely lift my arms, let alone fly any great distance."

His reply sounded more conciliatory in tone, and Mo smiled. "Love you, too. See you soon."

"Do you?" I asked, as she hung up.

"Probably not in the way he wishes, but there are many degrees of love." She shrugged. "I've lost my heart many times over the centuries, but passion that burns the brightest doesn't always last the longest. These days I prefer comfortable companionship over fervor."

Amusement twitched my lips. "The two are not mutually exclusive."

"They tend to be when you hit my age. Let's get your back sorted out." She tossed her phone onto her bed, then walked over to mine. "The bastard certainly took a good

23

chunk out of you. He only missed your spine by a few centimeters."

"Will it heal okay?" I already had more than enough scars on my body, thanks to damn demons—or half-demons, as was the case when it came to the melted-looking burn scar that now ran the length of my right side. I really didn't need anything else.

"Of course it will. Now lie still while I get to work."

My immunity to magic had never curtailed Mo's ability to heal the various cuts and scrapes I'd gotten over the years. Apparently, this was due to the fact that, although I'd never had access to the De Montfort gift of healing, it nevertheless resided somewhere in my DNA.

As explanations went, it didn't really make a lot of sense, but that was a very common theme when it came to Mo and answers.

She pressed her fingers to either side of the wound, then her power rose, a wave of heat that swept through my body, easing the aches and chasing away the pain. My skin rippled and twitched as it was healed from the inside out and, though it didn't hurt, it felt weird.

The warmth of her magic and her touch finally left my skin. "Right, that's all the major wounds healed. We'll check the scrapes tomorrow, but the holy water should have taken care of any possible infection there."

She flopped onto her bed, closed her eyes, and lightly rubbed her forehead. Guilt flickered through me, though I knew nothing I could have said or done would have stopped her. The best I could do now was look after her—though in a way that couldn't be considered 'fussing', as that was something she absolutely hated.

I swung my feet off the bed. "You hungry?"

"Enough to eat a horse."

I padded over to the small table. After flicking through the information booklet, I said, "We have the grand choice of Chinese, fish and chips, kebabs, or pizza if you want take-away. There's plenty of pubs, but given the state of my clothes, they're out."

"I feel like pizza—do they deliver?"

I flipped over the page. "No, but I can borrow your clothes and walk down there. It's not far." I hesitated, frowning at her. "Do you want me to pick something up for that headache?"

A smile tugged her lips. "If there's anything still open, that would be good."

Which meant the headache was bad. Mo hated taking tablets almost as much as she hated being fussed over—and for good reason. Most of her herbal concoctions worked far better and quicker than the pharmaceutical equivalent.

I glanced at my watch. It was close to eleven, so I was cutting it fine if I wanted to find a SPAR or Co-Op Super-market open. "You want anything else? A cup of tea before I go, perhaps?"

She shook her head.

I grabbed her pants and sweater and pulled them on. Thanks to the fact that Mo loved the loose Bohemian look, they fit perfectly, even though I was at least one size bigger than her. She also had a love for bright and clashing colors, though these harem pants were at least a staid pink floral print. They did clash rather alarmingly with the orange coat, however.

Once I'd shoved on my still-wet shoes, I grabbed the room key and her purse and headed out. Thankfully, the Co-Op was still open, so I ducked in to get her painkillers and some chocolate, then continued on to grab our pizza. They were already packing up for the night, but I obviously looked in need of a serious feed, because they good-naturedly made my order.

Mo was asleep by the time I got back, but stirred as I placed the pizza on the small table. "That smells good."

"And there's painkillers for starters, and chocolate for dessert."

"You're spoiling me."

"It's about time I repaid the favor." I tore the lid off the box, then placed half the pizza onto it. After handing it and the painkillers to her, I plonked down on the chair and reached for a slice. "What did Barney want to see you about?"

She grabbed the bottle of water from her bedside table and downed the painkillers. "His nephew enhanced the photos of the glyphs you found on the back of the throne, and he wanted me there to translate the words."

I raised my eyebrows. "And that couldn't wait?"

A smile tugged her lips. "You have to understand that this is probably the most exciting thing that's happened to him—and Ainslyn's council in general—in a very long time."

I laughed. "And here I was thinking *you* were the most exciting thing that had happened to him, but maybe I'm being biased."

She smiled. "On a personal basis, I most certainly agree. But aside from the occasional demon incursion, there hasn't been a whole lot for the council to deal with. Not for the last fifty years or so."

"They may find themselves quickly wishing the status quo had continued. Does he know the sword has been claimed?"

"Not as yet." She wrinkled her nose. "I thought a face-to-face would be best for that."

I picked up a second slice of pizza and bit into it. "If the main gateway does go down, what are we going to do? Uhtric had the advantage of a full witch army behind him. We haven't that option these days."

Only scattered witch councils and seven witch lines whose power and fighting skills had faded with every new generation.

"We do have the High Witch Council in London. They still have the power and the ability to draw all seven houses together."

The High Witch Council had once been the equivalent of the Privy Council, and responsible for advising the king and his executive on matters of the state. These days they were little more than an oversight council that settled disputes between witch houses. Of course, said disputes— while rare—were often brutal, bloody, and complicated, and only the most powerful spells could cut through all the crap and magic to ferret out the truth. Mo had once been one of five witches tasked with that ferreting, though it had been a long time before she'd stepped in to raise Max and me after the death of our parents.

"That's still not going to help if the main gate is opened and the entirety of Darkside floods out."

"Maybe not, but also remember that human weapons have seriously advanced since Uhtric's day."

"It was still witches who made the difference at the hospital when the demons went after Henry."

"Only because there were more demons than military present at the time. Had it been the reverse, it might have been a different story."

But still the same result. I squashed down the sadness and reached for a third slice of pizza. To say I was hungry was an understatement. "Has anyone actually informed the High Council what's happening?"

"Barney sent a missive when the tower's vaults were attacked, but there's been no chance to update them on more recent events."

The King's Tower situated in Ainslyn was the only intact remnant of Uhtric's castle. These days, it was little more than a tourist attraction and museum, though there was a secret witch repository tucked within the vaults—one that had recently come under attack from a witch working with both Darkside and the heir. A witch other than Tris, that is.

"And a cup of tea would be lovely right now," she added.

I smiled and rose, grabbing the kettle before heading into the bathroom to fill it. And decided to ask the one question I'd been avoiding up until now. "Why do you really think Max was there tonight?"

"I don't know."

"But you did cast some sort of truth spell, didn't you?"

"Only a minor one." She paused. "I'm surprised you picked it up and he didn't."

I came out and put the kettle back onto its stand. "I'm more familiar with your recent magic."

"True." She paused again. "There was no lie in anything he said."

"But?"

"But I wish I'd had more time and strength to question him. He's up to something, and I'd like to know what." She grimaced. "I'd also like to think he's not deeply involved in any of this, but Tris did contact him, and I've a feeling that wasn't a coincidence."

"Which never did make sense—I mean, Max is an heir, however indirect, so why would they allow Tris to contact him? Why wouldn't they just take Max out as they did the others?"

"There are lots of things not making sense at the moment." She shrugged. "Hopefully, I'll have more of a chance to question him tomorrow."

"That's if he turns up. He's just as likely not to, given he might have to help with the cleanup."

I picked up the two cups of tea; she accepted hers with a smile. "I believe curiosity is the reason he turned up tonight, and I think it'll be the reason he turns up tomorrow."

"Max and curiosity have never been bosom buddies."

"Unless there was a deal or money to be had."

True. I frowned. "There's not much of a deal to be had when it comes to Darkside. Especially for an heir."

"Tris thought otherwise. And, heir or not, Max might well think the same."

"Meaning maybe we should be doing something tomorrow about bugging him. Or, at the very least, put a tracker on his car."

She smiled. "This is why you're my favorite grandchild —you're practical but sneaky, just like me."

I resisted the urge to point out that—technically—I wasn't her grandchild or even her great-grandchild, as there were centuries more than *that* between us. "We might have to pull in either Mia or Ginny to help us. He'll be watching for the two of us, given our recent show of distrust."

Ginny in particular would be a good choice, as she could track people, animals, or vehicles via the color and currents they left behind after movement. She also happened to be a detective with the major crimes unit; if there was a shady, big-money deal going down in Ainslyn, she'd probably know about it.

"Good idea. In the meantime, you'd better send a message to your Blackbird, otherwise he'll be ringing at some ungodly hour of the morning again."

I gave her a deadpan look. "He's not my anything and never will be, given all he's interested in is a short-term fling."

"Flings can still be fun."

"Yes, but I'm over being considered a short-term prospect rather than long."

"So agree to one, and work on the other." Mischief twinkled in her eyes. "I speak from experience when I say it can certainly work."

I smiled. "I think it's safe to say that I don't have your good fortune when it comes to men."

"That's your problem—no self-belief."

I rolled my eyes. "If I can't hold the attraction of the man whose soul is supposedly linked to mine, what hope is there for me?"

"Plenty." She made a shooing motion. "Go contact him so we can get some rest."

I took a sip of tea, then headed into the bathroom to send him a text. It would have been far easier to call, but I was a little peeved at the man and avoiding direct contact where possible. His reply was quick and to the point —*where are you now?*

Recovering. Be home tomorrow.

I hit the mute button after I sent that, then put the phone down and walked out. Luc had made it very clear that his work as a Blackbird—the traditional protectors of witch kings—and his duty to the crown and the current queen were all he cared about or wanted in his life. The next step—if there ever was to be a next step in our so-far nonexistent relationship—had to be his. I'd certainly made it clear enough what I wanted.

We finished our pizza, topped it off with some chocolate, and then I settled down to watch some late-night TV while Mo slept. I must have drifted off fairly quickly, because a sharply ringing phone woke me hours later. I opened my eyes and was met by daylight.

"Tell them to bugger off," Mo muttered. "It's too damn early to get up."

I groped the bedside table between us, found her phone, and discovered it was seven, which wasn't that much earlier than our usual weekday waking time. I hit the answer button and said, a little groggily, "Hello?"

"Mo? That you?"

"No," I said, not immediately recognizing the woman's voice. "It's Gwen."

"Ah, the paradox. It's her friend—Jackie. Is she around?"

"She's asleep."

"Then you need to wake her. I've got some news she'll want to hear."

"I'm not waking her without good reason. She gets grouchy."

"I do not," Mo refuted.

"Then tell her," Jackie said, "that I've finally found Jules Okoro."

CHAPTER THREE

The mysterious Jules Okoro—who wasn't a relative of my mother's as far as we could ascertain—was an indirect heir to the Witch King's crown and, with the death of Gareth and Henry, now the only one ahead of Max. Why they were being killed instead of those whose bloodline could be traced back directly to Uhtric or even Layton was something Jackie had been researching.

Although did it even matter anymore, given the sword had been claimed?

Mo sat up and made a give-me motion. I handed the phone to her, then tossed the comforter aside and padded into the bathroom to check my clothes. My jeans and sweater were still damp, but my underclothes and shirt had at least dried. Demon scent still clung to everything, though. I grimaced and tugged them on regardless. I had a feeling we wouldn't be hanging about for long, and smelly clothes were better than no clothes when we got to wherever Jules Okoro might be.

Once dressed, I unplugged my phone and then glanced at the screen. Luc hadn't replied to my last text, and that niggled. Which was stupid and irrational, but then, when it came to desire, irrationality seemed to be a common theme in my life.

I shoved the phone and charger into my pocket and headed out. Mo was in the process of getting dressed.

"So where are we going?" I walked across the room and opened the window. The clouds were thick and gray, and the cold air filled with the promise of rain. Flying into a storm was not one of my favorite things to do, but it wasn't like we had any real choice.

"Thornaby."

"And that's where, exactly?"

She tsked. "Your knowledge of our great country is shocking."

"Maybe if I ever *do* get to your age, I'll know all the little places. In the meantime, where the hell is it?"

She laughed. "Over near Stockton-On-Tees."

Which didn't make me any wiser, but I kept that to myself. "How come he was so hard to find?"

"He was adopted as a babe—his legal surname is now Martin."

"Any record of his real parents?"

"According to the hospital records Jackie found, his mother's name was Hanna Okoro. No mention of a father. The mother disappeared from the hospital the day after he was born."

"I take it she was never seen again?"

"No."

Not a good sign. "Are there any theories as to why?"

"The retired nurse Jackie tracked down said it was obvious the girl had undergone major trauma."

"As in mugged? Or raped?"

"Unclear. But she said the girl was covered in old scars,

had the look of a frightened animal, and spoke gibberish. That's the only reason the nurse remembered her. She also said she wasn't entirely surprised when the girl disappeared."

"I gather the security cams were checked at the time?"

"Yes. It appeared she was dragged away by two invisible men. Or maybe even women. It's hard to guess gender when they're invisible."

Invisibility spells wouldn't hide the stink that came with demons, nor the click of steel-clad elf claws on floors, and *that* meant her abductors were probably human. Or, more likely, half human. "I take it her family were contacted?"

"Eventually, yes, and that's where it gets *really* interesting. They're not only a previously unknown branch of the Okoro tree, but they claimed Hanna Okoro died in an accident ten years previously."

"Curiouser and curiouser, as Alice was wont to say."

"Indeed. I've asked Jackie to keep digging." She glanced at her watch. "We'd better go. I'll head down to pay the bill and meet you outside in ten minutes."

I shifted shape, then grabbed my knives and flew out the window. While I waited for Mo, I drifted in lazy circles, enjoying the freedom of the skies and the ripple of wind through my feathers. Even on a cold, dull day like this, it was a glorious sensation.

Mo appeared below and strode down the pavement, no doubt looking for an empty side street before she took to the wing. While it was no secret the De Montfort line were shape-shifters, there were still some humans who got freaked out by the whole process. Which was weird, given the magic involved basically hid all the gory details of the shift. Thankfully, it also took care of the pain the process involved. I didn't think many of us would be switching forms too often if it didn't.

Once she'd joined me on wing, we flew on. By the time we got to Thornaby, it was drizzling. Jules's house was a small two up, two down situated in a cul-de-sac close to a meandering river. The small front yard had been concreted over, and there was a blue Ford parked in front of the attached garage. I flew over the tiled roof to check out the backyard; it clearly hadn't been mown in some time.

I swooped around and followed Mo past the trees lining the end of the cul-de-sac before landing beside her. Once I'd strapped on my knives, we climbed over a wire fence and walked to Jules's house. The place was quiet; dust and dead bugs lined the windowsills on either side of the door, and spiders hung between the glass and the net curtains.

Mo pressed the doorbell. The chime echoed inside but drew no response. The door was locked.

"Maybe he's out."

"Maybe." She stepped out from under the protection of the porch and peered up. "The curtains are drawn. It's possible he's asleep."

There was something in her tone that had my eyebrows rising. "But you don't think so?"

"No. My trouble antenna is quivering."

And *that* was never a good thing. "Should we enter via the back door? We don't need to be seen breaking in—"

"It's hardly breaking in when the door is left open." She pressed her fingers around the deadlock. Power surged, a brief flame that spoke of a power I'd not seen her use before. With a soft click, the door opened.

I gave her a long look. "And where did you learn to do that?"

"I once had a brief liaison with a king's thief. He taught me more than a few tricks."

Some of which weren't magic based, if the smile twitching her lips was anything to go by. "Why would a king need a thief?"

"How else was he to uncover the court's secrets? Courtiers weren't exactly known for their honesty or their piety."

I snorted and followed her inside. The small entrance hall held a coat stand under which sat a pair of well-worn brown boots. Beside it was a kitchen chair, and directly ahead a set of carpeted stairs. To our right lay what looked to be a sitting room.

The air smelled musty, suggesting it had been locked up for a while. But there was something else here, too, something I'd smelled before.

Death.

I swallowed. "Mo—"

"Yes." Her voice was heavy. "You check this floor. I'll go up."

"Be careful."

She smiled. "I don't think what lies up there is a threat to either of us."

While the smell suggested she was right, demons had been known to use the dead as lures. I shoved the thought away; if there were demons here, we would have sensed them by now.

And yet, a heartbeat of energy was now pulsing through Nex's blade. There might not be demons here, but there *was* something—someone—connected to them in the near vicinity.

As she climbed the stairs, I went into the sitting room. It was small but neat, with one lonely-looking armchair positioned in front of a massive TV. There was a radiator beneath the window, but the chill in the air suggested the central heating hadn't been switched on for a while. The kitchen was small—little more than a galley—with just enough room for a two-person table at the far end. Again, it was neat, with only a cup and plate sitting on the sink drainer. Jules, it seemed, lived a fairly solitary life.

I headed upstairs. There were three doors off the small landing. One was a bathroom, the other a box bedroom. Mo was in the third one.

"Did you find—" The rest of that sentence died on my lips as I entered the larger bedroom.

She *had* found the source of the smell.

It was a man.

An *old* man.

One who'd obviously been dead long enough for his stomach gases to release and his skin to discolor.

I wrinkled my nose and tried not to breathe too deeply. Even so, the smell was bad enough to have my stomach churning. "I'm guessing that's Jules Okoro?"

She waved his wallet. "According to this, it is."

"He's not what I expected. I mean, he looks to be in his mid-seventies, and that, in turn, begs the question—how old was the nurse Jackie spoke to?"

"She'd been retired a few years, so at least late sixties."

"Which makes her younger than him, and that's impossible if she was working at the hospital when he was born. What's his age according to his license?"

"Thirty-six."

I blinked and looked at the figure on the bed again. "Either he had some sort of degenerative disease, or something else was going on."

She dropped his wallet back onto his bedside table, then

squatted beside his bed. I remained exactly where I was. Getting any closer might just have last night's pizza making a grand reappearance. "Well, that right there could be part of the answer."

"What right where?"

She motioned toward his head. "His ears have a very slight point."

Which suggested he was a halfling—the offspring of a dark elf and a human. Elves, I'd recently learned, had a long history of stealing human women in an effort to refresh their own bloodlines. The resulting halflings were generally hermaphrodites, and while they didn't inherit the dark elf ability for magic, they did gain their ability to manipulate the weak willed. Like Tris, perhaps.

"Why would his being a halfling explain his advanced age? The other halflings we've come across didn't appear to have this problem."

"Because they were half human."

"What has that got to do with it?"

"There's been plenty of conjecture over the years as to why few witches were ever taken by the elves, but it wasn't until the discovery of a severely emaciated corpse outside a discarded Darkside gateway that we got a possible answer. There appears to be a gene incompatibility between our two races that results in multiple autoimmune diseases and premature aging. Whether it happens to all witch-elf offspring or only some is unknown."

"Do you think it was a coincidence—a simple matter of opportunity—that a woman from a previously unknown branch of the Okoros was taken?"

"I doubt it. It's pretty obvious someone out there knows a whole lot more about the lineage of the Okoros than we do."

Someone who had the missing family bibles, perhaps? "But why would they even bother? They'd have to know a halfling would never be able to draw the sword."

"They lose nothing in trying." She nodded toward Jules. "The price for this poor soul was a short and painful existence, but who knows how many other siblings he has running around Darkside or even here? Siblings that perhaps aren't as afflicted as he?"

"It still doesn't alter the fact that Darkside can't touch the sword." It killed them if they tried—a fact we knew from a legendary battle that happened in the days before Uhtric closed the main gate. His horse had been cut from beneath him and in the fall, his sword had slipped from his grasp. The dark elf who'd tried to claim the blade had been instantly incinerated.

"Full elves, no. But half-breed witches able to trace their lineage back to Uhtric? That's an unknown." She made a frustrated sound. "It would, however, seem I've been very lax in my duty."

I frowned. "I think if anyone is to blame for this mess, it's the Blackbirds. They're the protectors of King and Crown, after all, and they all but disappeared centuries ago."

She grimaced. "That might be true, but I'm a mage. With Mryddin locked in his cave and Gwendydd in Europe, it falls to me to hinder Darkside developments as best I can."

"Then maybe it's time you dug Mryddin out of his cave. It'd certainly be handy to have an extra mage about if the main gate is opened."

Her expression held a tinge of wistfulness. "As much as I'd love to, he's a very stubborn old man. Unless and until he wishes to come out, there is nothing either Gwendydd or I can do to budge him."

"So who was the woman who broke his heart and left him locked up and mourning in a cave?"

"Her name was Niniane, and she was his student. We did warn him that she was only after his power, but men in lust do tend to listen to the little head rather than the big."

A smile twitched my lips. "So she bled him dry and then walked away?"

"Ran is a more apt description. He tended to be a bit 'handsy.'"

That seemed to be a common theme amongst men of a certain age and generation, in my experience. "What happened to her after he locked himself away?"

"She attempted a spell beyond her capabilities. It consumed her."

"Fate does have a way of biting the butts of wrongdoers." I paused and studied Jules for a moment. "Do you think it possible that the person who drew the sword is one of his siblings?"

"Anything is possible, but I doubt it, if only because they wouldn't have attacked you on King's Island. It would have been more sensible *not* to draw attention to themselves that way."

"I'm thinking Darkside and sensible don't always go together."

She laughed. "They may not see things the way we do, but their thought processes aren't *that* different."

On that, we would always disagree. "If Hanna Okoro was snatched from the hospital by her dark elf keepers, why would they leave Jules there? Surely that was a bit risky—"

"Not necessarily," Mo cut in. "His ears aren't pointed enough to attract attention."

"But why not take him when they took his mother?"

"Invisible or not, it's still much harder to get into a natal ward." She shrugged. "Or maybe they simply did prenatal tests and knew he was flawed."

"It's kinda hard to imagine Darkside having hospitals and the like."

She raised an eyebrow. "Why? The only difference between our world and theirs is the fact that night is never-ending there."

"I guess it comes from thinking demons to be little better than rabid animals." I waved a hand toward Jules. "Do you think he died of natural causes?"

She reached out and lifted one eyelid. "His eyes are bloodshot, and there seems to be a faint stain of blue around his lips. Whether that's part of whatever condition he had or he's been smothered, I can't say. I think we need to get the preternatural boys out here to investigate."

The Preternatural Division was a secret section of the National Crime Agency, and had some of the strongest witches on their books as advisors to help investigate super-natural and magical crime. And, right now, that meant the death of anyone connected in any way to the Witch King and the sword.

"Have you got Jason's number?" she added.

Jason Durant was the head honcho of the team who'd investigated both Tris's and Gareth's murders. He also happened to be a good friend of Luc's. "No, but I could send a text to Luc."

She pushed to her feet. "Do it. Then we'd better get back home."

"You don't want to look around first?"

"I doubt there's much here to find, and we need to get back to Ainslyn."

I pulled out my phone; it was already past ten. "We're not going to get back there in time to meet the insurance assessor."

"No, which is why I rang your brother before I left the Lodge and asked him to get over there."

I grinned. "I'm sure he would have been absolutely thrilled to be woken at that hour." Especially if he and the entertainment had been partying all night.

"He did sound a little miffed, but that's not unusual these days."

No, it wasn't. I sent Luc a quick text, then shoved my phone back into my pocket. "If Jules has been murdered within the last forty-eight hours, does that mean Max is still in danger?"

Mo pursed her lips. "If Jules was murdered after the sword was taken, yes, because it suggests the heir is still taking out rivals."

"Meaning Max had better go back into hiding."

"Being hard to find didn't do Jules much good."

"Well, no, but our family is small enough." My voice was edged; worry and concern, rather than anger. "I don't want to lose anyone else."

She touched my arm lightly. "We won't."

I hoped not. I'd had more than enough grief in my lifetime already. I followed her down the stairs and out the front door. The drizzle had turned into a full-on storm, which meant it was a damn miserable flight home.

Max's Jag was still parked next to my red-and-white Mini when we finally reached Ainslyn, and there was a nondescript and unfamiliar gray Mazda next to Mo's Nissan Leaf. Which meant that maybe the insurance assessor was still here.

We shifted shape behind the cars and then walked

across the road. Healing Words—our store—was situated in a three-story, single-fronted building squeezed in between two larger terraces. Externally, at least, there wasn't much evidence of Darkside's attempt to collapse the building down on top of us. The red bricks might have a new layer of grime on them, but the heritage green-and-gold woodwork surrounding the front window and inset, half-glass door had been untouched. It wasn't until you looked up and saw the heavy tarps covering a good proportion of the roof that it became evident there'd been a problem.

The small bell above the door made no sound as we stepped through; a quick glance up revealed the clapper was missing. Which was odd—why would someone steal something like that? Unless, of course, they didn't want to be heard entering the building sometime in the future ...

I ignored the trepidation that rose with the thought and looked around. Aside from the dust and grime that lay upon absolutely everything, nothing else seemed to be out of place or missing—not at first glance, at least. There was certainly no sign of the destruction that lay above us.

Mo peeled off her coat and slung it over the hook to the right of the door. "You might want to lose those clothes, as the rain seems to have intensified the demon scent. I'll head upstairs and see what's happening."

I nodded and dripped my way through the various shelves containing books, Mo's healing potions and pretty soaps, and all the other oddities we stocked for the tourist trade, heading for the sectioned-off rear of the store. There were a number of smaller rooms here—an office, a storeroom, and, in a separate, magically shielded rear room, an old boiler and laundry. It had once provided the hot water for the building, but these days we basically used it to get rid of the occasional spell paraphernalia that couldn't be thrown out with regular rubbish.

I stripped off and chucked everything—including my shoes—into the boiler, then lit it. Once I'd cleansed my daggers, I grabbed a towel from the stack and wrapped it around me as I padded barefoot up the stairs to the first floor, running my hand under the banister as I did so. The bug Tris had placed was gone; hopefully that meant Ginny had cleared out the rest of them as well.

This level was divided into two areas—Mo's bedroom was at the rear of the building, and an open kitchen-living area lay to the front. The kitchen was filled with a colorful array of art deco cabinetry, and the upright stove came straight out of the sixties. But where the sofas and the big-screen TV had once stood there was now a large pile of plaster, wood, and roof tiles, as well as the remnants of what had once been my bed. I glanced up. The tarps over the roof were visible, and doing a good job of keeping the water out. At least we weren't getting water damage on top of everything else.

Aside from Mo, there were three others in the room—Max, a bald man I presumed was the assessor, and Luc.

Even though he wasn't looking at me, I felt the impact of his presence. It was fiercer than a punch to the gut, an indefinable force that was far deeper than just awareness and desire. It was almost elemental in feel, and spoke of a connection that stepped far beyond the physical, far beyond the emotional. It whispered of destiny and age, and of a bond not just days in the making, but decades.

According to Mo, it was the result of something called *anima nexum*, which basically meant soul connection. Apparently there were three different types—while it *could* sometimes refer to the type of soul connection that was little more than a meeting of gazes and a recognition of fate, it generally meant either souls that were doomed to battle each other through time eternal, or souls who were destined to keep on meeting until whatever had gone wrong in their initial relationship was rectified. Luc and I were supposedly the latter. Which was the pits, as right now it seemed highly unlikely we'd fix that wrong thing. Not in this lifetime, anyway.

He turned at that moment, and our gazes met. Just for an instant, something flashed across his expression—a heated mix of relief, joy, and desire—but it was very quickly shut down. While he might have admitted his attraction, he'd also stated he had no intention of getting involved with the sister of a suspect. And he still *did* consider Max that, thanks to the fact he'd been in the area the day the coronation ring had been stolen from the British Museum.

Luc's gaze flicked down my length; it felt like a caress and had heat stirring in all the right places. Or rather, wrong places when it came to *this* man.

"What happened to your clothes?" His voice was deep and velvety.

Everyone else looked around at this—Mo in warning. Obviously, the less said in the assessor's presence, the better. "Long story. Is it safe to head upstairs to my room?"

"The stairs are safe," my brother said, "But your room is pretty much a write-off."

"Can I get to my wardrobe?"

"Not yet."

"Grab something from mine," Mo said. "We'll worry about accessing your clothes later."

I headed into her bedroom and wasn't entirely surprised when Luc followed me. I dropped my knives onto her bed, then walked over to the wardrobe and began sifting through her clothes, looking for something that was more my style. Which was extremely difficult given her love of vibrant colors and patterns.

When it became obvious I wasn't going to say anything, Luc said, "I take it things got nasty at the gate?"

I glanced briefly over my shoulder. As specimens of manhood went, he was pretty damn perfect. He was tall, with well-muscled arms and lovely wide shoulders combined with the lean but powerful frame of an athlete. His short hair was as black as sin, his eyes the most startling shade of jade, and his face ... Simply saying gorgeous in no way did it justice. The man put angels to shame.

"You didn't ask Max?"

"Didn't have a chance—the assessor was already here when I arrived this morning."

"I'm surprised you didn't stay the night." I pulled out a pair of flowery purple pants and matched them with a fluffy white sweater. "Especially when Max said you'd come back here after heading across to King's Island."

"I was intending to stay, but I got a call from Jason."

"About what?"

"You answer my question, and I'll answer yours."

I snorted and walked over to the drawers. While I wasn't about to start wearing Mo's knickers or bras—the latter of which probably wouldn't fit anyway—she did have a few support tank tops that would probably stretch enough to do the same job short-term. And they were an infinitely better choice than having my breasts freefalling. *That* would get real uncomfortable, real quick.

I took everything over to her bed then dropped the towel and reached for the tank. An odd sound had me glancing around. Luc had turned away.

A smile tugged at my lips. "I know Blackbirds were the

chivalrous knights of old, but if I was worried about you seeing me naked, I'd have mentioned it."

He crossed his arms and kept his back to me. "Of that I have no doubt."

"Then why turn away?"

"It's for my own good." He paused. "Where did you get that scar running down your right side? It almost looks as if your skin has been melted."

My smile grew. If he'd noticed the scar, then he obviously hadn't turned as quickly as I'd thought. And while there was little chance a glimpse of bare butt would ever change his damn mind about the two of us, I couldn't help hoping it at least made his nights—and his dreams—a little more uncomfortable.

"In a sense, it was—I got hit by a dark whip. By the time I told Mo, the damage was already done."

"It was stupid to delay telling her."

"So Mo informed me. What did Jason want?"

I didn't have to see him rolling his eyes to know that's exactly what he was doing right now. "Remember I asked him to look at the traffic and security cams to see if he could spot the car that dropped Tris off the day he was shot?"

"He found it?"

"Yep. I joined him last night to raid the place."

I pulled on the fluffy sweater and then reached for the pants. "What did you find?"

"Not a whole lot—the place had basically been cleaned out by the time we got there."

"Probably right after they shot Tris." That seemed to be their modus operandi.

"Actually, I don't think so. It looked more recent and hurried."

That raised my eyebrows. "Does that mean you did find something useful?"

"Paperwork similar to the stuff you found in that deconsecrated church they blew up."

Meaning it was written in elvish. "Have you or the preternatural boys found anyone who can transcribe them yet?"

He shook his head. "However, Ricker remembers—"

"Who's Ricker?"

"A fellow Blackbird—"

"And related?"

It was a guess, but it made some sense, as Blackbirds were only ever sourced from the Durant line. Their ability to manipulate both light and shadow had once made them the perfect king's guard—and assassins, if the brief comment Luc had made was anything to go by. Weirdly, there were only ever twelve Blackbirds at a time and, even in this day and age, they were only ever men. It seemed that while Blackbirds might have dragged their chivalrous ways into the twenty-first century, the whole idea of equality hadn't accompanied it.

"Yes—cousin." He paused. "Why?"

I smiled, unable to resist teasing him. "Maybe I want to discover whether all Blackbirds have the same ironclad rules when it comes to attraction."

"Ricker is bound."

"Meaning married, I take it."

"Yes."

"Which still leaves me ten possibilities to explore."

He made a noise that sounded an awful lot like a low growl. "How about we concentrate on the business at hand rather than your hormones?"

I sighed, even as delight danced through me. "You're no fun, Luc."

"Ricker," he continued, obviously deciding to ignore my comment, "remembers seeing a translation scroll in the Glastonbury archives. He's been sent to fetch it."

"Did you find anything not in elvish?"

"A partial phone number. It matches the one you found in Tris's bag."

"Meaning it could belong to their controller."

"Or at least someone else connected to this whole murderous scheme. Jason's running a search, but considering it's only a partial, there's likely to be a ton of matches to check out."

"I'm dressed if you'd like to turn around."

He did so. His gaze skimmed me again and, deep in his rich eyes, desire smoldered. "I'm not entirely sure that sweater is much better than nakedness."

"I'll take that as a compliment—"

"You should, because the nakedness was pretty stunning."

I grinned. "So much for chivalrously turning around before you spotted too much."

"I'm a Blackbird, not a saint or a fool." His voice was dry.

"Mo would likely debate the latter."

"That's because she sees romantic issues through rose-tinted glasses."

"Romance? Is that an admission that there might be something more than lust happening here?"

He did the eye roll thing again. "Can you concentrate for five minutes?"

I made a show of glancing at my watch. "Five it is. I take it a warrant has been issued for the owner of the car?"

He nodded. "Her name was Karen Jacobs, in case you're interested."

"Was?"

"She was killed three weeks ago. Her body remains unclaimed at the coroner's."

"How was she killed?"

"Single shot through the head. Now, before my five minutes run out, how about you start answering some questions?"

"Only if you come closer." I sat on Mo's bed and patted the space beside me. "And don't worry, I won't bite—unless you beg me to, of course, and we both know that won't happen."

He shook his head and walked over. "And we both know why."

"Ignoring fate never ends well, Luc."

"This isn't fate. This is everyday, normal human desire and attraction—and it's something I can't act on while I'm working."

The image I'd caught in his mind—an image of a woman in a blood-soaked red dress—rose. "Because you did once before, and it ended in tragedy."

"Yes."

I sighed. It *was* a good reason, and if he'd been willing to explore the depths of what lay between us after all this was over, I might not be so annoyed with the man.

But he wasn't.

He was more than happy to pursue a sexual relationship, of course, but he'd already stated it would never be anything more than that. And I'd absolutely *had* it with relationships that were based on nothing more than sex. I wanted more. I wanted the box and dice—a man who loved me, who wanted to raise kids with me, and who, more than anything, wanted to grow old with me.

Tris had never been that man, and Luc wouldn't even consider the possibility. It seemed my luck with men really *was* on a roll—in the absolute worst way possible.

I quickly told him what happened at the gate and our discovery of Jules Okoro. "I'm actually surprised you didn't follow Max to the gate, especially given how little you trust him."

His amusement rolled across my senses, somehow setting them alight. "Until Jason's call, I was intending to. Did you search Jules's place?"

"No, because it may have been a crime scene, and we didn't want to spoil any possible evidence." I studied his beautiful profile for a second. "Why?"

He shrugged. "I was just wondering if he was connected to what's been happening—other than being a possible but unlikely heir, that is."

"If there's anything to find, I daresay Jason will find it—you did pass the information on, didn't you?"

He nodded. "He said he'd send a team up there immediately."

Mo appeared in the doorway. "We need to skedaddle over to Barney's."

I grabbed my knives and rose. My arm brushed Luc's and momentarily disrupted my equilibrium. I really did need to keep my damn distance from the man ... but that was likely to get harder and harder. I didn't have his will of iron, and I'd never really been all that good at fighting desire. My long, casual relationship with Tris after we'd officially broken up was evidence enough of that. "I take it the assessor's gone?"

She nodded as she turned away. "He's going to hustle the claim through so we can rebuild ASAP."

Luc followed me from the room. "Why are you going over to Barney's?"

"His nephew has enhanced the writing on the back of the throne. He wants me over there to transcribe it."

"And can you?" he asked.

"The glyphs look similar to the ones on Einar, so possibly. Won't know until we get there though."

Einar—Mo's dagger—had not only been carved out of a solid piece of black stone eons ago, but also had a life and heartbeat of its own. Its power was very different to that of Nex and Vita; it was almost as if the hunger and the means to kill demons and dark elves had been vital to its creation.

Mo cast Luc an amused look and added, "I presume you *are* coming with us?"

A smile tugged at his luscious lips. "Of course."

"Where's Max?" I asked, realizing he wasn't in the room. "Don't tell me he's nicked off again?"

"No, he hasn't" came Max's reply. "He's upstairs cleaning the mess in his room before Granny-dearest tells him off."

"Call me that again, and I'll come up there and box your ears, young man."

"I'll be out the window before you get to the top of the stairs, old woman."

"I wouldn't bet on that," Mo replied.

Max's laughter echoed down the stairs. "Actually, neither would I. Say hello to Barney for me."

Mo walked over to grab her purse. "I'd normally suggest we fly across, but given the weather and the fact Luc can't fly—"

"I'll drive," I said. "I doubt Luc will easily fit in the back of your Leaf."

"I'm not entirely sure the back of your mini will be much of an improvement," she said, amused.

"I'll be fine." His voice was dry. "I've been in tighter positions many times before."

"I just bet you have," Mo said. "And I'm betting they involved a lady or three, too."

Luc laughed and didn't deny it while I tried not to think about getting hot and heavy with Luc in the back seat.

I grabbed my coat and keys off the hook near the stairs and, once we were all in the car, drove through the cobble-stone streets until we neared Dame's Walk. Barney had an apartment on the first floor of a building that not only over-looked the Ainslyn River but also had parking for residents and guests out front—a rarity in this part of town. Once I'd stopped, we climbed out and walked over. Mo keyed us in, then led the way up the creaky wooden stairs; one thing was sure—no one would ever creep up these things without Barney knowing about it.

He opened the door as we approached, swept Mo into his arms, and kissed her soundly. "You took your damn time, woman."

The twinkle in his brown eyes belied the soft rebuke in his words. Mo laughed and patted his cheeks. "You know what they say about those who wait."

"Yeah, they end up with burned lasagna."

"You cooked?"

"I did. Figured you probably wouldn't take the time for breakfast." He glanced past her. "Gwen, Luc, nice to see you both."

He stepped back and waved us all in. His apartment was situated on the corner of the building and benefitted from windows on two sides. The bedroom and bathroom lay at the rear, while the kitchen and living areas were to the front. There was a surprising mix of features—high ceiling, ornate cornices, and ceiling roses juxtaposed against an ultramodern kitchen and furniture—but the room itself was light and bright and had the added bonus of glass doors down the far end of the room that led out onto a small balcony.

Mo took off her coat and strode over to the pin-neat glass-and-chrome dining table where three large photographs sat. "He's done a good job enhancing these."

Barney grabbed the oven mitts and pulled out a large tray of lasagna. It smelled absolutely divine. "The question is, are you able to read the glyphs?"

I stopped beside Mo and peered at the first photograph. The glyphs that had been almost impossible to see on the back of the throne were now crystal clear. It was also evident that each photograph held a different line, which surprised me. I'd only seen one when we'd been examining the back of the old throne—obviously the others had been all but hidden in the grime.

"The glyphs are older than the ones on Einar, but there're enough similarities to make a fairly reasonable guess." She paused, her eyebrows furrowed and expression intent. "The first line reads, *On the darkest day, in the darkest hour, when all hope has been extinguished—*"

"I'm not liking this," I muttered, "it's already sounding decidedly grim."

She ignored me and picked up the second photograph. "*The Blackbirds will rise, a hand will draw the one true sword,* and—" She paused and picked up the last photograph. "—*a lost throne shall be reclaimed.*"

"That's not a prophecy I've heard before." Barney

glanced at Luc. "Have you?"

"No, which is surprising given—" He stopped, his head snapping around.

That's when I heard it—the soft creaking of stairs. At the same time, Nex began to pulse.

"Barney," Luc said softly, "are you expecting any other guests?"

"No, I'm not." He placed the lasagna on a board, then took off the mitts. "There's an easy way to find out who it is, though."

He walked across to a small control panel on the wall to the right of the door and pressed a button. An image immediately flicked up on the screen. The two women climbing the stairs were dressed in plain blue overalls that had Ainslyn Express Couriers emblazoned on the left breast pocket. Both looked rather ordinary—one was short, stout, with a thick thatch of brown hair and skin that was perhaps a little too pale, the other her polar opposite.

But a closer look revealed their eyes were red more than brown, their painted nails ventured into claw territory, and their ears held a definite point.

Halflings.

And Nex had reacted to their presence. Interesting.

Luc reached back and drew the magically concealed Hecate. The spirit blade—which contained the soul of a witch whose penance on death was not only entrapment in the sword but to destroy the dark forces whose power she'd coveted in life—began to hiss.

But a soft scrape had my gaze darting toward the balcony. A figure dropped from somewhere above us, landing in a light crouch. As he rose, I spotted the gun in his hand.

And it was aimed at Mo.

CHAPTER FOUR

"Shooter on the balcony!"

I knocked Mo sideways and down as the glass doors shattered. The bullet aimed at her smashed into the wall behind instead, showering both of us with plaster. I twisted around and grabbed a couple of chairs, throwing them down lengthwise in front of us. It wasn't much protection, but it was better than nothing.

Hecate was screaming, a sound accompanied by the clash of steel against steel. The assassin at the window was still firing, and the bullets ripped through the apartment, tearing apart furniture, floor, and walls alike. Fragments of wood and glass spun through the air, deadly missiles that hit with an accuracy the shooter lacked. The metal chairs continued to protect us, but the shooter only had to take a couple of steps inside and we'd be easy targets. I needed to do something—and fast.

"Stay down," I muttered.

"Don't," Mo said.

I gave her the same sort of look she'd so often given me when I said something stupid and drew Nex and Vita.

After a deep, fortifying breath, I pushed up onto my knees, instantly drawing the shooter's attention, then slapped the daggers together and imagined a shield of sheer electricity. Lightning shot from the ends of both blades and whirled into a pulsing, dangerous net that caught and then incinerated every bullet flying toward us. But the only way to ensure we were really safe was to stop the gunman. I flicked a finger out, and a matching streak of blue-white light shot from the center of the shield. The shooter's eyes went wide even as he pushed up and back, but he wasn't anywhere near fast enough. The lightning hit him, incinerating him as easily as it had his bullets.

I twisted around to see what was happening behind me. Luc knelt over the body of a woman; the other was nowhere in sight. Barney climbed to his feet, and though he was covered in bits of plaster and wood, he looked unharmed aside from a small cut running along his left cheek.

I uncrossed the daggers, and the shield disintegrated, leaving me feeling washed out. But at least my eyes weren't bleeding; creating the shield and ashing the halfling hadn't drawn too much on my strength.

"Well, fuck," Mo said, holding out one hand. "Even I didn't know you could do that with those daggers."

I clasped her fingers and pulled her upright. "Neither did I, to be honest. It was a wing and a prayer moment."

"And one that means Nex and Vita have accepted you in a way they've not any other generation of De Montfort women."

I frowned. "Countless ancestors have used the lightning —there's multiple records of it in those old diaries you hold."

"Yes, but the immersion process never went deeper than surface level. There's no mention in any of those diaries of a lightning shield, and Vita hasn't ever saved the life of another De Montfort—not since Rhedyn, anyway."

Rhedyn was the first De Montfort to hold the daggers. She was also responsible for the tradition of passing them on to the firstborn girl at puberty—though I'd gotten them from Mo rather than my mother, simply because by the time I hit fourteen, she'd been dead for nearly eleven years.

"You never did tell me why Nex and Vita were forged, or even why they were given to Rhedyn rather than her brother."

All I really knew was that they'd been forged at the same time as the king's sword, and it had been the goddess Vivienne who'd gifted them to the De Montfort line. Which made no sense. No matter how friendly Mo appeared to be with the Lady of the Lake, why would she give them to *my* ancestor's over the Aquitaines? We might once have been warriors able to both give and take life, but the Aquitaines had always ruled and protected this land—until Layton's dismantling of witch rule, at any rate.

"No, I never did, did I?" Mo patted my hand. "That's a tale for a less dramatic moment. Go check the balcony while I examine our dead halfling."

I shook my head, then righted the two chairs and walked over to the shattered glass doors. Glass crunched under my feet, and the wind whipped in, its touch chilly and filled with the promise of more rain. It had already whisked away the ashed remains of the halfling—only a blackened circle of concrete spoke of the force that had hit him.

I carefully opened what remained of the door; a big chunk of glass smashed down, spraying glittering shards across the balcony. Above me, well beyond my line of sight, came an odd noise—one that sounded like the scrape of nails across concrete.

Light flickered down Nex's side in response. It definitely wasn't a human scrambling around up there ... I gripped her hilt tighter. Lightning spat from her sharp tip, hissing lightly as it hit the floor. If I wasn't careful, she'd set the whole damn place alight.

I stepped through the doorway and peered up. Unfortunately, the old stone lintel was wider than the actual door, and I couldn't see past it. The scrape echoed again, this time accompanied by a brief fall of dust. He was on the move—

A hand came down on my shoulder, and a squeak of surprise escaped as I swung around. Only quick reflexes on Luc's part stopped Vita scouring open his stomach.

"Damn it, Luc," I growled, keeping my voice low, "you know better than to creep up on me like that."

"Yeah. Sorry." He pointed with his chin to the balcony. "What's the problem?"

"Something's crawling around on the roof."

He reached back and drew Hecate again. Light flickered down her sides, but she wasn't hissing, and she certainly wasn't screaming like a banshee; but then, she only seemed to do that when in the middle of a fight.

"You keep watch here; I'll go up and see if I can grab them." He swung around and retreated. "Barney? I need you to unlock the roof's exit."

As the two of them left, I took a tentative step out the door. More dirt showered down past the stone ledge. I gripped the edge of the doorframe and leaned out. It took me a moment to spot him; the halfling's thin form matched the color of the brickwork so well, he was almost invisible. He was currently under the building's eaves, skittering sideways with an ease that very much reminded me of a spider.

I couldn't see Luc and Barney, nor could I hear them. Even if they *were* up on the roof, they wouldn't see the halfling; he'd already scuttled across to the next apartment. If I didn't do something, we'd lose him. Unfortunately, using Vita and Nex was out of the question; they were life and death, not capture.

"Mo, need your help here."

"What have you found?" She hurried over and peered past me. "Well, I haven't seen one of *them* for quite a long time."

"What is it?"

"A half-blood Aranea, from the look of him. They caused a lot of damage in Uhtric's time, as they could climb over any sort of defense."

"Not magical, surely."

"No, but they were able to weave a way through most of our spells."

I frowned. "Demons aren't capable of magic."

"Aranea are neither demons nor dark elves, but rather a Darkside version of humanity."

"A revelation that's guaranteed to give me nightmares."

"Here's another one, then—where there's one Aranea, there're usually others. They nest together."

"Great. Thanks." I watched the brown figure for a second. "Does the nesting thing apply to half-bloods?"

"That I don't know, as I've never come across one before. I've a feeling we'd better find out, though."

"Then you'd better fling a tracker spell, because he's about to escape."

"I will, but you'd better ring your brother. If they attacked us, they may well attack him."

I nodded and immediately called Max.

"What's up?" he said.

"We were just attacked by an Aranea—"

"*What?* Are you both okay?"

"Yes, but Mo thinks they'll also come after you."

"Why? The sword's been drawn—the game is over."

"Except it may not be—"

"What's that supposed to mean?"

"Nothing right now. Look, Mo's about to fling a tracker at the Aranea, so I've got to go. Hunker down and keep safe."

"Only if you do the same. I need you alive, little sister."

"Getting dead is not on my to-do list for today. Catch you later—"

I was talking to air. He'd already gone. As I put my phone away, Mo flung her spell. It hit the halfling's butt just as he went around the corner.

"Let's go."

She shifted shape and soared upward. I hastily lashed my daggers together and followed. The spiderlike halfling moved with surprising speed and dexterity considering he didn't actually have eight legs. I wondered if his full-blooded cousins did ... and shuddered at the images that instantly rose. I didn't need to be thinking about *that* sort of shit when we were about to enter a possible damn nest of the things.

The Aranea continued to scramble across multiple buildings, his coloring changing to match whatever brick-work he was currently on. He generally kept under the eaves but moved up to the roof whenever the size of a window made the crawling space too small. And while he didn't appear able to fly, he could certainly jump—the streets in Ainslyn's medieval section were fairly narrow, but beyond her walls, the streets widened out. He seemed to leap most distances with ease.

After another few minutes, he leapt onto the roof of a brown-brick Georgian building that had once been—according to the sign at the front—a funeral parlor, then clambered around the back and went in through an open window. I followed Mo down the small laneway that ran along the left side of the building and shifted shape under the convenient—but empty—carport.

I eyed the run-down garages that lined the building's rear fence, seeing a lot of cobwebs and half wondering if Aranea had spun them. "I don't suppose you can tell from here if we're dealing with one half spider thing or a nest?"

She smiled. "Well, no, and there're no obvious signs of occupation."

Maybe not, but we'd learned the hard way that didn't really mean anything. Three halflings had been monitoring our place from the building next door, and we'd had absolutely no idea until Ginny had mentioned the possibility.

"It's promising that we can't smell them," I said.

"We didn't smell the lot next door, either. Not until we raided the place."

And discovered they'd chosen to defecate all over the floor rather than risk us hearing the toilet flushing at a time when we knew our neighbor—Saskia—was away visiting relatives.

"But if we *are* dealing with a nest," Mo continued, "they'll be holed up underground."

The thought of tracking this thing into the bowels of the earth had my nose wrinkling. "Would halflings go underground, though?"

"Impossible to know until we get in there." She studied the building for several seconds, her expression hard to read. "Either way, we'd better not do so unprepared. It might be best if you fly—"

"Uh, no," I cut in. "It's not that I don't trust you not to go in alone or anything—but I don't."

"I'm mortified you'd say something like that." Though she feigned hurt, amusement shone in her eyes.

"I can't see why, when you raised me." I waved a hand toward the house. "We both know the minute I disappear, you're going to head in and kill the bastards."

The amusement got stronger. "Not all of them. We do need to question the fellow we followed to see who the actual target was."

I frowned. "He was obviously shooting at you."

"Let's not forget you were standing beside me, and they've certainly taken shots at you before."

Yes, they had, but I'd gotten the distinct impression that while the demons might want me dead, the dark elves didn't. I *had* thought that was because they wanted to get to Max through me, but after learning about Hanna Okoro, I wasn't so sure.

Which was yet another thought guaranteed to give me nightmares.

"All of which does not change the fact that it makes more sense if I stay—you're the one who's dealt with the Aranea before, and you're the only one who has some idea what it's going to take to deal with the bastards." I smiled. "And you can be damn sure I'm not stupid enough to go in there alone."

"That I'm not so sure about. I did raise you, after all."

I laughed softly. "Go. I'll watch in blackbird form. Hopefully anyone who spots me will think I'm a pigeon."

"Which will only work if the Aranea aren't aware who and what they're dealing with."

And *that* was extremely unlikely. She didn't say that out

loud, but she didn't really need to. "Then the sooner you go, the sooner you and the cavalry can get back."

"Just stay alert. It's always possible this is yet another trap."

I nodded. Once she'd left, I regained bird form and flew over to the small shed situated on the back fence of the house next door. I couldn't risk drifting on the breeze, because this was a well-established residential area, and a bird carrying knives wouldn't exactly be a common sight. It also risked drawing the attention of any watchers the Aranea had in place.

I landed on the shed's roof, deposited my knives in the gutter, and then strutted up to the roof's ridge. I wasn't high enough to see into the first-floor windows, but it did give me a view over the surrounding houses. There were obviously a lot of families in the area, because there were toys, trampolines, and bikes scattered throughout the various yards. Two boys chased each other around a few houses down, their laughter filling the air. It was a bright sound in a gloomy, rain-swept day.

There was nothing here that tweaked my instincts; nothing to suggest anyone living in this area was in any way aware that they had a nest of half-demons living right next to them. I doubted they'd so readily let their kids play unmonitored if they were.

I walked to the other end of the shed, then flew over the funeral parlor's roof to the building on the far side. As I did, a gray Merc drove into the narrow lane, then stopped in one of the marked parking bays in front of the old garages. I walked across to the chimney and used it for cover as I peered out. The driver didn't immediately leave his car; from what I could see through the heavily tinted windows, he was on the phone and—if his gestures were anything to go by—animatedly disagreeing with whatever the other person was saying. This went on for several minutes, then he thrust the door open and climbed out.

Shock rolled through me, and it was all I could do not to squawk in surprise. I may never have met the man below, but he matched the description Henry had given us and left me in little doubt as to his identity.

This was Winter—the halfling who killed my cousins and who'd more than likely ordered Tris's murder.

He was a delicately built man, with long white hair held back from sharp cheekbones by a black, trident-shaped, and very dangerous-looking hairpin. His features bordered on effeminate, and he was unmistakably from Okoro stock, even though his eyes were as blue as summer skies. But it was his skin that gave his true origins away—it had a grayish tint. His ears were also pointed.

When Henry had described him, he'd used the feminine pronoun rather than masculine. I wasn't sure why; despite his effeminate features, the man below clearly identified as male. But then, halflings were hermaphrodites and able to switch between functioning as a male and a female. Perhaps he'd taken on a more feminine look when he set out to murder my cousins. It would certainly explain how he'd gotten unchallenged into the house—Gareth had been a ladies' man. Maybe he'd quite literally invited death into his home …

Winter slammed the car door closed and stalked into the house. I shifted uneasily, wanting to see what he was up to but knowing full well moving from my hiding spot could lead to disaster. These people—this man—had been two steps ahead of us from the get-go. If we wanted to reverse that situation, then we—or rather *I*—needed to proceed cautiously. I shifted shape and called Mo.

"What's up?" she said without preamble.

"The halfling who killed Gareth and Henry—the one called Winter—just turned up."

"Don't you dare go in after her."

"He identifies as a male from the look of it, and I don't intend to."

"Promise me."

"Mo, he's going into a possible nest of creepy-crawly half-human things. There's no way known I'm going in alone."

She grunted, somehow managing to sound unconvinced. "It's going to take us a good fifteen minutes to get over there. Sit tight, and let me know if the situation changes."

"I will."

I shoved the phone back into my pocket and then resumed my other form. I had no idea if anyone was home in the houses opposite, but they were more likely to notice—and report—a strange woman huddled on a rooftop than a bird.

The minutes ticked slowly by, and it began to rain again. I fluffed out my feathers and huddled closer to the chimney; while it at least protected me from the worst of the wind, it nevertheless was damn cold and uncomfortable.

Winter came back out a few minutes later, jumped into his Merc, and quickly left. I ran across the roof to see which direction he went and then slid back, changed form, and called Mo.

"How far away are you?"

"Five—why?"

"Winter's just left. I'm going to follow him, but I can't take my daggers—they'll just slow me down."

"Where are they?"

"Sitting in the gutter of next door's shed. I'll ring as soon as I have a location."

She didn't say be careful. She didn't need to. I shoved my phone away, then shifted shape and leapt skyward. The speed limit around these parts was low, so it didn't take me very long to catch up. If there was one thing to be thankful for about this damn storm, it was the fact that my light plumage made it harder to pick me out against the sky. While there'd been a slight chance the Aranea didn't know I was a whitewashed blackbird, those odds were nonexistent when it came to Winter.

He drove past Ainslyn's main Hospital and Urgent Care Center and then turned left onto the highway. He left it again after a couple of kilometers, continued on for a few more, and then turned into a tree-lined country lane surrounded by farmlands. Eventually, he pulled off the road and parked in front of a field gate. I swooped down and perched on the branch of an ash—and not a moment too soon. Winter looked around as he climbed out of his car and then looked up, studying the skies for what seemed like an extraordinarily long time. I made like a rock. The ash's foliage was fairly thick, but one wrong move could easily reveal my plumage.

With a satisfied grunt that was barely audible from where I was perched, Winter locked his car and then walked down the road to an open water drain. After another look around, he ducked under the old wooden barrier, then jumped down and disappeared from sight. I hesitated, well aware that I was alone and without my weapons, then mentally smacked myself. Unless he had a gun, he couldn't actually hurt me—not when I was on the wing, anyway. I leapt out of the tree and swooped toward the drain.

A quick flyover didn't reveal where he'd gone. I swung

around and followed the other side of the drain for several seconds. Still no sign of the man.

I circled around and, after a brief hesitation, dropped low enough to view the large storm pipe that ran under the road. Nothing there, either. Nothing other than dripping water and thick strings of moss.

He *couldn't* have disappeared. He was a halfling, and incapable of magic. There *had* to be something here I was missing.

I eyed the drain warily for a few more seconds, then changed and dropped to the ground, brushing my fingers lightly against the wet grass to catch my balance. My appearance didn't draw any sort of response, and yet trepidation nevertheless stirred. I reached into my pocket to turn down my phone—the last thing I needed was it inadvertently ringing and advertising my presence—then cautiously walked on. The closer I got, the louder the steady drip of water seemed to get. It ate at my nerves and sent my heartbeat soaring.

I stopped again at the edge of the concrete pipe and brushed aside a slimy string of moss. There was absolutely nothing here.

And yet ...

I flared my nostrils and drew in a deep breath. I wasn't imagining it—the air now held a hint of acidity, and that meant there was at least *one* demon close by.

But where?

Other than this drain, there was no logical place for a creature that would be ashed by sunlight to hide, so why the hell couldn't I see him?

He couldn't be using a purchased concealment spell, because I'd see the threads of it. Mo might not have been able to teach me to cast spells, thanks to the inner lack of all magic aside from shifting, but she *had* taught me to how to see and track them. There was no spell—purchased or created—here.

Which left me with one other option—a hidden gateway.

I took a cautious step into the drain, my body practically vibrating with tension. Nothing jumped out at me. The water continued to drip, and that wisp of acidity remained faint.

Another step. Then another. Still nothing. I flexed my fingers and walked in deeper. The smell of rot and dampness now dominated the air; moss clung to the walls of the pipe, and it was a surprisingly lush forest of green. In fact, it was almost *too* lush—too thick and perfect. I frowned and lightly touched it. It felt like regular moss, though it was perhaps a bit more spongy than usual. I picked a bit off and examined it—and discovered it wasn't moss but rather some sort of artificial material. I walked a bit further down and picked off another piece, with the same result. Someone had gone to a lot of trouble to cover the inside of this pipe with this stuff.

I did another quick scan, my heart beating so hard if felt like there was a mad drummer inside my chest. The fake moss covered the middle section of the pipe and faded out toward the ends, but there was nothing here that immediately screamed door, hidden or otherwise.

I continued on, my fingers pressed lightly against the mossy wall. There was no seam in the artificial material, no break of any kind. If there was a gate on this side of the pipe it was very well hidden.

I moved across to the other side and repeated the process. Just off the middle of the drain, my fingers slid across a thin crack. The minute they did, the moss shimmered and disappeared.

Revealing a door into Darkside.

I sucked in a deep breath and fought the urge to run. While the gateway was unlocked—in fact, there was nothing to indicate witch magic had *ever* been used to lock it down—the door itself was closed rather than open. That could change in a heartbeat, of course, but given the thing looked and felt like it was made out of concrete, I doubted it'd open with any sort of speed.

And, of course, having thought *that,* the total opposite would now prove to be true.

I sucked in another deep breath that did nothing to calm my racing heart and studied the gate. It was six feet high, but rather than the doorframe being made of the otherworldly blue-black stone used in every other one I'd come across, this used simple concrete. The images carved into it, however, were as grotesque as ever, depicting demons of all kinds and shapes both cavorting with and destroying human figures. I could almost hear the screaming of all those being fucked, tortured, and hacked ...

I blinked, suddenly realizing I *wasn't* imagining it—there *were* people screaming.

As I instinctively stepped back, a pulse of power flickered around the arch and the door began to open.

I got the hell out of there.

I'd barely made it to the nearest tree when a figure exited the pipe and scrambled up the drain's grassy bank. It wasn't Winter—not unless he could utterly alter both his shape *and* height, and that was unlikely. Most shape shifts involved magic, and halflings weren't capable of it. Besides, there was no such thing as a witch who could alter their *human* shape, and surely if the ability *ever* existed, it would have been nurtured and used. Assassins might be rare these days, but hundreds of years ago it had been a profitable and much sought-after profession.

This man was long and thin, with spindly arms and legs and a way of walking that was almost spiderlike.

An Aranea. Whether it was the same one or not, I couldn't say, but I guessed it was possible—it just depended on how efficient the transport links were between the gates in Darkside.

He reached the top of the embankment and quickly looked around. Thankfully, he didn't scan the trees, because the foliage in this one wasn't particularly thick, and I had no doubt my white plumage would be visible.

He strode across the road and climbed into Winter's car. Which meant either the car was a universal one, used by all the halflings from this gateway, or he'd been sent on an errand by Winter.

As the taillights flashed on, I dropped to the ground and rang Mo.

She answered with a quick, "Where are you?"

"On some country lane outside Ainslyn's city limits. Winter went through a Darkside gateway, and I think it's either a new one or one that's never been registered."

She swore softly. "That's not the sort of news we need right now."

There was something in her voice that had trepidation stirring anew. "Why? What's happened?"

"We didn't find an Aranea nest under the house. We found another unregistered gateway."

A chill went through me. One unknown gateway might be brushed aside as an oversight, but two of them? In or around Ainslyn? That was highly unlikely.

"Why would Winter leave one gateway and drive all the way to another?"

"They don't all enter the same area in Darkside, Gwen. It could also be that it's easier to travel distances here rather than there."

Given how little anyone really knew about Darkside, that was more than possible. "It does sound like they've learned how to make new gateways."

"Or whatever caused the initial development of them has become active again. Either way, it is *not* a good sign." I could almost see her scrubbing a hand across her eyes in frustration. "Has Winter come back out?"

"No. But another Aranea has, and he's just jumped into Winter's car. Do you want me to follow him, or stay and watch the dark gate?"

"It's pointless staying—aside from the fact you can't in any way close it, you're weaponless. Follow the other halfling, but stay vigilant and keep me updated."

"I will."

I shoved my phone away and then flew after the Mercedes. He didn't, as I half expected, head back into Ainslyn, but instead drove around it and continued on to Leeds. Thankfully, he didn't appear to be in a hurry, so I was able to keep him in sight quite easily. He turned off before he reached the city, however, driving past a shopping center and down several residential streets before pulling into a lane lined with small, red-brick terraces.

He stopped in the driveway of the last house in the row but didn't immediately get out. The lace curtains covering the one ground floor window twitched, and a pale face briefly appeared. It was a child—a little girl—not an adult.

That sense of trepidation grew. Why the hell would a

halfling be sent to a house with a kid inside? Was the little girl also a halfling? Or was something stranger going on?

I flew on to the park at the end of the lane and, after a quick circle around to ensure no one was near, shifted shape and took up a position behind a tree so I could watch the house without being too obvious.

The spiderlike halfling still hadn't gotten out of his car, but he was looking down at something in his lap. If he was sending a text, then it gave me a chance to call Mo.

"Where have you ended up?"

"I'm just outside Leeds." I glanced at the nearby street sign. "Primrose Lane, just near the park there."

"And the Aranea?"

"He's sitting in the car outside a small terrace." I paused. "I know there's a kid inside, but I'm not sure who else is."

"The kid can't be his—halflings are usually sterile."

"Usually means there *is* some leeway."

"Well, yes, because we haven't examined all halflings." Her voice sounded a little exasperated, though I suspected it wasn't aimed at me.

"Have you and Barney sealed the gateway under the funeral place?"

"Yes, and a damn hard task it was too."

I frowned. "None of them are particularly easy to seal, so what made this one different?"

"There was a spell woven into the fabric of its construction that repelled other magics. It had to be unpicked first."

"Was it dark elf in origin?"

"Yes, and from a hierarchical level. If the nobility is now getting involved, they must be very certain the main gate will soon be opened."

My frown deepened. "If they know how to create gates,

why would they need the main gate opened? Why wouldn't they just create another big one and attack en masse?"

"Because the existing gateways weren't created by either their magic or ours, but rather a major force of some kind that briefly had the two planes intersecting. As a result, multiple coplanar points—or gateways—formed."

Which was the first time I'd actually heard it fully explained like that. For the most part these days, the gateways were simply shrugged off and accepted.

"Which doesn't address the point of them simply creating new ones."

"If they'd been able to create gateways in any sort of numbers, they would have done so by now. Remember, the coplanar points have existed for almost as long as recorded history."

"Yes, but—"

"The gateway under the funeral director's was sourced from the magic of at least three high-ranking elves," she continued. "The threads of said magic were entwined in a way I've not seen before, and contained the stink of death. I suspect the elves responsible for it may have died."

"The elves wouldn't care—not from the little we know of them, anyway."

"That may be true of the warriors, but the hierarchy is a different matter. They are more dangerous than the warriors and yet far fewer in number."

"Do you think the gateway I found under the drain is another fresh one? Its construction is certainly different to the one we found in Ainslyn."

"Possibly, although it could also be a previously unknown entrance that's been rebuilt in recent times. The existence of gateways has been known to fluctuate over the centuries—it's almost as if the connection between our worlds stretches and snaps, and then is slowly mended again."

"Huh." I glanced toward the house as the curtains twitched again. The pale face that appeared this time was a woman's. That the kid wasn't alone didn't in any way ease the tension within. "What do you want me to do?"

"Keep an eye on the place and see what the Aranea does. I might ask Luc to head over to help you out."

"The Aranea could move again before he's even halfway here, and we both know it. Stop meddling, Mo."

She chuckled. "I've spent my entire life meddling—why on earth would I stop it now?"

I rolled my eyes. "I'll give you a call if the situation changes."

"If you do happen to lose him, I'll meet you back home."

"Okay."

I shoved my phone away and then crossed my arms and leaned against the tree. The Aranea hadn't moved; if not for the faint glow of his phone's screen highlighting his thin features, it would have been easy to believe he'd fallen asleep.

The rain swept in again and big fat drops fell around me. I shivered. My coat was waterproof, but it wasn't exactly warm, and the day was getting colder. Or maybe it just seemed that way thanks to the fact the lower part of my body was utterly drenched.

Once again, time ticked slowly by. I couldn't help but wonder if the unmoving presence in the driveway at all worried the woman inside the house. If it'd been me, I'd have called the cops ... or grabbed my knives and gone out there to confront him.

My fingers twitched, and I couldn't help wishing I'd brought them with me. Something odd was happening, and

I really hated not having their comforting weight strapped to my thighs or feeling the inner pulse of their power.

As if in response to that thought, my fingers tingled and burned—a ghostly echo of the force that usually ran through the daggers. I frowned down at my hands, but the sound of a door slamming had me quickly looking up again.

The Aranea had left the car and now strode toward the house. He didn't ring the bell. He simply grabbed the handle, threw his weight against the door, and forced it open.

Voices followed. Raised voices. Angry voices.

Then the screaming began.

I didn't hesitate. Not for a second. I pushed away from the tree and bolted across the road, leaping over the small wooden fence then racing for the still-open front door.

The screaming was coming from upstairs ... but I was barely inside when it stopped. The silence that followed was ominous.

I grabbed the banister and ran up. Saw, at the last minute, a shadow move. Ducked low and felt the brush of metal across the top of my head. The bar that would have smashed my head open destroyed several balusters instead, sending thick splinters spinning thorough the air.

I thrust up and launched at the shadowy figure, hit him hard and sent him sprawling backwards. He wrapped long, scrawny hands around my throat, his fingernails cutting into my skin as he squeezed tight. The bastard was strong —*really* strong. I swore—a sound that came out a wheeze— pushed partially up, and thrust a knee into his groin. He grunted, and pain flashed across his thin features, but he didn't let go.

Blood flowed freely down my neck now, and his grip was like a vise. If I didn't get free soon, I wouldn't.

I clenched my fist and hit him hard, again and again and again. Blood and snot flew as his nose shattered and his thin lips split, but he simply chuckled. Even worse, he was getting off on killing me.

Panic surged, and with it came something else. Something fierce, electric, and born of storms. It burned through me, down my arms and into my hands, and then split into multiple forks of lightning that crackled across the Aranea's body. The force was such that he was ashed in an instant and the treads underneath were left smoking.

For several seconds, I didn't move. *Couldn't* move. Every bit of me burned and twitched, the inner heat so fierce that the sweat breaking out across my skin dried in a heartbeat. All I wanted to do was collapse and sleep for a hundred years, but I was in a stranger's house, and there was a woman and a little girl here somewhere. They could be alive, they could be dead, but either way, I had to find out.

I could worry about what had just happened afterward.

I pushed upright, then gripped the broken handrail as everything spun around me. Moisture dribbled down my neck and over my eyelashes, the latter briefly blurring my vision. Breathing remained difficult, though I had a feeling it had nothing to do with almost having my windpipe crushed and was more a result of the thunderstorm that had swept through me.

I stomped on a still-smoldering bit of stair tread, then dragged myself up the rest of them. My heart beat so heavily that by the time I reached the landing, I had to stop again and suck in great gulps of air. Everything—absolutely everything—continued to shake. Whatever that storm was—wherever it had come from—it had absolutely drained me.

I forced myself to move on. Two of the three doors off

the central landing were open—one was a bathroom, the other a kid's room. The third door no doubt led into the master bedroom. Dreading the possible horror I was about to walk into, I pushed away from the handrail and continued on. I paused again at the door, drawing in a deep breath, trying to fortify myself against whatever lay beyond.

One thing was certain—death waited beyond this door. I could smell it—smell the blood. The only question that needed answering was—was there one body or two?

I turned the handle and pushed the door open. It revealed a freestanding wardrobe and a double bed, but there was no immediate sign of the death and blood that permeated the air. The body—or bodies—had to lie to my right, behind the door.

I stepped in and turned that way.

A woman lay in a crumpled heap near the top end of the bed, her body battered and bruised. Her face ... Dear god, it didn't even resemble something that belonged to a human anymore. It was just a mess of pulped skin, bone, and hair. The Aranea had obviously used the metal bar he'd attacked me with on her; if not for luck and the storm that had surged through me, I might well have ended up in the same bloody mess as this poor woman.

The little girl lay in a crumbled heap behind the woman —a position that suggested the older woman had tried her best to protect the child. There was a red welt across her cheek, and blood dribbled from her nose and lip. She wasn't moving, and I couldn't immediately see any sign of breathing.

I carefully walked over, doing my best to avoid the splatters of blood and bone and brain matter, and pressed my fingers against the child's neck. Her pulse was light and erratic, but at least it existed. Relief hit, and tears stung my eyes. I sucked in air, trying to control my emotions, knowing the situation might yet change and that I needed to get help here fast.

I dragged my phone out and called Luc.

"Everything okay?" Though his voice was clear, the roar of his motorbike was evident in the background.

"No. I need you to call Jason and ask him to get his medics and a team here ASAP."

The Preternatural Investigations Team not only had their own team of medics who specialized in treating demon- and elf-related injuries, but also owned several high-security private hospitals—though I wasn't entirely sure they'd be the best option for this little girl. The high-security nature of the one Henry had been in certainly hadn't hindered Darkside in any way. Their attack on the place had been swift and violent, though just how they'd known he was there was a question that had yet to be answered. It did mean the girl might be no safer there than at any regular hospital.

Not that we could risk that, either.

"What's happened?" Luc said. "Are you okay?"

The tension and concern in his voice came through loud and clear, and it made me smile. He might not want anything long-term but he *did* care, even if he wasn't willing to admit it.

"I'm fine, but there's a dead woman and an unconscious kid here."

"I'll get on to Jason now. Be there in ten."

Meaning he wasn't that far away. Relief stirred, and I closed my eyes against the sting of more tears. Which was utterly unlike me and spoke to just how physically draining that storm burst had been.

I slid down the wall next to the little girl and lightly

gripped her wrist to check her pulse again. It remained thready, but I couldn't see any external sign of major injury. Hopefully, it meant she'd simply been knocked out.

Her face was Okoro in shape, her features almost ethereal, and her short hair thick and a rich burnished gold color. Her skin was on the pale side, but it was hard to tell if it held a gray tint or not. Her hands certainly didn't. Nor were they clawed.

Her build was on the wiry side, but her limbs were sturdy. She didn't in any way resemble the Aranea, and I very much doubted he was her father. I glanced at the woman. It was impossible to tell if she was the mother or merely a caretaker, but she had the same wiry build, and the bits of hair that weren't gore-covered were burnished gold.

Aquitaine, an inner voice whispered. Whether she was a halfling or a full blood wasn't immediately obvious.

So why did the Aranea want them dead?

Or had someone else given the order and he'd been forced to pass it on? He'd certainly spent some time in the car arguing with whoever had been on the other end of the phone—had he been trying to protect these two and been overridden?

Maybe.

Until we knew more about the woman and the child, it really wasn't a question we could answer.

I closed my eyes and leaned back against the wall. It probably wasn't the smartest thing to do, given I was in a house that might be connected to Darkside in more ways than just these two, but the light streaming in from the window was hurting my already aching eyes.

Time ticked by. Eventually, the approaching roar of a motorbike broke the hush surrounding the house. It stopped outside, and a few seconds later, Luc said, "Gwen? You still here?"

"Upstairs." It came out croaky, and I swallowed heavily. My throat felt like a desert. "Can you grab me a glass of water before you come up?"

"Will do." He moved away, and pipes rattled as he turned on a tap. Then he was back and coming up the stairs.

I forced my eyes open as he stepped into the room. His gaze swept the three of us and then returned to me. "Why are your eyes bleeding when you didn't have Nex or Vita with you?"

"It would appear I can use their lightning without actually holding them."

"I didn't think that was possible."

I accepted the cup he handed me with a nod of thanks and drank it down in several swift gulps. It didn't immediately ease the dryness in my throat, or the weakness clinging to the rest of me.

"Neither did I."

He squatted beside me and gently touched the wounds on my neck. "And these?"

"The Aranea dug his claws in while attempting to choke me."

"So it's his ashes on the stairs?"

I nodded. "I didn't get up here in time to save the woman, but the child is still alive."

His gaze briefly flicked to her, but his hand remained pressed against my neck, and the warmth of his touch pulsed through me, chasing away some of the weariness. "She doesn't look like a halfling."

"That may be the whole point," I said. "And it makes no sense that the Aranea was sent here to kill them. Why not move her—especially considering we didn't even know she existed?"

"They must have been under the impression that we did." He studied the girl for a moment. "It's also possible that they had no intention of killing the girl."

More than possible, when I actually thought about it. One blow could have easily killed her; instead, he'd simply hit her hard enough to knock her out.

The sound of approaching sirens invaded the brief silence. Luc glanced toward the window. "That'll be Jason's people. I'll head down and update them—you going to be all right for a few seconds?"

I smiled. "I'm not that fragile, Luc."

"Normally no, but whatever the force you used was, it's damn well drained you. You're looking decidedly gaunt right now."

"I'm too well rounded to ever look gaunt."

I said it as a joke, but he didn't look amused. "Elemental magic can kill the user just as easily as those it's set against—and you've barely recovered from the force you unleashed at the hospital."

"This wasn't elemental—"

"The smell in the air says otherwise."

I frowned. "Elemental magic hasn't got a smell—"

"That depends entirely on the element. Storm magic—or, more specifically, lightning—has sharp smell, not unlike something inorganic burning, such as electrical wires or plastic. That scent still rides the air here."

Did that mean the force coming from Nex and Vita was elemental in origin? That made absolute sense, given the king's sword drew on the power of all elements and the daggers were not only created in the same forge, but of the same steel. So why would Mo say they drew on the strength of their wielder?

I wearily rubbed the bridge of my nose. "Nothing is making much sense today."

"No, it's not." His fingers left my neck, leaving me feeling colder than I ever thought possible. I shivered and crossed my arms; Luc immediately took a blanket from the bed and draped it over me. "I'll be back with the medics in minutes."

"I'll be fine. Really."

He gave me a disbelieving look and then left the room. I tugged the blanket around my neck and tried to get warm. The fact that my borrowed pants, shoes, and socks were all soaked wasn't helping the situation. If I didn't wake up tomorrow with a chill, I'd be very surprised.

A sharp sound had me looking down. The little girl whimpered. I hesitated, and then wrapped my hand around hers. "It's okay, little one. No one is going to hurt you. You're safe."

At the sound of my voice, her eyes sprang open. Shock coursed through me, and a gasp escaped.

The girl's eyes were sky blue ringed by gold.

She was a De Montfort.

CHAPTER FIVE

B ut ... how was that possible?

De Montforts were few and far between here in England. There were certainly branches of the family living in multiple other countries, but there'd only been a dozen or so De Montforts located here in England when both Henry and Gareth had been killed. And Ada—their sister—hadn't yet had any kids.

Had her parents come here from overseas? If so, where were they? Or was she simply the result of Darkside's witch breeding program? My gaze jumped to the battered woman —surely if she was the girl's mother and *had* been impregnated by the dark elves, she wouldn't have willingly remained here. There were no obvious signs of restraints on her or in the house—though I guess that didn't mean there weren't unobvious ones.

The girl made another odd noise—it almost sounded like the mewling of a kitten—and seemed to shrink in on herself. Fear shone from her eyes, and her battered lips were quivering. "It's okay," I said softly. "You're okay. I promise."

Her gaze swept my face and then moved to the dead

woman. I flicked the blanket over the remains but not fast enough to prevent the child seeing what had been done. She didn't react. Not in any normal way. But her little fingers clutched mine more tightly and there was an almost unnatural strength in her grip.

Footsteps echoed on the stairs—Luc and a medic, from the sound of their conversation.

"The girl's awake," I called out softly. "Don't make any sudden moves, or you'll scare her."

Luc stepped aside, and a stranger appeared. The latter's build was long and thin, and he had dark skin and eyes. He could almost have been a De Montfort, although we tended not to be that tall. His facial structure was more Chen though and, skin color aside, he could almost have been Tris's twin.

As he turned toward us, the girl made another odd sound and leapt into my arms. I wrapped them around her wiry frame, aware of her trembling and breathing in her fear.

The medic hesitated, then got down and shuffled the remaining distance on his knees. The girl eyed him fiercely, but otherwise remained still. Only the trembling gave away her fear.

He stopped next to us and sat back on his haunches. "My name is Mark," he said, his voice soft and oh-so soothing. "I'm here to fix your nose—that's really sore, isn't it?"

She didn't respond. It made me wonder if she was in some way mute—it would certainly explain the odd sounds she kept making.

Unless, of course, the only language she knew was dark elf or demon ...

"May I touch your hand?" he continued. "You'll feel a

warm, tingly sensation, but that's just me checking your injuries. I promise it won't hurt you."

Meaning there *was* De Montfort in his bloodline somewhere.

The little girl continued to eye him fiercely, but, after a moment, held out one hand. She understood us even if she couldn't speak.

Mark lightly gripped her fingers, and his energy warmed the air as it flowed through his hand and up the little girl's arms. She shivered but otherwise didn't move. The bruising on her cheek rapidly faded, her lip healed, and her nose reverted to a more normal shape.

The energy retreated, and Mark gave a soft grunt of satisfaction. "She hasn't got any internal injuries, although we should still take her to hospital so she can be monitored—"

The girl made a garbled, distressed sound and flung her arms around my neck. "I'm thinking that means she doesn't want to go."

He frowned. "She's a kid. I hardly think she has any understanding—"

"I wouldn't be so sure of that," I cut in. "And we have no idea what other trauma she's seen or suffered."

"Yes, but that doesn't negate the fact that hospital—*our* hospital—is the safest place for her."

She made another mewling sound, and her arms tightened. She wasn't choking me by any means, but she didn't really have to to cause me pain—not with the bruising and the cuts already there.

I glanced past Mark to Luc. "We can't risk it. Not after what happened to Henry."

He frowned. "She'll be safer there than anywhere else—"

"We thought that about Henry, too."

He studied me for a second and then swept a hand through his thick hair. "Fine. But in that case, we need to get her out of here before Darkside realizes things haven't gone as they planned."

I nodded and glanced down at the little girl. "I'm going to stand up and take you away from this house and get you somewhere safe—okay?"

She nodded. I tightened my grip on her, then, with one hand braced against the wall for support, pushed upright. The room immediately spun, and it was all I could do to remain upright.

Mark half reached out, as if to grab me. "I'm thinking you're the one that needs to be in hospital rather than the girl."

"What's wrong with me will be fixed by a decent meal and a good night's sleep."

"But your eyes—"

"Are just the result of overusing elemental magic. I'm good. Really."

He hesitated, then slung his pack off his shoulder and opened it up. "In that case, take these with you." He handed me two bottles of tablets. Both were Panadol, but one was for kids, the other extra-strength and obviously meant for me. "Use them if you need to."

I tucked them into my pocket and then moved past him. Luc turned and led the way down the stairs—no doubt with the intention of catching me should I fall—then lightly gripped my elbow and guided me out the front door. A black car pulled up as we exited; the door opened, and a craggy-faced, silver-haired man in his late forties climbed out. Jason, the preternatural team's lead investigator and a good friend of Luc's.

"I should have guessed you'd be involved," he said, voice dry. "You seem to have a talent for attracting trouble."

"At least it's keeping you in a job," I replied mildly.

He snorted, and his gaze switched to Luc. "Why are you running off with one of our survivors?"

"Long story short, we can't risk a repeat of what happened with Henry."

Jason frowned. "Henry was an heir—"

"And in one of your most secure locations," I said. "It'll be better for everyone if we take her off grid."

"And we'll need to borrow the car," Luc added. "So if you can arrange transport for the motorbike, I'd appreciate it."

"I'll hold it hostage until a full explanation of what is going on is forthcoming," Jason said, voice dry.

Luc laughed. "As per usual. And you'll send an update as soon as you get the woman's ID?"

Jason rolled his eyes. "Yes."

"Thank you."

The two of them exchanged keys, then Jason went inside. I convinced the child to release me and belted her into the middle seat before climbing in beside her. She immediately pressed against me, her little fingers resting gently on my arm.

Luc did a quick U-turn then glanced at me through the rearview mirror. "I take it your comment about going off grid means Blackbird-related locations are also out?"

I wrinkled my nose. "No offense, but we can't risk it. It'll be safer for her and safer for anyone who guards her."

"Where do you suggest we go?"

"I have no clue." I shifted and dragged my phone out of my pocket. "But Mo will."

She answered on the second ring. "What the hell has

been happening? I've been getting all sorts of horrendous vibes from the cosmos."

"The Aranea killed the woman inside the house, but I managed to save the little girl."

"More went on than that. The vibes held the stink of a rising storm, and I haven't smelled something like that for generations."

"I'll explain all that later. Right now, we need somewhere secure to take the girl."

"Why isn't the preternatural team looking after her?"

"Because Henry wasn't safe with them, and I don't think she will be." I hesitated. "Mo, she's a De Montfort."

She sucked in a sharp breath. "That's ... interesting."

"I'm glad you didn't say impossible."

"I think the events of the last week or so have proven the impossible no longer is." Her voice was dry. "I take it you've already left Leeds?"

"In the process of, yes."

"Give me a few minutes then, and I'll make some calls."

She hung up without waiting for my reply. I dropped the phone onto my lap and then glanced down at the pale little face resting against my side. She was asleep. It was obvious she trusted me, despite the fact I was a stranger and, given my bloody eyes, probably a scary-looking one at that.

"Why do you think the Aranea was sent to that house to kill the woman and maybe this kid?" I said. "It really doesn't make much sense."

"Maybe they're simply getting rid of the loose ends."

"But the woman wasn't guarded—"

"Was Jules?"

"Not that we noticed."

"Then it's possible there was some sort of electronic or magic-based tracker involved."

That would explain why the woman had stayed in the house when the Aranea pulled into the driveway. Maybe she knew it was pointless trying to run and had grabbed the metal pole for defense—only to have it ripped from her grasp and used against her.

"It makes sense to track Jules—they obviously knew we were looking for him. But nothing we've come across mentioned an Aquitaine woman with a De Montfort child."

Nothing we could understand, at any rate. It was possible the partially destroyed notes we'd found in the deconsecrated church might have mentioned something, but everything had been written in elvish, and we were still trying to find someone to transcribe them.

"You're presuming the dead woman is her mother. She may not be." Luc's gaze met mine in the rearview mirror again. "As to the father—do you think she could be Henry's? Or Gareth's?"

"Gareth is the more likely of the two. He definitely had a way with the ladies." I wrinkled my nose. "I doubt he'd have kept her locked away like that, though. He might not have wanted children just yet, but he would have supported them both."

"There's no evidence as yet that he—or whoever else the father might be—isn't. She wasn't living in a run-down area, after all."

True. "I gather Jason will be doing a full background on her?"

"As a matter of course." He hesitated. "Could she be your brother's offspring?"

"He's homosexual, not bi."

"Which doesn't mean anything these days. Plenty of homosexual men have used artificial insemination and a surrogate to have children."

"Yes, but does my brother in any way look ready to settle down and support a kid? Hell, he can barely support himself half the time."

"All true, and yet it remains a possibility you can't deny."

I sure as hell *wanted* to. "The only way we'll ever find out is to do a DNA test."

"I'm sure either Jason or even Ginny could arrange for that to be done ASAP."

I frowned at the edge in his voice. "Why are you so certain she's his?"

"I'm not. I just think it's a possibility we have to remain open to."

I rubbed my forehead wearily, as much to scrub away the thought of my brother having a kid for nefarious purposes as to ease the still thunderous ache in my head.

"If it *is* true, then I guess the next natural question is, why didn't he tell us about her?"

"There's only one person who can answer that question, Gwen."

"And he's the one person we *can't* ask. Not yet. Not until we're absolutely sure she's his."

But surely we hadn't grown so distant that he was afraid to tell me he'd fathered a child via a surrogate? Did he think we'd in any way judge him for that?

Maybe, an inner voice whispered. *He's not the person you grew up with. Not anymore.*

And the flashes of emotion I'd seen under the bridge certainly underscored that.

"You can't keep making excuses for him, Gwen."

"I'm not, but he *is* my brother. My twin. I have to believe him incapable of working with Darkside. At least until there's indisputable proof saying otherwise." God, if they could turn my brother onto the dark path, who couldn't they get to?

"This kid might give you that proof," Luc said.

"A DNA test will only prove whether she's his or not. It doesn't prove a connection to Darkside." I hesitated. "And the very fact the Aranea killed her mother but left her alive means they might have been intending to use her as a hostage against him."

It also meant that Darkside knew a whole lot more about my family than either Mo or I did—and that was damn scary.

"That's also possible, especially if the new Witch King is intent on killing off the remaining heirs."

"So why are they still coming after me?" Or, at least, the demons were. I didn't want to think about the dark elves' intentions. "If they were aware of this girl's existence, wouldn't she make the better hostage?"

"It appears they might have come to that conclusion today. As to why they're still targeting you—maybe it's got something to do with the sword's reaction to you on the morning of the blessing."

"Why? It's not like I moved it or anything."

But even as I said that, an echo of the power that had raced across my fingertips when I'd gripped the sword's hilt rose, and I frowned at my hand. Was the storm that had roared through me this afternoon somehow connected to the sword? Perhaps the sword's reaction to my touch had somehow broken whatever barrier had prevented me accessing the full power of both Nex and Vita up until that point. Perhaps *that* was the reason they'd finally 'accepted' me.

It was undoubtedly another of those questions Mo would know the answer to and wouldn't share.

"It's still an indicator that Aquitaine blood runs in both you and Max," Luc commented.

I rubbed my forehead again. Thinking about all this was making the ache worse. "I really wish we had the De Montfort bible. I've a feeling it would provide more than a few answers."

The phone rang before he could answer. I glanced at the screen, saw it was Mo, and picked it up. "How'd you do?"

"Ginny's come through for us—she's arranged the use of a safe house in Wigan."

"Is that wise? She'd have to get permission from her bosses, and that probably means all sorts of forms and permissions—"

"If it was being done on the books. This isn't."

My frown grew. "I don't want Ginny getting in trouble or putting her job on the line—"

"She assures me she isn't."

Knowing my cousin as well as I did, that didn't reassure me one little bit.

"She hasn't volunteered to look after her as well—has she?"

"It wouldn't be practical, given her day job. Jackie and Ron—another old friend of mine—are coming in, but they won't get there until tomorrow morning. You and Luc will have to hold the fort until then."

"Is it safe to involve Jackie? She's been attacked once already, and she seemed convinced they'd try again."

"Which is why she went to ground days ago. They don't know where she is, and she's taken all precautions to ensure it remains that way."

I hoped she was right, because Jackie had already suffered enough at Darkside's hands.

"Stop worrying, Gwen," Mo added. "Everything will work out fine."

"It hasn't so far, so I've every right to worry."

She chuckled softly. "*That* is an inclination you got from your father. I'll send the address through when I hang up. Ginny will meet you there with a DNA kit. She'll prioritize the samples, so we should have the results back within twenty-four hours."

I wasn't surprised Mo had organized all this even though she hadn't been part of the conversation between Luc and I. We really did think the same way on most things. "I take it you've already given her some of Max's DNA?"

"His hair and toothbrush, yes. She said the two should provide enough to get a match—if there is one."

I really hoped there wasn't. Really hoped that if there *was*, then this little girl was nothing more than another of his rash 'wouldn't it be fun' schemes that he later came to regret. It might be a harsh desire, given there was a life involved, but better she be a mistake than part of a scheme involving Darkside.

"Will you be there?"

"I think it'd be safer if I wasn't."

"I'll see you tomorrow, then."

I hung up, and a second later, her text came through. Luc immediately programmed the address into the GPS, and the gentle hum of the engine soon had my eyes drifting shut.

I woke with a start sometime later to the realization that we'd stopped. I rolled my neck to ease the ache of resting my head awkwardly against the window, and then looked around. We were at the end of an unremarkable street filled with crisp, modern-looking two-story terraces. Each front yard was small but tidy, and there were at least a dozen children playing out in the street. Not the sort of area I'd expected a safe house to be in, and *that* was no doubt the whole point.

Luc walked around the back of the car and opened my door. "You want me to take her?"

I shook my head, undid our seat belts, then picked her up and climbed out. She woke but didn't say anything; she simply looked around, her expression showing interest but no fear. I couldn't help wondering why, given her mom had just been killed and two utter strangers had taken her away from her home.

The front door opened as we approached, and Ginny appeared. She was typical Okoro in looks, with long dark hair kept back in a plait and dark brown eyes. She was also barely five feet one and petite in build, but woe betide any criminal who thought either made her a pushover—as many crims now behind bars would no doubt attest.

"Are you sure you're not going to get into trouble for this?" I asked as she stepped to one side and motioned us through.

"Yes. I told the chief inspector I'm working on a witch kidnapping case in conjunction with the council. He's aware it has to be off books until we've collected enough incriminating evidence."

"I didn't think that sort of thing was allowed." I stepped inside. To the right of the small entrance hall was a living area, and directly ahead were the stairs leading up to the next floor. A hallway ran down to what appeared to be a kitchen diner. I headed down, my footsteps echoing.

"When it comes to dealing with anything human related, it isn't," Ginny replied. "Every operation has to be checked and re-checked, and then signed off by the higher-ups. But the rules when dealing with witches are more flexible simply because we're often dealing with magic that can alter perceptions and situations."

I glanced over my shoulder. "That's not very well advertised."

Her grin flashed. "Well, no. It'd hardly make our job easy if witch crims were aware they came under a very different set of rules."

The smell of fresh bread permeated the room, and my stomach rumbled a reminder that it'd missed the promised lasagna at Barney's.

"I bought food staples on the way here," she continued. "But there's a ton of tinned stuff in the cupboard and plenty in the freezer. It should tide whoever Mo's arranged to babysit over for a week or so."

"Are the neighbors aware of what this house is used for?" Luc stopped in the doorway, which was probably just as well. The kitchen was on the small side, and his big frame wouldn't leave a whole lot of room for the rest of us.

"I'm sure they probably suspect." She shrugged and walked over to the small bag sitting at the end of the kitchen counter. "Mo asked me to collect some DNA samples, if I can."

"How long do you think it'll take to get the results?"

"Items marked urgent normally take somewhere between eight and twenty-four hours."

"And you're sure you're not going to get into trouble for this?"

She flashed me a smile over her shoulder. "Quite. Barney's already discussed the 'operation' with my boss, so we're good."

She pulled out some gloves and a plastic-wrapped tube that held several long-looking cotton buds, and then motioned me over to one of the two stools tucked under the overhanging section of the counter.

"Do we know her name?" she asked.

"My name is Riona," came the soft, almost melodic reply.

Surprise rippled through me, but it was accompanied by an odd sense of dread. Riona—which wasn't a commonly used name these days—had been my mother's middle name.

Coincidence?

I wanted to think so. I really did.

"And how old are you, Riona?" Luc said.

"Five," she said, looking at him. "Not a kid."

"Well, it's nice to meet you, Riona." Ginny pulled on a pair of gloves, amusement twitching her lips. "I need to collect some of your mouth juices on this little swap. Will that be okay?"

The little girl fidgeted, her uncertainty momentarily staining the air. It smelled electric, like a storm on a distant horizon. "Will it hurt?"

"No, I promise you."

"Eat after? I want a sandwich."

"And you can have one."

Riona studied Ginny a bit longer, and then nodded, her expression solemn.

"Right," Ginny said. "All you have to do is open your mouth wide. I'm just going to run this cotton bud around the inside of your cheek a few times—okay?"

She nodded once again and opened her mouth. Ginny peeled the plastic away from the tube and the swabs, and then gently collected the DNA sample she needed.

"Right," she repeated, carefully placing the sample into the tube and then sealing it in a bag. "I'll get these to the lab straight away and give you a call as soon as I get the results."

"Thanks, Ginny."

She nodded and headed out. Luc followed, no doubt to lock the door after her. I introduced myself to Riona and then asked, "What sort of sandwich would you like?"

"Cheese and Marmite."

A combination that sent a shudder through me; I was no fan of Marmite. "I'm sure we can manage that—do you want to sit on the stool while I go make it?"

"Yes."

Once she'd clambered over, I investigated the fridge and then the pantry. When Ginny had said it was well stocked, she wasn't kidding. I pulled everything I needed out, not just to make her sandwich but also a couple for Luc and me.

"There're only two bedrooms," Luc said, as he came back into the room. "But the sofa looks comfortable—"

"Luc, I'm quite capable of sharing a bed with someone without ..." I hesitated and waved a hand. "You know."

"You may be," he said, voice dry. "But I'm not sure I am."

I tsked. "And here I was thinking Blackbirds were all about self-control."

"There's self-control, and then there's utter lunacy." He pulled out the stool I'd vacated, then sat down and offered his big hand to Riona. "I'm Luc. It's very nice to meet you."

She studied him shyly for a second and placed her tiny hand in his and solemnly shook it. "What happened to Naya?"

"Is that the name of the lady who was with you? The one the man hurt?"

She nodded.

"She's been taken to the hospital." He hesitated. "Was Naya your mother?"

She shook her head. "Mommy went out. Naya was minding me."

Holy fuck ... My gaze shot to Luc's. "We need to find her—ASAP."

He nodded but didn't immediately move or get his phone out. "Do you know where your mommy went?"

"She had to take Reign to the doctor."

"And who's Reign?" he asked softly.

"My brother," she said. "My twin brother."

Twins run in families. It was the first thought that popped into my head, but didn't really make all that much sense given twins ran through the maternal line *not* paternal. Max might well be their father, but his genetics wouldn't have played into the whole twin factor. It was a coincidence, nothing more.

I placed Riona's quartered sandwich in front of her. "Do you know what time it was when your mom left for the doctors?"

She shrugged. "It was in the morning. I was eating Coco Pops. I love Coco Pops."

"So do I," Luc said with a smile.

She frowned at him. "Pops are for kids."

"Maybe I'm just a big kid."

She appeared to consider this for a moment and then nodded, as if in acceptance. She picked up one bit of the sandwich and took a bite. "Reign never liked them. He used to pick on me because I did."

I smiled. "My brother picks on me, too. His name is Max—have you met him?"

She shook her head, but the denial didn't lessen the inner uncertainty. It would have been easy enough for him to be introduced under a different name.

"I don't suppose you can tell us your mommy's name, can you?" Luc asked. "It'll help us find her."

"Mommy's not lost. She went to the doctor."

The smile twitching my lips was echoed on Luc's. "Yes, but knowing her name will make it easier to find her at the doctors."

"Oh." Riona took another bite of her sandwich. "Her name is Gianna."

"Gianna Aquitaine?" Luc immediately said.

She shook her head. "Not anymore."

"What is it now?"

"Same as mine, of course."

"You didn't tell us your surname," he said, with the patience that came with having little sisters of his own.

"It's O'Brian."

"And your daddy's name?"

She shrugged. "I never met him. Only Reign did."

I blinked. "He never came to your house?"

She shook her head, her gaze rising to mine. There was a very old soul shining out from her blue eyes. "Reign is the important one."

I instinctively reached out and covered her hand with mine. "You're just as important as he is."

"Not to Daddy. Only to Mommy."

It was said so matter-of-factly that it was obviously something she'd grown up knowing and accepting.

"Are you going to bring Mommy and Reign here?" she added.

"Depends on how sick your brother is. He might have to go to hospital."

"He didn't look that sick."

And maybe he wasn't. Maybe Gianna had somehow

gotten wind of the Aranea's mission and decided to get her son out of there.

But if that were true, why not take Riona as well? Why abandon her daughter? Was it a case of believing—given Reign was the 'important' one—Riona would be safe with her minder?

I shook my head and wished the cosmos would start providing some answers rather than throwing us yet more questions. I glanced at Luc. "Do you know her mother?"

"Not personally. She's the older sister of an heir and went off the radar about five years ago." He rose. "I'll go ring Jason. The sooner he can find her, the better it will be."

'Better' meaning safer. I returned my attention to Riona and talked to her about all manner of things, from her favorite TV show to what she did at school and the play date she'd had with her best friend last weekend. Considering she was in a strange house with two people she didn't know, Riona was amazingly calm. But maybe *that* was a trauma response.

When Luc returned, he took up distraction duties. Several cups of tea did little to ease the ache in my head, so once we'd settled Riona down for the night, I grabbed a couple of Panadol from the bottle the medic had given me and then headed back into the living room.

"I'm calling it a night."

Luc rose from the sofa and walked over. He didn't touch me, didn't kiss me, but he nevertheless stopped close enough that his body heat flowed across my senses, warming me in so many ways. The desire to press my body into his, to feel all that strength and muscle against my skin, rose, and it took every ounce of willpower to remain exactly where I was.

If he wasn't willing to risk falling in love, then I had to

KERI ARTHUR

resist the pull of desire, no matter how strong it was. No matter how alluring the man.

"I'm glad." His deep, sexy voice had my pulse rate skittering. "Because you look like crap."

I laughed. "You really do know how to boost a woman's ego, don't you?"

He smiled and tucked a stray strand of hair behind my ears, his fingers so warm and gentle against my skin. "I meant it in a concerned way, not derogative."

"Which makes me feel so much better." I rose up on tippy-toes and brushed my lips across his. "Sleep well on your lonely little sofa, Blackbird."

I turned and quickly walked away before the temptation to do more than tease him with a kiss became too strong to ignore. His gaze followed me, a heat that burned into my back long after I'd stripped to my knickers and climbed under the blankets.

I woke many hours later to the realization I was no longer alone. An arm was draped across my waist and a big warm body pressed against mine. Unfortunately, there was also at least one layer of blankets separating us.

But he *was* awake ... and in more ways than one.

As I turned around, the blankets slipped from my shoulders, exposing my upper body to his gaze. His jade green gaze drifted slowly down my length and then came up so heated, my pulse leapt in anticipation.

"Morning, gorgeous," he murmured. "You're looking much better."

"And this statement has, of course, nothing to do with the fact I also happen to be mostly naked."

As was he. The blankets were sitting low enough on his hips to reveal the top of his boxer shorts.

"Of course it doesn't—though it has to be said that I

much prefer waking to the company of a lusciously naked lady than alone."

I raised an eyebrow. "And how often do you wake up in such company?"

"Far too few times for my liking."

A smile twitched my lips. "I thought you said Blackbirds weren't monks?"

"We're not. It's just that some of us are more discerning than others."

Or just more damn stoic. "What happened to the sofa?"

"It was too small and very uncomfortable."

"I believe I said it would be. Someone was too stubborn to admit I might be right."

"That someone was in self-preservation mode."

"And still is, if the divide of blankets is anything to go by."

"I won't start something I can't finish, Gwen. I can't."

It was a comment accompanied by a flash of old pain. I studied him for a moment and then said softly, "Who was she? The woman in red, I mean."

He sighed. "Her name was Aurora Aquitaine. I was assigned to protect her after a Darkside kidnapping attempt."

"Then how did she end up in a damn hecatomb?"

A hecatomb might have once been a place where the Greeks sacrificed either oxen or humans to their gods, but these days they were an exchange point—an arena where human life was offered up to Darkside for some kind of service or for information. We'd unfortunately uncovered one after Tris had inadvertently led us there—and we still didn't know what information he'd received in return for the life of the young woman he'd taken there.

"She ended up there because I was young and over-confident."

"We were all that once, Luc."

"Yes, but I was a *Blackbird*—"

"You're also flesh and blood, and mistakes come with that condition."

He didn't look comforted—hardly surprising, given how long he'd carried this guilt around. "So, what happened?"

"I fell for her—hard. It could have been lust, it could have been love—I'll never know for sure, because she died at my feet in that hecatomb." He drew in a breath and released it slowly. "We'd gone weeks without any sign of demons. Early one morning, I left her sleeping and went to the bakery to get some fresh croissants. I came back to discover the house had been ransacked and Aurora gone."

"How did you find her?"

"The one thing I *did* do right was place a tracer spell on her."

I frowned. "How? The Durant skill is manipulating light and shadows, not personal magic."

"My grandmother was a Lancaster. Her ability trickled down to two of my sisters and me." He raised an eyebrow. "How do you think I was able to lock down that gate we found in Ainslyn?"

"I thought you wove a light barrier around it."

"I did, but I also locked it down magically just to be safe. I should have done the same for Aurora."

I gently cupped his bristly cheek. "You can't keep blaming yourself for something that happened over ten years ago, Luc. You were young and inexperienced."

"All true. But it was a lesson learned and a mistake I'll not repeat."

"You can't go through life with your heart locked up. It's not healthy."

"When I'm working it is."

"And when you're not?"

Amusement tugged at his lips, chasing the lingering wisps of hurt and guilt from his eyes. "You're persistent, I'll give you that."

"Trust me, this *is* restrained. Remember who my grand-mother is." I let my fingers drift to his lips. He didn't say anything, didn't respond, but his eyes burned with heat. "But unless you're willing to risk that heart of yours, this will be the full extent of our flirtation, and certainly all I'm willing to offer."

His arm tightened around my waist and tugged me closer. Despite the layers of blankets between us, his erection was very evident. And lord, he was *big*. "Does flirtation involve kissing?"

I tried to get a grip on suddenly giddy hormones. "No."

"I'm owed one, you know."

"Are you just?"

"Remember the cave?"

"How could I forget?" Not only had we somehow managed to survive a tunnel collapse, but we'd also done so with the Witch King's crown still in our possession. It was now in the hands of the Lady of Lake. If it wasn't safe with her, then it wouldn't be safe with anyone.

"Then you'll remember our celebratory kiss was inter-rupted by the arrival of evildoers."

"So it was. And?"

"And, I doubt we'll face any such interruptions for the next few minutes. I aim to claim my kiss."

"I wouldn't bet on not being interrupted. There's a five-year-old in the next bedroom, remember." Amusement tugged at my lips. "And to quote your own statement, it would be utter lunacy to think either of us will stop at—"

The rest of the sentence was cut off as his lips claimed mine. There was absolutely nothing sweet about this kiss; it was all heat, hunger, and passion, and it made my soul sing and my heart soar. This was a kiss filled with the weight of centuries, even if it was very much of the moment.

And, oh, what a moment.

With our bodies crushed so close, I couldn't help but be intensely aware of every part of him, from the rapid rise and fall of his chest to the heated hardness pressing against my lower stomach. I wanted to explore his muscular splendor with hands and tongue. Wanted to kiss my way along the happy trail of hair that started at his belly button and disappeared under the blankets still covering his hips. Wanted to caress the long, wondrous length of him.

But I didn't caress him, and nor he me. Our connection was one of lips and soul only.

By the time he pulled away, sweat dotted my skin, my heart raced, and my body ached with need. But at least I wasn't alone in any of that.

A rueful smile touched his glorious lips. "That wasn't the wisest thing I've ever done. Not if distance is to be maintained."

"Not my problem—"

"Oh," he said, eyes glinting wickedly, "I think it is."

I snorted softly, but any reply I might have made was cut off by a soft squeal that came from the room next door. *Riona* ...

I flung the blankets off and grabbed my T-shirt, pulling it on as I bolted next door. A quick look around her room didn't reveal an immediate threat, but she twisted from side to side and punched wildly at the air. It looked for all the world like she was fighting something—or someone—off.

I sat on the side of her bed and gently touched her forehead. It was sweaty, suggesting she'd been fighting her dream battle for a while.

"Riona?" I leaned back to avoid one flying fist. "It's okay. You're okay. You're safe."

She continued flailing for several seconds and then her eyes popped open. Confusion and fear shone from her bright eyes. "Gwen?"

"Yes, and you're safe, Riona. No one will harm you while Luc and I are here."

"But *he* was here. He was in my mind."

I frowned and brushed the sweaty strands of hair out of her eyes. "Who was in your mind?"

"The gray man."

My stomach flip-flopped, and it was all I could to keep my voice calm. "And does the gray man have a name?"

She nodded and dragged the blankets closer to her nose as if to fend him off again. When she finally answered, it was in a fear-filled whisper.

"His name is Winter."

CHAPTER SIX

A thick fist of fear replaced the flip-flopping. If Winter had been in contact with this little girl, then we were in all sorts of trouble.

"What did Winter want?" My voice, I was relieved to hear, held no hint of the inner panic.

She bit her lip, fear evident. I smiled and tugged her up into my arms. Her little body was hot and trembling. "It's okay, Riona. Nothing you said to him will ever make us angry."

She hesitated, and then said, "I told him we were at a house in Wigan, but I don't know where."

We. Fuck. "And did he make you tell him who you were with?"

She pulled back, her lips trembling. It was answer enough. "It's okay, Riona. Really, it is."

"But he'll come for me. He always comes for me."

Something within went cold. "Where does he take you when he comes for you?"

"To the dark place."

Holy fuck ... I swallowed the rage and tried to remain

calm. I didn't want to scare her. "Does Winter talk to Reign the same way?"

She nodded. I swore. Silently—vehemently. Gianna might be on the run, but she wouldn't get far. Not if Winter could track her son via some form of sleep telepathy.

"Does you mom accompany you when Winter takes you to the dark place?"

She shook her head. "Just Reign."

"And what happens when you go to there?"

"They teach us to speak their magic and their language."

It wasn't unusual for witches to be taught magic at such a young age, but I hated to think just how badly Darkside would be twisting—fouling—the lessons. "So you can speak the dark language?"

She nodded. "They ... they scare me."

"They scare me, too," I admitted and hugged her for the longest time.

A soft noise had me glancing over my shoulder, though I was well aware it was Luc at the door rather than Winter or one of his half-demon thugs. "We'll need to get out of here."

He nodded. "I've already called Mo. She'll contact Jackie and Ron and get them to meet us at Waterloo. They'll take her off grid until it's safe."

"There is nowhere safe if Winter is able to communicate with her telepathically."

"Apparently Ron will be able to counter any further attempts."

Which suggested Ron's abilities ran to personal magic rather than elemental—unless, of course, there were non-magical means of countering telepathy. Given the preternatural team apparently had psychics on their books as well as witches, I guess it would make sense that a psychic means of countering such attacks existed.

I glanced down at Riona. "We'll have to leave. Do you want a hand getting dressed?"

"I'm big. I can do it myself."

"Good. But if Winter makes another attempt to contact you, let me know, okay?"

She nodded. "He only comes at night."

"Probably because the night gives him a stronger range and easier access to her mind," Luc said. "Shall I make toasted sandwiches for everyone?"

"Cheese and Marmite, please," Riona immediately said.

"Done. See you downstairs in a few minutes."

Riona got dressed, and then I brushed her hair. A few golden strands got caught in the bristles, so I plucked them free and wrapped them in a tissue. If Darkside did catch up with her, then Mo would be able to use them to trace her.

We headed into the other bedroom; once I'd fully dressed, she took my hand, and we headed down the stairs. It felt oddly right—felt as if we were family rather than two strangers—and I couldn't help wondering yet again if that was because her father was my brother. As much as I kept hoping he wasn't involved in this whole mess, there was a tiny part of me that welcomed her arrival. I could certainly deal with having a niece ...

Luc handed us each a paper-wrapped sandwich, then picked up the keys and ushered us out of the house—after first checking that it was safe to do so.

Once we were all in the car—Riona safely buckled into the back and happily consuming her sandwich and juice—we headed off. Thankfully, there was very little traffic on the road, so it only took little over half an hour to reach Waterloo.

As Luc drove through a myriad of streets, my phone beeped. I pulled it out of my pocket and glanced at the screen. "Jackie's waiting in the café. She wants to know if we want coffee."

He shook his head. "I think it better none of us hang about. The sooner we get Riona tucked safely away, the better."

I nodded in agreement and then turned around. Her blue gaze met mine, sharp with an intelligence that went far beyond her years.

"Because Winter might be trying to find us, we'll have to leave you for a few days. But a good friend of mine by the name of Jackie will be looking after you—will that be okay?"

Her lip trembled. "What about my mommy? And Reign?"

"We're going to find them," Luc said in a reassuring tone. "And when we do, we'll bring them to you."

"Is Jackie a witch, like you?"

I nodded. "And so is Ron, her friend. Between the two of them, they'll keep you safe and keep Winter away from you."

"He won't speak to me?"

"He won't speak to you," I echoed firmly.

"You'll come back for me?"

"I will. I promise."

Some of the tension left her little body, and she nodded. Contract accepted, I thought, and hoped like hell I could fulfill it.

We climbed out of the car and, with Riona holding my hand, walked down to the café. It was a long, odd-looking building standing behind what looked for all the world like a disused toilet block. But it looked out over the nearby park and, on a clear morning, you'd probably catch glimpses of the nearby shoreline from the long line of windows.

Jackie turned and smiled as we entered. She was of average height, with short gray hair and blue-gray eyes. Her face still bore the fading remnants of the bruises she'd collected from the demon that had somehow caught her unawares and beaten her up, but the swelling had at least gone down. She certainly looked far less of a mess than she had the last time I'd seen her.

"Morning, all," she said, her tone warm and cheery—deliberately so, I suspected. "Ron's just gone to the bathroom. He won't be long."

I nodded and glanced down. "Riona, this is Jackie, the lady I told you about."

Jackie immediately squatted in front of her. "Lovely to meet you, Riona."

Riona studied her for a second then said, "What happened to your face?"

"A demon beat me up," Jackie said, in a matter-of-fact manner.

"Is he dead?"

"He certainly is."

"Good. They scare me."

"They don't scare me. And they don't scare Ron." She glanced over her shoulder at the sound of footsteps. "This is him now."

Ron was a big man with snowy-white hair, a thick handlebar moustache, and a rotund face and figure. Add a beard, and he would have been a perfect Santa Claus.

He also oozed power, though I couldn't immediately pin whether it was personal or elemental. It seemed to contain elements of both.

He squatted next to Jackie—doing so with an ease that

belied his size—and smiled widely. "Do you like Elsa from *Frozen*?"

"Yes—why?"

"Because I was given a singing Elsa doll the other day, and it's not really my thing. I thought you might like it—would you?"

Riona nodded.

"Shall we go get her, then?"

She nodded again but looked up at me. "You will come back?"

I knelt down and gave her a hug. "I promised, remember."

"And Mommy?"

"We're going to look for her now."

She nodded, then stepped forward and almost shyly gripped Ron's offered hand. As they walked toward the door, Jackie gave me a slip of paper with a phone number on it. "Use this number if you need to contact us, as we've stashed our regular phones to prevent the possibility of tracking. Mo doesn't know where we'll be, and we intend to keep it that way. It's safer for everyone."

"Are you sure Ron can stop Darkside from contacting her via telepathy?" Luc said.

"It's more likely to be a dream bonding rather than direct telepathy—there's some evidence that halflings can manipulate the darkness to track and connect with their targets."

I guess that made sense, given one of their parents lived and breathed darkness. "But Ron can stop it?"

"Yes. He's got Durant blood, which has enhanced his own telepathic abilities and means he can sense darkness in someone's mind. If you do find the mother, send us a text. We'll arrange to meet off-site."

I nodded. "Just be careful, Jackie. Darkside want this kid back bad."

"They caught me unawares once. The bastards won't get a second chance at me." She squeezed my arm and then hurried out the door after Ron and Riona.

I glanced up at Luc. "It's worrying that we haven't heard anything from Jason about the mother yet. There can't be that many clinics in Leeds."

"I think we both know the mother is on the run. Do you want a drink to take with us?"

"A tea would be lovely." I took a moment to admire not only the grace with which he moved but also the underlying sense of power barely restrained. "If Darkside can dream speak to Reign, there's every chance they'll find her before we can."

"Which is why Jason's bringing in a psychic."

I frowned. "What sort of psychic?"

"A woman who uses psychometry to trace people."

The more I learned about the preternatural division, the bigger it seemed to get. "So what's our next move?"

He picked up the two takeaway cups and returned, handing one to me before motioning me on. "I dare say Mo will tell us once we get back to Ainslyn."

I glanced up. "So you've no plans of your own?"

He opened the door and ushered me out. "I've plenty, but none of them are practical right now."

I grinned. "I wasn't talking about sexual plans, Blackbird."

"Weren't you? That's a shame."

I raised an eyebrow. "That suggests there might be a slight deviation in the course you've set yourself."

"No deviation. Not until after all this mess is sorted, at any rate."

"You do realize that if the gate is opened and the dark horde floods out, you and I could die in a very frustrated state?"

He laughed and opened the car door for me. "If the gate does open and the horde does flood, I promise we'll meet death with smiles on our faces and satisfaction in our hearts."

I snorted. "Except we both know that if the gate is opened, you'll be standing alongside the other eleven Blackbirds attempting to hold back the tide."

"I doubt there'll be any sort of warning to the gate being smashed open. It'll just happen."

"To be honest, I'm surprised it already hasn't."

He shrugged. "From the accounts I've read of the Witch King and the sword, it apparently takes a while for the connection to establish." He pulled into the traffic and then glanced at me. "Much like what happened with your connection to Nex and Vita."

"Which makes sense, given they came out of the same forge." I took a sip of my tea. "What did you think of the prophecy that was on the back of the throne?"

"I thought the second line was oddly worded."

I nodded. "At first reading, you'd take it to mean the sword in the stone—the sword long believed to be the Witch King's—"

"Because it is," Luc cut in. "There's plenty of illuminated manuscripts and tapestries from his era that use that exact image."

"So why say one true sword? Why not simply say the sword of power?"

"He did use other swords—he didn't always take the sword of power into battle. Maybe that's what the line is referring to."

"Maybe." I took another sip of my tea. "I don't suppose there's a chance the prophecy is mentioned somewhere in the Blackbird archives?"

"If it's there, I'll find it." He glanced at me, a smile touching his lips. "A day or so of separation might not be a bad thing."

"Coward."

"But a realistic one." His smile grew, and my hormones did a wicked little dance. "Even the fiercest resolve cannot forever withstand the constant assault of sensory and sexual ambrosia."

I raised an eyebrow. "You're equating me to a dessert?"

"Ambrosia was first the food of the Greek and Roman gods, and it's one I would willingly consume, given the right time and place."

My already erratic pulse rate greeted this news with even more abandon. I did my best to ignore the images that rose in my mind and said, in a voice that held only the slightest trace of huskiness, "Shame, then, that your unwillingness to risk that heart of yours means it will never happen."

He didn't say anything to that. The silence stretched on, and I was perfectly fine with it. I just hoped his imagination was now offering the same sort of erotic images as mine and that he was consequently contemplating the wisdom of stating he would never have a long-term relationship.

He probably *wasn't*, but a girl had to hope. These were strange times, after all.

It didn't take us very long to get back to Ainslyn, thanks to the early hour and the fact daily commuters were generally heading out of the city, not in.

Luc pulled to a halt in front of our building, but kept the motor running. "I'll head over to Winchester and check the archives for any mention of the prophecy or other swords."

I frowned. "Winchester? I thought your headquarters was in London?"

"It is, but Winchester is the ancient home of the Blackbirds."

"But why? Ainslyn is where the Witch King ruled, not Winchester."

"While it's true that Uhtric spent a good portion of his time here, the other kings did not. There are multiple castles across the UK that can lay claim to being inhabited by one or more Witch King over the centuries."

"Huh." I opened the car door. "You'll call if you find anything?"

He nodded. "Be careful, Gwen. Remember, Winter knows we took Riona, and he might hit this place hard and fast in an effort to get her back."

"There's not much left of the place to hit." It was lightly said, but unease nevertheless pulsed through me.

I slammed the door shut, watched him drive away, and then headed in.

"That you, Gwen?" Mo called out the minute I opened the door.

"You already know it is, so why ask the question?"

She tsked. "You're a bit tetchy this morning—is that sexual frustration coming out? Is that why Luc roared away, rather than come in?"

I locked the door, then headed up the dust-caked stairs. "He said he's going over to Winchester to check the Blackbird archives for any mention of other swords, but basically, yeah, he's running."

Mo chuckled, a sound filled with delight. "Keep chipping away at his defenses, my girl. He'll be yours in no time."

"You keep saying that, and he keeps proving you wrong."

"No man—or woman, for that matter—can outrun fate for long."

"Tell him that."

Mo was on the sofa, her booted foot propped on the coffee table. Surprisingly, both it and the sofa were free of the rubble that still dominated the street side of the room, and the kitchen area practically shone. "You've been busy."

"I hired some professional cleaners. They'll be back tomorrow." She motioned toward the kettle. "And you timed your arrival perfectly—it just boiled."

I smiled and made a pot of tea. After adding a packet of chocolate digestives—Mo's favorite, not mine—to the tray, I carried it over and placed it on the almost new-looking coffee table. "I don't think I've ever noticed the grain on this table before."

"It is a lovely piece, but I've better things to do with my life than clean or polish wood furniture. Did the changeover go smoothly?"

I nodded and poured the tea. "I think Riona is a very old soul. She certainly took the situation far better than even most adults would."

"Riona?"

My gaze rose. "Yes."

"Oh dear."

"Yes. But I don't think we dare confront Max until we have confirmation that she—and her brother—are his."

"I agree." She sipped her tea, her expression contemplative. "It *is* always possible they belong to a branch of the family I do not know about."

"Really? You expect me to believe that?"

"A truly loving granddaughter would never question her grandmother's word."

"She would if she was raised by you." I sat beside her. "If they *are* confirmed as his, I guess the next question has to be, how deeply is he involved?"

"Deep enough that Winter has access to his children."

"And yet he's never come home stinking of demons."

"We both know there's ways and means around that." She pursed her lips. "Have the mother and brother been located yet?"

I shook my head. "She told Riona she was taking Reign to the doctor's, but it's pretty obvious she's on the run."

"And left her daughter behind as bait, thanks to her connection to Winter."

"Which was a pretty awful thing to do."

Mo screwed up her nose. "Yes, but I can understand her reasoning."

"I fucking don't." I took a deep breath and released it slowly. It didn't really ease the anger. "Jason is calling in a psychic to help locate her."

"That may not help, given Darkside are undoubtedly watching their movements." She reached for a biscuit and then dunked it into her tea. "Shame we haven't got something of the mother's to do a tracing spell with."

I reached into my pocket and pulled out the tissue-wrapped hair. "I do have a few strands of Riona's hair. I figured you'd use it to find her if Darkside grabbed her, but given they're siblings, could you also use it to trace her brother?"

"Yes." She smiled and patted my knee. "You always were the brightest child."

I snorted softly. "Not what you said when I was failing grades."

"And understandably, given you always had the ability but never bothered applying it." She finished her biscuit and reached for another. "Much like your magic, really."

"The magic you claim I never had."

"You tested as null—that's very different." She eyed me for a second, her gaze sharp and missing little. "What happened in that house?"

"I called on Nex and Vita's power even though they were in your possession, not mine."

"Which is why your eyes are bloodshot."

I nodded. "It felt like a storm swept through me, and it left me drained. That force wasn't De Montfort, Mo."

"No, it wasn't."

It was said in a matter-of-fact manner, and I narrowed my gaze. "You really do need to start giving me some answers."

She sighed. "Fine, although I will add that Vita *did* heal you, which indicates your De Montfort genes are not only present but viable."

"Except De Montforts have never been able to heal themselves." I motioned toward her booted foot. "For example."

"Well, yes, but few De Montforts have ever been able to access Nex's power in the way you have, and I suspect the same can be said of Vita."

Confusion stirred. "Doesn't their power come from centuries of De Montforts using them as conductors?"

"Yes, but that was not their initial intent. None of your more recent ancestors have accessed them in the way you have. Your mother certainly didn't."

"But I have vague memories of her using them—was she simply channeling her own force through them?"

Mo nodded. "Not even Rhedyn—who was the only other De Montfort to call lightning from the daggers—could access their full magic."

There was something in her voice this time that caught my attention. "Was she ... your daughter?"

Mo smiled. "No. She was my granddaughter."

Which meant she'd been alive well *before* Uhtric's time. I reached for another biscuit to help me cope with *that* gobsmacking revelation. "So you were already ancient when the main dark gate was breached?"

She whacked me on the arm. "In near immortality terms, I was barely out of my teenage years."

"So this would be your middle age?"

"It's perhaps a little more than that."

"So why didn't you know what was written on the back of the throne? Or even what's written on the King's Stone?"

"Because I left Ainslyn once Darkside had been re-caged."

"Why?"

She grimaced. "Uhtric and I ... we didn't exactly get along. He was an excellent warrior and a good leader, but as a man? He left a lot to be desired."

I raised my eyebrows. "Did you and he ever ...?"

"Good god, no! I think I have better taste in men than that." She took a sip of tea. "He was not only arrogant, but unfaithful to his wife—two traits I can't abide, even if it was quite common back then."

"How long were you away from Ainslyn?"

"Long enough to lose contact with my descendants here. I came into your father's life when he was barely two."

"I never knew that."

"Gregory—his father—died in a bus rollover. I stepped in to help Fiona raise the two boys. Sadly, she passed just before you and Max were born."

I topped up our teas and then said, "So why was Rhedyn given Nex and Vita in the first place? And what, exactly, was their original purpose?"

Mo pursed her lips. "Rhedyn was the Queen's Defender—"

"She was a Blackbird?"

"No. Blackbirds were the king's knights and protectors of the crown. They were—and are—always men, so it was impossible for them to guard the queen in all situations." A faint smile touched her lips. "The queen's guard came into existence after Gwenhwyfar's fall from grace."

Gwenhwyfar had been the first Witch King's wife. She'd apparently fallen madly in love with the Blackbird sent to escort her back to the court for the wedding and had paid a high price for it. She'd been forced to uphold the marriage contract and bear the king an heir and had eventually decided it was better to kill herself than remain with a man she did not love.

The Blackbird had things a whole lot easier, as he'd only been banished. He'd apparently gone to the Lady of the Lake seeking help, but the fact he'd left the kingdom *without* the woman he loved incensed Vivienne. She decreed their souls would be reborn down through the ages but would never find happiness until he held true to his heart rather than his duty and allegiance to king and crown.

Mo believed Luc and I were this generation's rebirth, and I wasn't about to argue—not only because of the instant and undeniable attraction that existed between us, but also because I'd been able to see into his memories with just a touch. I wasn't telepathic in any way, shape or form; the ability had apparently come from the fact that, with each rebirth, the bond between us strengthened; eventually, we would be one in heart, mind, *and* soul.

Of course, I'd only gotten a glimpse into his thoughts and memories that one time, so whether that meant our link still had development potential, I couldn't say. And I certainly wasn't sure I wanted to catch his thoughts on a more regular basis—especially if it confirmed his mind really *was* set on living an 'unencumbered' life, as he so charmingly put it.

"Were the queen's guard all De Montforts?"

Mo nodded. "We were warriors as much as healers back then, remember."

"So why was Rhedyn given Nex and Vita over any other De Montfort? Especially if she couldn't access their full power?"

"Rhedyn was the most powerful of the guard and head of the order. It was fitting the daggers were given to her."

"I don't suppose your relationship with Vivienne had anything to do with it?"

Mo laughed. "You don't have a relationship with the old gods—you're on speaking terms with them at best."

"Which you are."

"Only because our paths have crossed quite a few times over the centuries."

"Then why would Vivienne gift our line with daggers imbued with a power none can access?"

"The old gods never explain their reasons, although she did say that one day, the daggers and sword will be reunited."

"The only way that would ever happen is if De Montfort men could use Nex and Vita—and they can't." Max certainly tried often enough. I reached for another biscuit and dunked it in my tea, taking a quick bite before it got too soggy. "And De Montfort women can't use the sword."

"Remember what the prophecy on the back of the throne said, Gwen."

"A hand will draw the one true sword—"

"Hand is gender neutral."

"Are you saying what I think you're saying?" I couldn't help the incredulousness in my voice. "Because it's insane. *And* impossible."

"Nothing is impossible. Not when it comes to fate and the old gods."

"But Max—"

"Is not the true heir," she cut in softly. "I think you are."

CHAPTER SEVEN

I laughed—a sharp sound filled with disbelief. "Women can't raise the king's sword—plenty have tried over the years and none have succeeded."

"I wouldn't call two plenty, and they failed for very simple reasons; one, the sword is not part of Aquitaine rule, even if only one of their line can use it. It also can't be drawn in times of peace. And two, at the time, their link to the Aquitaine line was weaker than that of their male counterparts."

"The De Montfort claim on that heritage isn't exactly solid, either, Mo."

"I think it's safe to say that—given recent events—there *is* a direct link back to a Witch King somewhere in our bloodline. If it wasn't Uhtric, then it was one of his predecessors."

"If it was one of his predecessors, wouldn't you be aware of it? You were around well before Uhtric."

"Well, yes, but it wasn't like I was keeping tabs on the sexual shenanigans of all my kin." She paused. "It *is* possible Mryddin might know if there's a link between the

De Montforts and the Aquitaines—he did have a habit of interfering in the bloodlines of kings when necessary."

"So why aren't we breaking the old bastard out of his self-imposed exile? He really does sound like the only one who can give us some answers."

"In this particular case, I don't think we need his help." She placed her teacup on the table and then gripped my free hand. "Think, Gwen. If the twins *are* Max's, why would he seek out an Aquitaine to bear them when he's never expressed any desire to be a father?"

"To fortify a possible claim on the sword—"

"Or to fortify his succession intentions."

"And it doesn't matter either way, because someone else has claimed the sword."

"Do you still honestly believe that?"

I tugged my hand from hers, then pushed upright and headed over to the cupboard that held the whiskey. It might be early, but I needed a drink. "Right now, I'm not sure what to damn well believe."

Other than the fact that he'd obviously been planning all this for a very long time. And now there was an undeniable connection to Winter via these children ... *if* they *were* his children. Until the DNA results came through, I had to give him the benefit of the doubt. *Had* to.

I gulped down some whiskey, then glanced at Mo and wiggled the bottle. She shook her head and picked up her tea.

"Did you question him when he was here yesterday?" I asked.

"No—he arrived the same time as the assessor. Besides, I didn't want him to go to ground."

"You could have stopped him going anywhere with a quick spell."

"Even I can't cast a spell fast enough to have stopped him attaining blackbird form and flying away, Gwen."

I refilled my glass and then firmly capped the whiskey bottle and put it away. I did *not* need to be getting drunk just yet. There was still too much we needed to do. "Now that Winter knows we have Riona, Max would have to suspect *we* suspect. We may not see him again."

She grimaced. "Most likely, although given his tendency to do the unexpected, he might stick around, if only to gather information."

"He might keep in contact via the phone, but that's it." Max was many things, but he certainly wasn't a fool. Nor was he slow in the brain department. I dropped back onto the sofa. "None of this sheds any light on why the hell you think I'm the heir—especially if Max *does* have the sword."

She wrinkled her nose. "It's a combination of things, and it's possible I'm wrong—but we both know how rarely I am."

I couldn't help smiling. "Only when it comes to certain Blackbirds, apparently."

"That, my dear girl, is still a developing situation, and I continue to believe it will be resolved satisfactorily."

I once again hoped she was right—for the sake of my future selves if nothing else. I did not want to be going through this sort of sexual frustration in yet another lifetime. Of course, said sexual frustration could be easily solved if I was just willing to agree to a casual relationship ...

I took a quick drink and ignored the traitorous inner whisper suggesting it was better to have a short but passionate fling than maintain the current drought. "What things are we talking about?"

"For one, the inscription on the throne—it suggests there's more than one sword of power, and I know for a fact there isn't. Mryddin and I were there when Vivienne gave it to Aldred."

Who'd been the first Witch King. "I thought it and the daggers were created in the same forge?"

"They were—just not at the same time."

"If the sword in the stone *is* a fake, why wouldn't you know that? And why would it react magically to heirs? And to me?"

"As I said before, I left Ainslyn after Uhtric re-caged Darkside. The sword he held at that time *was* the real thing." She paused to sip her tea. "And the sword in the stone has always reacted to heirs—that's how kings were chosen. If it *is* a secondary sword rather than the original, then perhaps that was intentional. Mryddin always did have a penchant for creating magical swords—it was the godly blood in him."

"I thought he was the result of an incubus and human union?"

"Demon, god, they're all the same." She pursed her lips. "I do think the inscription on the stone—"

"The one that's impossible to read, you mean?"

She smiled. "There you go with that 'impossible' word again, but yes. I think it'll answer at least some of our questions."

I finished the whiskey, then moved back to the tea. "And the third thing?"

"Your brother's sudden appearance at the main gateway."

Which, I remembered, he'd explained *before* she'd placed her spell—but even without it, I hadn't really believed him.

I gulped down my tea and found myself fighting the

desire to grab some more whiskey. "You think he was there to test the sword?"

"I think it highly likely."

"He didn't have it on him in the canyon."

"Because he's not a fool. Besides, he would have sensed my magic from the roadside and known we were there."

"I should've fucking followed his car."

"You wouldn't have kept up, darling girl. Not in your weakened state."

I sighed. "So, what are we going to do?"

"Find Gianna and Reign as a matter of priority. If anyone knows for sure what is going on, it'll be Gianna."

"Unless she's just being paid to be an incubator and nursemaid and doesn't know who the father really is."

"No intelligent woman these days would go into a deal like this without at least investigating the man and the situation."

"Wouldn't it depend on her situation and the money offered? Surely not all Aquitaines are wealthy."

She wrinkled her nose. "The king's line has fallen from grace *and* gold since Layton handed full rule over to human royalty, but I wouldn't call any of them poor."

"Their ability to manipulate fire—like our ability to heal —has gone out of fashion since the industrial revolution, though. And even if they *can* call on all four elements, they can't do so without a conduit strong enough to withstand the force flowing through them."

And from the little Mo had said over the years, not only had very few conduits survived to modern times, but the number of people with the knowledge to create them was now limited to the old gods—and they didn't take a whole lot of interest in the affairs of humans and witches these days.

"All true, but I still don't believe she would have gone into this without investigation—but we can ask her once we've found her. Go kit up while I create the spell."

"Where did you put Nex and Vita?"

"In your room." She paused. "Check the backpack for tracer spells and bugs—Max did have it for a good period of time."

A thick lump of anger and pain threatened to choke me again. I swallowed heavily and was suddenly thankful I had something to do. Having any sort of time to dwell on my brother and all that he might have done—to Mo and me, to our cousins, and to others—would probably have reduced me to an angry, shaking, crying mess for hours on end. "I take it the floor structure up there has now been checked and cleared?"

She nodded. "Keep away from the hole, and you should be fine."

I handed her the tissue-wrapped hair, then grabbed another biscuit and headed up. My room was still a goddamn mess. There were gigantic holes in both the floor and the ceiling, where the witchling's magic had caused a collapse, and there was dust, plaster, and wood remnants covering everything else. My mattress—which had been torn off the bed and slashed open by the halflings searching for the papers I'd taken from Jackie's—partially hung over the edge of the hole, evidence of just how close I'd come to disaster.

I stepped warily into the room, but the floor didn't crack or bounce. My knives were hanging on the knob of the wardrobe, and the backpack was tucked just behind the door. I grabbed it, tipped out the contents, and then sorted through all the potions, charms, and even the first aid kit. There was nothing that shouldn't have been there. Relief stirred, but it didn't last long. When I unzipped the pocket on the side of the pack, I discovered a small silver disk the size of a button battery. Magic stirred across my fingers, a soft caress that tingled rather than burned, which meant a witch who followed the light had created it. I turned it over and studied the spell. It was some kind of tracer, but the design and feel of it was foreign. No witch I knew had made this, but the tell—the signature all witches left in their magic —was strong enough that I'd recognize it if I saw it again.

I sucked in a deep breath and tried to ignore the one very simple question that kept echoing through my brain—*Why?*

Until Riona's brother and mother were safe, and the riddle of the sword was solved, we couldn't risk asking that question. The minute we did ask, he'd go on the offensive. While I really wanted to believe my brother wouldn't physi-cally hurt either of us, the evidence to the contrary was mounting. The constant attacks from Darkside—be they demon or halfling—certainly suggested family blood wasn't holding him back in any way. Now, that might be simply because he held no sway over Darkside's actions, but if he *had* claimed the sword, surely the elves and the demons would at least play along with his games until the main gate was opened.

I left the pack where it was and went into his room— which was now back to its usual tidy self—to grab one of the old school bags from the back of his cupboard. Max might be a neat freak, but he also tended to be something of a hoarder and never threw anything out that might yet prove useful.

After repacking everything, I quickly changed into my own clothes, then slung the pack over my shoulder, grabbed Nex and Vita as well as the stone knife—which might have been overkill, but given how physically draining the daggers could be, having an option that didn't deplete my strength was a damn good idea—and then headed back downstairs. Mo remained on the sofa, but a sphere of gold now hovered in the air above the coffee table. Inside it were the pale strands of hair I'd taken from Riona's brush.

I grabbed my keys from the hook near the stairs and said, "Do you need a hand up?"

"No. And you're not driving—not after two glasses of whiskey."

"I'm not drunk—"

"Which doesn't mean you won't be over the limit in an hour or so. I've called Mia—she's happy to drive us, and it'll be handy to have another witch present if things get nasty."

Mia was a Lancaster, which meant she performed spells and drew on personal strength to give them life. "If things get nasty, she could be in trouble."

Mo quirked an eyebrow at me. "You've been friends with her nearly all your life, and you don't think she can protect herself?"

"I didn't say that. I simply meant that personal magic is by its very nature limited in scope."

"Gwen, stop worrying." She lifted her booted foot from the coffee table and rose. "Why have you got Max's old school bag?"

"Because my backpack had a tracer in it." I handed it to her.

"I'm not familiar with the tell, but I'll give it to Barney and see if he—or one of the other councilors—can track its creator down." She shook her head and put the tracer down. "I do wonder where I went wrong with that boy."

"I hardly think any of this is your fault, Mo."

She grimaced and carefully picked up the sphere. "Isn't it? I raised him. If I'd spotted the shadows in him earlier—"

"If I couldn't see them, how on earth could you be expected to?"

"Because I'm older. I should have recognized the signs." She took a deep breath and released it slowly. It was a soft sound of regret. "But perhaps it's not too late. Perhaps he's not too deep ..."

Her words faded. She knew, like I knew, there was little hope of either being true—and yet there remained a part of me unwilling to give up on him.

Not until we'd confronted him. Not until we'd given him the chance to explain his actions. I owed him that, if nothing else.

I led the way down the stairs, then locked up once we were out on the street. Mia's small white Fiesta pulled up a few minutes later; Mo climbed into the front seat while I claimed the back.

I took a deep breath and then sighed happily. "Is that freshly baked coffee scrolls I'm smelling?"

Mia chuckled. She was five foot ten, with blue-gray eyes, short brown hair, and a slender but wiry build. "It is indeed—the bakery next door just pulled them out of the oven as I was leaving. I couldn't resist. Mo, do you want to do the honors?"

Mo immediately handed me one of the three brown bags and then tore open a second and placed it on Mia's lap. "Head out of Ainslyn."

"Which gate?"

"Fisher, and then turn left."

Mia immediately sped off, zooming through the narrow streets and around the traffic with a skill that came from the countless advanced driving courses her parents had insisted on before she got her license.

Once we were out of the old town and heading toward the M6, she said, "So who are we looking for?"

Mo quickly updated her without mentioning we suspected the two children were Max's. There were some things better kept to ourselves—at least until they were confirmed, at any rate.

"What's the likelihood of us walking into a trap?" Mia asked.

"Fifty-fifty. It's daylight, so demons won't be a problem," Mo said. "But we have no idea how large an army of halflings they have."

"Quite a few, if they can afford to bomb a church load of them."

"Ginny told you about that?" I said.

She glanced at me through the rearview mirror. "Yes, and I'm damn annoyed I missed out on the action. Please do the right thing in the future and call me."

I snorted. "Be careful what you wish for, my friend."

"It's because I'm your friend that I'm insisting. This is a fight you two shouldn't be tackling alone."

Her words both warmed and frightened me. In all likelihood, I'd already lost my brother; I didn't want to lose my best friends as well.

And yet, how safe were any of us if the dark gate was opened? It wouldn't just be one or two lives lost, but thousands. Millions.

"Gwen always did have excellent taste in friends," Mo said. "Shame it didn't transfer to men—"

"Mo," I warned, even though I was well aware she was simply changing the subject.

"—but I do believe change is on the horizon," she continued, blithely ignoring me.

"Are we talking about a hot man in black leather?" Mia asked.

"We are," Mo confirmed. "Although he sadly doesn't wear his leathers anywhere near enough for my liking."

"Really? You're a zillion times older than him," I said, caught between amusement and exasperation.

"Which doesn't mean I can't enjoy the view. I'm old, dear girl, not dead."

I shook my head and tried to ignore the images of the hot man in question—the way his leathers hugged his butt, his thighs, his groin ...

The barely repressed deep-down ache reignited, and I silently cursed. If I couldn't break the damn man's determination soon, I might have to take matters into my own hands —especially if we shared another kiss as mind-blowing as this morning's effort.

Mia chuckled. "So where is the delicious man?"

"He ran away," Mo said.

"What did you do to him, Gwen?"

I snorted and licked some icing from my fingertips. "I threatened his equilibrium."

"What?"

"She kissed him," Mo said blandly. "It was apparently so hot and passionate he had to run to Winchester to cool down."

"Seriously?"

"No, of course not." I screwed up my paper bag and tossed it at Mo's head. "He's gone there to uncover more information about the sword."

"The one stuck in the stone?"

"Not anymore—the next Witch King has claimed it."

Mia shot Mo an incredulous look. "When?"

"A couple of days ago. And no, we have no idea who that person is as yet."

"There can't be a huge number of suspects, surely, given heirs were being killed left, right, and center."

"There isn't."

Mia raised an eyebrow, her expression amused. "I take it that means you won't confirm until you're sure."

"Exactly."

"She's frustrating like that," I commented.

Mia snorted again and swung onto the M6. We were an hour and a half into the drive when the golden sphere finally began to pulse.

"We're closing in." Mo straightened a little in her seat. "Turn right at the next roundabout and then left."

"Crooklands?" Mia said. "What the hell is at Crooklands—aside from our runaways, that is."

"Probably not a whole lot, and that may be the point," Mo said.

"It's generally easier to get lost in a big town than it is a country one," I said. "Country folk tend not to miss a whole lot—especially when it comes to strangers in their midst."

"Unless the town is used to strangers." She pointed to a sign that said Lancaster Canal Leisure Park. "She's in there."

Mia drove through the gates and then slowed down. There was a currently closed reception area to our immediate left and, to our right, a rainbow-colored collection of wooden holiday lodges that followed the sweeping curve of the road. There were only three cars visible, so maybe the park didn't have that many bookings thanks to the fact it was winter.

I undid my seat belt and leaned forward. "Which one is she in?"

"The last one on the left."

Which was pastel yellow in color with a metal roof and no car out front. "It looks unoccupied."

"Well, if I was on the run, I sure as hell wouldn't be advertising my presence by sitting the car out the front of it," Mia said. "Do we know what type of car she drives? It could be one of the visible three."

"Or it's simply out of sight," I said. "I can't imagine she'd want to be too far from quick means of escape if she was attacked."

Mia nodded and glanced at Mo. "What do you want to do?"

"Investigate, of course." She grimaced. "But I'm not liking the feel of this."

"You think it's a trap?"

"Maybe not one specifically aimed at us, but yes. Park here."

Mia immediately halted in front of a lavender-colored cabin. I studied the others, but couldn't sense anything untoward. There certainly weren't any visible signs of magic or spells, but that was to be expected. It'd hardly be worthwhile setting a trap if you advertised its existence with visible threads.

"How are we going to do this?" I asked.

Mo pursed her lips. "I'll take the front door, you take the rear—"

"Is there a rear door in these things?" I asked.

"It's a safety requirement to have a fire exit," Mo said. "Mia, you're on watch. If you see anything odd or suspicious—and I mean anything—toot the horn."

She nodded. "And if you get into trouble, I'll come running."

I frowned. "Mia—"

"Don't 'Mia' me," she bit back. "I'm fully capable of protecting myself—and not just with magic."

"Meaning?"

Her grin flashed. "I've been doing bo staff training with Jonny."

I blinked—more at the fact she'd been doing more with Jonny than simply fucking him. "What the hell is a bo staff?"

"Basically, it's an Asian form of the quarter staff, which is more thrust focused. The bo is all about the swing."

"It's also a discussion that can be had later," Mo said. "Gwen, let's go."

I grabbed the backpack, climbed out of the car, and drew in a deep breath. The air was crisp and held the faint promise of rain. It was utterly free from the taint of halflings and magic, but that didn't mean they weren't here. Didn't mean we weren't going to get caught in a fire blast ...

Unease stirred. I quietly closed the car door and followed Mo around the front of the Fiesta. "Are you sure Gianna's here?"

Mo nodded. "The tracking sphere isn't fooled by covering magic. It's not pinpoint accurate, however, and that means I can't be absolutely certain they're in the yellow cabin. Go around to the back of the cabins and keep an eye out. When you hear the doorbell, head in—but quietly if you can. We don't want to scare her."

"Because two strange women breaking into the cabin isn't going to be scary at *all*."

My voice was dry, and she smiled. "I suspect Gianna

has seen enough over the last few years not to be frightened by the two of us. Go."

I slipped down the small gap between two cabins. There were no sounds coming from the lavender one, but a couple was talking in the other. They sounded elderly, and I mentally crossed all things that they didn't get hurt in whatever was about to happen.

After clambering over the small fence, I followed the line of pines that separated these cabins from those in the next street. As I neared the yellow cabin, energy lightly caressed the air. There was definitely some kind of spell here, even if I couldn't see any threads.

After a quick look around to make sure no one was watching, I moved across to the small deck at the back of the cabin and silently padded up the steps. A quick check of the handle told me the door was locked. I drew the daggers; the blades glimmered in the day's dull light, but no flames caressed their edge. We might be walking into a trap, but at least there was no immediate threat from halflings.

From deep within the cabin came the gentle chiming of a doorbell. I took a deep breath and crossed the daggers to call forth the lightning. I wasn't sure whether my control was better or if the daggers were simply more attuned to what I needed, but the energy that arced from the tip of each blade held none of its usual force—simply enough force to melt the lock rather than blasting the whole thing apart.

I pressed my fingers against the door and pushed it open. No sound came from inside the house. The air was still and cold and smelled slightly musty. The sphere might be saying they were here, but it definitely looked to be a more general 'here'. This cabin hadn't been used or aired in some time.

I glanced over my shoulder at the cabin visible through the trees. Parked alongside was an old Ford Estate—the perfect nondescript car for someone wanting to hide.

We were searching in the wrong cabin.

A soft popping noise had my head snapping around. I gripped the daggers tightly, my gaze sweeping the area beyond the small boot room. Nothing moved, and I had no sense of anyone else except Mo. And yet ... something stirred.

Heat.

I hesitated and then took several more steps into the cabin. "Mo? You in?"

"Yes." Her voice was as soft as mine. "She's not, though."

"Obviously." I glanced over my shoulder again. "I've got a feeling she might be in the cabin *behind* this one."

"It's possible—as I said, it's hard to pin an exact location with—oh fuck! Gwen, run!"

Even as she said it, there was a second *pop*.

The trap had just been sprung.

I spun and ran for the door, fear lodged in my throat and fiery heat chasing every step.

Then, with little warning, the whole damn cabin exploded.

CHAPTER EIGHT

The force of the blast knocked me off my feet and sent me tumbling through the door. I crashed into the deck railings hard enough to daze, but self-preservation nevertheless kicked in. I threw my hands over my head and tucked my knees up close, presenting as small a target as possible as bits of wood, glass, and metal fell like rain all around me.

Through the roar of the flames now consuming what was left of the building, I heard another sound—a car engine.

I twisted around and saw the Estate speed out of its parking area. Gianna. It had to be.

But I didn't race after her—Mo was far more important to me than a mother on the run.

I scrambled upright and felt a sharp stab of pain in my lower leg. A quick glance revealed a thick sliver of wood embedded in the chubby portion of my calf. I yanked it out, then thrust upright and leapt over the railing. Black smoke filled the lane between the two cabins, cutting visibility and catching in my throat, making me cough. I tugged my sweater up over my nose, but it didn't seem to make much difference. The heat was so fierce, the paint on the other cabin bubbled and peeled—though how it was even standing, given the force of the blast, I couldn't say.

I raced around the front corner of the building and saw Mo lying in the middle of the road ... and she wasn't moving.

My heart leapt into my throat, and for several seconds I couldn't breathe. I dropped heavily beside her, skinning my knees and sending pain shooting through the rest of me. I ignored it and tentatively touched her neck.

Her pulse was strong and steady. I closed my eyes against the sting of tears and sucked in a deep breath. She was okay ... this time.

I ignored the ominous thought and quickly studied the rest of her. There were no obvious injuries—no broken bones or deep cuts—aside from the bloody scrape down her left cheek, which was no doubt a result of being flung onto the road. I pulled the first aid kit out of the backpack and grabbed a bottle of holy water to wash the wound.

The sound of running had me reaching for my daggers even as I looked around. Mia, rather than a stranger or a threat. Standing behind her on the balcony of their cabin were the elderly couple; the woman's expression was unfriendly, and she had a phone clutched in her hand.

"I've rung the police and fire brigade," she said, her voice a little too high to be forceful. "Don't you be running away, because I have your photographs."

"Could you also call an ambulance? My grandmother needs to be checked over," I said, then glanced up as Mia slid to a halt beside me. "You okay?"

"I wasn't anywhere near the damn blast—are you hurt? Is Mo?"

"No," Mo said, her voice a little hoarse. "I'm fine."

"Stay still," I commanded. "I need—"

"I'm fine, Gwen, as I said."

"You said that when you slipped down the stairs and fractured your damn leg," I retorted. "You just got blasted five meters through the air. Humor me and do what you're told for a change."

She opened her eyes. The blue depths held hints of amusement and pain. "I've heard that tone before, but it's usually mine rather than yours."

"It's your genes coming out in me again."

"In more ways than one, I suspect." She shifted her hands and pushed upright. Short of actually sitting on her, I couldn't stop her, but the pain in her expression deepened, suggesting she really hadn't totally escaped injury. She brushed her hands to get rid of the grit, smearing red. Her cheek wasn't the only thing she'd skinned. "I gather no one ran out of the house after that blast?"

"No, but the Ford Estate parked at the cabin behind certainly got out of here in a hurry."

Her gaze sharpened. "And you're not following? Why not?"

I rolled my eyes, torn between amusement and exasperation. "It just might have something to do with my grandmother lying unmoving and bleeding on the roadside."

She touched my cheek lightly. "I love you, you know that, but if you don't get your ass in the air and follow that car, I will be peeved."

I snorted, then grabbed my knives and quickly lashed them together. As the sound of sirens cut through the air, I pushed to my feet and handed Mia the medical kit and holy water. "Make sure she's examined by the ambulance crew before you allow her in the car."

"I hate to point out the obvious, but she can fly."

"And if she'd been able to do so, she wouldn't have ordered me after the Estate alone."

"You are altogether too quick sometimes," Mo murmured.

"That would be your genes again." I swung the pack over my shoulders. "I'll call when I get a location."

Mo nodded. "We'll use the tracker and follow in the car once we've dealt with this mess."

I glanced across at the older couple—who were still watching with beady-eyed interest—then shifted shape, grabbed my knives, and hightailed it out of there.

It didn't take that long to find the Estate—she might have driven out of the park at speed, but it appeared that once she was on the main road, she'd slowed down—no doubt to avoid attracting too much attention.

That was presuming, of course, this *was* Gianna and her son. Just because instinct said it was, didn't mean it was right. While I could swoop down to check, a bird carrying a set of knives would attract the attention of normal drivers, let alone one who may have been dealing with my brother for close on six years.

Once she'd turned onto the M6, her speed increased. I kept her in sight by flying across country, but I didn't push my speed. I had no idea just how long I'd have to fly after her, and I needed to conserve some strength.

The day grew darker—colder—and a drizzly rain set in. I cursed, but it was at least better than a full-on storm—although if the clouds on the horizon were anything to go by, that's what would soon strike.

The old Ford Estate continued toward Penrith, but didn't enter the heart of that lovely old city. Instead, she turned onto a road that went toward Redhills and then onto another road that wound its way through the gently rolling countryside, heading toward a large body of dark water. It was obviously one of the lakes, given we were now in the Lakes District National Park area, but I couldn't say which one. It wasn't Windermere, though—it was smaller and a different shape.

As she neared the top end of the lake, she turned onto a lane that looked to be little wider than her car and continued on, pulling over a couple of times—once to allow enough room for a tractor going the other way, and a second time to allow a fast-moving black van to get ahead of her.

The lane wound through a number of thickly forested areas, more or less following the lake's shoreline. Up ahead, in the distance, was a yacht club and another caravan area—was that her destination? If so, why? Surely she'd have to know that—come night—she wouldn't be safe. Not in the middle of a town, and certainly not in the middle of nowhere.

Either she didn't know Darkside—or at least, Winter—could track her children, or she'd purchased some form of protective spell.

I hoped it was the latter. I suspected it was the former.

The lane swept closer to the lake. As she disappeared into another short but thick-forested strand of trees, I flew over the canopy and waited for her to come out on the other side.

Two minutes passed, then three, then five. No sign of her. And absolutely no sign of that faster moving black van, which *should* have appeared at least a couple of minutes ago.

I swore—the sound coming out a harsh squawk—and arrowed down, swooping in under the canopy, but remaining high.

I smelled the fire before I saw her car. It was sideways across the road, the rear end hard up against the front of a black van. A second van blocked the road behind her; as I swooped closer, its rear door slid open and three men got out.

Gianna obviously didn't see them. She was too busy throwing flames at the two men from the first van. One of them was on fire, his clothes and skin sloughing from his body as he leapt over the roadside edge and plunged down the hill toward the water. The other had taken refuge behind the van; every few minutes he popped out from behind his cover, unleashed a couple of gunshots, and then jumped back. Bullets pinged off the Estate's roof, the road, and the nearby trees. Either he was a very bad shot or he was deliberately missing in order to keep her attention while the men in the other van crept up on her.

I dropped from the canopy and shifted shape as I neared the ground. The man behind the van spun as I landed and, in one smooth movement, he raised his gun and fired. I swore, dove away, and then rolled onto my knees and raised the daggers. I had no time to either untie or unsheathe them; I simply pointed and called to the inner storm. It answered swiftly and sharply, blasting past the leather tip of the sheaths with enough force that I was flung onto my butt. The twin bolts of lightning hit the gun, peeling it apart like butter before smashing into the man's chest. He didn't even have time to scream.

As his ashes fluttered to the ground, I thrust to my feet and raced around the rear of the nearest van. "Gianna, behind—"

I cut the rest of the sentence off as the van's door opened; the driver jumped out, his gun raised and blasting. A bullet burned across my forearm, another clipped my shoulder. He didn't get a third shot ... and nothing—not even ashes—remained.

I ran on. Saw one man on fire and another struggling with Gianna. Saw a third racing toward the other van with a little boy slung like a sack over his shoulder.

I tugged Nex free, screamed, "Gianna, drop," then, when she did, sliced open her assailant's face. As his blood spurted and his scream rent the air, I slapped the two knives together and took out the other van. A million bits of heated metal were flung skyward, the man holding Reign switched direction and plunged over the embankment, heading for the river.

It was then I saw the boat.

They'd come prepared for trouble.

I leapt over the small rock fence and raced after him. I didn't want to risk using the lightning on him for fear of hitting the boy, but I wasn't about to let him escape either. I cut sideways through the trees until I had a clear shot of the boat, then called to the lightning yet again. A sharp lance of fire cut through my brain—a warning I was now nearing my limits.

The boat and the man inside it were incinerated.

The man holding Reign swore, then spun and raised a gun. I dove sideways again, crashing through the under-growth and tearing clothes and skin. Bullets pinged off the tree trunks, showering me with sharp little daggers of bark.

I scrambled on all fours behind the tree and then took a deep breath. The pain in my head didn't ease, and the cuts on my calf, forearm, and shoulder all decided to join in on the fun.

Twigs crunched; the felon, on the move, heading toward me rather than away. I took another deep breath, gathering strength, but before I could move or react, fire burned down the ridge. As the undergrowth around me burst into flame and a scream echoed, I scrambled upright, hooked my knives into my belt, then leapt over the small wall of fire. The remains of the man who'd attacked me lay on the ground, burning. I detoured around him then ran on for the small, unmoving figure on the ground.

"Leave him alone, or I'll kill you" came a high, desperate demand.

I ignored her. She was hardly going to kill me if I held her son—not after her desperate efforts to save him. I scooped him up and hugged him close; he didn't stir. Either something was wrong or she'd drugged him to keep him compliant until they were safe. Though I wondered if drugging him would have made any difference to Winter's ability to shuffle through his mind, it wouldn't have made any difference in this case. The men in the two vans had obviously followed her from the leisure park. The trap had been too well coordinated to be a last-minute event.

I glanced up the slope. Gianna stood on the edge, flames flickering faintly around her fingertips. She was tall, with burnished gold hair and a thin, gangly frame. Her face was pale and dominated by what might have been called a 'commanding' nose in a male, but had no doubt been a source of derision for her as a child.

"Who are you?" she said, clenching and unclenching her fists. "What do you want?"

I might as well hit her with the bad news first. "I'm Gwen De Montfort, and I'm here to save your life."

"Likely story, if you're *his* fucking sister."

Meaning she knew Max well enough to know about me. I headed up the hill, only half watching where I was walking. The greater threat remained above me. "If I was after your son, I could very easily have killed you when I killed your assailant. And in case it escaped your notice, if the man behind the van had been a slightly better shot, you'd now be dead."

She didn't say anything to that, just clenched and unclenched her hands. Ready to unleash the minute I said or did anything threatening.

Which made asking the next question a little dangerous, but it had to be done—even if it was one that had the power to make or break me. "If you think so fucking little of Max, why did you agree to carry his children in the first place?"

She waved a hand. Fire followed the movement, bright in the gathering darkness of the incoming storm. "Because it seemed like a good opportunity at the time."

The answer—though more than half expected—nevertheless felt like a punch to the gut. For several seconds, I couldn't breathe, couldn't think, could only feel. And what I felt was pain. Deep, utter, soul-shattering pain.

Even so, one refrain echoed—why, why, *why?*

It was a question that could only be answered by the man himself, and one we dared not ask. Not yet.

I blinked back the tears threatening to stream down my cheeks and sucked in a deep breath in an effort to gather the shattered remnants of control. We might have defeated the men in the vans, but the three of us were far from safe, and until we were, I couldn't afford to dwell on the enormity of Max's duplicity.

"No doubt meaning he paid you extremely well to be a broodmare and nursemaid." I stopped several meters away from her, which put me at a slight disadvantage if she decided to attack. I doubted she would, though—not until she'd retrieved her son, anyway.

"He did—and there's no law against that, you know."

"So why did you run?"

She sucked in a breath and released it slowly. "I got a call from Max. He said he was sending his people over to collect Reign."

"That's not unusual, is it? According to Riona—"

"She's okay?" Gianna cut in quickly. Desperately.

"Yeah, no thanks to you."

"You don't understand—"

"You're right. I don't. Leaving one child to save another? Utterly unforgivable."

"But they wouldn't have hurt her or Naya—"

"Really? Because by the time I got there, Naya had been beaten to a bloody pulp."

Her face went white and a soft 'oh no' escaped. Her knees buckled, and she staggered back several steps until she hit the wall separating the slope from the road.

I moved further up the slope, but she didn't seem to notice. She thrust a shaking hand through her tangled hair and said, "No, it can't be true. I won't believe it."

"I can give you the phone number of the detective in charge of the investigation, if you'd like." My voice was harsh but I didn't care. She'd left her daughter behind to save her son. There was no excuse for that. No forgiveness.

"Where's Riona?"

"Do you care?"

Her gaze shot up. Despite the wash of tears, anger burned deep. "She's my daughter—of *course* I care."

"And yet you made her a sacrificial lamb in order to save your son."

"Because I believed they wouldn't hurt her—they have plans for her, just as they have plans for Reign."

"Do you have any idea what those plans are?"

My voice was grim and she frowned. "Of course—Max

intends to resurrect Witch King rule, and Reign will secure the line of succession."

Hearing our suspicions confirmed in such a matter-of-fact manner somehow made it all that much harder to take. When it was just conjecture on Mo's part, I could keep pretending he wasn't the brains behind this hideous plot. But now? Now I had no choice but to accept my twin was a traitor. A killer. A betrayer.

What probably hurt the most was the fact that he'd obviously been planning all this for well over six years—and neither Mo nor I had had even the faintest idea.

How could we have missed it? Surely there must have been some sign of what was happening—of the dark path he was being led down. Or had we grown so used to his secretive manner that we ignored all the clues?

I didn't know—and probably never would. Not now.

I shook my head in a vague effort to get rid of the agony that burned within and the tears that still threatened to burst free. "And you didn't think him crazy?"

"Of course not. He had the coronation ring—he showed it to me."

Was it the one stolen from the museum, or the one the Blackbirds supposedly had in safekeeping? "And how do you know it was the real thing?"

"Because I've seen it before—or rather, seen the replica —at the British Museum."

Which didn't clarify which one he'd possessed. I'd have to ask Luc to check whether they were still in possession of the real one when I saw him again.

"You surely didn't agree to bear his children on the sighting of one old ring. Or was it the money that convinced you?"

She hesitated. "He did—and does—pay very well, but there was also the bible—"

My gut clenched. "What bible?"

She gave me a strange look. "The De Montfort bible, of course. It wasn't in great condition—had some fire damage, from the look of it—but it showed a clear line of succession to the current crop of De Montforts."

Where the hell had he found *that*? How had he managed to find it, when it had supposedly been destroyed in a fire that had partially destroyed the family home just before the First World War?

And if they had that, why had the demons been searching for the Valeriun family bible? Or was it more a matter of Darkside and my brother not wanting us to get our hands on it, because it would have confirmed there was a direct link between the Aquitaine and De Montfort lines?

There were too many damn questions, and far too few damn answers.

I scrubbed a hand across burning eyes and said, "You do know he plans this resurgence of witch rule with the aid and power of Darkside—"

"What? No—"

"What do you think Winter is?"

She frowned. "He's strange, yes, but—"

"He's a half-demon."

"Half-demon? No, he can't be—"

"Have you ever asked your children where Winter takes them?"

Her frown deepened. "To school. Max wanted them to learn languages. I told him they were too young but—"

"And do you know where that school is?" I cut in.

"Not far from where we live."

Meaning there was a dark gate near them? Another

thing I needed to tell Luc. "Darkside. They're taken into Darkside."

She stared at me. "You're insane."

My smile was grim. "Maybe I am, but that's what Riona said when I asked, and I have no reason to disbelieve her."

"But—" She stopped. "I can't believe—"

"Really?" I broke in again. "Then why did you run when Max called to say he was sending someone over to pick up Reign?"

"He said that things had escalated sooner than he'd hoped and that he was taking him away for a while." Her quick smile held little humor. "Whatever you may think of me, I'm not a bad mom. Something felt off, and I didn't have much time to think. I just acted, as any mother would."

Any mother would *not* have left their little girl behind. I pushed the anger down and glanced up as fat drops of rain began to fall. "We better get moving—not only is it about to bucket down, but we're not safe here."

"Why?" She frowned. "We've taken care of your brother's men."

"And how do you think they found you here, when you didn't leave a note or any other indication of where you were going?"

She opened her mouth and then closed it again.

"Winter can speak to—and track—your children when they're asleep." I glanced down at the child in my arms. He had my brother's features, and it was a knife to the heart. *Max, how could you do this? Why would you do this?*

I swallowed heavily and added, "Given they did find you relatively quickly, they were obviously close behind you when we sprang the trap in that cabin."

"That was you?"

"Yeah. And if you'd succeeded in killing us, Reign would now be on his way to Darkside."

"No—" She stopped. "How do I know you're speaking the truth? How do I know I can trust you?"

"All I can do is let you speak to Riona, but until Reign wakes, I'm not taking you anywhere near her. It'd put her and her guardians in danger of an immediate attack."

Her gaze swept me, lingering briefly on the blood staining my shoulder and sleeve. "You risked your life to save us. I guess I really have no choice."

For now. She didn't say that, but it nevertheless seemed to hover in the air.

"Let's get back to your car and get out of here," I said, as the skies opened up.

"My son—"

"I'll carry him."

Annoyance flicked across her expression, but she nevertheless climbed over the fence and strode toward the car. I followed. After clipping Reign into his car seat, I clambered over the console and dropped into the passenger seat. It would have been easier to use the doors, but there wasn't a chance in hell I'd risk getting out of the car. The bitch would have taken off—the slight smile tugging at her lips was evidence enough of that.

"I take it you have a plan of action?" she said in a friendly and yet still snippy way.

"Yep. Get us out of here before someone calls in the cops."

She shoved the car into gear and flattened the accelerator. As the old car shook, I grabbed my phone and called Mo.

"Where are you?" I asked the second she answered.

"Approaching Penrith. Did you find her?"

"Yes, but Darkside got there first. We're all okay, though."

"Good." The relief in her voice made me smile. "I'll arrange for Ron to come fetch them."

"I'm not going anywhere with a damn stranger," Gianna said.

"You already are, and you'll continue to do so if you want to save your son's life," I snapped back. To Mo, I added, "What do you want us to do in the meantime? Reign's been drugged—"

"Because he was screaming for his damn sister," Gianna muttered. "It was attracting attention."

"Perhaps he knew his sister was in danger."

She snorted. "He's five."

"And a twin. We twins have a special bond." And I couldn't help but wonder when the one between Max and me had broken—and why I hadn't even noticed.

"Just drive," Mo said. "It may not be safe to stop, as it's unlikely Winter got Gianna's location details from Reign if he's been drugged and hasn't stirred."

Something I hadn't actually thought about. I glanced quickly at Gianna. "Did you pack anything of Reign's that Max or Winter gave him?"

"Just an old teddy—"

I swore and twisted around. The teddy had been strapped into the middle seat next to the car seat. It was indeed old—a grubby-looking bear with threadbare cheeks, black ears, and a natty blue waistcoat. It was also, I thought with a stab to the heart, Max's bear—one that he'd absolutely cherished as a kid.

Maybe, despite all his plotting, some part of him did actually care for his children—or, at the very least, his son.

And maybe I was just grabbing at something—anything

—that meant my brother wasn't totally lost. That some love, light, and decency remained.

"Hang on a sec, Mo." I put the phone on loudspeaker, placed it on the console, and then leaned back to grab the bear. A quick but thorough examination revealed the existence of a small, circular object. The tracker, no doubt.

"Your instincts are spot-on, Mo—there's a tracker in his teddy."

"What?" Gianna said, horror in her expression.

"It may not be the only one, either," Mo said. "Your brother's never been one to leave things to chance. Ditch the teddy—"

"No," Gianna said. "He won't sleep without it."

Max hadn't either. I blew out a breath and drew Vita. After carefully unpicking a few stitches, I squeezed the small disk out of the bear's fat little backside. "The tracker's little bigger than a ten pence piece."

"Which means it probably hasn't a huge range. They might still be following you."

I opened the window and tossed the tracker out. "We'll drive around Penrith until you can give us a location," I said. "If there is a second tracker, then at least there's less chance of them hitting us in a busy market town."

"Hopefully. Just be careful."

"I will."

I disconnected and then glanced at Gianna. "Have you got anything else of his—or even yours—that Max or Winter gave you?"

"The teddy and a few clothes was all I had time for." She glanced at me. "Who's Mo?"

"Our grandmother. Did Max never mention her?"

Her expression was amused. "This was a business deal, not a love match."

"I certainly didn't think it was love—he's homosexual."

She snorted. "Well, that explains his awkwardness over the whole sex part of the arrangement."

I blinked. "You and he actually had sex?"

"How else does one get pregnant?" She raised an eyebrow, amusement evident. "Him being gay does explain the decided lack of enthusiasm and why proceedings stopped the minute I *did* fall pregnant."

This was certainly a day for shocks. I wasn't sure I could take too much more, especially where my brother was concerned.

"Do you have his phone number?"

Her eyebrow rose again. "You don't?"

"I course I do, but it might not be the same one."

She immediately rattled off the number. It was the same one.

"What about Winter? Do you have his number?"

She nodded. "But I don't know that one off by heart—I was warned never to use it except in emergencies."

"I'll need you to give it to me so we can track it."

"I will, as soon as I can access my phone." She glanced at me. "Winter is ... unpleasant."

If that wasn't the understatement of the year, I wasn't sure what was. "Trust me, I'm well aware of that."

Her gaze slid over me, then rose to the bloody sleeve of my arm. "If you knew what Max was up to, why haven't you stopped him?"

"Because we didn't know. Not until very recently."

"But he's your twin—"

"And we don't live in each other's pockets. Who was Naya?"

She blinked hard, several times. "My cousin. Max was paying her to homeschool the twins, as she's a qualified

157

teacher. She also had babysitting duties when I had to go out." A lone tear trickled down her cheek. "Is she really dead?"

"I'm afraid so."

One tear became two. She bit her lip and lightly shook her head, as if to loosen the grip of sadness. "Her parents will need to be informed."

"The investigators will handle that." I paused as she turned right around the roundabout and continued on to Penrith. "Did you ever meet Winter or Max outside your home with the twins? Or did they always come to collect them?"

"Generally the latter, but there was one time where I had to meet Winter in London. It was a fucking long train trip with two kids in tow, let me tell you."

My heart began to beat a little faster. While it was very unlikely that whatever address they'd used would still be in use, it would at least give us a starting point. Right now, he very much remained an enigma. "Can you remember where in London?"

She wrinkled her nose. "It wasn't far from Euston Station—Goodge Street, I think. There was a Botanicals place opposite it. I remember that because Reign pointed out the bear on the sign."

"Can you remember what floor?"

"Top, I—"

The rest of the sentence ended in a yelp as the Estate was hit from behind and sent flying toward the side barrier and the thick pole of the overhead sign that stood behind it.

Darkside hadn't quite finished with us yet.

CHAPTER NINE

"**B**rake!" I yelled, automatically bracing for impact.

The tires squealed and the car fishtailed violently as Gianna fought to keep control. But we were going too fast to stop so quickly, and we hit the metal barrier with a bone-jarring crunch that threw us both forward *and* sideways. As the seat belts snapped taut, the airbags exploded, filling the cabin with smoke and dust. It felt like someone had deployed a sledgehammer against my chest, and for several seconds, breathing hurt.

I sucked in the foul, powdery air and caught a glimpse of movement in the side mirror—a man walking toward the vehicle, a gun held against his right leg. They definitely weren't playing this time.

"Gianna?" There was no immediate response, and I risked a quick glance at her. There was blood on the side of her face, and she was out of it. She must have smacked her head against the window when we'd slammed side-on to the barrier.

I swore softly, dragged Nex and Vita free of their sheaths, and then glanced at the side mirror again. The stranger with the gun had reached the back of the Estate. I undid the belt but didn't immediately release it, allowing it to retract slowly to lessen the chance of the stranger seeing the movement.

Then, after silently praying the deflating airbag didn't get tangled in my legs, I thrust the door open and pushed out.

The stranger was quick, I'll give him that. There was a soft *thwock, thwock* and several bullets hit the lower part of the door, close to my torso.

I unleashed the power of the daggers and burned him to a crisp, then quickly glanced under the car and saw a pair of sneakered feet edging toward the rear door. I flicked a stream of lightning at him, heard a yelp that cut off abruptly, and watched his ashes spray across the ground. A heartbeat later, an engine roared to life; the truck that had sent us into the barrier was reversing. Whether he intended to leave or he simply wanted to gather enough momentum to finish us off, I couldn't say. I certainly wasn't going to wait and find out. I crossed the blades and sent a deadly arc of lightning straight at him. The front windshield exploded, and the driver disintegrated. With no one on the accelerator or guiding the wheel, the truck swung back into the barrier and stopped.

Our means of escape, if we moved fast enough.

I scrambled upright and tugged open the back door. Reign didn't appear to have been injured—the car seat, with its inbuilt five-point harness, had obviously done its job, though it was hard to be certain given he remained fast asleep. I reached past him and shook Gianna. She swore— whether at me or in pain, I wasn't exactly sure.

"Gianna, you have to wake up. We need to get out of here." And before someone came around the corner and stopped to offer assistance. We'd been lucky so far—both sides of the road had remained empty, but I doubted such luck would hold for long. "Gianna? Move—now!"

"What happened?" She thrust a hand through damp hair. Her fingers came away red. "Why am I bleeding?"

"We got hit from behind and pushed into the side barrier," I said. "Either something in your belongings is bugged or this car is. We have to abandon it and get out of here."

"Abandon?" she said, sounding a little out of it. "Why?"

"Because I said so." Impatience edged my voice. We didn't have time for this. "You'll have to climb over the console and get out through the passenger door—your door took the brunt of the collision."

She muttered something under her breath, but nevertheless undid the belt and unsteadily obeyed. I quickly undid the tether points on the kid's car seat, slashed through the top point because I didn't have the time to fiddle, and then dragged the whole thing over to the other side of the car. It would be damn awkward to carry, especially with Reign still strapped inside.

Gianna stood next to the open passenger door, the old teddy gripped firmly in one hand as she looked around a little owlishly. "Where are we?"

"Outside Penrith. Can you see the blue truck behind us?"

She glanced that way. "Its windshield is broken."

"Yes. Get into the passenger seat."

"I can't leave Reign—"

"I'm bringing him. Go."

She walked away unsteadily. I grabbed my backpack and her shoulder bag, then sucked in a deep breath that did little to ease the growing tide of aches and weariness. After wrapping my arms around the car seat, I hauled it free of the car and lugged it over to the truck. The world was spinning by the time I reached it, the pain in my head so bad my sight was blurring. Given everything also had a reddish tinge, I suspected my eyes were bleeding. No surprise, given just how much I'd called on the inner power over the last twenty-four hours.

With a grunt of effort, I placed the car seat into the back of the truck and attached the two still viable points before hauling the regular belt over the top to make doubly sure it was secure. I dumped my pack in the footwell, then tipped the contents of her purse onto the back seat. A quick ferret through didn't reveal anything unexpected, but I nevertheless checked the purse's side pockets. The tracker was in one of them. I tossed it onto the ground, crushed it underneath my heel, then scooped everything back into the purse and dumped it beside the pack.

Once I'd brushed away the ashes of the previous occupant, I climbed into the driver seat. Gianna was blinking owlishly, and her skin was pale. Concussion, I suspected.

"Gianna? You need to belt up."

As she mechanically obeyed, I checked the mirrors and then pulled out. We'd barely passed the overhead sign when a car came around the corner. I kept an eye on it, but it neither sped up when it saw us nor slowed down when it saw the remains of the Estate.

I released the breath I hadn't realized I'd been holding, and my inner strength washed away as quickly as a tide. I swallowed heavily, tightened my grip on the wheel, and did my best to concentrate. We had to get out of here; had to get somewhere safe. Nothing else mattered right now.

By the time we were close to the center of Penrith, I was barely holding it together. I spotted a big golden M through the elms lining the right side of the road and swung into the parking area. It was reasonably full, which meant the only spots available were the ones at the back of the parking area—perfect for us. I reversed into a spot and then switched off the engine and leaned my forehead against the steering wheel, sucking in great gulps of air. The inner shaking had expanded to the rest of me, and my stomach felt like it was about to unleash.

"Where are we?" came Gianna's soft question.

I glanced at her. She'd been floating in and out of consciousness for the last fifteen minutes, but for the moment looked lucid. "Penrith. I think you've got a concussion—do you want some Panadol?"

She nodded and rubbed her forehead. Flakes of dried blood fell away, which at least meant the wound on her head had stopped bleeding and couldn't have been too serious.

I twisted around, grabbed my backpack, and retrieved the bottle of painkillers. After handing her two, I popped a couple out for myself. There was no way they'd be strong enough to calm the mad orchestra inside my head, but maybe they'd take the edge off.

She frowned at me. "Why are your eyes red?"

"It's a consequence of using my powers." I grabbed my phone, then dumped the pack behind the seat again. "You must have some backlash after using all that fire."

She nodded. "It drains me. I usually sleep for at least a day afterward."

Meaning maybe she wasn't concussed; maybe she was simply zoning out after draining her system of energy.

I hit Mo's number; the phone barely had time to ring before she was saying, "We're about five minutes away from your current location, if this tracker is to be believed. What the hell happened back there?"

"Another attack—we're now in our assailant's truck."

"Were they halflings or witches?"

"I didn't really take the time to ask." I hesitated. "They were armed, though, so they might have been regular thugs for hire."

"Possibly. You keep smoking their troops, and they surely can't have an endless supply of them, even if they have been planning this for decades."

"If they've been planning this for decades, I wouldn't bet on that." I glanced toward the road as a small white Fiesta came around the corner and slowed down. "We're in the parking area, right at the back."

The car turned in, and a few seconds later, they'd parked beside us. Mo climbed out and opened the truck door.

"Well, don't you look like shit?" She leaned past me and added, "And I'm guessing you'll be Gianna. Wish we could have met under more pleasant circumstances."

Gianna nodded, but her expression was uncertain. "Are you sure we're going to be safe? They've found us pretty easily twice now."

"There are magical means of preventing tracking spells and physical means of preventing the use of regular tracking devices, but I can't one hundred percent guarantee it won't happen," Mo said. "What I *can* guarantee is that the best shot you and your children have of remaining free of Dark-side control will be with us."

Gianna was silent for a moment, her gaze sweeping the two of us. Her uncertainty remained, and the annoyance that had been buried under the avalanche of adrenaline and fear flickered to life. I'd almost died protecting her and her goddamn son ... my *nephew*. I drew in a slow, deep breath and tried to calm down. Her reactions were perfectly natural, especially given how closely related we were to the apparent leader of this whole fucking mess. Heaven only knew what Max had told her about us.

"Fine," she said eventually. "Where are we going?"

"It's better if that remains a secret." Mo glanced into the rear. "Damn, that boy looks like his father—but what the hell did you give him to make him sleep so soundly through all this?"

"A third of one of my Ambien tablets."

Mo sharp inhale was a sound of disapproval. But then, she'd always preferred herbal medicines to manmade, especially when it came to children.

"Let's get you both out of here—I'll check him and take a look at that cut on your head once we're safe."

Gianna frowned. "He's okay—"

"And you've both been in a crash that totaled your car. Humor an old healer and let me check you both out." She waited until Gianna had climbed out of the car and then said, her expression concerned, "How bad are the gun wounds and the weariness?"

"I'll survive."

She snorted. "To throw your own words back at you, you'd say that even if you'd broken every bone in your goddamn body. Give me your hands."

I obeyed. Her magic stirred around me, a warm caress of power that chased away the chills and weakness even as it closed over the worst of my wounds. I still felt washed out, and my head still pounded, but that was to be expected given she could hardly waste all her strength on me when she had Gianna and Reign to protect.

She released me with a sigh. "That'll have to do for now."

"Thanks." I leaned forward and lightly kissed her

scraped cheek. "What are you going to do once you settle Gianna and Reign?"

"Head on over to Barney's—"

"Will that be safe?" I cut in. "They've already attacked him once."

"I don't believe they'll attack again—they were after the photographs rather than us."

I frowned. "And how did you deduce that? They certainly weren't pulling their punches when it came to shooting at us—"

"Except that they were—do you really think the chair would have protected either of us if they'd actually wanted us dead?"

"It *was* well made."

She snorted. "Not that well made. The photographs were snatched while we were chasing the Aranea and the two men were on the roof."

Meaning the attack had simply been a distraction. "Why would they bother, though?"

She shrugged. "Maybe your brother and his Darkside mates decided they'd better uncover what the prophecy on the throne actually said."

"But they tried to destroy it—"

"No doubt to stop *us* getting to it. And that's the reason Barney and I are going over to King's Island this evening. I want to grab some pictures of the King's Stone's faded glyphs, just in case they attempt to repeat the destruction there."

"I guess if anyone can bring out what's written on that stone, it'll be his nephew. Just ... be careful. I really want to believe Max wouldn't hurt either of us, but he may not be running the entire show."

Mo smiled and squeezed my hand. I knew her well

enough to know she didn't believe Max was anything else but the ringleader. Pain stabbed through my heart once again, and I battled back the stinging tears.

"I doubt it's going to be safe for you to return home alone," she said. "I contacted Luc, and he's given me the address of a temporary safe house. He'll meet you there."

She handed me a bit of paper, and I glanced down at it. It was for an address in Southport. "It'll take me at least five hours to get to there from here, and I don't want to be driving around that long, especially in this truck."

"Dump it somewhere close and grab a cab, then. I'll see you tomorrow sometime. Make sure you rest up."

"I will."

Mo and Gianna hauled the car seat and the still sleeping child over to the Fiesta. Mia gave me a wave and a thumbs-up as they left, and I suddenly felt very alone. And very exposed.

I glanced at the address again, then programmed it into my phone rather than the truck's navigation system. Given I intended to dump the truck, it'd be nothing short of stupidity to give them an easy means of finding us.

I tugged my purse out of the backpack, then went through the drive-through and grabbed a large fries, chicken strips, and a bucket of coffee. Munching on them as I headed back out of Penrith at least kept the weariness at bay, perhaps more so than the coffee.

I dumped the truck close to the Harris Museum in Preston and then caught a cab the rest of the way to Southport. It was expensive, but I was beyond caring. Dusk had given way to night by the time I arrived at the safe house Luc had arranged for us. I paid the cab and climbed out, staring at the building in awe. It was a large and impressive Tudor mansion, though it wasn't, I realized after a few minutes, a particularly *old* building—the roof tiles were too new and the black-and-white framing too crisp and clean. It didn't matter—it was simply stunning.

The main door opened, and a sharply dressed elderly gentleman with neat white hair and merry blue eyes came out.

"Ms. De Montfort?" he asked, in an ultra-polite, but friendly manner. When I nodded, he added, "We've been expecting you. This way please."

He waved a gloved hand toward the door, and I half smiled. We De Montforts certainly weren't poor, but neither were we so crazily rich that we could afford to build a mock Tudor mansion in an area like this, so close to both the sea and the golf course, and then have a multitude of staff catering to every whim.

The entrance hall was a vast space whose main feature was a turned oak staircase leading up to a galleried landing. The floor and deep skirting boards were also oak, and a huge gold-and-crystal chandelier hung from the double-height ceiling, sending rainbow sprays of color across the white walls every time light hit the teardrops.

"Would you like a shower, Ms. De Montfort?" the elderly gentleman continued. "Or would you prefer something to eat first?"

"A shower would be fantastic. And please, just call me Gwen."

He inclined his head. "I'm Henry, the majordomo. This way, please."

We walked up the sweeping staircase to the landing and then down a wide and very plushly carpeted hall to a bedroom bigger than the entire first floor of our building.

"The bathroom is to your right," Henry said. "You'll find all necessary items in the nearby shelving. If you wish your clothes laundered and mended, please place them on the bed. Just press the buzzer beside the light switch in the bathroom, and Jenny—the maid—will fetch them."

"Thank you, Henry."

He nodded and left, quietly closing the door behind him. I drew in a deep breath and resisted the urge to flop down onto the ginormous bed and sleep for the next twenty hours. The bedding was pristine white, and I was a blood-soaked, sweaty, grimy mess. The two were not compatible.

I stripped off then folded my clothes and placed them neatly on the top of the blanket box at the end of the bed. The three daggers I shoved under the pile of pillows, out of immediate sight but close to hand when I was sleeping.

The bathroom was another revelation. Like everything else in this place, it was vast and opulent; the white marble was veined with gold, and the two basins and all the taps were gold. The shower was big enough to have a party in, with three ceiling-mounted showerheads and two flexible wall ones.

I pressed the buzzer to call Jenny, then collected sham-poo, body soap and sponge, and a tent-like towel from the inset storage area. After turning on the middle shower and two side ones, I stepped under the hot, hot water and simply stood there, soaking away the grime, the blood, and the aches, for so long that my skin began to prune.

Once I was dry and my hair combed into some sort of order, I padded back into the bedroom, my feet sinking deep in the thick carpet. A dressing gown had been placed on the chest where my clothes had been, but I didn't bother grab-bing it. I pressed the button to close the curtains and then climbed in under the blankets and went to sleep.

I woke who knows how many hours later to the aware-ness I was no longer alone. I slid a hand under the pillow to grip Nex's hilt, then the warm mix of musk, sandalwood, and cinnamon teased my nostrils. I smiled even as my heart began to dance and a deep-down ache stirred to life.

The damn man was going to be the death of me—if one could die of sheer frustration, that is.

I released my grip on Nex and opened my eyes. Luc wasn't lying on the other side of the ginormous bed, as I'd half hoped, but had instead dragged up one of the well-padded armchairs and was asleep in that, his sock-covered feet resting on the end of the bed. He looked at peace. At home. *Gorgeous*. My fingers itched with the need to reach out and caress the muscular splendor barely hidden by the almost too tight shirt; I longed to kiss my way down his chest and stomach, to explore what lay beyond the waist of his jeans ...

I drew a deep, shuddery breath, and his eyes opened. The green depths sparkled with amusement, as if he knew exactly where my thoughts had been and what that intake of breath had meant.

"How are you feeling?" His voice was a deep, sexy rumble that created havoc with my already erratic pulse.

"I'm good. Hungry, but good."

Desire flared in his eyes, along with amusement. The damn man knew I wasn't talking about food. "When did you get in?"

"About six hours ago."

"So why are you sleeping here in a chair rather than in your own bedroom? I'm sure a mansion this size has plenty of them."

"It does, but from the little Mo said about the reasons this retreat was needed, I figured I'd better not leave you alone."

"Nex and Vita are under—"

"And you've used them enough that the whites of your eyes are still pink, despite being asleep for over twelve hours."

"Twelve hours? No wonder I'm damn hungry."

A sexy smile teased his lips. "I think *that* is a constant state with you. Some of us do have—"

"If you say more control, I'm going to throw a mountain of pillows at you."

The smile grew wider and he raised his hands. "A stomach that doesn't need to be fed every couple of hours."

We both knew that wasn't what he'd intended to say, and maybe it was time to prove a point. I stretched like a cat, and the blankets fell away, revealing the upper portion of my body.

His gaze swept me, a heated caress followed by a wave of desire so fierce it made my nipples pucker and my breath catch in my throat. I briefly closed my eyes, drawing in the warm sensation, savoring its strength and power. But I didn't react in any other way, and I certainly didn't cover up.

"How did your search in Winchester go?" I said after a moment.

"Hit and miss." His voice held a throaty edge that warmed me deep inside. "There was a brief mention of a ceremonial sword in one journal but no mention whether it was part of the prophecy or indeed held power of its own. The archivist is currently searching through our other archives to see if he can find anything else."

"I take it he'll call you if he finds it?"

He nodded. His gaze slid from my face to my breasts, and the desire in his eyes left me breathless and buzzing. "I don't suppose you'd consider covering up?"

"Nope."

"I didn't think so." He sighed. "You're going to be the death of me, you know that, don't you?"

I raised an eyebrow. "Really? Why's that?"

"Don't play innocent. It doesn't suit you at all."

I grinned. "Maybe not, but hey, you're the one with all the rules and an unwillingness to risk that heart of yours."

"I know." He sighed again. It was a deep sound of frustration. "What if we come to a compromise? Will you stop flaunting your glorious body at every opportunity?"

I chuckled. Even I had to admit it was a decidedly evil sound. "It totally depends on the compromise."

"We concentrate on finding the sword and stopping Darkside. No more teasing. No more kisses—"

"You kissed me, I seem to recall."

"Yes, and will you just let me finish?"

I waved him on with a grand flourish.

"If we both survive the battles that are undoubtedly coming, then you and I start dating—and hopefully having mad passionate sex several times a day, at least—and we'll see if this thing between us leads to something more serious."

"What if it leads to being 'bound,' as you so charmingly put it earlier?"

The smile that twisted his lips was oddly self-deprecating. "The drive to Winchester did clear my head, but not in the manner I'd wished. It forced the conclusion that there would be far worse fates—"

"Oh, be still by giddy heart," I cut in dryly.

"—than to go through life," he continued, an odd sort of seriousness in his expression and eyes, "without ever exploring the full extent of what lies between us—not just physically but also emotionally."

My heart did another of those odd flip-flops. For a

moment, I couldn't even breathe. I just stared at him, unwilling to believe—after everything he'd said, after all the heartbreak and the determination I'd felt in him when I'd so briefly shared his memories of the woman he'd loved and lost—that he'd so readily pushed them all aside and was now willing to explore a relationship with me.

Of course, there *was* the caveat of surviving the Darkside apocalypse first.

"Nothing to say?" His expression was warm and amused. "That has to be a first."

"I'm just—" I stopped and shook my head. "Shocked by the fast turnaround, that's all. I mean, even after that kiss yesterday, you were all 'no way, no how.'"

"I won't ever regret that kiss, but damn, I should have known it would only lead to the decimation of my ability to stand firm."

I rolled my eyes. "You're such a romantic."

"The romantic will make an appearance if and when we both survive. Do we have an agreement?"

"Yes. Do you want to seal it with a kiss?"

"No. Do you want to cover up?"

"You surely have more control than to be undone by the sight of a half-naked woman?"

"I thought so, until I met you."

"You have to at least shake on it."

He gave me a narrow-eyed gaze. "Only if you promise to behave."

I rolled my eyes. "We're both adults. We can do this."

His raised eyebrow suggested he fully expected this to be another of my ploys. I smiled and held out a hand. He took it, and we shook.

"Deal done. There's no backing out of it now."

"There was no backing out of it almost from the minute

we first met, up at the King's Stone." A wry smile touched his lips. "Tell me what happened yesterday."

I tugged the blankets up. "Mo didn't tell you?"

"Only in general, as I said."

I quickly updated him on everything and was caught by surprise by the deep sympathy in his expression. "I'm so sorry, Gwen. While I've always suspected Max, I'd also always hoped I was wrong. For your sake, and for Mo's."

I swallowed heavily. "Thanks. I guess ... I guess I just didn't want to see what was blindingly obvious if I'd only sat down and thought about it."

"No one ever wants to believe those they're closest to could betray them, but it happens time and again." He paused and interlaced his fingers. I suspected he was resisting the desire to reach out and hold me. "How do you plan to deal with him?"

"I honestly don't know." I ran my fingers through my tangled hair. "I daresay Mo has ideas, but right now, she's with Barney taking pictures of the writing on the King's Stone. They're going to attempt to transcribe it."

"That inscription is just another piece of information lost to time and mismanagement," he muttered. "It's very frustrating."

It was. "Did Ricker find the translation scroll in the Glastonbury archives?"

He nodded. "I'll be meeting—"

"We'll be meeting."

"—him in London this afternoon. And I'll have to clear your entry into our headquarters with the rest of my order before I take you anywhere near it."

I raised my eyebrows. "I knew your lot were old-fashioned, but surely the men's-only club thing went out with the dark ages?"

A smile teased his lips. "Far from it—and there are plenty of them in London to prove it. But in our case, it's not just women but anyone unrelated to the order—for safety reasons."

"That I can understand." Especially at the moment. "But I'd really like to transcribe the list we found at the church after they blew it up, and to do that, I need to see the scroll."

"I take it you took photographs of the notes?"

I nodded. "What time do you have to meet Ricker?"

He glanced at his watch. "At five. It's just gone ten now, so we've plenty of time to grab breakfast and get ready."

"Well, then, if you don't want to be flashed—"

"Just to be clear here, I can think of nothing I'd rather be doing than watching you parade around naked." A wicked twinkle entered his eyes. "Well, maybe one or two things. I also have no doubt that I might yet end up regretting my bargain."

"Well, I'm quite willing to break it—but only if you jump into this bed right now and we have hot monkey sex for the next ten hours."

He laughed and pushed out of the chair. "As much as I love that idea, I think we'd better stick to the deal. Distractions can be deadly, especially when you think you're safe."

I'd expected no other answer, but nevertheless felt a twinge of disappointment. "Then you'd best go ring your people and get my clearance. I'll meet you downstairs for breakfast."

He shoved his big feet into his boots and then headed out. I sighed and crawled to the end of the bed to grab my phone out of the pack.

Mo answered on the second ring. "Well, I hope your evening was a whole lot simpler than mine."

Just for an instant, fear surged. Which was ridiculous, given she was on the other end of the phone and obviously quite okay. "With Gianna and Reign?"

"No, the changeover went fine. Ron and Gianna connected instantly, which is a blessing. I suspected she might have been plotting escape routes up until then."

"It's possible she still is."

"She's not—Ron checked before they left. I did place a nebulous obedience spell on her, just to ensure she didn't change her mind, though."

Which was probably a good idea, given what I'd seen of Gianna. "So what else happened?"

"It seems either Darkside or your brother had the same idea we did. Thankfully, we got there sooner and were able to take some photographs before the bastards attacked."

"You and Barney obviously weren't hurt."

"Barney got some ricochet shrapnel in his butt, but he's fine after my tender ministrations overnight."

And not *just* healing ministrations, I suspected. At least someone in our little family unit was getting some. "Do you think they would have destroyed the King's Stone if given the chance?"

"Very likely, as I don't think they're aware the sword they have might not be the true king's sword."

"Which is all the more reason for them to keep it, surely? Besides, it's basically just a stone sheath—it holds no power in and of itself."

"If it held no power, any Tom, Dick, or Harriet with enough strength would have been able to pull the sword free. Magic held it in place."

"But not enough, given we De Montforts have had to protect the sword for centuries. I take it you've now protected the stone?"

"I've reinforced the blessing. That should hold them off for the moment."

I grunted. "Would there be anything in the archives—in the diaries from our ancestors, perhaps—that mentions what the inscription says? It can't have always been illegible."

"It's possible, but let's see if our photographs can be enhanced first. What are you and Luc up to today?"

"His cousin is meeting us in London with the translating scroll. We're going to use it to look at the paperwork found at both Karen Jacobs's place and at the old church."

"And Karen Jacobs is ...?" she said.

"The owner of the gray car that dropped Tris off right before he was shot. She's dead."

"Seems to be a continuing theme with these bastards. I did think your brother was better than all this."

"He always had grand schemes for great riches." My voice was tight with suppressed emotion. "And isn't snaring the Witch King's throne and restoring witch rule to all of England the grandest scheme of all?"

"Not with the backing of Darkside. That boy has rocks in his head if he truly believes they'll allow him to rule in their stead."

"Maybe he has a grand scheme for that, as well."

"The sword is not a source of unending power. It is a means to draw on and combine the power of all four elements, but its strength—its ability to combat and contain darkness—truly depends on the strength, the heart, and the soul of the person whose hand grips it. Uhtric's soul wasn't exactly pure, and that fault almost killed him."

"Is that why it took him so long to contain Darkside?"

"Yes. He was only one man, and the strength of the witch lines was fading even then."

"Then heaven help us."

"As I've said before, modern day weaponry is far superior to anything Uhtric had in his time. Demons and dark elves are not immune to bullets."

No, but in the case of many demons, they were generally faster than any but the most highly trained soldier could pull the trigger.

Besides, Max was well aware of modern-day weaponry. I had no doubt he'd been stockpiling guns and other shit for some time now. The fact he'd planned the whole heir thing six years ago was statement enough of just how long he'd been involved in all this.

God, how could I have missed his slip into darkness?

Was I so used to his offhand manner and get-rich schemes that I'd willfully ignored the signs when they became something more? Had I missed them all simply because I hadn't wanted to believe my twin—the other half of me—could have fallen so far?

All current evidence certainly suggested I had.

I swallowed the bitter surge of self-anger and said, "What I don't get is, the power of the Aquitaine line is fire. How exactly is the sword—which is supposedly nothing more than a conduit—able to combine and draw on the power of all four elements?"

"Because it was created by gods, and gods like doing crazy shit like that."

I snorted. "I'll bow to your experience when it comes to the foibles of gods."

"As you should." Amusement echoed in her voice. "The sword is more than a conduit, though. It gives the user the means to step beyond flesh and into the unseen dimension—the gray space—in which all energies move and exist."

"Well, that makes total sense."

My voice was dry, and she laughed. "Think of it as the

existing world but one step back. There are no people, there are no buildings, and there are no animals. There's just the earth and the sky and the natural energy that lives within and without."

"And it's this energy that the user can draw on?"

"Yes. But there's a price, as there always is when it comes to the gifts of the old gods."

"Uhtric survived."

"Cedric did not. He was vaporized by the powers that swept through him—although thankfully not before he'd contained the Darkside threat."

Cedric being the second Witch King. "If he was vaporized, then who placed the sword back in the stone?"

"I presume it was the Blackbirds."

"That being the case, you'd think they'd damn well know if the sword in the King's Stone was the real one."

"It was all a long time ago, remember. Things that were well-known then are little more than vague rumors on the wind now."

"Which is a very poetic way of saying they forgot."

She laughed again. "I've called a council of war for tonight—"

Unease slid through me. "And just who is going to be involved in this council?"

"All the usual suspects."

Meaning Ginny, Mia, and Barney. "Mo—"

"Better they be at the safe house than running around Ainslyn at the moment." Her tone said her mind would not be changed. "Your brother knows our weak points, remember. The last thing we need is for any of them to be used against us."

I hadn't even *thought* of that possibility. I rubbed my eyes and wished I didn't believe that Max would willingly—

and deliberately—hurt my friends as a means of getting to me.

"We're not meeting Ricker until five, so we're not likely to be back tonight."

"That's okay. I'll update everyone on what's been happening, and we'll see you in the morning."

"Be careful, Mo."

"You too, darling girl."

I smiled and hung up. I had a quick shower to chase away the last vestiges of sleep, then got dressed in my freshly cleaned and pressed clothes, and headed downstairs.

Henry met me in the foyer. "Breakfast, Ms. Gwen?"

"That would be fabulous. Thank you."

He nodded and led the way to a small and decoratively restrained dining room. He must have seen my surprise, because he said, "This is the family's preferred morning room. The main dining hall is far too large, and this does have glorious views over the garden."

And the distant sea, I discovered after a quick look.

Once Henry had seated me, another man unfolded my napkin with a snap and then asked what I wished for breakfast. My vegetable and bacon omelet—along with a gold rack of toast, butter, and a selection of jams—promptly appeared a few minutes later.

I was halfway through my third piece of toast when Luc finally appeared. "Did I get clearance?"

"Not as yet." He took a seat, ordered his breakfast, and then added, "It'll take a few hours to get hold of everyone."

I frowned. "What happens if I don't get clearance?"

"Then we'll take the scroll down to the café and work there."

"You have a café in your building? How is that safe?"

"It gives us the perfect cover for coming and going, and

it also provides a very good income, as the building is close to the theatre district and Drury Lane."

"Huh." I picked up a triangle of toast, then used it to indicate the room. "Who actually owns this place?"

"A friend."

"Male or female friend?"

"Does it matter?"

Meaning a woman owned it. "Only once we start dating, and only if she's one of your casuals."

"She was once, but now we really are just good friends."

I nodded. "Is she old money?"

"No. An investment banker who's done very well for herself. Her main residence is in London—this is really just a weekend retreat."

It was one hell of a retreat. "Is your place like this?"

"Meaning over-the-top opulent, I take it?" When I nodded, he raised an eyebrow. "Do I look like the type to you?"

"Well, no, but it's not like I actually know you that well. You could be a hidden cross-dresser for all I know."

He laughed. "One of my brothers actually *is*."

"I thought you had sisters?"

"I do. Lots of them. I also have three brothers." He grinned. "My parents didn't believe in contraception—not until the ninth child, at which point my mother decided enough was enough."

"I hope you believe in contraception, because there's no way I intend having nine children."

"I do, but let's not get ahead of ourselves. Sex first, explore possible relationship second, then commitment and children if it all works out."

I pointed my remaining bit of toast at him. "You can be sure I'll hold you to all that."

"I expect nothing less." His smile grew. "My place is a simple country manor in the middle of Somerset. I do have staff to look after it because I'm often away and the place is open to the public in summer and spring. It could never be described as opulent. More ... traditional."

"I look forward to seeing it."

"I look forward to showing you."

The heated glow in his eyes suggested what I'd mostly be seeing—at least for the first couple of weeks—was the inside of his bedroom. And I was perfectly okay with that.

I ordered another pot of tea and drank it while he finished his breakfast. After returning upstairs to do my teeth and grab my pack, I met him in the foyer, and we headed out.

It took ages to get to London, thanks not only to a couple of pit stops—one for a toilet break, and one to collect a very vital cup of tea for me and a coffee for him—but also the traffic around Regent's Park.

Once we were near Drury Lane, he swung into a parking lot, flashed the app on his phone at the reader, and then found a parking spot. I grabbed my pack and met him at the back of the car.

"This way." He motioned toward the exit then pressed his fingers lightly against my spine to guide me. Delighted tingles radiated from the epicenter of his touch and washed through the rest of me.

We made our way down Drury Lane, turned into Tavistock, and then finally into Catherine Street. The Blackbirds' headquarters was midway down; it was a four-story red-brick building with three arched, ornate windows on each of the top three floors. The ground floor windows were square, with the top portion being simple stained glass squares. There were a couple of small round tables sitting at the front—both of which were occupied—and it looked to be fairly full inside.

He opened the door, then once again touched my spine and guided me through the maze of tables to the rear of the old but charming café. After going through another door and past the public bathrooms, we came to an elevator.

"I take it this means I have clearance to enter hallowed grounds," I said as he shoved a key into the lock and turned it sideways. The elevator began to descend with a loud—and worrying—clanking sound.

"Yes. Sorry, the call came through at our bathroom stop."

The door opened, revealing an old-fashioned but grand cage elevator. I stepped in somewhat gingerly and resisted the urge to huddle close to Luc as he pressed the top floor button. I didn't mind elevators when they had four solid walls, but these things had always given me the willies.

The door closed, and the elevator slowly began to ascend. It came to a bouncy stop, then the door opened, revealing what was obviously a library archive. There were soldier lines of bookcases stuffed with all manner of books, and what looked to be vintage wooden map drawers lining the wall opposite the elevator.

Luc stepped out and then turned left, walking down a narrow corridor to an area at the back of the building. The arched windows had been covered with some sort of opaque film that diffused the light—maybe to protect the books in the nearby bookcase, which looked and smelled far older than the volumes nearer the elevator. The space between the bookcase and the rear wall was obviously a designated reading and researching area; not only were there half a dozen antique-looking mahogany tables, but also a number of comfortable leather lounging chairs. Near the rear was a small kitchenette.

"Would you like a cup of tea?" Luc asked. "I'm afraid we've only tea bags, not leaf—"

"Bags are fine." I looked around. "The scroll's not here."

"No, but Ricker will have been informed that we've arrived and bring it up."

I pulled out a chair and sat down at the nearest table. The wood was almost black with age and heavily scratched and dented by time and use. "Why isn't it already here, in the archive?"

"Because the main meeting area is on the second floor, as it's the most secure. It's also where the round table is located."

"Meaning I'm not going to see this mythical table of yours? Damn."

"No one sees that table but Blackbirds." He filled the kettle and then placed it back onto its stand and flicked it on.

"Shame, because there's definitely a tourist market for anything involving Witch King antiquities."

He glanced at me, amusement twitching his lips. "I actually can't tell if you're serious or not."

I grinned. He rolled his eyes and added, "Not."

As he made our drinks, the bell above the ratty old elevator pinged, and the doors clanged open. The man who appeared a few seconds later was older than Luc by about ten years, if the amount of silver in his short black hair was anything to go by. His face also lacked the utter perfection of Luc's, thanks mainly to his jawline, which was much squarer and had a bold indent. His eyes were the same glorious shade of jade but his build longer and leaner. In his right hand was what looked to be a rolled-up bit of leather.

"Luc! Good to see you again, buddy." His deep voice was filled with warmth, but his bright gaze centered swiftly on mine. "I'm Ricker, and you're no doubt Gwen. I hear you're causing Luc all manner of problems."

I grinned and briefly shook his offered hand. "And it's all well deserved, let me tell you. Is that the translation scroll you're holding?"

"Yes." He carefully unrolled it along the table. "It's a bit hard to read, though, thanks to the fact it had been shoved into the back of a damn cabinet and forgotten about. Time has not been its friend."

The scroll was made out of some sort of hide that had a faintly disgusting smell, but the center portion of it was supple and had a rich patina of color. Its edges were dried out and cracked.

I crossed my arms to prevent accidently touching it and leaned closer. It was written in Latin rather than English—no real surprise given the age of the thing, but annoying given it wasn't a language I knew.

Luc handed me a mug of tea. I thanked him with a nod and tried to ignore his big warm presence as he stopped beside me. "Can either of you read it?"

Both men nodded. Ricker pulled some papers from his pocket and placed them on the table. Not only did most of them look ratty, but they also appeared to be stuck together with sticky tape.

"The notes you found at Karen Jacobs's place, I take it?"

Ricker nodded. "We've already partially transcribed them. These two"—he lightly touched two of the five sheets of paper—"are nothing more than a record of purchases."

I frowned. "What sort of purchases?"

"That's where it gets interesting," Ricker said. "They appear to be stockpiling weapons."

"That's no real surprise given who has claimed the sword," Luc said.

Ricker glanced up at him sharply. "Last I heard, we didn't actually know who'd drawn the sword."

"And we still haven't absolute confirmation," he said. "But it's almost certain that Max De Montfort was that person."

Ricker's gaze cut to me. There was a decided coolness there now. "Have you talked to him?"

"No, and I'm not sure I want to, given that any confrontation is likely to get very ugly."

He studied me a few seconds longer and then nodded. Some warmth crept back into his expression. "They mention five locations. We've been in contact with the witch councils in all five areas; a coordinated, simultaneous assault will happen at dawn tomorrow."

"We'll have people at each location, I take it?" Luc asked.

Ricker nodded. "That's why the attack was delayed—it gives us time to get there."

"Good." Luc glanced down at me, something I felt more than actually saw. "Do you want to Bluetooth the photos you took of the papers in the church across to the printer? It'll be easier than trying to read them on a small screen."

I placed my tea on the chair next to me so there was no danger of me knocking it all over the translation scroll and then grabbed my phone and made the printer connection.

As Ricker walked over to retrieve the printouts, I leaned over the table and took several photos of the scroll. While it might be perfectly safe here in the heart of the Blackbird's headquarters, there was probably little chance of me ever returning to view it. It'd be handy to have something to use if we found anything else written in Darkside script.

As I shoved my phone into my pocket, dust fell like a fine rain from the ceiling. I frowned and glanced up; a small hairline crack was inching across the ceiling and the pendant light swayed lightly. But it wasn't the only thing on the move—a jolt ran through the building, and everything sitting on the kitchen counter crashed to the floor.

Ricker stopped abruptly, and Luc surged to his feet. As his chair fell backward with a crash, an alarm sounded, its shriek so loud it hurt my ears. It was followed by a loud *whoomph,* and the whole building shuddered. The crack in the ceiling widened, and bits of wood joined the plaster and dust raining around us.

I'd seen all this once before—in my bedroom when Darkside's witchling had attempted to bury me under the collapsing roof.

The Blackbirds' headquarters was under attack.

CHAPTER TEN

L uc grabbed my arm and hauled me upright. "We need to get to a safe—"

"There is no fucking safe place," I snapped back, ripping my arm from his grip. "This is what they did at our shop—and this time, Mo's not here to stop the whole building from coming down. We need to get out."

"Not even they have the power to bring the whole building down," Ricker said. "Not a building this size, anyway."

"Do you want to risk the lives of everyone in this building on that?" I grabbed my knives out of the pack and strapped them on. "As I said, the only reason they didn't succeed with us in Ainslyn was thanks to the fact that Mo was able to counter the attempt. So unless you've got a goddamn mage handy, this place is coming down."

He didn't get a chance to respond. The building shuddered violently and then twisted oddly, sending him staggering into a table.

"Trust what she says," Luc growled. "And call an immediate evac."

Ricker swore and staggered across to a panel on the wall. He flipped a switch and then said, "This is an all-points emergency. Darkside is attempting to collapse the building. Evacuate immediately. I repeat, evacuate immediately."

His voice blasted out of unseen speakers throughout this floor and no doubt the others. As another shudder went through the old building, I lunged across the table and grabbed the scroll and Ricker's notes, hastily rolling them up before tucking them safely into my belt. I might have photos, but the real thing was always better.

"This way," Luc commanded, and ran for the emergency exit sign. As he hauled open the door, a huge chunk of concrete fell down, crushing the railings and taking out several steps.

"The lift is likely to be even more dangerous," Ricker growled. "We're fucking trapped."

"There's still the windows," I said.

"The windows are barred, and it's a fucking four-story drop," Ricker growled. "And neither Luc nor I can fly."

"No, but Gwen can and she can also—" He grabbed my arm and dragged me back. A heartbeat later, a huge chunk of timber crashed down. We would have been crushed had we still been standing there. "Ricker—get a rope."

As the older Blackbird staggered toward a cabinet whose doors were swinging widely in time to the increasingly violent gyrations of the building, I dragged my daggers out of their sheaths and called on the lightning. It streaked through the thick, dusty air and shattered the nearest window's glass, sending glittery shards flying outwards into the night. I flicked the energy around in an arc, cutting a wide enough hole in the thick metal bars for the two men to climb through.

I'd barely shoved the daggers back into their sheaths when there was a massive crack and a good portion of the floor between us and the other man began to disintegrate.

"Ricker," Luc shouted. "Move—now!"

Ricker looped the rope around his shoulders then ran straight at the ever-widening gap. As he neared the edge he leapt high, but the gap had already grown wider than his leap.

He wasn't going to make it.

Luc swore, leapt over the table, and lunged forward, grabbing his cousin's outstretched hands just as he was beginning to drop. The force of his abrupt stop had Luc grunting in effort and, for several seconds, the two men were immobile, one prone on the increasingly unstable floor and the other swinging lightly over a dark and dusty drop. Then, with another grunt of effort, Luc slowly but surely hauled Ricker upward until he was close enough to grab the edge and drag himself the rest of the way.

More ceiling fell, and huge cracks began to appear in the walls. I swore and staggered over to the window. The thick dust in the room was now funneling out the broken window, making it almost impossible to see what lay beyond.

Luc grabbed the rope off Ricker. "There's an external fire escape on the building opposite. Secure the rope, and we'll shimmy over."

The floor under the end of the bookcase closest to the seating area dropped several feet. Wood split, and the lovely old books were tipped out, disappearing into the ever-widening gap.

"And hurry," Ricker added unnecessarily.

I undid my knives and thrust them at Luc. "Lose them and I'll kill you."

With that, I shifted shape, grabbed the end of the rope with my claws, and flew out the window. The fire escape that zigzagged down the rear of the other building didn't look all that well maintained, which was surprising given the spate of new rules that had come into existence a few years ago after several horrible residential tower fires.

I shifted shape and landed with a clang on the metal landing, then quickly secured the rope, using the bowline knot we'd been taught when Max and I had gone through a brief 'we need to learn sailing' stage. Which was well before we'd hit our teens and—in Max's case at least—discovered flesh-based passions.

The rear wall of the Blackbirds' building began to splinter, and chunks of bricks and slate crashed down to the yard below. I leaned over the railing; it was only then I saw the forming sinkhole. Fear slammed into my chest.

"Luc, Ricker, get over here now!" I couldn't see either man; the billowing smoke and dust was just too thick. "Half the building is about to collapse into a sinkhole."

Ricker leapt out of the window, caught the rope, then crossed his legs over it and shimmied across. As I helped him over the railing, Luc leapt out and repeated Ricker's movements.

He was halfway across when, with a noise that almost sounded like the groan of a dying beast, part of the rear wall gave way and tumbled to the ground, taking the rope—and Luc—with it.

"No!" I darted back to the railing and peered over, trying to see through the thick dust and rubble. "Luc? Answer me!"

For several gut-wrenching seconds, there was no reply. Then, in a voice hoarse with pain, he said, "Here. Two flights down."

It was only then that I noticed the rope was taut rather than slack. The collapsing building might have taken it down, but Luc had somehow hung on. I bolted down the stairs, the clatter of my steps lost to the groans of the still-dying building.

In one of the still-functioning, calmer back sections of my brain, I fervently hoped the building was the only thing that was ...

By the time I got to Luc, he was already climbing over the railing. I threw myself at him and just clung on for several seconds. His arms went around me, and his lips brushed the top of my head.

"I'll no doubt have a pretty array of bruises come tomorrow," he said softly, "but I'm okay. And so are your knives."

"Good." It was telling that I hadn't even thought of the daggers. I pulled back as Ricker joined us and added, "They'd have to be fairly close to be causing this sort of defined damage."

"I hardly think it's defined," Ricker growled. "They're bringing the whole fucking place down."

"But not the ones on either side." Which was odd, really, because surely it would have taken less effort to just collapse them all.

Unless, of course, Max didn't want too many innocents caught in the destruction—which was a bit of a laugh considering the mess Darkside would make of everyone if and when he managed to open the main gate.

"They can't be on the street—this sort of magic takes time, and it'd be too obvious," Luc said. "They have to be underground—in the sewers."

"There's a manhole not far from here," Ricker said. "Let's go."

We scrambled down the remaining stairs, darted through the dust and debris still crashing down, somehow avoiding getting crushed in the process, then clambered over the fence dividing us from the next property. Ricker crashed through the rear door of a building two down from the Blackbirds' and led the way through the maze of back rooms into the main café area. Though the place was empty, meals and coffee lay abandoned on a number of tables, and multiple chairs had been tipped over, suggesting everyone had left in a hurry. Dust fell freely from the ceiling, and the alarm was strident and ear-piercing. It wasn't alone though —multiple alarms were going off up and down the street.

Ricker flung open the front door, paused briefly on the sidewalk, and then ran left, bellowing at everyone milling on the pavement to get out of his way. Most did—those who didn't were brutally shoved aside. Luc and I followed, though I struggled to keep up with the two of them.

We went left around the next corner. Halfway down the street was one of those plastic yellow triangle barriers surrounding an open manhole cover.

Ricker came to such an abrupt halt that Luc had to jump sideways to avoid crashing into him. Thankfully, I was far enough back to slow down normally.

"Surely they wouldn't be so—"

I cut the rest off as Ricker held up a hand. "Listen."

For several heartbeats I couldn't hear anything beyond the wail of the approaching emergency vehicles, the rumble of nearby traffic, and the screams of the frightened and confused.

I tuned it all out the best I could and eventually heard it —the soft echo of footsteps on metal. Someone was climbing up the sewer's ladder.

"They'll have to have transport waiting," Ricker said softly, looking around. "They can't walk through the streets stinking of sewage—it'd attract too much attention."

Luc handed me Nex and Vita. "Ricker and I will handle the sewer rats. You head across the road and take out the car when it arrives."

I waited for a gap in the traffic, and then darted across. Parked cars lined this side of the road, so I tucked in behind the largest—a Land Rover—and lightly gripped Nex's hilt. A soft pulsing immediately started deep in her metal heart, and energy briefly caressed my fingers. She was ready— eager—for action. The gods had definitely given her a blood-thirsty edge.

There was no sign of the two men on the other side of the road; they were obviously wrapped in darkness. My gaze went to the manhole, but no one had come out as yet. I took a deep breath and flexed my free hand. It didn't do a whole lot to ease the inner tension.

A few seconds later, a man in plastic-looking coveralls and knee-high wellies appeared. He climbed out of the manhole and casually looked around. I ducked behind the Land Rover, my heart pounding so fiercely it felt like a drum—and a loud one at that. When I looked back, the man in coveralls was studying the shadows haunting a doorway several buildings further down the street. Was that where Luc and Ricker stood? Did he suspect they were near? I had no idea and could only hope that he didn't.

After another few seconds, he leaned down and said something, then pulled a phone out of a breast pocket and made a call. I flexed my fingers again. This was it.

I walked to the front of the Land Rover. It was out of the stranger's direct line of sight, which meant there was less chance of him spotting me.

A black van appeared further down the street, and my pulse rate leapt. It was the same sort of van that had been involved in Reign's attempted kidnapping.

Lightning flickered down Nex's side, and her energy pulsed through me. Or maybe it was the other way around; it was hard to be certain, given the strengthening connection between me and these daggers.

The van crawled closer, its progress hampered by the evening traffic. I glanced back across the road; three men were now out of the manhole, but they were obviously waiting for others. None of them was our witch. Someone strong enough to bring down a building with such ease should radiate power. These three felt human, and that meant they were probably just guards.

I returned my gaze to the van. It wasn't yet close enough to do anything about, and even if it was, I couldn't react— not until everyone was out of the sewer.

It crawled closer. Four people were now standing inside the yellow triangle, and the witch behind the destruction still hadn't appeared. Maybe he wouldn't; maybe they'd decided it'd be unwise to bring him out too close to the scene of so much destruction ...

But even as that thought crossed my mind, a small, youngish figure appeared. A halo of power surrounded him, but its force was muted. Spent. His skin had a gray tinge, and lines of dirt, or maybe even blood, trailed from the corners of his eyes. His face was gaunt and his shoulders so thin they looked pointed. Even his arms and chest ... I stopped. Breasts. *He* was a *she*.

Why that sent such a deep wave of anger through me, I couldn't really say. It wasn't as if she was the first witchling we'd come across, and she certainly wasn't the first halfling. Maybe it was just the knowledge that the dark elves would no doubt use her for breeding purposes once she'd hit puberty—if they weren't already doing so.

I wished we could save her; I really did. But it was already far too late—and it wasn't just the lack of both expression and animation in her demeanor telling me that. It was her tell—it ran deep with darkness. She hadn't been as lucky as Jules—she'd been born and raised in Darkside. Its stain ran through all that she was.

I silently sent the gods a prayer for her soul to be granted a happier life next time around. Then I shifted my weight and drew Vita. Fire ran along her edge and then flicked across to Nex. The two were connecting without me crossing their blades.

The black van stopped in front of the barrier, much to the displeasure of the driver in the car behind him. As the horn blasted long and loud, the van's window slipped down, and the driver made an obscene gesture at the car.

Which did not go down well at all. The car's driver got out and stalked toward the van, shaking his fists and screaming abuse. I quickly sent a thin streak of lightning at the van's rear tire. It burst with a loud *pop*, making the car driver jump and swing around. The van driver climbed out and lumbered forward. He was a thickset giant of a man with fists the size of shovels.

The car driver immediately held up his hands and backed away. The giant stalked to the tire, bent to study it, and then snapped upright, his gaze shooting across the road. I darted backward but not fast enough to prevent him spotting me. With a bellow that was fierce and bloodcurdling, he bolted forward, his thick features red with rage and his fists raised, ready for action.

I raised the daggers, but a car hit him before I could unleash the lightning. He toppled over the hood but somehow managed to land on his feet. He spun around and was hit again, this time by a truck. It knocked him down and then ran over the top of him. He didn't move.

I had no idea if he was dead, and I didn't really care. He was, for the moment at least, immobilized, and that was all that mattered. As the truck stopped and the driver got out, I darted across the road and pulled the black van's side door open. There was no one in the passenger seat or in the back, so I continued on to the pavement—just in time to see Hecate dispatch the last of the halflings. The small girl was nowhere to be seen.

Luc shook free of the shadows, Hecate gripped in his left hand. Blue fire sparked across her steel and burned away the blood splatter. His gaze swept me and came up relieved, but he nevertheless asked, "You okay?"

"Yes. Where did the witchling go?"

"Back down the sewer." Ricker's expression was grim. "I've called in reinforcements to go after her."

I frowned. "Why? Between the three of us, we should be able to find one little girl—"

"Who could cause untold damage to both the sewers or the Underground if she's cornered. We not only need a means of tracking her down fast, but also a way of countering whatever magic she attempts."

"But if we don't get down there soon, we could lose her."

"We won't." Ricker's gaze moved to Luc. "You two had better go. I'll take care of this lot and deal with the cops."

"I'm working with the Preternatural Division at the moment, remember. It'll be easier if I deal with the police." Luc glanced at me. "But it probably would be better if you head back home."

I smiled. "You're not going to get an argument out of me—"

"*That* would be a first."

His voice was dry, and I smiled. "I have some papers to transcribe."

He glanced down at the scroll tucked into my belt. "Did you also grab Ricker's notes?"

"Yes."

"Good." He fished the car keys out of his pocket and offered them to me.

I raised an eyebrow. "I can fly, remember?"

"It's a damn long way, you'll be carrying your daggers, and that will just exhaust you. Given Darkside are upping their attacks, that's not a state you want to be in. So just humor me and take the damn keys."

I smiled and took the keys. "How do I get out of the parking lot without a pass?"

"Ah. Hang on." He did something on his phone, and a few seconds later, mine beeped. "Just flash that at the reader, and the gate will open."

"Thanks." I resisted the urge to rise onto my toes and kiss him goodbye—and if the sudden flare of heat in his eyes was anything to go by, I wasn't the only one thinking along those lines. I smiled, said goodbye to Ricker, and walked away.

The drive home was long and tedious. I made multiple stops for coffee, chocolate, and bathroom breaks, so it was well after midnight by the time I pulled into the mansion's driveway.

The house lights came on as I parked, and a few seconds later, Henry appeared, looking utterly unruffled and unconcerned by my late arrival.

"Good morning, Ms. Gwen," he said, with absolutely no

indication he'd probably been fast asleep only a few minutes ago. "Would you like a hot drink? Perhaps a late-night snack?"

"Thanks, Henry, but I think I'll just head up to bed." I hesitated. "Did my aunt and friends arrive this evening?"

"Yes. Ms. Moscelyne said she'll meet you in the morning room for breakfast at nine."

I nodded, thanked him, and then headed up to the bedroom, where I stripped off, shoved my phone onto the charger and the daggers under my pillow, and climbed into bed. I was as grimy as all get-out, and I didn't give a damn. Not this time. I was asleep three seconds after my head hit the pillow.

Bright sunlight woke me who knew how many hours later. I blinked owlishly for the several seconds it took me to remember where the hell I was, and then stretched like a cat, feeling warm and rested. But also very hungry.

I tossed the blankets off and padded into the bathroom for a shower. Once dry, I came back out to discover that not only had the cleaning fairy been in to grab my grimy pile of clothes, they'd left a small carryall sitting on top of the blanket box. Inside was an assortment of fresh clothes. Mo's doing, rather than actual fairies or the maid.

Once dressed, I grabbed the scroll and the notes and headed downstairs. Everyone else was already there, enjoying breakfast.

"Morning all." I nodded a thank-you to Henry as he seated me. Once he'd taken my order, I added, "How's the butt, Barney?"

"In full working order," he said with a grin. "Although if your grandmother hadn't pushed me off the rock when she did, more vital body parts could have been injured."

"Which is why I pushed," Mo said, voice dry. "The butt

I don't care about. I do, on the other hand, have a deeply personal interest in keeping your knob in full working order."

"Well, isn't this a fabulous conversation to have over breakfast," Ginny said, clearly amused. "So much more interesting than listening to my mother drone on about babies and me needing to have them before I hit the crone years—which, in case anyone is interested, she insists start at thirty."

I tucked the old leather scroll safely under my chair, then reached for a piece of toast and smothered it in butter and raspberry jam. "I thought you were dating the very lovely but very human detective in your division to shut her up?"

"I am." Her cheeks dimpled. "She's less than pleased, but it hasn't yet stopped her. It might take another few dates —which won't be a hardship, let me assure you."

"Speaking of no hardship," Mia said. "Where's that luscious Blackbird of yours?"

"Taking care of the mess in London."

Mo frowned. "What happened in London?"

"You didn't hear?" I asked, surprised.

"Obviously not, if I'm asking the question."

Despite the seriousness of the whole situation, I couldn't help grinning at the tartness in her tone. "Darkside attacked the Blackbird headquarters with an earth-powered witchling."

Mo sucked in a breath. "Many casualties?"

"I don't know, but I wouldn't think so. We had enough warning to order an evacuation. I suspect their library and artifacts store is now buried under a mountain of rubble, however."

"Which might have been the whole point," Barney said grimly. "The Blackbirds held the real coronation ring and crown, didn't they?"

"They certainly had the ring," Mo said. "And it would be easy enough for demons or even elves to slip into a collapsing building and steal the thing—especially if one of their own controlled the collapse and kept it to certain areas."

"And if the building was utterly destroyed afterward," Barney said, "it could take months before anyone realized it was missing."

"But why would anyone want to steal the coronation ring?" Mia asked, confusion evident. "It's only a bit of jewelry left over from witch rule, and these days isn't even used in actual coronations."

"There's a theory the power of the sword can only be accessed by the crowned king." Mo's expression was contemplative. "I personally think the ring was *not* the sole intent of the attack, however."

"Taking out the Blackbirds does clear the path of opposition somewhat," Barney said. "None of the other witch houses are as truly ready for battle as them."

"Yes, but I think it's deeper than that." Her gaze met mine. "Didn't Gianna say that the new Witch King intended to resurrect witch rule?"

It was interesting that she didn't actually name Max. I could understand her not wanting Mia or Ginny to know, but surely Barney had to—he was the head of Ainslyn's witch council, after all, and would by necessity be involved in any countermeasure we made against either Max or Darkside.

"Yes," I said, "but to do that, he has to attack the crown

and the queen, and she's still protected by Layton's spell. No witch house has ever been able to break it."

"So there *have* been attempts to do so?" Mia asked, surprised.

Mo nodded. "Three or four, at least, over the centuries."

"Then what makes you think the new Witch King will succeed where those others failed?" Ginny asked.

"Because none of the others held the sword of power."

"And in reality, he might not, either," I said.

Mo's gaze met mine. "Whether the sword he drew was the real thing or a substitute, it *does* hold power. We just don't know what kind and whether the new claimant will be able to access it."

"So why don't we ask the woman who made the king's sword in the first place?" I said. "Surely she'd have some inkling of what the substitute is capable of." Not to mention where the real thing was.

"And just who made the sword?" Mia asked.

"Vivienne—the Lady of the Lake," Mo said. "Don't they teach you anything in schools these days?"

"Myths and legends are part of the primary school curriculum," Ginny said. "But none of my teachers ever mentioned the fact she's real."

"Well, she is," I said. "And quite damn impressive too."

Mia's eyes went wide. "You've met her?"

I nodded and flashed Henry a smile of thanks as he placed my bacon and eggs down on the table. "She can lay down a scary fog like no other, let me tell you."

"If she still exists, how come no one knows about it?" Mia asked. "I mean, you'd think there'd be a whole religious industry developed around her presence."

"Which might just be why she's kept her presence

unknown," Barney said, voice dry. "The old gods got over the whole 'adoration and tributes' thing centuries ago."

"I suspect that might have been forced on them thanks to humanity turning to more organized religions," Mo said, clearly amused. "However, I agree it would be a good idea to speak with her as soon as we possibly can, even if it is not ideal to make such an attempt during the day."

"If the attempt fails, wait until evening," Barney said. "There's plenty of usable power at the end of a day—it should be enough to call her forth."

Mo nodded and patted his arm. It was a somewhat patronizing motion, though Barney didn't seem to notice.

"All of us?" Mia said hopefully, "Because I'd really love to meet an old goddess—"

"I doubt she'd appreciate being called old, and it would be better if only Gwen and I attended her. There are plenty of other problems that need sorting out in the meantime."

"Like those notes we found in the church they blew up." I reached under my chair and pulled out the scroll. "Luc's cousin found the translating scroll."

Mia wrinkled her nose in distaste. "Wow, that smells old."

"It would be," Barney said. "I think the last mention of the Darkside language being transcribed was by monks in the time of Aldred's father."

He made a give-me motion, and I handed it over. He carefully unrolled it and then placed the notes to one side. "It'll need stronger light than this, but it seems straightforward enough—it's just a matter of switching Darkside symbols for various letters of the alphabet. It will take some time to get through all this paperwork, though."

"There's a second lot on my phone," I said. "I'll shoot them across to you."

He nodded and glanced across the table. "If the three of us tackled the problem, it should only take days rather than weeks."

I frowned. "Ginny, don't you have to work?"

She shook her head. "Mo suggested I take a week off, just in case the fallout from the safe house debacle somehow found its way to my door."

Meaning Darkside—and probably Max—rather than any sanctions from her bosses.

"And I," Mia said, "will snatch any excuse not to be working at the bar. I love my parents and all, but I've never had a grand desire to learn the ropes and run the place after their death, no matter how much they want me to."

She'd also gone against the Lancaster tradition of selling spells to the general public that countered their personal and medical problems and had instead gone to university to train as an accountant. She generally only helped out at the bar over the winter period, when her taxation services were in less demand.

And while I really didn't want either Mia or Ginny involved in this mess any more than necessary, as Mo had already said, they were far safer here than anywhere else.

Presuming, of course, Max didn't have a means of finding us all. He might not be capable of that sort of magic himself, but simple tracking spells using hair or even a toothbrush were easy enough to purchase—especially in Ainslyn, where there were plenty of Lancaster witches selling magical goods and services.

Trepidation stirred, though I wasn't sure whether it was simple fear or a premonition of what was about to hit us.

I really, *really* hoped it wasn't the latter. Deep down in the stubborn part of my soul, I still desperately wanted to believe that, no matter what else he might be doing, he wouldn't attack Mo or me. Wanted to believe that, in the end, blood ties would be stronger than the call of darkness.

After all, hadn't he said not so long ago that he was working on a deal that would change our lives? Our lives, plural, which surely meant he wasn't envisioning either of our deaths.

"Then we have a plan," Mo was saying. "While you're finishing your breakfast, Gwen, I might lay a few redirection spells around the place—just in case."

Barney rose with her. "Let me throw in a couple—the more spells involved, the harder it'll be to break through them."

The two of them left. I grabbed my cutlery and tucked into my breakfast.

"I get the feeling there's a whole lot of stuff you and Mo aren't telling us." Ginny studied me over the rim of her coffee mug. "The currents around you are a swirl of green and red, and that generally means stress and anger."

"I'm guessing the latter is aimed at Max," Mia said. "Because he's done his usual disappearing trick at a time when he'd be handy to have around."

"Oh, big flare of frustration and rage," Ginny said. "Which means Max is definitely involved somewhere along the line."

I shoved some bacon into my mouth and munched on it for several seconds while I desperately figured how I could answer without actually lying. Ginny would pick up the latter and only push further. I had no idea why Mo wanted them out of the loop when it came to Max, but I wasn't about to gainsay her until I'd at least asked her about it.

"I think it's fair to say I'm more than a little angry with him." Which was nothing but the truth. "He hasn't surfaced since the attack at Barney's—hasn't even contacted us."

"He may not be aware of that attack," Mia said sensibly. "Or even how bad the situation is getting."

"This is Max we're talking about." There was an edge in my voice I couldn't quite help. "If it happens in Ainslyn, he's aware of it."

"Then ring him," Ginny said. "Demand he get his ass back here to help us ASAP."

"Mo has said she'd handle it, so we'd best let her. But if he does happen to ring either of you, fob him off. " I scooped up the last bit of egg and then pushed upright. "I better go get ready. Just ... be careful today. Don't lower your guard, and keep your weapons handy. Given how easily they got past the protections surrounding the Blackbird building, it might not matter how many spells Mo and Barney lay down here."

"Thanks for that cheery thought," Mia said, voice dry.

I smiled and headed out. By the time I'd brushed my teeth and retrieved my phone and all three knives, Mo had finished spelling and was waiting near the front door.

"Where's Barney?" I shoved my arms into my coat and followed her outside.

"He and the girls have gone into the library so they can spread out the scroll and the notes." She clicked open her car. "I'll drive."

"You've got a broken foot, remember?"

"And the car is automatic. Get in. I'll be fine."

I knew that tone of voice well enough, but I neverthe-less felt obliged to keep arguing. "So why did you call in Mia to drive us around?"

"Because I thought we might need help. And I was right."

I rolled my eyes and gave in. "If Max is intent on finding

us, he's got plenty of options—a whole damn building filled with them, in fact."

"I know." She grimaced. "I did gather—and burn—your toothbrushes, combs, and brushes so they couldn't be used in any sort of tracking spell."

I glanced at her sharply. "But not yours?"

"I'd rather he come after me than you."

"I wouldn't."

She chuckled and patted my knee. "It'd take some pretty strong magic to take me out."

"It's not magic I'm worried about. They used a goddamn metal bar on Gianna's cousin, remember."

"I doubt they'd attempt that with me. Max is aware how swiftly I can raise a retaliation spell."

"Even you can't retaliate against a bullet."

"Which is why I think—once we speak to Vivienne—we need to turn the tables on him."

"He's never been easy to track down. I doubt that's going to change, especially now."

"I suspect it will depend how much he thinks we know."

"He'd have to be aware we have Gianna and his kids."

"There were no survivors from either the attack at the house or the attempted kidnapping in the forest, so it's possible neither he nor Darkside are aware it was us rather than the preternatural boys."

"Preternatural doesn't have witches who can smoke bad guys with lightning that shoots out of daggers, so I think that's pretty much a giveaway."

"Why would he assume it's you, when you've never been able to access the power of the daggers?" She glanced at me, eyebrow raised. "And how do you know the preternatural team don't? More importantly, how would he know? He'd have far less contact with them than us."

"That would depend on whether he—or whoever he's working with—has one of them on the payroll."

"True." She paused, waiting for some traffic to pass before pulling out onto the road. "We still have to try, though."

"I take it you gathered some of his items when you cleaned out mine?"

"Of course I did, though it *was* a bit of a risk. If he goes home and notices, he might decide to hit us first."

"I really don't want to believe that he'd hurt us, Mo."

She didn't say anything for a very long time, concentrating instead on the road and the morning traffic. Once we were past Preston and on the M6, she glanced at me. Her expression was both serious and sad. "You do realize that—if all this goes down as I suspect it will—we may have no choice but to—"

"Don't say it," I cut in. "I don't want to hear it."

Not now. Maybe not ever. He was my twin, for god's sake ... I swallowed heavily and fought the rise of tears. The need for confrontation and drastic action would come, and there was nothing I could do to avoid it. But as long as I didn't acknowledge it, I could still believe there was a chance—a hope, however slight—of redemption.

"What we need—what *I* need," I continued, aware of the catch in my voice but unable to do anything about it, "is to talk to him first."

"I agree we need to talk to the lad, but we can't risk a true showdown just yet, Gwen. We need to learn far more about his Darkside connections first."

I sucked in a breath and released it slowly. It didn't do much to ease the inner tension, and I wasn't entirely sure whether its cause was Max or something else. "Can you track him via his phone? At the very least, it would be handy to know where he is at the moment."

"I'm afraid when the roof collapsed into the living room, it took out the tracker phone. I haven't yet had the chance to pick up another and replicate the spell."

I forced a smile. "Well, why not? It's not as if you've been busy doing other things."

She snorted and slapped my leg. "Cheeky wench."

"Had a good teacher." I watched the passing landscape for a while, although there wasn't much more than grass and treetops to see, thanks to the sloped embankments on either side of the road. "What's our next step if Vivienne can't offer any info about the real sword?"

"We might be forced to try the impossible."

I raised an eyebrow. "And that is?"

"Wake the old bastard from his slumbers." She grimaced. "As I said, it won't be easy. But he did have a penchant for creating magical swords; if the sword in the stone *is* one of his, he'll certainly be able to tell us why it was created and what it's capable of."

"Did I not suggest this course of action some time ago?" She gave me what some might call the evil eye, and I grinned. "That look doesn't scare me, you know."

She sighed. "What is this world coming to when my best means of frightening small children and nonsensical adults no longer has any effect?"

"I'm not sure I'm pleased to be called nonsensical."

She reached across and patted my knee. "Present company excepted, of course."

It was at that precise moment, when her attention was more on me than what was happening around us, that we were hit.

Not by another vehicle. Not even by energy or magic.

By wind.

Wind so fierce and strong, it was as if we were suddenly in the middle of a cyclone.

It lifted us up and spun us around so fast, we were flung about bonelessly. Then it spat us out over the metal guard barrier and down into the wide river below.

CHAPTER ELEVEN

The water woke me. It crept up my legs, its touch icy. The car sounded like a dying beast, hissing and groaning as it tilted forward and down. It was only the seat belt holding me in place.

What the hell had happened?

For too many vital seconds, I puzzled over that question, even as I struggled to open my eyes. My head pounded like crazy, and there was moisture—warm moisture—running down the side of my face. Then memory hit, and so too did panic.

We were in the fucking *river*!

I sucked in air and tried to calm down, to *think*. We could escape this, but only if I acted calmly and quickly.

I forced my eyes open. For an instant, all I saw was dark water. It had risen halfway up the windshield and was slowly climbing ever higher. It also poured in through the vents and from who knew where else.

We had to get out. *Now*.

I kicked off my boots and then braced one hand against the dash and undid my seat belt. The movement made the car rock unsteadily in the water, and I fought the surge of fear.

"Mo?" My voice was urgent. Desperate. "Mo? You need to wake up."

The window on her side of the car had been smashed; the water creeping up the windshield trickled in through the lower edge. A few more minutes and it would be a tide.

"Mo! You need to wake up. We need to get out of the car—now!"

Still no answer. I leaned over and pinched her cheek. Her response was muted—weak. And there was blood—lots of blood—on her face.

I swore again and pressed the button to open the front windows on both sides of the car. The gods were obviously on our side, because the electronics hadn't shorted out yet. As water began to trickle in through the windows, I slung the backpack over a shoulder, then grabbed the edge of the doorframe and pulled myself out into the river. The pack made movement a little more awkward, but it contained my knives and there wasn't a chance in hell I was about to leave them behind—especially when I had no idea if this drowning attempt was but the first of a string of planned attacks. Or even if our assailants were, right now, watching from above and readying another ...

I thrust the thought away. Another attack was the least of my worries right now. The water was pouring into the car at a faster rate, meaning I had maybe twenty seconds, if that, to get Mo out.

I quickly swam over the submerged engine bay to the driver side of the car, then grabbed the shoulder of her coat, pushed her back against the seat, and leaned in to undo the belt. She murmured something I couldn't quite catch, but hope nevertheless stirred. Partially conscious was better than nothing.

"Mo," I yelled, even as I pulled her closer to the window. "You need to grab the top of the door and pull yourself out of the car. Now! Please!"

For a second, she didn't respond. The car was sinking fast, and the force of the water flowing into it made it all that much harder to hang on to her and keep us both afloat.

"Gwen?" The sound was remote and weak, but nevertheless music to my ears. "What happened?"

"Later," I said urgently. "Just grab the top of the door and pull yourself out of the window."

It took a few attempts but, with my hands under her arms for support, she eventually pulled herself out of the car. I kept a grip on her and slowly kicked backward, away from the steadily sinking car and toward the shore and those who were now swimming out to help us.

I wasn't entirely sure what happened after that, as it was all a motion- and voice-filled blur. When full consciousness did return, it was to an awareness of soft beeping, people talking, and something tight around my arm. Blood pressure monitor, I realized after a moment.

I forced my eyes open and looked around. I was obviously in a hospital emergency ward, and there was a middle-aged woman smiling down at me. "Glad to see you're awake."

"Glad to be awake. Where's my grandmother?"

"In the cubicle next door—"

"I need to see her—"

I tried to get up but was pushed down by both the woman and the younger male nurse standing to my right.

"She's fine. Let's worry about you first."

"Define fine," I said. "And where's my backpack?"

"On the chair," the doctor said. "Your grandmother has a large cut on her head that's currently being tended and bruising down the side of her face."

"Has she undergone a CT scan?"

"Yes, as have you—you're both clear of any head or brain trauma." Her tone was friendly enough, but it definitely held a hint of steel as she added, "Now, please settle down while we complete the rest of our tests."

I sucked in a deep breath and obeyed. They checked my memory, concentration skills, and other stuff, and eventually came to the conclusion that, other than possible concussion and the two-inch-long cut near my temple, I'd been pretty lucky.

Once patched up, the cops came in and took my statements. The curtain between Mo and me was opened at my insistence, and I was relieved to see that she really was okay. We were kept under observation for a few hours and then set free with strict instructions to rest up and take it easy for the next couple of days.

Like *that* was going to happen.

I called a cab once we were outside and silently thanked past me for following the intuition to grab a waterproof phone when I'd updated. The cab driver took us to a nearby Travelodge, and the receptionist didn't bat an eyelid at our sodden and woebegone state. Maybe because I asked for the business floor with everything included, or maybe because it was winter and no business could really afford to turn away good money even if we looked like semi-drowned rats.

"I need a shower," Mo said wearily. "It feels like there's still ice in my veins."

"Do you need a hand?"

"I'm concussed, not an invalid," she said crossly. Then

she sighed and patted my arm. "Sorry, I'm not angry at you. Just me."

"There's no reason to be angry at yourself. You couldn't have foreseen that attack."

"But I should have—especially given I all but set myself up for it." She grimaced and peeled off her sodden clothes. "But the anger stems more from the fact I didn't take the proper precautions when you were with me."

I crossed my arms and leaned my butt against the wash-basin. "It's just as well I was, because you would have drowned."

"Probably."

"Meaning what, precisely?"

"Water is an element I have some control over, remember. I suspect the coldness hitting my face might have insti-gated survival mode." She turned on the shower and held a hand under it, testing its temperature. "Is there tea in this place? I feel the need for a good cuppa."

"There's no doubt tea; whether it's *good* or not is another matter entirely."

I filled the kettle and flicked it on, then stripped off and hung my clothes over the back of the desk chair. By the time I'd wrapped myself in a towel and made the tea, Mo was out of the shower and climbing into bed. I handed her one of the small cups and then sat down on the other bed.

She took a few sips and then sighed. "Not great, but better than nothing."

"You're just a tea snob."

"At my age, I'm allowed to be."

I guess she was. "So, what's the plan now?"

"We rest, as ordered."

"Why? Dusk isn't that far away—"

"I know, but Vivienne always preferred dawn."

I studied her for a moment. She looked pale and slightly out of sorts, and that had rage rising. For the first time in my life, she seemed vulnerable, and while I knew it was probably just a combination of concussion and the shock of the attack, I really didn't like it.

And I certainly didn't like the fact my goddamn brother had more than likely been behind it.

I took a sip of my tea and discovered she was right. It wasn't great. "I suppose it's likely there'll be fewer people around at dawn."

The rage wasn't evident in my voice, and for that I was thankful. It'd only make her worry about me doing something stupid—like ringing my goddamn brother. But what she'd said earlier made absolute sense—if I unleashed now, it'd not only drive him away from us but also drive away any chance we had of uncovering who he was working with.

To kill a hydra, you first had to kill its minor heads. Only then could you tackle the immortal one.

My brother wasn't immortal, but it was looking more and more like he was the hydra's main head.

I gulped down some more tea, burning my throat in the process, and then added, "That being the case, I might go out and grab some fresh clothes for us both. We can't run around in our current ones—they stink of river mud."

She nodded. "Grab something to eat on the way back. I'm feeling a mite peckish."

"Anything in particular?"

She waved a hand. "Nothing too greasy."

I nodded and finished my tea. By that time, she'd drifted into an easy sleep. After pulling my sweater and wet jeans back on, I shoved my feet into her shoes and headed out.

By the time I returned just over an hour later, dusk had settled in, and the skies were ablaze with color. *Red sky at night, sailors' delight* ... I hoped there was some validity in that old saying, because we could really use some calmer waters right now.

The kettle's whistling greeted me as I reentered the hotel room. Mo smiled. "You always did have perfect timing when it came to a cup of tea. What did you grab for dinner?"

She was, I realized with relief, looking and sounding more like her normal self. "Beef in ginger, garlic, and coconut, nasi goreng, and dumplings. I also grabbed a banoffee pie for dessert, because we both deserve it."

She grinned. "Perfect—though I may not fit into my new clothes after all that."

I handed her a couple of bags, dumped mine onto my bed, then headed across to the small desk to open the containers and set out the paper plates and plastic cutlery. As the rich aromas filled the room, I hurriedly stripped off my still-damp clothes and wrapped the towel around me again. I could shower later; my stomach was loudly reminding me I hadn't eaten since breakfast.

Mo tugged on a loose, bright-yellow sweater, then joined me at the desk, tucking one bare leg underneath her as she sat down. "So, did you succumb to temptation and ring your brother?"

A smile twisted my lips. "No, but I did arrange a hire car."

"Clever girl." She grabbed the beef and spooned some onto her plate, then repeated the process with the nasi goreng and dumplings. "However, I've been thinking, and it might actually be prudent to contact him."

I frowned. "Why?"

"Because if he *is* behind this attack—"

"Do you honestly think there's a chance he's not?" I

concentrated on filling my plate, rather than dwelling on the sudden and stupid leap of hope.

"It's possible," she said. "If only because we still have our uses overall—he must know by now the sword he claimed is not the true king's sword."

"Why?" I repeated. "He obviously hasn't tested it against the gate, because you would have felt it."

"Yes, but as I explained earlier, the king's sword is, in very many ways, something of a gateway itself. It is the only way the Witch King can seal—or indeed open—Darkside's main entrance."

And until that gateway was open, there could be no major attack, thanks to the fact the others were too small to allow a mass incursion. It gave us time. Gave us hope, however minute.

"Even if he *is* unaware that his sword might not be the real one," she continued. "He has to feel the difference in its energy output. It wouldn't fit the descriptions given in the great ballads."

I raised my eyebrows. "What great ballads?"

She waved a hand airily. "The ones written after Uhtric's victory, of course."

"I think *that* part of my education is missing."

My voice was dry, and she shook her head, her woebegone expression spoiled by the amused glitter in her eyes. "I find it very sad that the current generation knows so little about their history."

"Hey, if you wanted me to know, you should have said so." I pointed my beef-filled fork at her. "Especially given you were around at the time and could have provided a firsthand account of both the event *and* the scribes who wrote the damn things."

"There are many things I currently regret not doing."

The laughter faded from her expression. "Not teaching you more about your history and even your powers are certainly two of them."

"I haven't got any powers." Or, at least, I hadn't. It was hardly her fault I was a very late bloomer. "And none of this addresses why you want me to ring Max."

"If we don't ring," she said, around a mouthful of beef. "He may suspect we suspect."

My smile was a little bitter. "I think merely suspecting him went out the window a few days ago."

"Maybe, but given we can't be absolutely certain of *anything* right now, we need to play the game."

I sighed. "Fine. I'll ring him after I finish this."

I motioned toward my plate and she nodded. "Just don't forget to play up how badly I was injured, and mention we'll have to lie low for a few days. It might give us some breathing space."

I snorted. "He'll probably just ask what hospital you're in and then send in the troops."

Once again, there was a bitter edge in my voice, and Mo tsked. "You know he's not that stupid."

"I thought I knew him. I can't help but wonder if that was *ever* really true."

She reached across and squeezed my free hand. "No matter what else he does, no matter how badly darkness has stained him, he *is* your twin, and I do not for one second believe he can or will cast that aside lightly. Not without great cause, at any rate."

"You *raised* him. That should have held some weight, too."

"You shared a womb. I did not."

I laughed, as she no doubt intended. "The way things

are panning out, that possibility wouldn't actually have surprised me."

"Only Mryddin has the reverse life gene; even then, he only regresses to a certain point before his life clock ticks forward again."

I studied her for a second, uncertain as to whether she was being serious or not. The mischievousness in her expression suggested not, but she did have a long habit of hiding truths in outlandish statements.

"Really?"

She nodded and airily waved her fork. "It's his incubus heritage; it does weird things to the genes. It's also what allows him to hibernate for centuries on end."

"Huh." I picked up a dumpling and munched on it. "Are you going to start aging backward anytime soon?"

She chuckled. "Definitely not. I'm stuck with this face and body until death eventually claims me."

Given she could only die of unnatural causes, I was praying death kept her grimy claws away until well *after* she'd claimed *me*—which hopefully wouldn't be anytime soon.

Or, at least, not until I got some Blackbird action.

I finished my meal, then tossed the paper plate into the bin. I half thought about grabbing a shower to delay calling Max a little bit longer but decided against it. I might just need to wash the anger and sense of betrayal away afterward.

"It'll be all right," Mo said softly.

It would never be all right, and we both knew it. I sucked in a breath and then made the call.

"Gwen," he said, voice warm and a touch surprised. "This is an unexpected pleasure—or has something gone wrong yet again?"

Yes, it has, asshole, and you know it. I sucked in another breath and said, "Thought you'd like to know that Mo and I were attacked this afternoon. We both ended up in hospital."

He swore vehemently. Angrily. It sounded so real, so unpracticed and genuine that for a moment, uncertainty stirred. But only for a moment. He'd been lying to us for a long time now and was no doubt well practiced in producing the necessary emotions on cue.

"Are you okay?" he asked eventually.

You. Not Mo. *You.* I wanted to scream and rant at him, but I somehow held it back.

"Yes," I said, somehow managing to sound normal. "Concussed and a little bruised, but otherwise, okay. We were damn lucky, though."

"You want me to come home? At the very least, I can keep you both supplied with tea and chocolate until you're both better."

Once again, he sounded so genuine—so concerned—that tears stung my eyes. *Damn it, Max,* I wanted to scream, *I know. I just need to know why.* But I didn't. *Play the game. Find the hydra's minor heads first ...*

"We won't be home for a day or so," I said. "Mo's been ordered to rest up, so we're going to hide out and take it easy."

"All the more reason for me to be with you."

This time the concern in his voice was edged with deep anger, but I had a suspicion it wasn't aimed at us. It *might* have been caused by his troops missing their kill shot, but instinct suggested that wasn't the case. Did that mean Mo's guess was right? Had this action been taken without his knowledge or consent?

"As much as I'd like nothing more than to finally have

you play errand boy, it's too much of a risk." But not for the reasons he'd undoubtedly think.

"And one I'm willing to take. Damn it, Gwen, you've spent plenty of time looking out for me after my various misadventures—"

"Misadventures? That's putting it a little mildly, isn't it?"

"Depends on your definition," he said, laughter in his voice.

"We had thugs pounding on our door at midnight because you'd done a sleight-of-hand car deal—"

"Which was nothing more than a misunderstanding."

"What about the irate woman who threatened to cut your nuts off because you sold her a strip of land that you didn't actually own?"

"A simple delay in the paperwork and easily solved."

"And the idiot who took potshots at you?"

"Stopped as soon as the situation was explained to him. I dare say these attacks will stop, too."

"Something I thought would happen after you'd claimed—"

I stopped, my eyes widening as horror flooded me. But he either didn't hear what I'd almost said or he hadn't yet processed it.

"Damn it, Gwen, you're my sister! I'm not going to sit back and do nothing."

Then call off your people, I wanted to yell, *tell them to goddamn stop*. I sucked in a deep breath and pushed the anger back down again. While it was unlikely he'd missed my near slip, his anger might have overridden the comment enough that he wouldn't dwell too much on it. But I couldn't risk a repeat.

"If Mo doesn't look to be recovering too well, I'll call

you. But I really think she just needs some rest. It's been a busy few days."

He made a low, frustrated sound. "Have you heard anything from the preternatural boys or even Luc about Tris's murder?"

Rage stirred anew. Prodding me for information, no less ... "Why would I?"

"You were there when it happened, weren't you?"

"Yes." But I hadn't told him that; either he'd been there himself or he'd been informed of the fact afterward. "But that doesn't mean they'll keep me updated. They're all playing their cards very close to their chests."

"Even Luc? I mean, the attraction between you two is pretty obvious."

"Attraction doesn't equate to sharing a bed or bedtime secrets. I'm not you or Tris."

It was out before I could stop it. I winced and glanced at Mo. She wiggled her hand—a movement that suggested as comments went, it wasn't the worst thing I could have said.

"And what the hell is that supposed to mean?" There was anger in his voice, not suspicion, and for that I was grateful.

"Oh, come on, you're the one who boasted about sleeping with a certain merchant to get some insider information a few years ago."

He grunted. "That's true, but let's face it, it was a very profitable experience."

"There's no profit in me sexing secrets out of Luc. If I need to know something, I'll damn well ask the man."

"And he'll totally answer, because Blackbirds are not known for keeping secrets at *all*."

"With good reason, Max."

He snorted. "And yet they couldn't stop the sword

being claimed. Hell, they couldn't even stop their own building from being attacked."

"Because no one expected Darkside to attack damn foundations."

He was silent for perhaps a second too long. "How do you know they did that?"

How did he? He shouldn't have, if he was as innocent as he was claiming. "Because I was there. I felt the magic."

"Damn it, Gwen, you need to stay away from both Luc and the Blackbirds. Please."

"I can't. It was my duty to protect the king's sword, Max, and I failed in that duty."

"Hardly, given it was claimed by the heir."

"An heir who's working with Darkside." My heart was thumping so loudly as I said that, it was a wonder he couldn't hear it. "I feel duty bound to rectify the situation."

"That's stupid. De Montfort women aren't warriors—"

"We were once."

"That was a long time ago, and you're no warrior, Gwen. You haven't even been able to access Nex and Vita's full capabilities."

My gaze rose to Mo's. How did he know their full capabilities when she'd only recently told *me* about the true extent of their powers? Or was it merely a small snippet of information gleaned from everything else he'd gathered over the many years this plot had been in the planning?

"That's not the point—"

"That *is* the point," he cut in. "Darkside's out to destroy the Blackbirds—"

"Or maybe they're simply out to grab the Witch King's artifacts they hold."

"That's merely a side benefit." He paused. "Please, Gwen, do as I ask. I don't want you dead."

And if I kept going, that would be my fate. He might not have said it out loud, but that nevertheless was the implication.

"Hey," I said with forced lightness. "I don't want me dead either."

"Then stay away from the Blackbirds. It's not like they've been successful in stopping anything, anyway. They're past their prime *and* their time."

"Darkside would be stupid to underestimate them, Max, and so would you."

"I don't underestimate anyone. I never have."

You underestimate me. You underestimate Mo. I swallowed heavily. "Anyway, none of this is important. Mo's calling out for a cup of tea, so I'd better go. Keep safe, and keep in contact."

"You too."

He hung up. I sucked in a deep breath, then put my phone down. "He didn't deny claiming the sword. He heard me almost say it, and he didn't deny it."

"No, he didn't."

"Fuck." I scraped a hand through my hair. "I really had been hoping that we were wrong, that it wasn't true, that I wouldn't have to—"

Confront him. Maybe even kill him.

But the truth was out now, and there really was no going back from it.

Mo took my hands and held them tightly. Tears prickled my eyes again, and this time, I didn't fight them. I simply grieved for the brother I'd already lost in both heart and soul, even if not yet physically.

Mo didn't say anything. She simply waited, silently offering me comfort and strength. Eventually, I sucked in a deep, shuddering breath and said, "Well, at least I got *that* out of the way."

"Never be afraid to cry, Gwen. I have, plenty of times over the centuries. It might not free the soul of anguish, but it certainly prepares you for what is to come."

"I don't know if I can—"

"In the end, your job isn't to kill your brother but to restrain Darkside. Remember that." She squeezed my hands, then released me and stood up. "I think a good cup of tea and a huge slab of banoffee pie is in order."

Whiskey would have been better, but I'd unwisely forgotten to pick that up. "What happens if your presumption that I'm the true heir rather than Max isn't actually correct?"

She flicked the kettle on and then stooped to pull the pie out of the small fridge. "I'm never wrong, darling girl. Misdirected sometimes, but never wrong."

I laughed—it was a wan sound, but it was better than resorting to tears again. "Do you want me to ring Ginny and let her know we won't be back tonight?"

She shook her head. "I have to ring Barney for an update on their progress, so I'll tell him then."

I accepted the slab of pie with a nod of thanks. "The other thing he confirmed was them going after the artifacts during the destruction of the Blackbirds headquarters."

She nodded. "I suggest you ring Luc and find out if they succeeded. If they didn't, we'll need to secure that ring."

"With Vivienne, I take it."

"Yes, although in truth, even then it won't be totally safe."

"I doubt even Darkside would be stupid enough to attack an old goddess."

"They won't need to. If you are the heir—and if they *do*

226

work that out—then they can simply force you to get it for them."

I opened my mouth to deny the possibility, then snapped it closed again. In reality, all they'd have to do was to capture and threaten Mo, and I'd be putty in their hands —and Max was well aware of that.

Of course, the key to *that* particular scenario was to actually capture her.

"Then let's make damn sure they *don't* work it out." I munched on my pie for a bit; the thick layers of caramel, banana, and cream might not do much for my waistline, but it certainly made me feel happier. "Although it's not as if Vivienne will answer my call."

"She will if you're the heir."

I glanced at her sharply. "Has she answered the summoning of Witch Kings before?"

"Once or twice." She shrugged. "It depends on what mood she's in."

"Then here's hoping she's in a good mood tomorrow."

"As I said, she does love her mornings. I'll call her, though. It's better to leave the possibility of you being the true heir mired in uncertainty until we get all our ducks in a row."

"Our ducks being the real sword and the coronation ring, I'm gathering?"

"Yes."

"And are we going to tell Luc of your suspicions?"

"No."

"Why not?"

She raised an eyebrow. "I adore the man, and I'll love him like my own son when you two marry—"

I snorted. "I like this fantasy world you're living in."

She gave me the look. The one that said *don't be daft.*

227

"But can you honestly see him—or indeed any of them—accepting the fact that the Witch King's heir might well be a woman?"

"No."

"So why say anything until it happens?"

"To warn them."

"Why waste time and energy? There're too many other things we need to be doing right now. What's the time?"

I glanced at my phone. "Just after seven."

"I'd better ring Barney, otherwise he'll get worried." She held out her hand. "I'll need your phone. Mine's still in the car, along with my purse."

"Hopefully the cops will return it once they fish it out of the water."

"Hopefully." She made a give-me motion with her hand.

While she made the call, I finished my pie and then headed in for a shower. I stood under the hot water for what seemed an eternity, but it didn't do much to erase the inner chill. The ties that bound Max and me were very deep; he was my twin, and he would always be a part of me. But to survive what was coming—to survive what I might yet have to do—I had to totally lock my feelings and emotions down. If I didn't, I might hesitate at the worst possible moment, and that could have dire consequences. Not just for Mo or me, but also for the world. The inner chill was the beginning of that lockdown. It was a barrier of ice forming around my emotions and memories—a shield that would hopefully protect me when I needed it the most.

And I *would* need it.

I closed my eyes and raised my face to wash away the reemergence of tears. But there would be plenty more before all this was over, of that I was sure.

By the time I got out of the shower, Mo was making another cup of tea. I grabbed the phone from the side table, then slipped under the duvet and called Luc.

"Hey," he said, his voice warm but weary. "How's the transcribing going?"

"Good, I presume. Ginny and Mia are working on it with Barney."

"Then where are you and Mo?"

I gave him a brief rundown of events, and he swore vehemently. "Maybe you should both back off—"

"And do what? Watch the world burn around us?"

"No, but that's two close calls now. You might not be so lucky the third time—"

"If you want to be technical," I said lightly, "it's actually three close calls—I also survived the roof collapse, remember."

"Damn it, Gwen, I'm being serious here."

"So am I. We De Montforts lost the sword, Luc. It's our duty to get it back."

"I think *that* horse has well and truly bolted."

"That depends entirely on whether the sword in the stone was the true king's sword or not, doesn't it?"

He grunted. It was not a happy sound. "Has Mo managed to transcribe what was written on the King's Stone yet?"

"She's still waiting for Barney's nephew to send through the adjusted images."

"Which should be by the morning," Mo said as she placed a fresh cup of tea on the bedside table.

I passed the comment on and then added, "I talked to Max this evening. He all but confirmed today's attack was as much about grabbing the coronation ring as destroying Blackbirds."

"Then they failed in both aims."

"The ring wasn't there?"

"No, we moved it and a few other precious artifacts to safer locations when the museum theft happened."

Relief stirred. Max might believe the Blackbirds were past their prime, but at least they'd been one step ahead on this particular occasion. "Good. But I need you to grab it for me."

"I doubt that would ever be approved—"

"Luc, the safest place for the ring right now is with the Lady of the Lake. Darkside won't get it off her anytime soon."

"Why would Vivienne deign to safekeep the ring? She hasn't gotten involved in the affairs of men or witches for decades."

"This is different." I cast a questioning look at Mo, and she shook her head. No telling him about the crown, then, despite the fact he—and the Blackbirds—had a right to know. "It's only a matter of time before they attack your other locations looking for the ring, Luc. It needs to be protected by the goddess who made the sword."

"I doubt any of us has the capacity to raise her—"

"Mo's interacted with Vivienne in the past," I cut in. "And besides, we've nothing to lose by trying."

His doubt and disbelief seemed to vibrate all around me. "Look, all I can do is talk to the table and see what happens."

"And when is that likely to be, because there's a bit of urgency here—"

"We're meeting in half an hour," he said. "I presume that's quick enough for even Mo."

I ignored the slight edge of sarcasm. "Given your headquarters is a ruin and the round table undoubtedly buried under a pile of rubble, where are you meeting?"

"We've a choice of buildings nearby, and the round table is fine—it was one of the artifacts moved out under the cover of darkness. As I've said before, it's irreplaceable." He paused, murmuring something I couldn't quite catch. The soft reply was also inaudible, but I recognized the voice—Ricker. "Sorry, duty calls, and I'll have to go."

"The ring?"

"I'll ask. If there *is* consensus on its relocation, where do you want me to meet you?"

"At Windermere Museum, tomorrow morning if you can."

"I'll be there, with or without the ring."

"Just be careful, Luc. Darkside is ramping things up."

"I'd ask you to do the same, but we both know you'll do what you want, regardless of what I say or think." The warm amusement in his voice had my pulse doing a happy little dance. "Sleep well, and I'll see you in the morning."

He hung up. I shoved the phone on the table and picked up my tea. "So, what did Barney say?"

"They're making slow progress. Most of what they've transcribed so far appears to be admin stuff—payments, stock lists, etc."

My eyebrows rose. "Payments to who?"

"They're all coded, so it's hard to say. He's going to pass them on to preternatural for further investigation." She reached for the remote and turned on the TV. "He'll give me a call the minute he does find anything. In the mean-time, what do you feel like watching?"

"Something that doesn't take much brain power."

We settled on an old episode of *Escape to the Country*. I

finished my tea and then snuggled under the duvet. In no time at all, I was asleep.

A soft beeping woke me many hours later. I opened one eye and looked around balefully before I realized what the sound was—the alarm on my phone. I swiped it off and then saw the time—it was barely 4:00 AM.

"Fuck, Mo, why so early?"

She chuckled softly—some might say evilly. "Because we need to get to Windermere before sunrise. Up, lazy bones."

I swore at her—which only made her chuckle again—then tossed off the duvet and shivered my way into my clothes. After pulling on my new boots, I dug the wrist sheath holding the black stone knife out of the backpack and strapped it on. I had no idea why I felt the need for additional protection, but I wasn't about to gainsay it. I then strapped on Nex and Vita and stuffed everything else into the backpack. As we headed out, I grabbed the remains of the pie. Dessert for breakfast was perfectly acceptable at this ungodly hour of the morning.

We climbed into the nondescript Focus I'd hired, and I drove out of Preston. There wasn't much in the way of traffic on the M6, so we reached the turnoff in good time. From there, it took us another twenty minutes to reach Windermere. Dawn was just beginning to tickle the clouds with color, and a thick gray fog crawled through the empty streets, hiding the quaint old houses and giving the old town a decidedly spooky feel.

Once we'd reached the Windermere Jetty and Museum, I pulled into the small parking lot and stopped. The minute I climbed out, a rush of awareness flowed around me, cocooning me in a blanket of warm caring.

Luc was here.

My gaze went to the darkness hovering close to the museum's entrance. "How long have you been waiting, Luc?"

He shook off the shadows and walked toward us, a smile tugging at the corner of his lips. "It's just as well Darkside hasn't your skill at sensing our presence, or we'd be in deep trouble."

"I think it's more you she can sense than Blackbirds in general." Mo's voice was dry. "It's that whole connection of souls thing you don't believe in. Did you get the ring?"

"Surprisingly, yes."

"Excellent. This way, both of you."

She quickly set off, marching across a bridge that spanned the concrete water channel and then through the heavily treed park beyond.

Luc fell in step beside me, his big, warm body protecting me from the slight chill rising off the dark water. "How long has it been since she talked to Vivienne? Does she really believe she'll get a response?"

I shrugged rather than outright lie. "It apparently depends on what sort of mood Vivienne is in."

Another smile tugged at his lips, though it was something I felt deep inside rather than actually saw. "It's hard to imagine a goddess being 'moody.'"

I snorted. "Why? There's countless tales of vengeful gods wreaking havoc on both human and witch populations."

"Yes, but I always thought them to be nothing more than tall tales meant to scare us into obedience."

"Some were," Mo commented without looking back at us. "But some atrocities were very real and very understated. Not all the old gods were as benevolent as Vivienne—and even she had her moments. Now, quiet, both of you."

She stopped at the shoreline. The fog clung to the dark water, hiding the end of the jetty and the boats moored nearby. It felt as if we were in the middle of nowhere, despite the multiple houses that lay on the other side of this small inlet.

Mo knelt and pressed her fingers into the gentle waves lapping the shore. They rose around her hand as if in welcome.

"Lady of the Lake," she said. "Heed my call, I beseech you."

Her voice was soft and yet filled with a power that echoed across the foggy stillness. The water remained still; no deeper power stirred in response.

"Lady of the Lake," she repeated. "Your presence and your help are requested. Please, heed my call."

The fog remained still and the night absent of any power beyond Mo's. Maybe our goddess was in one of her moods.

"Vivienne," Mo said. "We really do need your help. Please, heed the call."

This time, the fog moved, sluggishly at first and then gaining traction and power as it rolled toward the shore and over us. It erased what little of the lake and museum had been visible and seemed to dull all external sounds. Even the gentle lapping of water against the shore was mute.

"What is it you wish of me, Moscelyne?"

The voice was softly feminine and yet full of power and force. An odd sort of thrill ran down my spine. To be in the presence of an ancient goddess once was amazing enough, but I'd now done it twice.

I glanced at Luc. Though his expression was unreadable, his awe echoed around me as sharply as if it were my own.

"I have a question and a favor to ask," Mo said.

"What is the question?"

"The sword that was locked in the stone on King's Island—was it the sword you gifted Aldred's line or was it a substitute?"

"I know nothing of a sword locked in stone," Vivienne replied. "But Elysian will surface once the true heir has risen."

"Elysian?" I glanced at Mo. "The king's sword has a name?"

"All great swords do," the goddess said before Mo could respond. "To keep them nameless would be to disrespect their power."

Maybe, but the Greeks had believed Elysium was the final resting place of the heroic and the virtuous, and *that* was ominous. "Swords aren't sentient beings unless they're held by Blackbirds and hold the soul of a dark witch."

Vivienne's amusement spun around me. "It may not be sentient, Gwenhwyfar, but it does hold great danger to one who still fights to believe."

That she called me Gwenhwyfar was ... unsettling. Mo might have already declared me the reborn soul of the first Witch King's wife but hearing the name drop from Vivienne's lips somehow felt like a death knell. "Gwenhwyfar was never meant to draw the—"

"Gwenhwyfar's fate has *always* been tied to the sword," she cut in. "Destiny and blood has simply converged in the current timeline."

Mo's gaze met mine, a warning clear in her gold-ringed eyes. I swallowed the rest of my questions on the matter and asked instead, "Then how do we find the real sword?"

"When the true heir claims the coronation ring, Elysian will rise."

"Why does the ring make a difference?" Luc asked. Though the question was soft, it echoed through the confines of Vivienne's white blanket. "Even in times when witches ruled, it was nothing more than a symbol of the crown."

"Those who know little of true history may consider it so, but it has always been a guide, one only the heir can use." The fog stirred in agitation. "Who speaks?"

"Luc Durant, Lady Goddess."

"Ah, the Blackbird." A hint of amusement touched her voice. "It is good to see your order still serves the crown after all this time."

"Serving the crown was both our penance and our duty—"

"Indeed, but there are few enough these days who believe in either." Long fingers of fog moved around him, probing, judging. "You will face a familiar choice in coming days, Blackbird. Choose your path wisely, because this time, the fate of this world may ride on it."

"There is no choice when it comes to duty," he replied evenly.

She laughed softly. "Ah, the certainty of youth. Were we ever so foolish, Moscelyne?"

"I dare say there are plenty who would say that I still am," Mo replied, amusement evident.

"And there are none who would say that of me, if only because most of my peers have fallen into the long sleep." She sighed. "As to the identity of the sword locked in stone, I would suggest you stir the great enchanter."

"I feared that would be your answer."

"He can be challenging, even for one such as I," Vivienne agreed. "But it is well past time he stirred again. What is the favor you wished, Moscelyne?"

She half turned. "Luc, can you give Gwen the coronation ring?"

He raised an eyebrow, but carefully pulled a worn and very plain leather pouch from the inside pocket of his jacket. I held out my hand. He opened the pouch, then carefully tipped it upside down. The gold ring that fell into my palm was absolutely glorious. A huge red ruby dominated its center; on its surface, a cross and a rose—the symbols of the Witch King—had been carved. At least twenty small diamonds surrounded the ruby, and even in the fog-clad darkness, they sparkled brilliantly.

"It's heavier than I expected," I whispered. "It must be worth a fortune."

"Its monetary worth is nothing compared to its historical value to crown and country," Luc said. "And that's true now more than ever, given the goddess's statement of its power."

I held it out to Mo. "Here you go."

She didn't take it, and her expression held an odd mix of surprise and perhaps even doubt. She turned back to the lake. "The favor I would ask is that you accept this ring for safekeeping."

"That I can do," she said. "Throw it to me."

"Gwen?"

I stepped to the shore and, with all my might, threw the ring out across the water. Red light pulsed from the gem at its heart, but unlike the crown we'd given Vivienne for safekeeping not so long ago, that light didn't cut a path through the fog.

A hand as pale as ice, with nails that gleamed the color of fresh blood, rose from the dark water to catch it. Vivienne held the ring aloft for several seconds, as if studying it, and then pulled it back into the water.

"This ring is not the true coronation ring," she said, "And I suspect you know this well enough, Moscelyne."

"Impossible." The word all but exploded from Luc. "We have guarded that ring since before Layton's betrayal of the crown. It *is* the real thing—it can be nothing else, given it was taken from the Uhtric's hand on his death."

"It may be the ring he wore on his death, but it is not the one that will call forth the sword. Your order has been deceived, young Blackbird."

"Well, *fuck*." Luc thrust a hand through his hair and then added a hasty, "Sorry, I didn't mean—"

"I have heard far worse from the mouths of men, trust me on that." Vivienne's amusement was evident. "Do you wish the ring returned or shall I keep it?"

Mo hesitated. "I think it best returned. Aside from its value, we can use it as a lure."

To catch a hydra? I wondered, and ignored the swift rise of heartache.

Bloodred flashed deep in the heart of the white. Mo caught the ring and handed it back to Luc. "Keep it safe."

"We have been," he murmured. "For hundreds of years we've kept this damn thing safe, and all apparently for naught."

I wrapped my fingers around his arm; he glanced at me, his expression rueful. Once he'd tucked the ring back into his pocket, he caught my fingers and lightly squeezed them. He didn't immediately release them, and for that I was glad. There was something very comforting in his touch, and I had a bad feeling I'd better enjoy it while I could.

"I will no doubt see you again before this game plays out, Moscelyne," Vivienne said. "In the meantime, walk warily. The dark forces gather exponentially, and as this nation's last guardian, you will be in their sights."

"I know, but thank you."

And with that, Vivienne left. The thick white fog disappeared with her, leaving only murky wisps of gray stirring around the nearby trees and boat masts.

"What did she mean when she said you were the last guardian?" I asked.

"Nothing major." Mo rose and wiped her fingers on her coat. "I'm the last surviving mage here in the UK, that's all."

It was more than that, but it was pointless pressing. She'd tell me when she wanted me to know, not before. "Does that mean Mryddin is dead?"

"No, but as she said, he *is* hard to wake. Perhaps 'last active mage' would have been a better choice of words."

"What are we going to do about the ring?" Luc said. "And if the one we held isn't the original one, then does that mean the one stolen from the British Museum *was*?"

"If it was, then it would be in Max's hands and he'd know the truth of the sword in the stone."

"*We* don't know the truth as yet," I said. "Not with absolute certainty."

Mo patted my arm. "As Vivienne said, you cannot forever deny the truth, however much you might wish to."

"I've got a bad feeling I'm missing some necessary information to fully understand that particular statement," Luc said, frustration evident in both his voice and his expression.

"You are," Mo said equably. "But given it's information you're not yet equipped to deal with, let's concentrate on setting a trap and waking the dead."

Luc scrubbed a hand across his face. "You are the most frustrating woman—"

"Isn't she just," I muttered.

He gave me a side eye. "Now there's a case of the pot

calling the kettle black, if ever I heard one. What's the plan?"

"First, we go somewhere for breakfast," Mo said. "I cannot think on a stomach that has had nothing but banoffee pie for breakfast."

"Why on earth would any sane person even consider eating something like *that* for breakfast?"

"Chocolate cake would have been better, I agree, but we had to make do with what we had." She patted his arm. "Come along."

She headed off briskly. He shook his head, his expression bemused. "I take it she *has* got a plan, but isn't willing to share it yet."

"She's always got a plan," I said. "And I daresay she's already putting it into action."

A comment that proved utterly correct when she directed me back to the M6 and then on to Carlisle rather than home. Or at least, our temporary home. I glanced in the rearview mirror to ensure Luc was still behind us— briefly taking a moment to enjoy the sight of a well-built, leather-clad man on a glorious motorbike—and then said, "Where are we actually headed?"

"To Mryddin's Cave, of course. We need answers, and he might be the only one who can give them to us."

"Yes, but where is his cave? And is that its actual name?"

"Yes, and it's in Physgill, near Whithorn."

"Which clarifies absolutely everything."

She lightly slapped my thigh. "I'll definitely have to sit you down and give you geography lessons."

"Why? It's not like it will matter, now or later."

She tsked. "A good queen should always know the history and geography of the lands she rules."

"Even if I *am* destined to claim Elysian, it's not like the throne will ever be mine."

"That's not the point."

It actually *was*. Even if Darkside managed to destroy Layton's protections, they would never erase the entire royal line. The Blackbirds wouldn't allow it. They'd fight for the crown's existence, even if human royalty now wore that crown rather than witch.

And while there were undoubtedly plenty of witches who'd love to see the reemergence of witch rule, there were just as many who'd fight to keep the status quo—mostly those whose businesses and wealth were very much tied in with the current system.

"When did you realize the ring wasn't the real one?" I asked eventually.

"When it didn't react to you."

I glanced at her. "Which might have just meant you were wrong and that I'm not the heir."

"Hardly, when Vivienne all but declared it as truth."

Meaning that whole convergence thing, no doubt. "Then how are we going to find the real ring, especially if the Blackbirds took the current one from Uhtric's hand?"

"I suspect Mryddin might be able to answer that one."

"Why? Hasn't he been in hibernation since the time of the first Witch King?"

"I believed so, but perhaps this is one of those very rare occasions when I'm wrong." She pursed her lips thoughtfully. "I did leave after Uhtric re-caged Darkside, remember, and all these intrigues certainly have Mryddin's feel. Plus, Vivienne did say it was time for him to stir again."

"What if he *doesn't* have the answers we need?"

"Let's cross one bridge at a time, darling girl."

I snorted softly but nevertheless switched my full attention back to road. By the time we neared Carlisle, dawn had fully risen, and the day looked gray and ugly. Mo directed me off the M6 and through a number of streets until we reached a small café on the outskirts of the main town center.

I stopped out front and climbed out. Luc pulled up beside us; after storing his helmet, he glanced up at the café's sign. "Coffee Climax? Seriously?"

Mo chuckled. "Mary does have a bent sense of humor, although there are plenty who would attest to her coffee being as close as you'll get to an orgasm without having sex."

I locked the Focus and followed Mo across to the café's bright blue door. "I take it she's a witch?"

Mo nodded. "She specializes in sexual dysfunction, be it male or female, though her café is real enough. It pays to diversify in this day and age."

She rapped on the door. The noise echoed, suggesting emptiness, but a few seconds later, a sharp voice said, "Who the hell is it?"

"Me, you old fool. Who else would it be at this hour?"

"Not my customers, that's for sure. They know better. Why the hell are you knocking? You've been cleared to enter at any time."

"I have people with me, Mary. I wanted to give you time to put clothes on."

"Ha! They prudes, are they?"

"No, but this is a business visit, not pleasure."

"Well, fine. I'll get dressed. Come in and help yourself to coffee."

"We need breakfast, not just coffee."

"You always push it, Moscelyne. Just as well I fucking like you."

Mo chuckled and pressed her hand against the door,

just above the heavy, medieval-looking lock. Power stirred, and bright sparks ran across Mo's fingers for several seconds. With a loud click, the door opened.

The room beyond was quaint—stone walls, low ceilings, heavy beams. A small inglenook dominated the rear wall; to the right of this was an open wooden door that led into a kitchen. A rickety old staircase stood on the other side. Along the wall to our right was a servery counter, a cake fridge filled with mouthwatering delights, and a surprisingly large and modern coffee machine.

We followed Mo through the room and entered the kitchen. It was also surprisingly modern, with lots of stainless steel benches and appliances. A tall, willowy woman with vivid purple hair tied into a messy bun stood in front of the stove, flipping eggs and frying bacon. She was wearing a loose, translucent kaftan that revealed fleeting glimpses of flesh with every movement. Mary's idea of being dressed was as left of center as she seemed to be.

Mo strode over and dropped a kiss onto an offered cheek. "You look younger every time I see you."

Mary snorted and slapped at Mo's arm with the egg flipper. "I'm already cooking you breakfast—what else are you damn well after?"

"Advice."

"Ha. You're never just after advice." She glanced over her shoulder. Though she looked to be in her mid-forties, the fine lines around her eyes and the crepey neck skin suggested she was at least ten if not twenty years older than that. "Who are these two?"

"My granddaughter, Gwen, and Lucas Durant."

"Her beau?" She looked him up and down. "Worthy of her, I'd say. Looks to have some stamina in him, which is what you always want in a keeper."

I bit my bottom lip to stop a laugh escaping. I didn't dare look at Luc, though I had no doubt there was some eye-rolling happening, at the very least.

"You'd better sit down," she continued, this time waving the egg flipper somewhere off to our right. "Breakfast is almost ready."

"Shall I ready the tea and coffee?" Mo asked.

"Well, you ain't here for your good looks now, are you?"

Mo's lips twitched, but she nevertheless grabbed the softly whistling kettle and poured the water into the waiting teapot. I turned and saw a small table tucked into the corner of the room. The bench seat surrounding two sides of it barely looked big enough to fit Luc and me, let alone Mo. There was one kitchen chair, so at least the four of us weren't squeezing in together.

I scooted in behind Luc while Mo brought over the drinks, cutlery, and plates. Mary dished everything onto a platter, then sashayed over and placed it on the table.

"I ain't dishing it up, so help yourselves." She plonked down on the chair and led by example. Around a mouthful of food, she added, "Now, what's this about you needing information?"

Mo piled bacon and a couple of eggs onto her plate, then handed me the tongs. "I need to know what the situation is with Mryddin."

Mary pursed her lips. "His cave is closed for conservation works. There've been some rockfalls of late."

"Natural or magic based?"

"Bit of both, I believe."

"Do you think Mryddin is stirring?"

"Possibly only in his sleep. His locks remained engaged." She picked up the teapot and filled the cups. "What's this all about?"

Mo grimaced. "The sword on King's Island has been drawn."

"Not by anyone friendly, I'm taking it?"

"No."

"Well, fuck."

She leaned back in her chair; the kaftan tightened across her chest, revealing pert breasts unchained by a bra. A woman not afraid to flaunt what she had—a woman after my own heart, I thought with a smile. Luc caught my eye when I offered him the tongs and then wiggled one finger back and forth between Mary and me. Suggesting, I suspected, that the two of us were as bad as each other. Or that I'd be her in a few years time.

I didn't mind either.

"What are we going to do about it?" Mary continued. "Other than talk to the old grump—if he deigns to grace us with his presence, that is."

"Right now, we need to chase down Uhtric's ring—"

"I don't think his ring would be worth finding these days —not considering how long he's been in the ground," she said, a devilish glint in her blue eyes.

I just about choked on my bacon. Mo tsked softly. "Mind out of the gutter, Mary. This is serious."

Her amusement fell away. "How serious?"

"End of the world, main gate into Darkside opening serious."

"Well, fuck. There goes my plan to spend summer in Paris."

"You've been there before."

"Not in this lifetime."

"It hasn't changed *that* much." Mo scooped up a last bit of bacon and then leaned back with a contented sigh.

"Don't suppose you've heard anything on the grapevine about the coronation ring, have you?"

"There were some undefined whisperings about Windermere Lake a week ago, but I suspect you already know about that. If his mob don't have the ring"—she pointed with her chin at Luc—"then there's two options— Mryddin or the arcane."

"Was Mryddin active after Uhtric's death?"

"I believe so. He also woke after Aldred's victory."

"Do you know why?"

Mary shook her head. "I was on the point of passing."

"Damn." Mo picked up her teacup and took a drink. "Any idea how best to find the coronation ring, then?"

Mary pursed her lips. "I'll ask the ancient ones tonight, but I can't make any promises. They've been very uncommunicative of late—no doubt because of what you said about Darkside and the sword."

"Let me know either way," Mo said. "And use the alternative channel—it's safer at the moment."

Mary nodded. "If Elysian's been claimed, what's the king currently doing?"

"We're not entirely sure the sword on King's Island is Elysian—that's why I want to talk to Mryddin."

"You think he's done a switcheroo?"

"Possibly."

Mary frowned. "He wouldn't have done it without a good reason."

"I know."

Mary glanced at her watch. "You'd best be getting along, then. It's a bit of a scramble to get to the cave, and the tide will be coming in again soon."

She immediately rose and walked away. A woman who

didn't dither and who had no time for those who did, I suspected.

I grabbed my last bit of bacon and munched on it as I followed the two older women out of the kitchen.

"If you *do* manage to wake the old bastard," Mary said. "Remind him he owes me a drink and that I expect him to pay up."

Mo laughed. "I wouldn't. He was never one to honor his debts."

Mary opened the door and ushered us out. The devilish glint was back in her eyes. "It depends entirely on the debts and whether the payment was monetary or physical."

Mo shook her head. "I'll never understand your attraction to the man, Mary."

"Looks are a poor second place to bed prowess, as you well know."

Mo laughed again. "We'll talk later tonight."

"After midnight. The ancients get antsy if I wake them too early." Mary's gaze fell on me. "I see your strength in her, Moscelyne, and damn, she's going to need it."

"Everyone will if we're to survive what's coming." Mo's tone was grim. "But more so those of us who'll be on the front line."

"Wasn't it ever so?" Mary sighed and slammed the door shut.

"Well, that was an interesting experience," Luc muttered. "I gather she's another mage?"

"No," Mo said. "She's what I call a soul soldier—a soul destined to be reborn into a new body in times of great darkness, be it a Darkside, human, or witch-based catastrophe."

"Is she only ever reborn in times of need?" I asked. "Or is it a continuous cycle?"

Like Luc and me, I wanted to add, but thought better of it. He still really hadn't accepted the possibility, and I wasn't about to say anything that might jeopardize our recent agreement.

"She only ever enters new flesh as needed, and it is ever her destiny to die on the battlefield." Mo gestured at Luc's motorbike. "Climb aboard your steed, Blackbird. We need to get moving."

He obeyed. I offered Mo the car keys. "I take it you want to drive?"

She nodded and opened the car. "It'll be easier if I do, given I know the way and you don't."

I waited until she'd reversed out of the parking spot and we were on our way again before asking, "So if Mary isn't a mage, what are her powers? Besides being able to talk to the dead."

"Not just *any* dead," Mo said. "But the ancient druidic council. Or the six masters of mayhem, as we like to call them."

I raised an eyebrow. "Why? Or shouldn't I ask?"

"They had a nasty habit of stirring up trouble to justify their own existence." She shook her head. "We butted heads many a time with them."

"'We' being you and Mary?"

"And Mryddin, Dyddy, and any other soul soldiers who happen to be around in that century."

"Dyddy?"

"Gwendydd." She glanced at me. "You were named after her, you know."

I raised an eyebrow. "I thought I was named after Gwenhwyfar?"

"Your mother never knew about Gwenhwyfar or that you were her soul reborn. Hell, I didn't realize it for far too many years." She neatly avoided an idiot in a van who stopped for no good reason that I could see. "She found an ancient tome about Dyddy's exploits and declared her first daughter would be named Gwen. She was eight at the time."

"Why on earth was she thinking about children when she was *eight*?" I wasn't even thinking about them now, and I was nearly thirty.

"She was always determined to have kids young," Mo said, with soft regret. "I often wonder now if she knew her life would not be a long one."

I didn't say anything. The only clear memories I had of my mother were of her dying in the hospital after the car crash that had already taken my father's life. Which was sad, I supposed, but not unexpected given I'd only been three.

"Aside from spirit talking," Mo continued, "Mary's a strong spell caster."

"I'm not entirely sure the ability to raise limp dicks will be much help when we're battling Darkside."

Mo laughed. "She can do more than that, trust me."

"I would hope so." I studied the long row of red-brick terraces that lined either side of the street for a minute. "Is she the only soul soldier born into this timeline?"

"They generally work in pairs, at the very least, but we don't have a lot of contact until trouble rises." Mo shrugged. "They have to hide their presence because Darkside hunts them down."

"How would they even know a soul soldier from a regular reincarnation?"

"It's all about the aura and smell—Tartarus hounds are specifically trained to hunt them."

"What is a Tartarus hound? Or don't I want to know?"

Her lips twitched. "Probably the latter, but given they'll

undoubtedly be unleashed before all this has ended, they're basically the mythic hellhound. Only bigger."

"Well, isn't that something to look forward to?" And I couldn't help wondering how many other nightmare creatures I'd learn about before this fight was over. "What kills them?"

Nex and Vita obviously would, but on the off chance I couldn't access their power, it'd be handy to know.

"Anything sharp and silver."

"Note to self—start collecting all things sharp and silver."

"No need—there's a cache of demon-killing weapons hidden in the King's Tower."

I frowned. "Where? I didn't see it when we were down there."

"Well, it'd hardly be hidden if you could see it, would it?"

We were approaching another bridge, and my breath caught in my throat. Nothing happened, of course, but it was nevertheless a relief once we were on the other side.

"Does the fact Darkside hunts soul soldiers down mean they can't be reborn into the same century?" Then, before she could answer, I added, "I guess it does, thanks to the whole 'having to grow up before you can fight' problem."

"Actually, soul soldiers are born into the bodies of the freshly dead and inherit whatever personality and magical abilities their meat case has."

"Meat case? That's seriously gross."

"But nothing more than the truth once the original soul has left."

"What happened to the real Mary? And what's the current version's actual name? Or were they never born human in the first place?"

"Mary had an allergic reaction and passed before medical help could get to her." Mo flicked on the blinker and turned onto the road leading to North Glasgow and Edinburgh. "Soul soldiers are chosen from those who made a vast difference to the lives around them. I believe she was christened Kwyn."

"What did she do to become a soul soldier?"

"From the little she's said, I think she led her people to victory against greater odds after their king and his generals had fallen."

"Handy to have in a fight, then."

"Yes, though sword fighting is not a part of her skill set in this generation."

"Given how few people actually train to use a sword these days, that's hardly surprising."

"No, although they generally do choose the best available meat case at the time of their rebirth."

"And now I have an image of a celestial supermarket where the newly dead are displayed, all with little tags nominating their strengths and weaknesses."

Mo's mouth twitched. "It's probably not that far from the truth."

I snorted and fell silent. It took nearly two hours to get to Whithorn, though the cave itself was accessed from a park area that was basically in the middle of a farming community a few miles out of town. I climbed out of the car and stretched the kinks from my body. Once Luc had arrived, we headed off down a muddy path that skirted around the farm buildings and headed into a thick wood. The closer we got to the sea, the sharper and colder the wind got. A pebbly beach soon came into view; it was quite pretty even though the sea looked gray and cold.

The crunch of our footsteps echoed across the stillness, but we'd barely taken five steps when Nex pulsed.

A heartbeat later, there was a sharp blast of power.

A power filled with malevolence rather than darkness. Not that the source really mattered. What *did* was the target.

Mryddin's Cave was under attack.

CHAPTER TWELVE

"Fuck," Mo said. "They're trying to collapse the cave. You two, go. I'll try and keep the thing intact."

She hunkered down and pressed her hand against the ground; power thrummed under our feet, a deep pulse that spoke of anger.

I drew my daggers and followed Luc down the beach. He'd drawn Hecate, but she was silent for the moment. Which logically meant that—given Darkside couldn't survive sunlight and halflings had no magic—the people behind this attack were witches. It was a fact backed up by that malevolent pulse of power.

And yet ...

There was something else involved. There had to be. Nex wouldn't be reacting so eagerly if we were merely dealing with halflings.

The cave sat above the shoreline on a rocky promontory jutting out toward the sea. The cave's sides were vertical with a jagged top that made it look like a rough crown. Dust and bits of rock tumbled down the hillside from above the cave, and cracks were appearing in the rocks above the crown. I suspected it was only Mo's countering magic that was keeping the place intact. We had to get in there and stop the bastards before the whole place collapsed.

But it was damn hard to move with any speed with the beach shifting so drastically underfoot.

We reached the embankment and began to climb. There didn't appear to be anyone guarding the entrance into the cavern above, but that didn't mean they weren't inside, especially given the sunlight wasn't strong enough to penetrate any more than a few feet. I raced on, clambering over rocks damp with sea spray, scraping my hands on their sharp edges. As we drew close to the plateau, something finally moved in the shadows haunting the cavern's entrance. Nex's pulsing sharpened; she was definitely hungry for action. I definitely wasn't.

I jumped over the last rock and landed in a half crouch on the plateau. The shadows were moving with increasing agitation, and an unpleasant stench now rode the stiffening breeze.

"Luc," I said softly.

"I see them."

"I don't think whatever is in there is human."

"They aren't." He strode on, Hecate still gripped casually in one hand.

"Then what are they?"

I rose and padded after him. The stench got stronger the nearer we got, and I wrinkled my nose in distaste. It smelled off, like meat left too long in the sun.

"Some form of demonic animal."

My grip tightened on the daggers. Lightning flickered down their sides, bright in the grayness of the day. "But demons can't move around in daylight."

"So the theory goes."

I glanced at him sharply, though he remained several steps ahead of me and wouldn't have seen it. "There's been no evidence to suggest otherwise."

"No, but if they're kidnapping women to produce cross-breeds, what makes you think they're not doing the same with animals?"

"I never really thought about it." And certainly didn't want to now.

The shadows ahead no longer stirred. I didn't think that was a good thing.

Luc glanced around at me. "Ready?"

Fuck no. But I nevertheless raised my daggers. Lightning shot from the tips of the blades and angrily snaked back and forth. "You want me to clean out the shadows?"

"Worth a shot, though I daresay there'll be other problems deeper inside."

He was altogether too calm about this whole matter, but then, I guess this *was* his job.

I crossed the blades and directed several bolts of energy into the cavern's mouth, sweeping them back and forth in an effort to get anything that might be hiding in a crevice beyond our line of sight. The thick stench of burned skin and hair stained the air, and my stomach turned uneasily. I'd certainly gotten something ... and I wasn't looking forward to discovering what.

The cracks above the cave's crown were growing larger and the rain of dirt and stone heavier. Mo's efforts weren't stopping the witch, and I had to wonder why.

Luc moved on, keeping to the right while I went left. We paused again in the cave's mouth, just beyond the reach of the increasingly heavy curtain of debris. The stench of burned hair was now so thick I could taste it. I swallowed heavily and tried breathing through my nose. It didn't help much.

"Hecate, burn," Luc said softly.

A deep and bloody light radiated from the sword's blade and quickly burned away the shadows. Ash stained the air, but beyond the immediate circle of death were the burned remnants of the demons the lightning hadn't quite reached. They were grossly misshapen dogs with razor-sharp talons and leathery tails spiked with barbs. Beyond them, much deeper in the cave, were a number of humanoid shapes; Hecate's light wasn't strong enough to reveal anything more than that, unfortunately.

But between them and us stood at least two dozen demons.

"So much for Darkside not being able to move around in daylight," I muttered.

"There has to be a gate nearby. It's the only reasonable explanation." He glanced at me, one eyebrow raised. "Shall I do the honors?"

"Luc, you can't—"

"I can. You need to find and stop the witch before she brings the whole damn cavern down on top of us."

As much as I hated to admit it, he was right. There were only the two of us, and the earth witch had to be our priority.

"Fine," I muttered. "But if you get dead, I'm going to be seriously pissed."

He laughed, then raised Hecate and, with a roar that echoed through the shadowed stillness, charged at the waiting horde. The demons immediately came to life, their screams echoing through the chamber, a fierce and hungry sound. Luc plowed into the middle of them, using Hecate like a scythe, sending limbs, torsos, and heads flying.

I sucked in a breath and darted to the right, leaping over a line of rocks into what appeared to be a small water channel. It hugged the wall and swept away from Luc and the horde, allowing me to get past them without being seen—

A bloody scream quickly shattered *that* illusion. Deadly claws slashed through the shadows, forcing me to jump sideways in order to avoid being carved in half. My shoulder smashed into the cavern wall, and pain slithered down my arm. I ignored it and, as the demon's bitter stench filled my nostrils, did a one-two slash with the daggers. Vita's sharp edge sliced through the talons reaching for me even as Nex's lightning crawled up the demon's arm, incinerating his flesh in the process. His scream of fury became one of pain but was quickly cut off as his face disintegrated. I leapt over what remained of his body and ran on, using Vita's pulsing light as a guide.

With a loud crack, a huge chunk of rock fell from the ceiling. It hit the floor close to the channel and splintered into hundreds of needle-like shards that sliced through the air with deadly intent. I swore and threw myself down into the trickle of water, using the rocks lining the channel as protection. Splinters snagged my hair, but for the most part I escaped major damage. But the flickering, pulsating light coming from the daggers highlighted the growing number of dangerous cracks. If I didn't stop the witch soon, we'd all be in deep trouble.

I pushed up and ran on.

There were nine figures ahead; three were kneeling, their hands pressed against the cavern's stony floor. The pulsing energy that surrounded all three told me they were earth witches. No wonder Mo was making little headway; she might be a mage, but not even she could counter the combined magic of three full earth witches.

The other six stood in a circle facing them. It would be easy to believe they had no interest or knowledge of what else might be happening in the cavern, but I suspected *that* was highly unlikely.

I ran on through the rain of dirt, skirting fissures, leaping over rocks, trying not to think about how close to collapse the cavern had to be. Trying not to worry about the man who still battled the screaming, hungry horde behind me.

I was still some distance from the witches when the six figures turned as one and linked hands. Then, again as one, they began to spell, the words too soft for me to hear. The resulting hum of energy sent unease prickling down my spine even though it didn't appear to hold an immediate threat.

Was it some form of protection?

I suspected it was, but there was only one way to find out. I called the lightning from the daggers and split it into three, sending two at the circle and the third at the kneeling witches.

The figures didn't move. Didn't react in any way. Their pale faces were expressionless, and if it wasn't for the soft rise and fall of their chests, it would have been easy to believe they were simply robots—even if no currently existing technology could make such perfect human replicas.

Just as my lightning was about to hit, light speared the darkness and formed a dome around the silent figures. It was a deep, sickly brown-green in color and pulsated with an energy that appeared to be a warped combination of earth magic and darkness.

My lightning hit it and, with a sharp crack, exploded.

I swore, gripped my daggers tightly, and ran straight at

the bastards. The only way to break *any* circle of power was to move or remove one of the elements. I had no idea if it would work here, simply because I had no idea what magic was being employed. But if it *didn't* work—if the dome protecting the earth witches didn't fall—we were in deep trouble.

My footsteps echoed loudly, despite the roar of the battle behind me, and the deep, quivering groan of the earth. It was close—so close—to succumbing to the pressure being applied by the witches; the fall of debris was now so bad the daggers' light provided little in the way of guidance. I was running on instinct and hoping like hell that instinct and my footing didn't betray me.

My heart pounded so fiercely, it felt ready to tear out of my chest, and each breath was a sharp rattle of fear.

I could do this.

I *had* to do this.

There was no other option. Not if we wanted to survive; it was very evident survival was *not* in the minds of the nine.

With another resounding crack, the cavern's ceiling began to crash down in very large chunks. It was now or never ...

I sucked in a deep breath, then launched myself at the nearest guardian. She didn't move. She didn't even look at me. Didn't react when I hit her feet first in the gut. The force knocked her backward, ripping her hands from the grip of the two motionless figures on either side. The sickly green dome immediately began to pulsate.

But it didn't fall.

I hit the ground, rolled onto my knees, then slashed Nex across the calf of the guardian to my right. The sharp blade cut through tendons, muscle, and bone with ease, and her lightning cindered the lower portion of his leg. He collapsed, but he didn't lose his grip on the woman beside him, and the dome remained intact.

I swore, scrambled over the top of the collapsed man, and severed his hand, thereby breaking another link in the chain.

The dome began to retract; as a hole in the still-pulsating wall of energy formed, I flung in three bolts of lightning.

Between one heartbeat and the next, the three kneeling witches were cindered, and the dark caress of their energy stopped feeding the collapse.

But the cavern still shook, and I had to wonder if perhaps I'd been too— The thought cut off as a scream rent the air. Or rather, six screams that sounded like one.

Before I could react, they hit me, tearing at clothes and skin with nails as sharp as knives. I instinctively raised my arms to protect my face and then called on the lightning again. It burst from my body rather than the blades, a wicked wave of death that cindered everything in the near vicinity. As their ashes rained around me, pain erupted through body and brain even as blood filled my eyes. I sucked in air, trying to calm the painful pounding of my heart, trying to gather the strength to at least *move*.

The danger wasn't over yet. Not only did the cavern remain in a perilous state, but Luc was still out there, still fighting.

I wiped the blood away from my eyelashes and pushed to my feet, coughing as the sooty remains of the guardians stirred around me. I couldn't immediately see Luc or the demons—the debris and dust remained too thick. But after a few minutes, I caught the flare of bloody red.

Hecate.

Luc was still standing.

The relief that swept me was so fierce, my knees just about buckled under its force. I sucked in another breath, then staggered forward. I'd barely managed two when Hecate's glow softened and Luc's big body appeared out of the dusty gloom. There was a bloody cut across his cheek and another down his left arm, but otherwise he appeared unhurt and whole.

His grin was fierce and bright. "Now *that* was a whole lot of fun."

He smelled of sweat and blood and strength, and I wanted nothing more than to step into his arms and inhale it deep. "You're insane, Blackbird."

"That's been said before." He caught my chin and gently swiped at the trickle of blood running down my cheek. "How bad is the headache?"

"I can see."

"That's not what I asked."

I sighed. "It's ten times worse than any migraine I've ever had, but I'll survive."

"You shouldn't even be upright," came Mo's comment. She appeared out of the dusty shadows, her expression concerned as it swept me. "Sit down before you fall down. Luc, can you go find how these bastards got in here? I'll fix our girl and then check whether this racket has managed to wake Mryddin."

"The cavern won't fall in on us?"

"I've shored things up as best I can in the circumstances, but keep alert. There may be some fissures that defy my efforts and resort to collapse."

"Keeping aware is a motto all of us should be living by at the moment," he said, voice a little grim. "Recent attacks have certainly proved that."

He stepped around me, then strode deeper into the cavern, the sound of his steps quickly receding.

Mo squatted in front of me and placed her hands on my shoulders.

As her magic rose around me, I said, "Don't—you need to conserve your strength."

"Containing the earth didn't take that much out of me, and the fact is, you're useless to us all in your current state."

"It's still more important to contact Mryddin—"

"Yes, and I'll need all my concentration to do it. It'll leave me an easy target, which means I need you fit enough to defend me if necessary."

"Which is a totally convincing argument to anyone who doesn't actually know you."

She grinned. "Your inability to take the things I say at face value is yet another reason why you're my favorite grandchild."

I smiled, but stopped protesting. Her healing energy washed through me, a warm wave that stopped the stinging in my eyes and erased the worst of the pain in my head. The niggling ache that remained was at least survivable, and there were painkillers in my backpack I could take once we got back to the car.

With a slight sigh, Mo released me and then sat cross-legged in the guardians' ashy remnants. "This could well take hours. Keep alert."

I nodded. "How do you actually connect?"

"Astrally. Kind of. Hence the reason he's always been hard to wake—it's very easy to ignore an astral projection."

"You can't use magic to poke him?"

She shook her head. "He has all sorts of wards set around the cavern's inner chambers. Truth is, even if Darkside had succeeded in collapsing this part of the cavern, Mryddin would probably have been safe."

"Then why were they even trying?"

"Wouldn't you, if you were Max? Mryddin's exploits are well enough written about, and I have no doubt Max has done his research. He'd be aware of my connection with him." Bitterness edged her voice. "And he's certainly heard me say often enough that it's always better to erase a problem before it actually becomes one."

I placed a hand on her knee. She cupped it and gently squeezed. "I'll be fine. I'm just ... annoyed I didn't see what was in front of my eyes before it was all too late."

"I had no idea what he was up to, and I'm his goddamn twin. You can't blame yourself for something you can't possibly have changed."

She raised an eyebrow, amusement evident in the bright glint of her eyes. "Sage advice coming from the woman who has done nothing but blame herself."

"Well, I *am* your granddaughter—what do you expect?"

She smiled and drew the car keys from her pocket. "If this goes on for too long, you might have to send Luc for sustenance. Just remember the tide is coming in—if you *do* want something to eat and drink, you'd better go get it sooner rather than later."

I nodded. She placed her hands palm up on her knees and closed her eyes. In very little time, she'd slipped into an astral trance.

I crossed my legs, then placed the daggers in front of me; they'd at least give advance warning of any approaching demons. As for human foe—well, hopefully I'd spot their shadows against the skyline as they entered the cavern. Depending, of course, on how long the still-swirling dust took to clear.

Time ticked by slowly. It was tempting to pull out my phone and check what was happening in the world—or at least on social media—but inattention was the surest way to tempt an attack.

Eventually, awareness tingled down my spine. I glanced around as Luc appeared out of the gloom. "Did you find anything?"

"A dark gate at the rear of the cavern. Freshly created, too."

He sat down beside me and lightly pressed his shoulder against mine. Warmth flowed between us, and it felt oddly energizing. As if he was somehow sharing his strength—or that I was siphoning it. I frowned and shifted fractionally, breaking the connection. The flow of strength immediately stopped. I glanced down at Vita; golden light was fading in the heart of her blade. Obviously, there was more to her healing abilities than Mo had previously mentioned.

But that was something I could worry about later.

"Are you certain it's actually new?" I said. "Or is it simply a gate broken by the stretching of time that's been recently fixed?"

"There's no real way to tell a recommissioned one from a new, but either way, it doesn't bode well."

No. "I gather you've sealed and alarmed it?"

He nodded. "And I sent a message to Janet, who's in charge of the Carlisle council. They'll monitor it."

I frowned. "Isn't there a council in Dumfries? It's a bit closer."

"There's only a regional monitor there these days. He hasn't really got the power to shut the gate down again if something breaks through my locks."

"Ah." I brushed some dirt off my face and wished I could

so easily brush away the tiredness. "Mo's not sure how long it'll take to get a hold of Mryddin. If we want something to eat, we'll have to grab it now, before the tide becomes a problem."

He glanced at me. "Do *you* want something to eat?"

I hesitated. "I could do with a cup of tea and some chocolate, but it's a long way back—"

"If you want them, I'll go get them. Keys?"

I handed them to him. He leaned forward and gently brushed a kiss across my lips. I raised a hand, cupped his bristly cheek, and deepened the kiss. For far too many minutes, there was nothing but this man and this kiss. A kiss that felt like a homecoming. Like I was exactly where I was always meant to be.

His gaze, when it finally met mine, burned with desire, but there was something else in those green depths now—something I hadn't unexpected. Something that made my heart soar.

It was an acceptance of fate.

He might never admit it to me or to anyone else, of course, and maybe—given the uncertainty of our situation and the fact we might not survive what was coming at us—that was wise. And even acceptance didn't mean anything in the true scheme of things. The two of us had apparently fallen in and out of love many times over the centuries, and there was no guarantee that this rebirth would be the one to change any of that.

But still ... there was always hope, and given the dark times that lay ahead, it was at least something to cling to.

"You're a witch. You know that, don't you?" His voice was soft, husky.

"Well, technically, so are you."

He laughed and brushed a stray strand of sweat-curled

hair from my eyes. "I better go, before I give in to temptation again. I won't be long."

"You better not be, because you really don't want to see me in a tea-deprived state."

He grinned, stole another—this time all too brief—kiss, then rose and strode away, whistling softly. I leaned on my knees and watched, a silly smile on my face. Hope. There was no better pick-me-up.

Once he'd gone, I glanced around at Mo. Her face was serene, but energy flowed around her, rainbow bright in the shadows. From the little she'd said about astral travel, those colors meant she was no longer in 'residence' of her body. The energy was basically a warning system, meant to sound an alarm and drag her soul back into her body if it was attacked or something else went wrong.

I just had to cross my fingers—and all other things—that nothing else *did* go wrong. We'd really had more than our fair share of bad luck in the last twenty-four hours.

It took just over half an hour for Luc to return. The tide was obviously a fair way up the beach, because his jeans were wet up to his— The thought stalled as a familiar and very much welcome scent teased my nostrils. I dragged in a deep breath and smiled happily. Aside from freshly baked bread, there wasn't a better smell in the entire world than that of fish and chips.

"I do so like a man who anticipates his lady's needs, even when she's reluctant to admit them."

He grinned and sat beside me. "Mo did warn that I should never let you get too hungry if I wanted a long and peaceful life."

"Did she now?"

"It's one of the many pieces of advice she keeps imparting whenever you're not around to protest." He handed me the tray holding not only my tea and his coffee, but also three bottles of water, then began unwrapping the fish and chips. "Oh, and before you ask, I did get a full range of chocolate, as I wasn't sure which one you preferred."

"Any chocolate is good chocolate." I paused and wrinkled my nose. "Except the Bounty Bar. Way too much coconut for the amount of chocolate provided."

"Many would find that a controversial statement."

I raised an eyebrow. "Do you?"

"Hell no, totally agree."

"I see glimmers of hope for a successful relationship."

"And I'd hope a successful relationship would depend on far more than chocolate compatibility."

"Well, yes, there *is* the whole sexual satisfaction thing to consider, but you need to know going in that I consider chocolate one of the five essential food groups."

"Then I shall keep a constant supply to hand when we get around to having a relationship." He motioned to the fish and chips. "Eat up before it gets any colder."

We ate in companionable silence, but by the time I'd finished my tea and a couple of chocolate bars, tiredness threatened to wash me away.

Luc tucked the rubbish under a rock so that it didn't get blown away by the chill breeze now funneling into the cavern.

"Why don't you grab some sleep," he said softly. "I can keep watch."

"That's not fair—"

"Gwen, you look like shit—"

"I do love the way compliments fall so very readily from your lips."

A smile tugged at said lips but failed to reach his eyes. "I'm being serious—"

"So am I."

"You are *so* annoying, woman." He wrapped an arm around my shoulders, then dragged me into his big warm body. I did what I'd resisted earlier and drew in a deep breath. His warm, spicy scent ran with the musk of man and sweat, and it had an oddly calming effect. Or maybe that was a result of the tenderness with which he held me and the steady beating of his heart under my ear. He was strength and caring and connection ... An image of a woman in red rose like a ghost in my mind, her blue eyes bright with laughter. But that laughter was fading, just as she was fading. I had no idea whether he was actually thinking of her at that moment or if the connection between us allowed me to catch another memory. Either way, I couldn't help but hope the fact she was fading meant her grip on his affections was also fading.

I closed my eyes and within minutes was asleep.

The dust had settled and the cavern was pitch black when I finally woke. Luc's arm remained around me, but the heat emanating from his body couldn't entirely erase the iciness in the air. The crashing of waves upon the shore seemed louder—closer—than it had before, but more concerning was the rush of water inside the cavern. The water channel sounded flooded, and there were at least three or four mini waterfalls to be heard.

"Is it raining outside?" I pulled away from him and rolled my neck to get rid of the crick.

"Has been for hours now."

"That explains the chill, but not all the water in here."

"Darkside's assault opened a few major fissures and has given the weather access. I daresay it'll collapse the whole cavern in a hundred years or so."

"We won't be around to care."

"No, but Mryddin might." His gaze swept me, warm with concern. "How are you feeling?"

"Better." I drew my knees up and wrapped my arms around them—as much to keep the chill away as to stop myself from reaching for him. "How long was I asleep?"

"Close to six hours."

I stared at him. "No."

A smiled twitched his lips. "Yes."

"But the sea still sounds high."

"Because it still is. The tide has only been in retreat for the last hour or so."

"At least we should be able to get out." I glanced around at Mo. Despite her having been astrally traveling for close to eight hours, there was no sign of consciousness returning anytime soon. But the rainbow surrounding her had muted, and that meant it was now taking a toll on her strength.

Anxiety stirred, but I knew better than to try and wake her before she was ready. Not only would it annoy her, but it could also endanger her life.

I scrubbed a hand across my face; dirt and dried blood flaked away under my touch, and I wanted nothing more than to soak the chill and the lingering aches away in a deep, hot bath. But that prospect wouldn't be in the offing for at least another couple of hours.

I pushed to my feet and did some stretches. My backside was decidedly numb after sitting for so long on cold rock.

"I've more chocolate, if that'll help," Luc said.

"It would, but we'd better leave some for Mo. She'll need an energy kick after this."

"I did buy twelve bars, so there's still plenty left." He handed me a Snickers and then added softly, "I had time to think while you were asleep."

My stomach plummeted. "Oh, that sounds ominous."

"Not about you and me."

"Good, because karma never appreciates the breaking of a handshake deal."

"I think karma has too many other things on her plate to be worried about whether or not we follow through on our deal *if* and when we survive the next few weeks."

"Given karma is a romantic, I wouldn't bet on that." I studied him for a second, seeing and not liking the seriousness in his expression. "So, what's the problem?"

He hesitated. "What are you going to do about your brother?"

"Find him, of course."

"And then? He's been hatching this scheme for a very long time, Gwen. I think it's too late now to try and talk sense into him."

"I have to at least try. I don't want to kill him." I tore open the Snickers and took a bite. It tasted like sawdust and felt like a lump of concrete when I swallowed it. I wrapped the bar back up and shoved it into my coat pocket.

"And if he gives you no other choice?"

"I honestly don't know. He's my brother, my twin, and —" I broke off, but Luc nevertheless understood. It was evident in his expression, and in the gentle swirl of emotion that briefly flared between us. I sucked in a deep breath and then added, "But he chose Darkside over his own damn flesh and blood."

Luc reached up and twined his fingers through mine. His grip was warm, but I found no real comfort in it. Not this time. "Despite everything, I don't actually believe he's chosen them over you. If he truly wanted you dead, Gwen, he could have killed you and Mo well before any of this started."

"Perhaps he didn't understand what either of us was capable of. He hasn't exactly called off any of their attacks on us."

"He may not be responsible for those. Just because he's working with Darkside doesn't mean he's in full control of them."

I studied him curiously for a second. "Why are you suddenly defending him?"

"I'm not, but—" He hesitated. "This is going to sound strange, but you dreamed while you slept, and it played out like a movie in my mind."

I blinked. The connection went both ways. "That's ... a very interesting development."

"Alarming, more likely, given I'm not telepathic."

"Neither am I, but it didn't stop me catching your memories of Aurora." I hesitated. "What did you see?"

"Aside from a few ... shall we say ... tantalizing images of what exactly you plan to do with me when the deal begins, you mean?"

I grinned. "You can't blame me for having erotic dreams when you can't keep your lips off me."

"True." His amusement faded. "I saw the connection between you and your brother, Gwen. *Felt* it. I can't believe he could or would readily betray such a bond. Not without great cause."

Which was an echo of what Mo had already said.

"I hope you're right." And feared neither of them were. "In case you're worried, the ability to see into each other's minds doesn't happen all that frequently and seems to center on memories rather than thoughts."

"Good, because there're certainly some thoughts I'd much rather keep to myself."

I grinned. "Where's the fun in that? I mean, I'm sure

there's an occasion or two where you'd like to know exactly what's going on in my mind."

"Undoubtedly," he said, voice dry. "But luckily for me, I generally don't need to access your thoughts to know that. A poker player, you will never be."

"I wouldn't be betting on that, Blackbird," Mo commented, her voice soft and filled with weariness.

I spun in surprise and hurried over to her. "How are you feeling?"

"My backside is numb, my legs are ice, and I feel like I've been hit by a train." She sighed and glanced up, her face pale and drawn. "Which is all pretty normal for an astral event of any length. Help me up."

I grabbed her hand, waited until she uncrossed her legs, and then carefully hauled her upright. I didn't let go until she was steady on her feet.

Luc undid the lid of the remaining bottle of water and handed it to her. "Did you manage to contact him?"

She smiled her thanks and took a long drink. "Yes, although he was being his usual tiresome self about it all."

"Did you ask him about the sword?"

"Of course." She squeezed my hand and then pulled away and did some leg stretches, wincing with every movement. "He *did* create a secondary sword for Uhtric."

"Why? He had Elysian—why would he need another sword?"

"The gifts of gods always come with a price, Luc. Nex and Vita are evidence enough of that." She grimaced. "Uhtric apparently had no wish to use Elysian unless it was absolutely necessary."

I frowned. "Then what did the replica do? And was it the one in the King's Stone?"

"The sword in the stone is the one Uhtric used to mop

up the remaining hordes," Luc said. "I'm certain of that, as we're the ones who placed it there on his death."

Mo patted his arm. "And that sword is a replica of the original, according to Mryddin."

"So why did images in that book I found at Jackie's show Uhtric using a very plain sword?"

"What book?" Luc said sharply.

"A book of fables that features tales of all the old kings."

"Ah, there's your explanation. Fables are not fact."

"But fables are often based on fact," Mo commented. "And now that my memory has been jogged, I do recall that Elysian was a much plainer sword."

"It still doesn't explain why Blackbirds of the time sheathed the fake in the King's Stone rather than Elysian," I said. "Surely they would have known the difference?"

"Yes," Mo said, "and to me it suggests they did so at the order of the king."

"If that were true, there would have been some mention of it in our archives," Luc said. "There isn't."

"There wouldn't be if they were acting under the orders of the king," Mo said.

Luc frowned. "Why would Uhtric have ordered that?"

"Perhaps he—or more likely, Mryddin, given it is one of his great gifts—foresaw a future in which Uhtric's line no longer ruled and wanted to protect the three items of power."

Luc grunted. It wasn't a convinced sort of noise.

"What *is* the replica's power? Did Mryddin say?" I asked.

"It echoes Elysian's ability to draw on all elements without the need to move into the unseen dimension. It was also designed to react to heirs in the same manner."

"Isn't the unseen dimension the only way to close the gate?"

"Yes, and that's why finding the coronation ring has jumped to prominence. Neither we nor Max can find the true sword without it."

"Did Mryddin happen to know where the true ring is?" Luc asked. "Because we were certainly under the impression it was the one in our possession."

"It was placed in the King's Stone a month after Uhtric drew Elysian; it was in that time Mryddin secretly made the replica."

"So why weren't you aware of it?" I asked curiously.

"Because neither Uhtric nor Mryddin deemed it necessary for me to know, obviously." There was just a touch of annoyance in her tone, though I didn't think it was aimed at either of us, but rather at a past that couldn't now be changed.

"Hiding the ring within the King's Stone makes no sense, though," Luc said. "The place is unsecured—why would they take such a risk? Especially when we didn't return the sword until decades later?"

"The King's Stone was never unsecured, Luc. We De Montforts have always protected it, even when there was no sword for others to covet." She paused, her gaze moving past us. "Has the tide fallen enough for us to get back to the car?"

"Yes," Luc said, "although we might get wet feet."

"Wet feet I can cope with. Let's move. We have a ring to find."

She marched off with surprising speed, leaving the two of us scrambling after her. The plateau beyond the entrance and the rocky path down to the shore were wet and treacherous. Luc led the way, assisting Mo down despite her protests that she was perfectly fine, then helped me over the last few rocks. The waves lapped at our toes and the wind was damnably icy, but at least it was no longer raining.

Luc opened the Focus's door and ushered Mo in. As I climbed into the driver seat, my phone rang, a sharp sound that echoed loudly across the otherwise still night.

I tugged it out of my pocket and glanced at the screen. "It's Barney."

Mo made a give-me motion. I handed it over, then pulled on my seat belt. Luc leaned on the door, obviously waiting to see what news Barney had.

Mo listened for a few minutes and then said, "Send me the address. We'll meet you there in five hours. Do not—I repeat—do *not* go in without us."

She was silent for a few seconds and then said, "Just tell them to be wary, Barney. After what happened at the funeral parlor, they'll be on high alert at all their residences."

He obviously agreed, because she made no further remonstrations and hung up.

"What's happened?" I immediately said.

"The unexpected." She paused. "It appears they've succeeded in transcribing a lot of the paperwork found at Karen Jacobs's place."

"And?"

"And they've got an address."

My heart began to beat a whole lot faster. "Whose address?"

But I knew. It was the only possibility that explained the undercurrent of excitement in her voice.

"Winter," she said. "They've damn well found Winter."

275

CHAPTER THIRTEEN

"Why on earth would Darkside have written his address down *anywhere*?" I said. "They haven't been careless to date, so why start now?"

"It could be a trap," Luc commented. "It would certainly explain the haphazard manner in which that place was cleaned out."

"Barney is aware of the possibility," Mo said. "He's contacting the Manchester council and will arrange for the place to be monitored until we all get there. You coming with us, Luc, or following?"

He hesitated. "With you. Darkside is well aware I ride a motorbike and might be on the lookout for it."

"You can't leave it here," I said. "It'll be stolen or stripped for parts within hours."

"I'll call in a tow-truck and pick it up from them later. And I'll drive—I'm not as tired as either of you."

I didn't bother arguing. While he made his call, I helped Mo move, then claimed the front seat. Luc climbed in, started the car, and drove off.

As the headlights speared the night, highlighting distant

buildings, he said, "If it *is* Winter's address, he'll no doubt have the place well secured."

"Barney's no fool, even if I sometimes treat him as such." Mo gave Luc the address and then added, "There's a convenience store down the road—they'll wait for us there."

"We're going after Winter?" I said, a little surprised. "What about the ring?"

"It's safe enough for the moment. Winter has to be a priority, as it's very obvious he's a major player in this game."

"I take it by the 'they'll' comment," I said, with more than a little trepidation, "that Ginny and Mia will be with Barney?"

"You didn't think he was ever going to get out of that house without them, did you?"

"Well, no, but I do keep hoping common sense will finally kick in."

Mo snorted. "When has either of them backed away from an adventure?"

"This is all too deadly to be called a mere adventure."

"Perhaps, but they've always had your back, no matter what was happening, and that's not about to change anytime soon."

"I know, but—"

"In dark times, we all need people we can absolutely depend on and trust," she cut in. "You'll need those two before this is all over, trust me on that."

I looked around at her. "What have you seen? What else did Mryddin say?"

"I've had no visions, if that's what you're worried about. As for Mryddin—he spent half the time admonishing me for both forgetting so much and for losing track of vital items even though he's the one who failed to pass on vital information. He really is a cranky old bastard."

A smile twitched my lips, despite knowing she'd half avoided my question. "Did he say anything else useful? Or offer to help us?"

"He'll help, but it's going to take him a while to dismantle all his protections. He'll be there for the final battle, if necessary, but I'm not counting on him for support until then."

"I'm really hoping it doesn't get to the final battle," Luc said. "I'm not sure any of us are prepared for it."

"No one ever is," Mo said. "Aldred certainly wasn't, and that's probably what cost him his life."

"I thought using Elysian killed him?" I said.

"It did, because he wasn't prepared for the cost. Because he battled the sword rather than becoming one with it. Remember that, when the time comes."

"Which," Luc said, with a slight edge, "brings me back to something Vivienne said—what did she mean when she said Gwen's fate was tied to the sword?"

"Technically, she said Gwenhwyfar—"

"No games, Mo," he cut in. "I need to know what the hell is going on."

"But are you ready to actually hear it?" she bit back. "I don't believe so."

"Tell me," he said, that edge stronger.

Mo sighed. "Fine. I don't believe Max is the true heir. I believe Gwen is."

He didn't immediately snort in disbelief, even if I felt the wave of it. "No woman has ever drawn the sword."

"Which doesn't mean no woman ever will."

Luc flashed her a glance over his shoulder. "Max drew

the replica—surely that's proof of his claim, given only the true heir has ever drawn it."

"The sword reacted to Gwen, remember, and at a time when there were still other heirs alive."

"Reacting is not proof."

"True enough," Mo said. "But you also have the words of the goddess herself—destiny and blood have converged in the current timeline."

He made a deep sound that sounded like a growl. "I cannot believe—"

"Cannot?" Mo cut in. "Or will not?"

His expression was an interesting mix of disbelief and anger. "Surely if the goddess had intended the sword to be borne by either sex, there would have been some indication of it before now."

Mo snorted. "*That* simply shows your ignorance when it comes to goddesses."

"We have a record of what she said when she gave the sword to Aldred. There was no mention of the sword being borne by a woman."

"There was no mention of it being borne only by men, either," she said. "I was *there*, Luc. She decreed, 'The sword can be raised in times of great darkness by those who bear Aquitaine blood and who hold the crown by right.' She didn't ever say it was restricted to the males of that line. That's merely a presumption on the part of men who were never there, but nevertheless documented it."

He was silent for several moments. I had a suspicion it was at least partially caused by the realization just how old Mo actually was. "That's why you asked me to give the coronation ring to Gwen, isn't it?"

"Yes. I wanted to see if it reacted. When it didn't, I suspected it was fake."

"Most people would think that a bit of a leap."

"Most people haven't been alive as long as me. My memory might not be as good as it once was, but my hunches are rarely wrong."

"What made you suspect I was the heir?" I asked. "You never really said."

"The sword reacting to you was the beginning of it, but it was the deepening of your connection to Nex and Vita afterward that all but confirmed it."

I frowned. "Why? The fake sword isn't connected to Elysian or the goddess—it wasn't even created in the same forge."

But even as I said that, I remembered the storm-kissed energy that had risen when I'd crisped the Aranea sent to kill Gianna. It had felt very similar to the energy that had caressed my hand when I'd gripped the king's sword. It might not be the real thing, but if it had been designed to echo Elysian's powers, then its emissions would be similar. And while accessing the power of the daggers in a way no other De Montfort ever had might not be definitive proof to most, Mo—as she'd already noted—wasn't most. She'd witnessed both Aldred and Uhtric using the sword and was very familiar with both what it could do and what its energy emissions felt like. She might not have been there when I'd touched the sword on King's Island, but she'd certainly witnessed me using the deeper energies of the daggers multiple times now.

"Fake or not, the sword in the stone remains a gateway to great power," Mo said. "Maybe not enough to open the main gate, but certainly plenty to cause mass destruction on *this* side of it."

"Perhaps even enough to destroy the protections around the queen and resurrect witch rule?" I asked.

"Possibly." Mo's voice was grim.

"So if Mryddin *did* foresee that Layton would cede the witch crown to human rule," Luc said, voice again sharp, "why wouldn't he at least warn those of us who were meant to protect both the crown and its artifacts?"

"Because, as a general rule, mages do not interfere in the destiny of men. We guide where practical and join the battle when necessary, but we don't usually alter the path fate has decreed."

Luc snorted. "And yet history is littered with examples of mages doing exactly that. Did not Mryddin disguise one king so that he could seduce the wife of an ally?"

"Well, yes, but with good reason—the child borne of that union was Aldred's ancestor."

"What happened to the seducer?" I asked.

"He and his family were slaughtered. They were turbulent times."

"Then why didn't Mryddin warn the king and ensure the safety of his family?" I reached into my pocket and drew out the remains of the Snickers. Thankfully, it tasted better the second time around.

"Because to have done so would have ensured the continuation of a line destined for failure."

"That's pretty cold," Luc commented.

"Yes, but sometimes such decisions are necessary when the country tears itself apart with war. That child not only brought peace to his people, but decades of stability."

Luc grunted. "All of which is interesting but doesn't address the main question—the idea that Gwen is the heir."

"Does your disbelief stem from chauvinism, or the fact that it's Gwen?"

"Chauvinism is an inbuilt characteristic in Blackbirds.

Sons are always prized more highly than daughters, as only sons can join the table."

His gaze met mine; fear stirred deep in the emerald depths. Not for himself or the battle that now loomed way too fast on the horizon. Rather, it came from the realization that my role in all this might be far greater than any of us initially thought.

"We're all aware of the toll war takes on men," he continued, "and history tells how close Uhtric came to death when using Elysian. I don't want either for you."

"I don't want them for me either," I replied softly. "But there may be no other option."

He cast a dark and broody look my way. "There're always other options, Gwen, even in the bleakest of moments."

I reached out and gripped his thigh. His muscles jumped in response, and that connection between us stirred to life. The woman lying at his feet in that hecatomb no longer wore a red dress. Instead, she wore jeans, boots, and a brown mac. She also had pale skin and blonde hair.

He was envisaging me dying. Envisaging me dead.

I hoped, with all my heart, it was a vision born of fear rather than foresight.

"Except there *is* no one else to draw the sword," I said softly. "Not now."

Max and his cohorts had made damn sure of that.

"Which brings me to another point, Mo." He briefly placed his hand over mine and squeezed my fingers. The vision faded, but not the fear I sensed in him. "You said Mryddin designed the fake to echo Elysian's reactions to heirs. Max subsequently drew it. To me that states he *is* the true heir."

"There have never been twins born in the king's line

before," Mo stated. "It's possible the hand that draws one will not draw the other. I actually suspect now that the writing on the King's Stone will reveal something along those lines."

"Has Barney said whether his nephew has sharpened the images or not?" I asked.

"No. I think he's been so totally invested in transcribing the notes that he simply forgot about it. I'll prompt him once we deal with Winter."

Dealing with one problem at a time was certainly the way to go right now—especially when the problems just kept getting bigger.

We drove on through the night. The freeway was relatively quiet, which meant Luc was able to put his foot down more than was probably wise. Mo slept while we discussed random, inconsequential things like movies, food preferences, and places we'd one day like to travel. His list, I noted with some amusement, almost perfectly matched mine.

Dawn was just starting to tint the clouds with rose hues by the time we pulled into Manchester. Luc followed the altogether too perky directions of the GPS, then turned the annoying device off as we crossed a red-brick bridge spanning a fairly wide canal.

"That," he said, pointing to a house on the left-hand corner of the crossroad ahead, "is our target."

It was a pretty basic red-brick two-up two-down end of terrace house in an area that looked ... average. "I'm not exactly sure why, but I didn't expect Winter to live in the middle of everyday suburbia."

"No." There was an edge of sleepiness still evident in Mo's voice. "I certainly had him pegged as a 'lights and disco' sort of guy."

"Disco?" Luc said with a half laugh. "That stopped being a thing decades ago."

"Really? That's a shame. I was rather fond of the Bee Gees."

I briefly glanced around at her. "That sounds like you knew them."

"Met them backstage at the Nelson Mandela Birthday Tribute at the Wembley Stadium in eighty-eight. Nice young men they were."

"They were middle-aged by that time," Luc said, voice dry. "That's hardly young."

"Compared to me, they were practically in their infancy." She paused. "There's a ribbon of energy surrounding that house."

I swung back around and narrowed my gaze. After a moment, I saw it. It wasn't just one ribbon, but multiple, and they all had a sickly, twisted look to them. "That's Darkside magic."

"Yes, and I'm having difficulty reading its intent."

"I can't even see the ribbon," Luc said, frustration evident. "Is it a spell? Or something else?"

"It seems a touch more organic than a spell. I suspect the only reason Gwen and I can see it is because we're trained to read presence trails."

"Could the ribbon be a result of Winter's energy field?" I said. "And if it is, then why didn't we see or sense it earlier?"

Like when we spotted him at the funeral parlor?

"I don't know," she replied. "But there's a minor ley line running through this area; maybe he's tapped into it. It would explain its more organic appearance."

"Only earth witches can tap into ley lines," I said. "And he certainly hasn't the look or the feel of an earth witch."

"Which means nothing given he's also half dark elf." She paused for a second. "The ribbons skim the common wall but don't fan protectively across the entire roofline, and there doesn't appear to be any immediate protection around the two skylights. They might be our way in."

"They might also be a trap," Luc said. "They're aware you're blackbirds, remember."

"Something I can hardly forget, given my grandson is working with them."

Mo's reply was decidedly mild, but I nevertheless felt the flash of her annoyance. She hadn't appreciated the comment, though I suspected it came more from her still smarting from Mryddin's remonstrations than Luc's gentle reminder.

"Turn left into the side street and park a little up the road," she added, "I need to study the energy a bit longer."

Luc stopped the car in front of the small house behind Winter's. Cone-shaped pines lined the fence dividing the two, and while it lessened any chance of him spotting us from the two small top-floor windows, it also only left the end portion of the terrace fully visible.

The dark ribbons continued to move in a slow, snakelike manner around the building. As Mo had said, there wasn't any magic evident across the visible section of roof, and the skylight was conveniently open. Either there were alarms up there we couldn't see, or it was a trap, as Luc had already suggested.

"Have you come across anything like this energy before?" I asked eventually.

"No," Mo said, absently, "but that's not surprising. Uhtric's lockdown gave the dark elves plenty of time to develop new spells and energy subversions."

"Did that also happen in Aldred's time?"

"Yes. But there were three of us active then, which made it quicker and easier to develop counters."

"Then maybe it's time you called Gwendydd back." Especially if Mryddin took his time to make an appearance.

"I have spoken to her," Mo said. "She has a few commitments she needs to look after first, but should be here within a week or so."

"A week or so might be too late," Luc said. "Especially if Darkside decides to flood its people through the minor gates."

"They've tried that in the past. It didn't work. Now, hush for a few minutes, you two—I need to concentrate."

The faint caress of her energy touched the air—a gentle but very careful probe that reached for the house. The dark ribbons reacted with alacrity, snapping back and forth like the angry snakes they resembled. Mo quickly withdrew the probe, then sent it skimming skyward, angling it over the unprotected section of the roof.

"Interesting," she murmured eventually. "I think we'd better go meet the others now."

"What did you see?" I asked, as Luc started the car then pulled away from the curb.

"What seemed like nothing actually isn't."

"Meaning there *is* a spell laying over the roof?" Luc asked.

"Yes, but it's little more than a general alarm. Given there's no reason the ribbons couldn't be employed to cover the entire building, it's obviously a deliberate choice—especially given the open skylight is without any sort of protection."

"It's a trap, then."

"Some form of, yes, and one I think we should spring."

My head snapped around. "Are you crazy? Why?"

Amusement twinkled in her bright eyes despite her serious expression. "Sometimes the best way to snare your quarry is to be caught first in their net."

"That depends on exactly what the net's intention is," Luc said.

"I don't think capture is the intent here," I said. "Not given the way the ribbons reacted to your probe, Mo."

"I disagree," she said. "Why else would they make it so easy to get in that house via the skylight?"

"Um, maybe to collapse the whole thing in on us when we're inside it?" I said. "They've shown a propensity for doing that."

"If the skylight *is* bait," Luc said, "then why not subvert their plans? One of the windows on the first floor is open. You could go in through that."

"That would mean tackling the ribbons," I said. "And I personally don't think that would be wise."

"Let's wait and see what Barney and the girls have to say before deciding on a course of action," Mo said, in a manner that suggested she knew exactly what that course of action would be and nothing anyone said would change her mind.

Luc pulled up behind a gray VW a few houses down from the convenience store. After tugging my coat's hood over my head to shadow my face, I climbed out of the car. A surge of energy had me looking around; Luc had disappeared.

I raised an eyebrow. "Is that really necessary?"

"Any watchers in that house may overlook two women in hooded coats hurrying toward the store." His reply indicated he was moving around the front of the Focus. "But two women accompanied by a man bearing the manner and coloring of the Durant line? Unlikely."

"And a door opening and closing without sign of anyone getting out or even appearing in the driver seat isn't going to snare attention at *all*."

"A door randomly opening is far less noticeable than a six-foot-two-inch man, especially given the distance. We can't afford to be incautious, Gwen, especially when getting it wrong could get us all killed."

And that was me told, I thought.

"Stop with the verbal foreplay, you two, and come along," Mo said as she strode toward the store.

I hurried after her. The building was a double-story, brown-brick affair, with a front wall of glass that was covered by all sorts of advertisements. Four protective metal bollards stood halfway between the street and the store, making me wonder if ram raiding was a big problem around this area.

The door swished open as we neared; the interior was packed with shelving and grocery items. There was a payment area to our right, and to our left, a service counter and large coffee machine. A small blonde woman made coffees while a taller woman took orders from the small line of waiting customers. The scents that filled the air were rich, aromatic, and exotic, a result of not just the coffee but also all the loose herbs and spices sitting in open boxes or hanging from the ceiling.

A small, rotund figure appeared from the middle aisle and gave us a wide smile. "Mo De Montfort?"

"I'm she," Mo said.

"Good, good, your party waits for you upstairs in the office. This way, please."

She bustled away. We followed in single file—between the closeness of the shelving and all the items stacked on the floor, there really wasn't another choice—to the rear of the store. After passing through thick plastic strips that divided the main store from the rear storeroom, she led us left and up a flight of stairs. A bathroom sat directly opposite the landing, and there were two other doors—one down a short corridor to the left and another to the right.

The woman stopped and motioned us toward the left door. "They wait inside. Would you like coffee?"

"No, but thank you very much," Mo said.

Luc—who was still melding the light around his body to remain invisible—stepped quickly to one side as the woman nodded and went back down the stairs. We continued on, the floorboards creaking under our feet. The door ahead opened, and Mia appeared.

"You took your time," she said cheerfully. "Sadly, that means all the food we bought has now been consumed."

"I think eating is the last thing on their minds right now," came Barney's friendly rumble somewhere to the right of the door.

"A statement that shows your ignorance when it comes to Gwen." Mia moved aside and motioned us to enter.

The room was large and appeared to serve as both an office and a break room. Filing cabinets lined the left wall, and in front of these were a couple of tidy desks. To the right were two sofas and a coffee table; Barney had claimed the smaller of the two sofas and had two-way radios, his phone, and some other electrical paraphernalia lined up on the table in front of him.

Ginny was perched on an office chair she'd dragged over to the window, but glanced around as we entered. "There's been no movement into or around the terrace for the last hour, and no indication that anyone is currently inside—though it's still early and they might be asleep. There *is* some sort of weird air movement around the building, though. It's something I've not seen before."

"That would be energy ribbons." I grabbed the other office chair and rolled it over to the second window.

"Ribbons?" she said, eyebrow raised.

"Darkside evilness, basically," I said.

"Ah, well, that certainly explains the weird vibes it's giving me."

"It'll do more than give you weird vibes if you get close to it," I said.

"Does that mean you won't get past it?" Barney asked.

"No. It just means we have to be bit more cunning in our approach." Mo quickly updated them on everything and then added, "What's the situation with the Manchester council?"

"There's a councilor keeping an eye on earth vibrations from the terrace next door, another watching from the parking area near the gardens, and a third in a van parked in the street behind the terraces."

"Have they got any record of a witch living in that house?" Mo asked.

Barney shook his head. "Thanks to the city's growth in the research and manufacturing sectors, Manchester's witch population has become transient. It makes it harder to keep tabs on everyone."

I frowned. "Why would they even want to?"

"The witch registration rule was brought here after a number of violent events in the early nineties—some witch based, some not," he said. "It was a means of keeping tabs on troublemakers—of which there were plenty at the time, believe me."

I grunted and glanced back to the street. Nothing had

changed and yet a tiny niggle that appearances were mighty deceiving stirred.

"Whatever we're going to do," I said. "I think we need to do it sooner rather than later."

Mo glanced at me sharply. "What are you sensing?"

"I don't know. Something."

"Then we move." Her voice was crisp. "Barney, I gather you're in contact with the councilors?"

He nodded and tapped one of the two-way radios. They all had in ear receivers, so at least using them would be less noticeable. "I've tuned them to the same channel and will coordinate."

"And Gwen and I?"

"Are on a separate channel so you don't hear all the chatter—that could prove dangerous inside. I'll alert you if anything happens."

"Good. Ginny, you'll remain on air watch, but you can't do it from up here. You and Mia need to grab a coffee, then stroll to the seat under that plane tree in the park. Just remember, our foes may or may not be obvious. They might even be spell concealed. Luc—"

"He's here?" Mia's gaze darted around.

"Near the door," came the reply, amusement evident. "Didn't want to shock the store's friendly inhabitants by suddenly revealing myself."

"Huh." Mia studied the doorway for a second. "It's a little spooky to witness, as there's absolutely no—"

"Can we concentrate?" Mo cut in. "Time is a-wasting."

And it might already be too late … but for what? I had no idea. It wasn't like the terrace itself provided any clues—it remained still and dark, and the undulating ribbons of energy hadn't in any way altered.

"Luc," Mo continued, "we'll need you close by, just in case entering the house leads to an external attack."

"Have you got an attack radius for the ribbons? I can't see them, remember."

"Best estimate, based on its reaction to my probe, is six feet."

"Then I'll leave seven, just to be sure."

"Probably wise, given we're dealing with the unknown." She accepted the radios Barney handed her, then tossed one to me.

"Are you both going in?" he asked.

"It depends entirely on how those ribbons react," Mo said. "I'll let you know either way."

"Good."

I switched on the two-way, tucked it into my pocket, and shoved the receivers into my ears. Then I unstrapped my knives and lashed them together. "We need to move. Now."

"Go," Barney said. "I'll notify the troops. And be careful, all of you."

I strode out the door, following the still invisible Luc down the stairs and back out into the street. Thankfully, my awareness of him allowed me to not only keep an even distance between us but avoid crashing into him when he stopped.

"Here, take these." He pressed the car keys into my hand. "If someone is watching they'll think it odd if you don't leave in the car. I'll be out the front; yell if you need me."

"I will." Whether he'd get into the building if I did get into trouble was another matter entirely.

I squeezed his fingers, then released him and hurried back to the car, starting it up as Mo climbed into the passenger side. I waited for a car to pass, then did a U-turn and took the first left, driving around to the rear of the terraces.

Once parked, I leaned my arms on the steering wheel and studied the building. The rear gate was open—an invitation I wished we didn't have to accept—but the carport beyond was empty. That didn't mean the house was, of course. I bit my lip and thrust away the growing trepidation. It was nothing more than fear of the unknown, and it wasn't like I was going in there either unarmed or alone.

My gaze shifted to the energy snake. It continued to undulate around the house, but for some reason, it felt more dangerous than it had before. But maybe that was a result of knowing we were about to tackle the thing.

"How do we play this?"

"I don't think there's any benefit to sneaking around—that'll just attract attention." Mo glanced at me. "You ready?"

I half smiled. "Am I ever?"

She laughed and patted my shoulder. "You'll be fine, darling girl. You're stronger than you know."

"That's not saying much."

"That's the old you speaking," she said. "The new you knows better."

I sighed. "Yeah, but the new me is also scared witless."

"And yet you keep going when angels would falter."

"Which is no doubt your genes coming out in me once more."

She laughed again and climbed out of the car. I grabbed my knives and followed her down to the carport. The ribbons continued their sinuous journey around the building, seemingly unaware of our presence. That would change soon enough.

"So, what's the actual plan here?"

"I noticed earlier that the ribbons' energy withdrew to the middle of the building when it attacked the probe, leaving the roof and base momentarily free. I'm going to set up a timed probe spell; with any luck, its approach will echo what happened earlier, and give us the chance to get in through that top window."

"And getting out?"

"Will undoubtedly depend on what we discover inside."

"I do love your 'seat of the pants' method of doing things. It fills me with such confidence."

"Ha!" she said and got down to the business of spelling.

I crossed my arms and watched intently. Spelling wasn't my gift, and I'd never be able to replicate it, even if Lancaster blood did run distantly through my veins thanks to her. But that didn't mean I couldn't lock the information away just in case I came across something similar in the future. As Mo tended to say, what you didn't understand, you couldn't unpick.

It took nearly five minutes to complete the spell, and the result was a spinning sphere of tangled streaks of light that hovered several feet away.

I carefully walked around it. A finger of light darted toward me, paused when it got close, and then retreated.

"I take it it's designed to dart about and draw the attention of the ribbons?"

Mo nodded. "We'll have a couple of minutes to get inside before it withdraws."

I glanced at her. "Withdraw? Not fade?"

She nodded again. "It'll last an hour; that should give us time to get out if we need it. Ready?"

I motioned her to proceed. She flicked the sphere

toward the house, then shifted and flew upward. I changed, grabbed my knives with my claws and followed, hoping like hell that the neighbors weren't looking our way. They might not notice a hovering blackbird, but they'd look twice at one carrying sheathed knives.

As the sphere neared the house, the ribbons snapped toward it, lashing back and forth in angry warning. The sphere twirled out of their way, then darted across to the building's communal wall. The ribbons snaked after it and, in the process, fell away from the roofline and down past the window.

Mo immediately flew in. I tucked my wings close and swept under the window frame and into the room. But I cut it too close, and the daggers hit the windowsill's edge. A ribbon immediately appeared, snapping after us, forcing us to fly on into the hall.

The ribbon paused at the door, then retreated to the middle of the bedroom, where it snapped back and forth for several seconds before slowly retreating.

I shifted shape and dropped to the ground, tension vibrating through my body as I studied the hallway. There was only one other room up here, and, from what I could see, it appeared to be another bedroom. There was no bathroom, but there were stairs that led up into the loft. The place was as silent as a grave and, ominously, smelled like one too.

I pushed to my feet and studied the room we'd flown through. It held a single bed and a chest of drawers, but neither had been used in some time—there was simply too much dust sitting on the top of both. I walked over to the loft staircase and peered up. Nothing but shadows up there, despite the skylights.

Mo looked over my shoulder. "There's definitely a snare spell up there. I can't see it, but I can feel it."

"Then we don't go up there." I strapped on my knives, then drew Nex. No light flickered down her sides, which at least meant Darkside inhabitants weren't nearby. "I'll check out the other bedroom. You watch the main stairs."

I stepped around her and moved down the hall. One step into the room was more than enough to see both the room and the source of the stench. I clamped a hand over my nose, but breathing through my mouth didn't seem to help; the wretched smell of decay coated my throat regardless.

The woman in the bed had obviously been dead for some time; the blankets might be tucked up around her neck, but it was pretty evident the decomposition was well advanced—a fact backed up by the number of maggots visible.

I retreated. There was nothing I could do for the woman and, given the state of decay, no way to uncover what had killed her. That was a job for forensics.

"It's an elderly woman," I said. "She's been dead for quite a while."

Mo grimaced. "Poor thing. I daresay they killed her in order to use her house. The question is, why?"

"Could it have something to do with the ley line?"

"There's only one way to find out. Let's head down."

I grabbed her arm. "Me first. Nex will react if there's anything nasty down there."

"Nex can't see magic—"

"No, but I can, remember?"

Her gaze narrowed. "I have a suspicion your protective gene is unnecessarily kicking in again."

"Possibly, but only because if I do have to raise the

goddamn sword and shut the gate, I'm going to need you on perimeter defenses to keep the bastards off me."

"A very good excuse for said protectiveness, and one I'm not buying in the least."

I grinned and slipped past her. "Tough. Come along."

She snorted and followed. We moved cautiously down the stairs, pausing every other step to listen. The house remained silent. Dust lay thick on the banisters, and the only coat hanging on the hook near the front door was a vivid pink that obviously belonged to the woman upstairs. From the little I'd seen of Winter, he hadn't seemed the type to wear such a fluorescent color.

I paused on the last step and studied the immediate area; there was neither a magical nor physical alarm. And yet trepidation was spiking. I stepped down and studied the long corridor. It had three doors off it—the one directly in front of me led into a small living area, while the one down the far end went into a kitchen. The other belonged to whatever had been built under the stairs.

I motioned toward it. "Whatever I'm sensing, it's coming from that."

"Do you want to make sure the rest of the house is clear? I'll investigate the cupboard."

I nodded and went into the living area. The small room was immaculately tidy, holding a small sofa and armchair, an electric heater, and a large TV perched on a cabinet stacked with Blu-rays. Double glass sliding doors at the rear of the room divided this room from the dining room. I went through. The kitchen lay to the right of the dining table. Behind it was a small bathroom.

I retreated back to the hall. "Found anything?"

"Yes," she said. "And not what I'd expected at all."

I walked over. Lightning flickered down Nex's side, and trepidation switched to fear. "What is it?"

"A staircase."

"Into a cellar, I take it?"

She glanced at me. "Yes, but there's something far worse down there than that."

"It's not another fucking hecatomb, is it?"

"No, it's even worse."

"I didn't know anything could be worse."

"Of course there can be; a hecatomb—while gruesome—is little more than an information exchange point. It hasn't the capacity in and of itself to alter the fabric of the world in any way."

My gaze returned to the stairs disappearing into darkness. I *really* didn't want to go down there, but I wasn't about to let Mo venture on alone, especially if what lay in wait was worse than a hecatomb.

"And that's what we're dealing with here?" I asked.

"Unfortunately, yes," she replied heavily, "because what lies down there somewhere is a goddamn dark altar."

CHAPTER FOURTEEN

Confusion stirred through the fear. "But they're not usually associated with Darkside."

"Darkside has witches working with them, remember."

How could I forget, when Max was one of them? I pushed away the ache of betrayal and pain; there was nothing I could do about him right now, and it was far better to concentrate on the problem in the cellar than worry about the confrontation that was coming.

The rising air smelled of earth and dampness, but as I drew in a deeper breath, I caught something else—energy. It was sharp and crisp, reminding me a little of the electric scent that came before the onset of a storm. I suddenly understood why she'd claimed this was far more dangerous than a hecatomb.

"They've tapped the altar into the ley line."

"Yes, and we need to detach it before it's forever stained. I think it best if—"

"Forget it. You're not going down there alone."

"Gwen, it *is* the sensible thing—"

"And how do you work that out?" I cut in. "You can't

protect yourself when you're spelling, and this may well be a trap."

"I doubt it. They wouldn't risk an altar in order to trap and kill us. We're not worth that much to them."

"If we weren't worth much, they wouldn't be trying to kill us all the goddamn time," I said. "Why don't you contact Barney and let him know what we're doing. I'll go down and check out the cellar. Wait up here until I give the all clear."

A smile touched her lips, and her eyes shone. My gaze narrowed. "What?"

"Nothing. Go." She touched the two-way. "Barney? You there?"

I gave her an annoyed look but nevertheless headed down, one hand on the old brick wall and the other holding Nex out in front of me. Despite her light, the darkness closed in, deep and thick. The smell of dampness grew stronger, but the caress of energy remained distant. That suggested the dark altar wasn't directly under this house.

I paused on the bottom step and held Nex higher. Her light fanned out, revealing a small, bricked room no bigger than the kitchen above. The wall to my left was covered in a rusty assortment of hammers, screwdrivers, saws, and other bits and pieces. There were also at least a dozen dust-covered wine bottles lying on a rack directly ahead. At the other end of the cellar, an opening had been roughly cut into the wall. The tunnel beyond was narrow and dark, and the strength of the breeze flowing out of it suggested there was an external opening somewhere.

One thing there wasn't here in the cellar was a dark altar, and that meant we'd be tackling that small, damp tunnel.

I took a deep breath, then, as Mo started down, shifted Nex to illuminate the stairs.

"Discover anything?" she said.

"A tunnel. How far away is the ley line?"

"A few hundred feet at the very least."

I frowned. "Why would they make the main entrance to their altar so far away? There'd surely be houses far closer to it than this."

"Undoubtedly," Mo said, voice grim. "But perhaps it simply came down to the point that there was a greater chance of the occupants in the other houses being missed."

My gaze returned to the tunnel. "There's no magic protecting the entrance."

She stopped beside me. "There's definitely magic somewhere deeper in, though."

"Could it be shoring up the passage? The thing doesn't look particularly safe from here."

"It feels reactive rather than protective, but without getting closer, I can't say for sure."

"Great," I muttered. I drew Vita and felt a little bit safer with the weight of both daggers in my hands.

The narrowness of the tunnel meant having to slide in sideways, but even then, it was tight. Moving with any sort of speed was impossible; defensively, the position sucked.

Thankfully, Nex's pulse didn't alter; there might be Darksiders down here, but they were still some distance away.

Progress was slow but steady. As the tunnel began to slope downward, the caress of the ley line's energy grew stronger and the air decidedly hotter.

I swiped at the sweat trickling down my face. "It feels like there's a damn furnace up ahead."

"That's because we're getting closer to the ley line."

I glanced at her. In Nex's pale light, the golden rings around the blue of her eyes glowed so brightly, it put the rest of her face into shadows. It was an eerie sight. "I wasn't aware the ley lines held heat. It certainly wasn't mentioned in any of the books I've read about them."

"That's because most witches use the lines at a surface level. Very few go underground."

"Then why do dark witches? Is it just a matter of being safer?"

"No. It's easier to tap directly into the energy of the lines from underground. Of course, with that ease comes greater danger."

"Because of the closeness?"

"Because to fully tap into a line—as most dark altars do—you must first step into its flow. The unprepared can be washed away."

Unease stirred. "Does that mean you'll have to step into the flow to disentangle it?"

"Yes."

"Have you done it before?"

"Once. It was a most unpleasant experience, I can tell you."

Given her habit of understating dangers when she was tackling them, that no doubt meant she'd come close to losing her life. "And is the flow ahead stronger or weaker than that one?"

"It's about the same." There was a smile in her voice, even if I couldn't see it. "Stop worrying. It'll be fine."

"You keep saying that, and half the time it never is."

She chuckled softly. "You really do have your father's pessimistic streak. He was always worrying about things and situations he couldn't control."

Which only made me wonder if he'd worried about the

trip that had killed both him and my mother. I didn't ask, because I really didn't want to know. The sad fact was, most of my memories of my mom came from when she was dying in the hospital; I didn't even have *that* much of my father.

The tunnel eventually widened enough to allow us to walk normally, though we remained in single file. The damp smell of earth got stronger, and from somewhere up ahead came a steady dripping sound. Water now seeped down the walls and the floor was slick with moisture.

Then, from not too far up ahead, came a soft shimmer.

The threads of magic.

I stopped abruptly. Mo stepped to one side and peered over my shoulder.

"It's a perimeter alarm," she said eventually. "I might be able to divert it—it'd be safer than disconnecting."

Because disconnecting the spell was likely to have the same result as tripping the damn thing. I swung sideways and sucked in a breath, giving her the room to slip past. Once she had, I raised Nex to provide light. The last thing I needed was her slipping and breaking her leg again.

The perimeter alarm was a fairly simple spell, and it didn't take Mo long to tuck the lower strings into the upper, allowing us room to duck through it without disturbing or tripping the spell.

After a dozen or so more steps, the tunnel opened into a surprisingly large cavern. The water tumbling past our feet ran down a stony incline into a wide, shallow pool that covered most of the cavern's floor. In the middle of this was a long, darkly stained stone table. Sitting in a shallow basin in the middle of the table was a dark, oily-looking liquid. A long copper rod rose from this, and cut deep into the line of energy that flowed through the middle of the cavern

The ley line was unlike anything I'd ever seen before.

At first it appeared to hold no color, and yet the longer you stared at it, the more beautiful it became. It was a rainbow of perfection, a pulse point of immeasurable power, an artery that belonged to the earth itself.

And a goddamn dark altar was feeding off it.

I gripped Nex tightly and fought the urge to send a blast of lightning at the table to smash its grip on the ley line. I had no idea how dangerous that would be, and suspected it'd be better not to find out the hard way.

I drew in a calming breath and looked beyond the rainbow river. The cavern was oval in shape and, at first glance, didn't appear to have a second exit. It wasn't until I spotted shallow stairs cut into the side of the wall to our right that I saw it partially hidden behind an outcrop of rock on a ledge about halfway up the wall opposite where we stood.

I returned my gaze to the altar. "How long will it take to disconnect that thing?"

"Anything between ten minutes and half an hour." She grimaced. "Unfortunately, the minute I start disentangling it, they'll know."

"Then let's pray for the shorter disconnection time over the longer." I pointed Nex at the ledge. "I'll contact Barney, then wait up there for the bastards."

Mo nodded. "Be prepared for a major attack."

My gut twisted at the thought of facing them alone, but I nevertheless smiled and dropped a kiss on her cheek. "Don't get washed away by those currents."

"That may one day be my fate, but today isn't that day." Her eyes twinkled with mischief and an odd sense of knowing. "I've got a queen to see crowned, a dark enemy to defeat, and Blackbird grandbairns to help raise first."

"We haven't even had sex yet, and here you are antici-pating grandchildren."

"Because fate will not be denied."

"She has been for multiple centuries—why should that all change now?"

"Because timelines are converging. What was destined will now come to pass."

"I hate it when you talk shit like that."

She laughed and began taking off her shoes. I walked over to the rough-cut stairs and, as I climbed, activated the two-way. "Barney, you there?"

"Sure am—what's happening? Where's Mo?"

"We've found a dark altar connected to the ley line in a cavern under the house. Mo's about to disconnect it, and the shit is likely to hit the fan. Can you warn me the minute there's any sort of unusual activity up there?"

"Sure will. Is there only one way in and out of the cavern?"

"No—there's a second tunnel, though I'm not leaving Mo alone to investigate it."

"In what direction does it run?"

"I have no fucking idea."

"Use the compass on your phone." His tone was that of a teacher talking to a not-too-bright pupil.

"Oh." I dragged it out and opened the app. "Okay, it's saying we're northeast. Why?"

"I'll get our earth witch to suss it out. If she can find the tunnel's other end, she might be able to seal it."

"Why not just collapse the whole thing?"

"Because we're in the middle of a large housing estate. The last thing we need is a tunnel collapse taking out a house or two. Tell Mo to be careful."

"I will."

I signed off and glanced across at her. "Barney sends his love."

"He did not."

I grinned. "Well, maybe not in so many words, but that's what he meant."

"Get your lying bones over to that ledge and keep sharp."

I laughed and bounded up the remaining steps. The tunnel half hidden by the outcrop of rock was a lot wider than the house tunnel, and certainly looked better built. It also didn't have anywhere near the amount of water leaching from the walls, though the taint of earth and moisture still hung heavily on the gently stirring air. That breeze at least meant I'd smell the demons before I ever saw them— though Nex and Vita would no doubt 'see' them far earlier than even that.

I moved back several feet, then leaned against the cavern wall. While it was unlikely they'd attack from the house tunnel, we couldn't afford to take any chances. If I lost Mo now, I wasn't sure what I'd do, or how I'd even recover ...

I swallowed heavily. Given what she'd said about being swept away, she obviously had a good idea as to when death would finally claim her. Unexpected accidents could happen, of course—my parents were proof of that—but that just meant I had to remain a little more alert.

Mo had stopped a couple of feet short of the ley line. After taking a deep breath, she flung her arms wide, as if in welcome, and stepped into its river. It flared so brightly in response that I had to raise a hand to protect my eyes. For several long minutes, there was no sign of Mo; the light had completely engulfed her. When it finally faded and she reappeared, she was without clothes. Her silvery hair was unbound and flowing around her like a cape, totally ignoring the laws of physics and the directional flow of the energy. Her skin, like her eyes, glowed as brightly as the force through which she now waded, giving her the appearance of otherworldliness. Of godliness.

I shivered, both awed and frightened by the sight. But I now knew what she'd meant when she'd said it would be easy to be swept away by the power; she hadn't meant by the strength of the energy flow itself, as much as the fact that it literally passed *through* her. By entering that stream, she'd become something more than mere flesh.

But as her hands came down on the altar, a scream rent the air, distant and angry.

They knew. They were coming.

And if the number of footsteps echoing through the air were anything to go by, there wasn't just one or two but twenty or more. And *that* suggested there was a gateway down there somewhere.

If there *was*, we were in deep trouble ...

I stepped away from the wall, Nex and Vita held at the ready. As the scent of ash and evil grew stronger, the daggers reacted. Their blades glowed, and sharp whips of lightning snapped through the air; they were ready and eager to fight.

All *I* wanted to do was run.

I shifted my feet to strengthen my stance. Closer and closer the demons drew, until all I could smell was their wretched scent and all I could hear was the pounding of their feet.

A lone demon shot out of the entrance. He was obviously a scout, because his gaze swept the area before coming to a halt on me. He screamed something to the unseen multitudes behind him, then attacked. I unleashed the lightning, and he was ash in an instant. So were the six who immediately followed.

But there were many more deeper still in the tunnel.

I stepped closer to the entrance and speared the lightning inside. A thick wave of ash rolled out, momentarily cutting visibility but not sound. The demons still screamed, but their steps had momentarily stopped. I pulled back the lightning, sucked in a breath, and glanced across to Mo. Light flickered from her fingers and spun up the copper pole, though I didn't immediately understand what she was—

A scrape had my gaze snapping back to the tunnel. A red demon flew out into the cavern, moving so fast, his wings were a blur. I backpedaled and raised Nex, slicing across the claws reaching for me even as I sent a weave of deadly light spinning from Vita. He flicked his wings and soared up and over the net; it continued on, ashing those behind him, sending a thick cloud of black dust into the air. The red demon did a sharp roll through it and slashed at me with wickedly barbed feet. I ducked away, but not fast enough. His claws scoured my back, slicing through coat, sweater, and skin. A scream of pain leapt up my throat, but I somehow held it in check, not wanting to frighten Mo. I leapt upward with Nex, stabbing the red bastard deep in the crotch before twisting the blade sideways, cutting through his genitals and leg with equal ease. As his blood sprayed through the air, I twisted around and unleashed more lightning at those in the cavern. Their screams were abruptly cut short.

But the red demon wasn't finished yet. He swooped low, coming in fast, his eyes afire with determination and his blood a black stream behind him. I raised Vita; another net of energy formed in front of me as I readied for impact. The red demon hit it hard enough to force me back several feet. One foot hit the cavern wall, and I braced against it as the net consumed the demon. Not even ash remained.

As Vita's energy drew back to her blade, an arrow of utter agony shot through my head. It was a warning I had no choice but to ignore. I sucked in several breaths that did little to ease the fire in my brain and glanced again at Mo. Her magic still spun up the copper probe, and though its point now seemed lower than before, it remained attached to the ley line.

No resting just yet, then ...

The two-way squawked in my ear, making me jump. "Gwen?" Barney said, voice urgent. "You there?"

"Yep. What's wrong?"

"We're under attack. At least six people got inside the house—"

"How the hell did that happen?"

"Long story short, they hit with magic and muscle from several angles. You've probably got a couple of minutes, if that, before the six are on you. We've stopped the rest."

"Good." I hesitated. "Anyone hurt?"

"One of the councilors is down, but other than that, no. The ribbons are still active though—Luc attempted to get in after them and was attacked. He's burned but fine."

Burned didn't equate with fine in my opinion. I ignored the flood of concern and then glanced sharply at the nearby tunnel. While there was no immediate indication of another wave of demons, something was coming. Something that had dread crawling down my bleeding spine ...

"Gotta go," I said. "Please don't let anything else in."

"We'll do our best."

I moved cautiously toward the tunnel. It remained silent, and yet the sense that *something* approached was definitely stronger. I didn't think it was a demon, but it didn't feel like a dark elf, either.

I *should* bring the whole damn tunnel down on whoever —whatever—approached. But Barney's comment echoed through my mind; the last thing I wanted to do was endanger anyone whose house lay above us.

I glanced back to the house tunnel. They were closer than whatever was coming down this one. I needed to take care of them first, especially when surprise would give me the advantage.

But that didn't mean I dared leave this tunnel unguarded. I stretched several hair-fine slivers of light across the tunnel exit. Hopefully, the ley line's brightness would conceal their presence, because I had a bad feeling I'd need the warning to survive.

I spun and ran down the stairs. A quick glance at Mo revealed there was now only an inch or two of the copper probe set within the ley line's flow. But sweat slicked her glowing skin, and I could feel her strength waning—something that shouldn't have been possible, given I didn't have the De Montfort gift.

And yet, Vita had healed me. Was she the key to unlocking what I supposedly didn't have?

Before I could contemplate *that* particular thought, a soft scrape had my gaze snapping back to the house tunnel.

The bastards were coming.

I ran through the water and braced against the wall close to the tunnel exit. There was little to be heard now other than the steady dripping of water; whatever these six were—human, halflings, or even demons—they were certainly far more cautious in their approach than those who'd erupted from the other tunnel.

My heart pounded so hard it felt like it was reverberating through the wall behind me. I swallowed to ease the dryness in my throat and swiped at the sweat running down my face. It was damnably hot in here ... or was that simply a by-product of exertion and fear?

I flexed my fingers on the daggers' hilts and felt comforted by their steady pulsing. My head might be on fire, but the steady heartbeat running through the two blades suggested it wasn't at a cataclysmic point just yet.

A solitary scrape echoed. Deliberately, I suspected. I waited, my gaze on the other tunnel even if every other sense was tuned to this one. The unknown presence still strode toward the cavern; an odd sort of trembling rose in my soul, one that was deeply entrenched in fear.

Not of the person, or even what I would have to do, but rather of the consequences that would follow.

Which made absolutely no sense.

There was another soft scrape of sound—the slip of a boot on rock. It came from a little further than a few feet inside the tunnel. They were baiting me.

My breath caught in my throat, my grip so tight on Vita and Nex that my knuckles shone. Then, in complete and utter silence, four men flowed as one out of the tunnel, running directly for Mo ... and the bastards had guns.

I didn't waste breath on swearing. I simply called to the lightning and ashed them all. Pain hit, and my vision momentarily blurred. I blinked away the blood and half turned toward the tunnel. Caught movement and leaned back, but not fast or far enough. Something smashed into my jaw and sent me flailing backward. Blood filled my mouth, and pain shot through my jaw as my head reeled. I blinked, trying to see as I fought to remain upright. Saw a blurred figure standing several feet away and the glimmer of metal. Gun. I dropped and lashed out with a booted foot, sweeping at his legs. As he leapt over it, I unleashed a bolt of light and burned the fuck out of him. Another figure emerged from the tunnel. I launched forward, hitting him low, sending him sprawling backward. This one, I didn't ash. I simply raised Nex and stabbed her deep into the bastard's heart. He didn't die immediately, but he wasn't in any state to go anywhere in a hurry, either. Right now, that's all that mattered.

I collapsed back against the wall and sucked in air. Everything hurt. My head, my jaw, my back. But it wasn't over yet. Mo remained in the ley line, and the unknown person still approached.

I rolled onto hands and knees, remained there for several seconds until the cavern stopped spinning, and then climbed slowly to my feet. I was barely upright when a roar went up and demons surged out of the other tunnel.

So much for the strings of light giving me advance warning. So much for the feeling that it *wasn't* demons.

I flicked lightning their way, both through the air and across the water, in an attempt to fry even more of them—all the while ensuring Mo, who stood in the middle of the stream, remained untouched by the water-conducted electricity.

But for every one I ashed, two more took their place. They clambered up the walls and ran down the ledge, a black stain of evil that only had one goal—Mo.

There was no way known they were ever going to reach her.

Power surged through me, exploding from skin and both daggers. It ballooned outward, becoming multiple forks of intertwining light that swept left and right. It surrounded the table and encased Mo in a pulsing, white shield that stretched from floor to ceiling, cutting directly through the ley line river but seemingly unaffected by it.

The demons flung themselves at it from every angle. The shield pulsed and spat, crisping demon after demon. Their ash filled the air, but they didn't seem to care. But with every hit, the pain in my brain worsened, until all I could feel was fire and all I could see was blood.

I staggered into the house tunnel and dropped to my knees. If the demons decided to attack, I'd at least have a speck of protection here. A speck was better than nothing.

The blood blurring my vision poured over my lashes. If the demons didn't stop soon, it would be the end of me.

My only real hope lay in Mo finishing her task and joining the fight. But that was unlikely to happen anytime soon, given the point of the rod remained locked in the ley line's flow. And even if she *did* manage to detach the rod, the sweat sheening her face and body suggested she might not have enough strength to swat a fly, let alone dozens of demons.

I took a deep, shuddery breath and sent a silent prayer for help to whatever gods might be listening.

One of them must have been, because the attack abruptly stopped, though it took me a minute or two to realize it. I swiped at my eyes with the sleeve of my coat to clear my vision and peered into the soot-filled cavern.

What I saw made absolutely no sense.

The demons remained in the cavern, but they were now standing still and silent against the wall opposite. Maybe they'd decided enough of them had died in the cylinder's fire, but why retreat rather than attack *me*?

What were they waiting for?

But even as that thought crossed my mind, I knew.

My gaze went to the other tunnel, my heart pounding

somewhere in my throat and my breath little more than an uneven stutter.

He was coming ...

I swallowed heavily and pushed to my feet, determined to meet him upright and ready.

The breeze stirred around me with renewed vigor, bringing with it familiar scents—cardamom, bergamot, and lavender. It was combination I'd smelled at least twice before—on King's Island the day I'd performed the blessing, and in the tunnels underneath the King's Tower the morning fire had ripped through the genealogy archives.

This man had not only been in both places, but he could control the demons in a manner I'd not seen before.

He was a leader ... but was he *the* leader? The man who'd liberated the sword from the stone?

Was it Max?

CHAPTER FIFTEEN

As far as I was aware, Max had never purchased aftershave that had those specific undertones, but it wasn't like he'd spent all that much time at home in recent years. He might have tons of the stuff in his London apartment.

If it *was* Max, it would certainly explain the weird, soul-deep vibes I'd been getting. While we'd never shared the telepathic-like connection twins were supposed to have, there'd been a few times over the years when I'd instinctively known he was in trouble, and vice versa. The vibes could simply be a variation of that—although surely if it *was* him approaching, I'd have a clearer sense of him.

A flicker ran down Nex's side. Not Max, then, as she'd never reacted to him in such a manner. She *had* reacted that way to halflings, though.

A heartbeat later, a man walked out of the tunnel and stopped close to the ledge's edge.

It wasn't Max.

It was Winter.

Relief hit so hard, my knees briefly buckled, and I had

to grab the nearby wall to remain upright. I might still be in grave danger, but I'd at least gained a fraction more time to prepare for the confrontation with Max.

Although I was pretty sure a lifetime wouldn't be enough.

"Well, well, well." Winter's voice was soft and surprisingly melodious. "If it isn't the meddlesome sister. Why don't you come out of that tunnel?"

"Why don't you come in and get me?"

His brief smile didn't touch the coolness in his sharp blue eyes. "We both know you can't hold that protective cylinder around your grandmother forever, especially if the attacks on it are renewed. Do as I say or watch her die in utter agony instead of receiving a clean death."

"I prefer the third option—ashing your ass the minute your demons attack."

He chuckled softly; the sound reverberated around the cavern and sent a chill skittering across my skin. "If you had strength enough to kill me, you would have done so already. Come out, or I'll force you out."

Why was he so unconcerned about the prospect of me attacking? He might be right about my strength, but given the damage I'd caused to his brethren over the last week or so, he shouldn't be as certain as he sounded.

Or was it more a case of being certain that I couldn't hurt him if I *did* attack?

I lightly swiped at the blood dribbling over my lashes in an effort to clear my vision. That's when I saw it—the faint but undeniable shimmer surrounding him. He was shielded.

Several demons stirred, drawing my gaze. A warning, nothing more. In truth, while I did have enough strength to attack, he was right in that I wouldn't last long if *they* did.

And once my strength gave out and unconsciousness swept me away, I'd be at the mercy of whatever the bastard planned.

Even worse, so would Mo, because the minute I fell, so too would the cylinder. And she was close, so close to removing the copper rod. Whether that would be the end of it and she could join the fight, I had no idea, but I had to give her time.

Even if time was scarce at the moment.

"You're going to kill me whether I'm out there or in here," I replied evenly, "and I'll last longer in here."

"I have no desire to kill you," he said. "Not unless there's absolutely no other choice."

"And why would I believe you?"

"I'm not asking you to, but let's be realistic, dear Gwen. You've only got two options. Come out and take the chance that I mean what I say, or I order an attack and wait for you to collapse."

"You forgot about the third option."

He smiled. It was a pleasant sort of thing, totally at odds with the growing ice in his eyes. "I think we both know that won't have any effect. You've never been stupid, Gwen. Please don't act like it."

I stared at him for several seconds, a knot forming in my stomach as his warning recalled a memory—I'd been on a phone call to Max, and two people had been arguing in the background. While one of those voices had been familiar—though I hadn't been able to place it—the other had belonged to a stranger. That was no longer the case—it had been Winter. He'd used exactly the same phrase to whomever else was in that room.

And with *that* realization came a deeper, darker suspicion.

No, I thought. Surely not.

A short sharp *pop* made me jump and had my gaze darting back to Mo. The end of the copper rod was out of the energy river, but its length was still retracting, and Mo's concentration remained solely on it. Time. I just had to give her more time.

I took a deep breath and walked out from the tunnel.

Winter's expression bordered on approving. Energy flicked through me and echoed through each of the daggers. I wanted nothing more than to unleash, but the minute I did, all hell would break loose. Until I knew what sort of magic protected him, I was better off playing his game.

"Now," he said benignly, "lose the daggers."

I raised an eyebrow. "I'll lose them the minute you order your forces back into the tunnel."

"And why would I do that?"

"You want me to trust you. I want you to prove you're worthy of it."

He was clearly amused, but the demons nevertheless turned en masse and scrambled back into the tunnel. All but six.

Winter waved a hand in their direction, then clasped it behind his back again. It made me wonder what he was holding out of sight. A gun, perhaps?

"Consider them my insurance policy. Attack me, and they'll return the favor. Now, the daggers."

I carefully bent and placed both on the ground. I didn't need to be holding them to use them, even if the toll it took on my body was greater, but Winter obviously didn't know that.

But then, neither did my brother.

Even without the knives or the lightning, I still had my

stone knife strapped to my wrist. Only trouble was, to use it I had to get closer. Much closer.

"Now, walk over to the stairs and come up here."

I slowly obeyed. Every second I delayed was one more second for Mo. "What do you want with me, Winter?"

"Me? Nothing at all. But you are the blood price, and even he can't get around that."

The halfling who'd been Tristan's contact had also said I was the 'price,' and at the time we'd presumed she'd meant Tristan's. We hadn't known then what we did now.

Part of me still wished I didn't.

I swallowed heavily. "Max would never offer me as a blood sacrifice, no matter how desperately he needed help."

"You're right, he wouldn't. And he didn't. But there are other means of paying debts."

Like breeding half elf bastards ... Revulsion churned through me. Surely Max wasn't so far gone that he'd wished that fate on me? I was his goddamn twin—how could he not know I'd prefer death to something like that?

"Please do move along," Winter added. "I have a business meeting to get to."

I climbed the rough stone stairs, one hand pressed lightly against the wall to steady me. My vision was moving in and out of focus, and there was a deep roaring in my ears. Not good, I thought. Not good at all.

Winter shifted fractionally, keeping front-on to me. He was definitely holding something behind his back. Add that to his comment about a clean death, and it was pretty much certain he was holding a gun. And while I'd used a shield similar to the cylinder to protect us from gunshots at Barney's, Winter would surely have been told about that. He wouldn't have come here with a gun if he didn't believe it would work.

My gaze flickered past him. If I could collapse the tunnel's entrance and trap him in here with me without the majority of his demon force, we might yet have a chance ... but only if I could also take out the six demons that remained here at the same time.

May the gods be with us ...

I flexed my fingers and tried to ignore the gathering tension and fear. I could do this. I *had* to do this.

I pushed away the clamoring doubts and said, "A meeting with Max, I take it?"

There was something in his eyes, something in the smile that now played across his lips, that had my gut churning and all but confirmed those dark suspicions.

"Yes," he said. "We're a very good team, he and I."

"I take it you're the consort to his king?"

He laughed. "That's a fair summation. How did you guess, given you've never seen us together?"

I shrugged and stepped onto the ledge. Ten feet separated us; close, but not quite close enough. I couldn't risk throwing the knife, not when there was a fire in my brain and I was seeing double. "Your expression was evidence enough."

"He always said I wasn't very good at concealing my emotions." His hand came out from behind his back. In it was a gun. He smiled. "I'm not saying I don't trust you, Gwen—but I don't."

With that, he fired. I swore and threw myself sideways, but my reactions were far too slow. Something tore into my shoulder, and I glanced down. It wasn't a bullet. It was a goddamn dart. *Fuck.*

I wrenched it free and rolled upright. Became aware of an odd tremor in the earth and spotted demons flowing out of the cavern. I called to the lightning within me and flung it, with everything I had, at the tunnel rather than the demons. The twisting, tumbling streaks of light hit the wall and exploded with the force of a bomb. As the stone under our feet trembled and huge chunks of rock crashed down, hands grabbed me, pulling me sideways, pushing me down. A figure appeared in my vision, fist raised. I reached for the lightning again, but there was nothing left. Nothing except blinding, searing pain.

But this fight wasn't over yet. I flicked the stone knife into my hand and stabbed upwards, even as that fist descended. Flesh met stone; the sheer force of his blow vibrated up my arm even as the blade sank hilt-deep into his hand. I twisted the blade sideways, sliced through muscle and bone, severing arteries. Blood spurted, and he screamed, the sound high and furious. But he wasn't about to release me.

He dropped his weight onto me, one knee thumping into my gut and forcing an explosion of air from my lungs. With the other knee, he pinned the hand holding the knife. Then he wrapped his good hand around my throat and began to squeeze, his fingers digging deep into my carotid. If I didn't end this soon, he would.

I bucked, trying to dislodge him. He chuckled softly, his expression cold. Hard. No matter what his orders were—no matter what Max or the dark elves might want—he was going to kill me.

And he was going to enjoy every second of it.

The black hole of unconsciousness roared toward me. I twisted and bucked, hitting him with my free hand, trying to gouge his eyes with my nails. He swore and ducked away from each blow, his grip unfaltering even though I clawed his cheeks and mouth and neck. My lungs burned for air, and my heart raced so hard it felt like one long scream. I had no idea if it was the drug or his strangulation, and in truth it didn't matter, because I was dead if I didn't do something in the next few seconds. Punching and bucking wasn't working, which left me with only one choice.

To use what had already flamed out.

I stopped fighting, stopped sucking in air. Reached beyond the pain, beyond the fire, and past the depleted reserves of strength. For several, agonizing seconds, there was nothing but a curtain a gray.

Death, I thought.

Then the curtain moved, and I stepped onto the edges of another plane. It was a place beyond flesh—a place that was this world, and yet not. A place in which there were no demons or death or a halfling bastard trying to kill me. There was simply the earth and the air, and all the energies moved and existed between them.

In this place, Nex and Vita blazed, one gold, one a cold white. Life and death. I reached for death, saw Nex respond both within this otherworld and without. She shifted, rose, and cut through time and space, her blade comet bright, leaving a trail of sparks behind her.

Winter must have sensed something was off, because at the very last moment, he turned to face the cavern.

Nex plunged into his left eye, deep into his brain. He was dead between one breath and another.

As his body began to fall sideways, I reached up and withdrew Nex from his eye socket. Her blade still pulsed, but that shadowed world had retreated, and I was once again in a body wracked with pain and holding no strength.

And the demons who'd escaped the rockfall were coming straight at me.

I tried to move, tried to get to my feet or at least raise either Nex or the stone knife to defend myself. My limbs were leaden and refused to obey. The fucking drug, I thought distantly. He'd won after all.

Damn him. Damn him to hell.

I closed my eyes, not wanting to see what was coming. If I'd been capable of taking my own life, I probably would have; better a death by my own hand than being torn apart by demons.

Seconds became minutes, and life went on.

I opened my eyes. The demons had gone. Disappeared. I blinked, wondering if somehow this was merely the peace that came after death.

Then a familiar figure stepped into view and clicked her tongue. "Well, you're a right old mess then, aren't you?"

I smiled. Or at least tried to. My lips weren't responding too well at the moment.

Mo touched my cheek, a caress that was warm and healing. "Go to sleep, my girl. We're safe, and the ley line is free. You did good here today."

So did you. But the words never made it to my lips as the darkness finally swept away the last vestiges of awareness.

I woke in a cocoon of warmth and to the awareness of being watched. For several seconds, I neither moved nor spoke but simply enjoyed the heat of awareness and caring.

Luc.

Once more watching over me as I slept.

I flipped the blankets away from my face. "Me waking from a healing coma to find you lounging nearby with your feet propped up on the end of my bed is becoming something of a habit."

"Yes," he drawled, his green eyes bright with an emotion

he wasn't quite ready yet to voice. "And it's one I seriously hope you'll consider breaking. I really don't think my heart could take another episode like this."

Which was as close to an admission of his feelings I was likely to get at the moment. I smiled and pushed upright. The blankets slid down my body, and his gaze followed them. It felt like a caress. Felt like heaven.

"I do hope," he said, his voice deepening fractionally, "that you'll be just as uncaring as to whether you're clothed or not when we are finally dating."

"Our deal involved more than just dating," I said evenly. "I do believe there was mention of mad passionate sex several times a day. At least."

"A commitment I'm not likely to forget—especially at a moment like this." He sighed and removed his feet from the end of the bed. "I better go get Mo—she wanted to be notified the minute you woke."

My gaze flickered to his hands. "Barney said you'd been burned—how bad was it?"

"Bad enough." He flexed his fingers. "I've still full use of my sword hand, thanks to Mo."

Thank god for that, because we were going to need both him and Hecate before this was all over. "How long was I out this time?"

"Only twenty-four hours."

"Which is far less than when I killed the winged red demon and his witchling." And I couldn't help but wonder why, given I'd done far more—pushed myself to the utter limit and then some—this time.

"A fact I'm very thankful for." Luc climbed to his feet. "Would you like some breakfast?"

I nodded. "Pancakes, bacon, and poached eggs, all smothered in maple syrup would be brilliant."

He shuddered. "I think your dietary habits are going to take some time to get used to."

"Don't knock the combination until you actually try it."

"Thanks, but no thanks."

He moved to my end of the bed, then leaned over and kissed me. Not sweetly, not teasingly, but with hunger, passion, and intent. It was a both a promise and a declaration of what he couldn't—or wouldn't—put into words. It made my heart soar and my body sing, and it was over all too soon even if it went on for ages and ages.

"I look forward to the day when you're a permanent fixture in my life." His breath brushed my lips with heat, and his eyes were afire with desire. "Until that point, however, please consider the well-being of my heart and stop taking horrendous risks."

I laughed softly and touched his bristly cheeks. "It's not like I'm going out there looking for trouble—"

"A statement not even *you* believe." His voice was wry. He kissed me again, all too briefly, and then quickly left the room—before temptation got the better of him, no doubt.

I sighed and glanced around. We were back at the mock Tudor mansion in Southport from the look of things. I flung off the blankets and padded into the bathroom. Mo might have healed me, but grit and grime felt lodged into every pore. I needed to get clean. Needed to wash away the feel of Winter's fingers on my neck and the taint of his breath across my face.

Needed to *not* think about how Max was going to react to the news that I'd killed his consort.

I switched on the water, waited for it to reach the right temperature, then stepped under and raised my face. It washed away the grime, but not the fear of the heartbreak that was yet to come.

It was several minutes before I realized I was no longer alone in the room. I turned around. Mo was sitting on the edge of the ginormous bath, watching me.

"You okay?"

I smiled, though it held very little in the way of amusement. "As well as I can be, given I killed my brother's lover."

She blinked. "I had no idea that Winter—" She paused and sucked in a breath. "It explains so many things."

"Yes." I grabbed the shampoo and started washing my hair. "Where do we go from here, Mo?"

"We find the ring, though in truth it's little more than a perfunctory action now."

"I meant with Max."

"I know." She drew a deep breath and released it slowly. "And there's only ever been one option once the truth was revealed."

I briefly closed my eyes against the sting of tears. It didn't help. Nothing would. And there was nothing I could do or say to avoid the coming confrontation.

I swallowed back the bitter rise of bile and said, "What actually happened in that cavern? What did I do?"

"The impossible."

"Helpful."

She smiled. "Remember what I said about Elysian forging a connection between this world and the unseen in which all energies move and exist?"

I nodded. "But I wasn't holding Elysian. We don't even know where she is at this point, let alone if I'm the true heir."

"Do you truly believe you're not, given what you did and achieved in that cavern?"

I wanted to. God, how I wanted to. "That doesn't

negate the fact that I didn't have her, so how the hell did I manage to step onto the edge of the gray?"

"The ability to see the unseen is one that runs through the Aquitaine line, and it's why many females of the line were revered seers."

"Seeing what may be is a little different to stepping into the gray, though," I said. "And it certainly doesn't explain how I did."

"Nex and Vita were created by the same hand that made Elysian; it's natural they could tap into fields in a similar manner if so directed."

I frowned. "But I didn't—"

"Perhaps not consciously. Perhaps it was a by-product of desperation and need."

"Possibly." I rinsed out my hair, then turned off the taps and reached for a towel. "I take it the dark altar is no longer a problem?"

"It's destroyed, as are the tunnels that led into that cavern."

"I daresay they'll try to reopen them."

"I daresay they will—and they'll find a lovely little surprise for them if they succeed."

"You spelled?"

"Yes and no."

"An enlightening answer, as usual." I wrapped the towel around me and stepped out of the shower. "Are we heading across to King's Island today?"

She nodded. "I think the sooner we get there and find the real coronation ring, the better."

"You don't think Max knows it's there, do you?"

"No, but it did occur to me that, rather than attempting to breach our protections, he might simply destroy it."

"Why would he do that?"

"To ensure the sword cannot be returned to it."

"But why?"

"Because he plans for his heir to wield it after him."

"Then Reign and Riona are his?"

She nodded. "Ginny got the confirmation back this morning."

I drew in a deep breath and released it slowly. While the results were no surprise, it was still a reminder of the chasm that now separated us. "Only trouble is, neither Elysian nor the sword in the stone work that way."

"We know that, but I'm not entirely sure he does," she said. "For all that he's studied our line, for all that he's researched history, for all that he's planned and schemed, he doesn't appear aware that the sword he holds is a Mryddin-created replica. I have no doubt he would have contacted us for information if he had suspected."

He'd certainly shown no qualms about doing so to date. Pain rose yet again, but there was nothing I could do except ignore it. Nothing I could do but accept that the ache was going to be with me for the rest of my life.

"I'll grab some breakfast, then we can head out." I hesitated. "I take it you retrieved Nex and Vita?"

"And the stone knife. It saved you once. I think it'll do so a few more times before this whole thing is resolved."

"Well, *that's* good to know."

My voice was dry, and her smile flashed. "Magic cannot solve all problems. Sometimes, the old-fashioned methods of dealing out death are the best."

"Perhaps when it comes to a gun. But a short knife that requires you to get far too close to your assailant? Not so much."

She laughed. "Get a move on, darling girl. I'd like to get to the King's Stone by midday if possible."

"Any particular reason?"

"Maximum daylight protection." She rose. "I'll meet you downstairs."

I quickly dressed, then strapped on the wrist sheath, grabbed Nex, Vita, and my coat, and headed out.

Breakfast was waiting for me in the small morning room. Luc was absent, as were Barney, Mia, and Ginny. I glanced around as Mo walked in, a cup of tea in hand. "Where is everyone?"

"Luc's been summoned back to Covent Garden."

"That was sudden, wasn't it?"

"Yes, he got the call a few minutes after your little tête-à-tête upstairs. From what I heard, it had something to do with the protections around the current queen and the need to boost them."

"Fair enough, but he left without saying goodbye. I'm affronted."

A wicked twinkle gleamed in her eyes. "And *he* was all front. Such a very well-built young man."

I just about choked on my bacon. "Mo!"

"I can't help noticing what is very obvious," she said mildly. "And I daresay the extent of that hard-on is the reason he didn't risk another encounter."

I shook my head. I'd basically lived with her all my life, and she still had the power to shock me. *And long may it continue.* "What about the others?"

"Barney and Ginny are still dealing with the mess in Manchester—"

"I thought that had already been taken care of?"

"The tunnels, yes. The witches who were working with Darkside, not so much." She grimaced. "I believe the preter-natural team has been called in to help interview and process them all."

"There must have been a few."

"They were determined to protect their asset."

I grunted and tucked into my meal. "And Mia?"

"Had to go back to Ainslyn—it's her mother's seventieth, and there's a family party."

"I hope you told her to be careful."

"Of course. Not that she needed the warning."

Maybe not, but it nevertheless needed to be said. Max would want revenge for the murder of his lover, and he might just start by taking out everyone I cared about.

Once I'd finished my breakfast, we headed out. The day was bright and sunny, the skies blue. It was still winter, so a chill remained in the air, but all in all, it was a perfect day for flying.

We shifted shape and, after I'd scooped up my knives, followed the coastline until we reached King's Island. We landed on the open ground just before the ring of stone monoliths that surrounded the King's Stone. I swung around, studying the area. Nothing moved, and nothing seemed out of place. The sky was clear, and all of Ainslyn was on view, from the old docks at the far end of the walled section to the many high-rises in the business sector.

Mo was already moving toward the stone circle. I hastily followed, my gaze on the stone that had once held the sword. Physically, it looked no different and yet ... and yet, something was different. The feel of the place was different.

"Mo—"

Her pace didn't slow. "I know."

"What is it?"

"Someone's tried to shatter the blessing."

I frowned. "How? Only you and I—" I stopped. "Max."

"I would guess so. The blessing might be the province of

De Montfort women, but he's witnessed me performing it often enough to have a keen understanding of it."

"But he's not capable of magic. Not the blessing sort, anyway."

She glanced over her shoulder, her eyebrows raised. "Technically, neither were you."

"Yes, but—" I stopped. The lines between what should and shouldn't be possible had definitely blurred over the last week or so. "Is there any visible damage?"

"Nothing that's immediately obvious."

I stopped at the base of the knob and stared up at the hump of rock that had once held the sword. Its sides were smooth, worn down by time and weather. The soft shimmer that briefly ran around its base told me the blessing remained in place, but it certainly wasn't as strong as it should have been. I placed a hand into a hollow smoothed by countless others doing the exact same thing and stepped up. There was no slot at the top of the stone to indicate a sword had ever been sheathed within it.

"Any idea where the ring might be hidden?" I asked.

"Afraid not. Mryddin simply said it was in the stone."

"In? Like the sword was in?"

"Possibly. He didn't actually clarify exactly what he meant." She stopped near the step-up point and shoved her hands on her hips. "Can you see anything? Feel anything?"

"No." I ran my fingers across the top of the stone, and just for a second, energy stirred. It was a distant echo of the electricity that had caressed my fingers when I'd gripped the sword in the stone. "Yes."

"What?" Her voice was sharp.

"There *is* something here." I narrowed my gaze and, after a moment, saw a slight indentation. It was the soft shimmer in the air above it that said it was something more.

I hadn't noticed it before now simply because the sword had always dominated my attention. It had been the reason we'd climbed up here every year, after all, and it wasn't as if any of us had been aware that the stone held a secondary treasure deep in its stony heart.

I hesitated, then pressed my thumb into the dent. For a second, there was no response. Then, with a soft click, a slot appeared in the stone. From deep within came a bloodred gleam.

My breath caught in my throat, and for several seconds, all I could do was stare. This was it. This was the point of no return. This was where I found out if I was the true heir or not.

This was the moment where my life would forever change.

Mo didn't say anything. In truth, there was nothing she could say. This decision, this action, was mine and mine alone. I could accept destiny or I could walk away and watch as everything I knew, everything I loved, was destroyed.

As decisions went, it was far harder than it should have been.

But in the end, I reached in and retrieved the ring.

Like the one the Blackbirds had held safe for centuries, this ring was dominated by a huge red ruby onto which a cross and a rose had been carved. But its band was simple silver rather than gold, and there were absolutely no diamonds encrusting it.

At my touch, a bloody fire flared to life deep in the heart of the ruby and began to pulse, quickly falling into a rhythm that matched the rapid beating of my heart.

It had recognized me. Accepted me.

I met Mo's gaze. Her smile was bittersweet. "I was right, though in many respects, I wish for once I wasn't."

"You and me both." I accepted the hand she offered me and jumped off the rock. "What about the rock? Do we need to protect it?"

Mo nodded. "Yes, but spells alone won't do that. Not if my fears are right. Keep watch."

I nodded and stepped away. As she knelt and pressed a hand to the cold gray stone that formed the base of the monolith circle, I pulled Vita free and dropped the ring into her sheath. Not only would it be safe enough there, it was the one place Max would never think to look.

I crossed my arms and kept guard as Mo literally moved the earth—after sinking the real knob deep into the ground, she fashioned another above it. Even I was hard pressed to see any differences between the fake and the real stone.

She pushed unsteadily to her feet once done and scraped a hand through her hair. "That should do it."

I hoped so. "Shall we go?"

She nodded and immediately took to the sky.

I took a deep breath and then followed. The day wasn't over yet.

We had a sword to find.

And, god help me, a brother to confront.

ABOUT THE AUTHOR

Keri Arthur, author of the New York Times bestselling Riley Jenson Guardian series, has now written more than forty-eight novels. She's won a Romance Writers of Australia RBY Award for Speculative Fiction, and two Australian Romance Writers Awards for Scifi, Fantasy or Futuristic Romance. She was also given a Romantic Times Career Achievement Award for urban fantasy. Keri's something of a wanna-be photographer, so when she's not at her computer writing the next book, she can be found somewhere in the Australian countryside taking random photos.

for more information:
www.keriarthur.com
kez@keriarthur.com

The Black Tide (Dec 2017)

Souls of Fire series

Fireborn (July 2014)

Wicked Embers (July 2015)

Flameout (July 2016)

Ashes Reborn (Sept 2017)

Dark Angels series

Darkness Unbound (Sept 27th 2011)

Darkness Rising (Oct 26th 2011)

Darkness Devours (July 5th 2012)

Darkness Hunts (Nov 6th 2012)

Darkness Unmasked (June 4 2013)

Darkness Splintered (Nov 2013)

Darkness Falls (Dec 2014)

Riley Jenson Guardian Series

Full Moon Rising (Dec 2006)

Kissing Sin (Jan 2007)

Tempting Evil (Feb 2007)

Dangerous Games (March 2007)

Embraced by Darkness (July 2007)

The Darkest Kiss (April 2008)

Deadly Desire (March 2009)

Bound to Shadows (Oct 2009)

Moon Sworn (May 2010)

Myth and Magic series
Destiny Kills (Oct 2008)
Mercy Burns (March 2011)

Nikki & Micheal series

Dancing with the Devil (March 2001 / Aug 2013)
Hearts in Darkness Dec (2001/ Sept 2013)
Chasing the Shadows Nov (2002/Oct 2013)
Kiss the Night Goodbye (March 2004/Nov 2013)

Damask Circle series
Circle of Fire (Aug 2010 / Feb 2014)
Circle of Death (July 2002/March 2014)
Circle of Desire (July 2003/April 2014)

Ripple Creek series
Beneath a Rising Moon (June 2003/July 2012)
Beneath a Darkening Moon (Dec 2004/Oct 2012)

Spook Squad series
Memory Zero (June 2004/26 Aug 2014)
Generation 18 (Sept 2004/30 Sept 2014)
Penumbra (Nov 2005/29 Oct 2014)

Stand Alone Novels
Who Needs Enemies (E-book only, Sept 1 2013)

<u>Novella</u>

Lifemate Connections (March 2007)

<u>Anthology Short Stories</u>

The Mammoth Book of Vampire Romance (2008)

Wolfbane and Mistletoe--2008

Hotter than Hell--2008

CPSIA information can be obtained
at www.ICGtesting.com
Printed in the USA
LVHW041459161020
669012LV00001B/72